AF385831

Tell Tale

Also by Claire Parkin

The Final Hours of Muriel Hinchcliffe

CLAIRE PARKIN

Tell Tale

MACMILLAN

First published 2026 by Macmillan
an imprint of Pan Macmillan
The Smithson, 6 Briset Street, London EC1M 5NR
EU representative: Macmillan Publishers Ireland Ltd, 1st Floor,
The Liffey Trust Centre, 117–126 Sheriff Street Upper,
Dublin 1 D01 YC43
Associated companies throughout the world

ISBN 978-1-0350-2852-8

1 3 5 7 9 8 6 4 2

A CIP catalogue record for this book is available from the British Library.

Map artwork © Hemesh Alles

Typeset by Palimpsest Book Production Ltd, Falkirk, Stirlingshire
Printed and bound in the UK using 100% Renewable Electricity by CPI Group (UK) Ltd

Visit **www.panmacmillan.com** to read more about all our books
and to buy them.

In loving memory of my father and mother –
Leighton Williams (22 July 1930–14 September 1984)
Barbara Williams (28 February 1932–16 July 1994)

You can't depend on your eyes when your imagination
is out of focus.
> *A Connecticut Yankee in King Arthur's Court*
> MARK TWAIN

Hiraeth (*noun – Welsh*). An intense, bittersweet longing
for a person, thing or place which is absent or lost;
yearning, nostalgia or homesickness for the past.

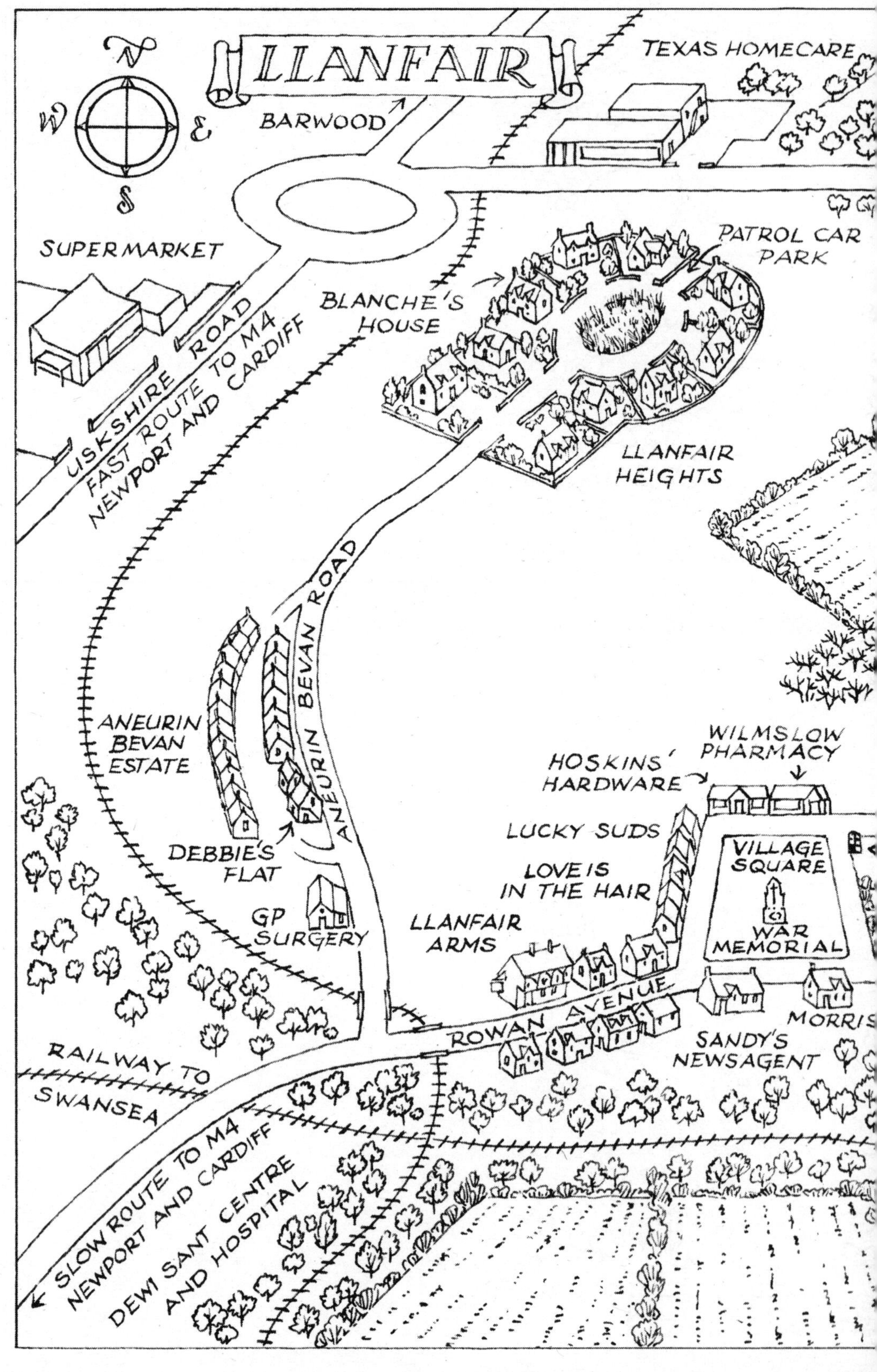

N
W
E
S
LLANFAIR
TEXAS HOMECARE
BARWOOD
SUPERMARKET
PATROL CAR PARK
BLANCHE'S HOUSE
USKSHIRE ROAD
FAST ROUTE TO M4 NEWPORT AND CARDIFF
LLANFAIR HEIGHTS
ANEURIN BEVAN ROAD
ANEURIN BEVAN ESTATE
WILMSLOW PHARMACY
HOSKINS' HARDWARE
DEBBIE'S FLAT
LUCKY SUDS
LOVE IS IN THE HAIR
GP SURGERY
LLANFAIR ARMS
VILLAGE SQUARE
WAR MEMORIAL
ROWAN AVENUE
MORRIS
RAILWAY TO SWANSEA
SANDY'S NEWSAGENT
SLOW ROUTE TO M4 NEWPORT AND CARDIFF
DEWI SANT CENTRE AND HOSPITAL

BARWOOD MOUNTAIN
LAY BY
STOCKHOLM VILLA
QUARRY
LLANFAIR WOODS
FIELDS
VICARAGE
LLANFAIR CHURCH
SCOUT HUT
COPPICE
SCHOOL VIEW ESTATE
LLANFAIR LANE
TELEPHONE BOX
HOLLYHOCK COTTAGE
NURSE PUGH'S HOUSE
BARBARA'S GARDEN
LLANFAIR COMMON ROAD
LLANFAIR VALLEY
VILLAGE SCHOOL
RAILWAY TO LONDON
CARDIFF ← M4 → LONDON
HEMESH ALLES

Prologue

1.05 a.m., Monday, 7 September 1964

In a Morris Minor on the A5876, halfway between Barwood and Llanfair

Herbert Wilkins wants to shout.

Mainly with joy at his good fortune, but also because the ash from his Cuban cigar has dropped onto the left leg of his dress-suit trousers. The distraction of his burning thigh, and the frantic slapping of trouser that follows, nearly propels Herbert, his beloved Morris Minor, and his passenger – Eleri Ellis – into the concrete embankment of the A5876.

Another near-miss. Herbert's had rather a lot of those lately. He dabs at his forehead with his monogrammed handkerchief, keeping his eyes fixed on the twisted mountain road ahead. The clouded sky is moonless and starless; the route dark and perilous, lit only by a row of cats' eyes that vanish repeatedly, only to reappear in the nick of time as Herbert navigates hair-pin bend after hair-pin bend. His jaw is firm, his gaze steely, his gloved hands unyielding on the leather-bound steering wheel, despite his having had a skinful of whisky and a spectacular knee-trembler with Eleri Ellis in the deserted car park behind The Barwood Arms just now.

Herbert slips his handkerchief back inside his trouser pocket and casts a victorious glance at the sleeping woman at his side – her slender neck curved towards the passenger window, button nose level with the beady eyes of her fox-fur stole. Platinum waves tumble over her soft white shoulders, a gentle purr ripples from her plump carmine lips as she snores, and Herbert wants to shout once more. She's worn out – worn out by him *– and, it has to be said, by several encores of 'Bread of Heaven' at the Barwood Miners' Club. Llanfair had done it again – South Wales Choral Society for the third year running! It was all too much, really it was. What a night it had been. What. A. Night.*

Just another half a mile or so until the turning for Llanfair Lane. Herbert stamps his foot on the accelerator, driving it into the floor. The cool September night air, smoky-sweet with mountain heather, swirls through the open windows, ushering Eleri's Chanel No 5 towards Herbert's flaring nostrils. He's a king – an absolute king! How fortunate, he tells himself, that Eleri and I share a love of choral singing, the perfect cover for our affair. How fortunate our respective spouses happen to be tone-deaf. How fortunate my oldest friend – Huw Ellis – is a drunken buffoon, who suspects nothing of my affair with his wife, and my own wife, Mairi – who does – neither loves nor desires me enough to care. As long as I bring home the bacon, she gives not a stuff for my tomcattery.

But – The Brat.

Herbert frowns. Yes, there was always the problem of The Brat, who would care very much indeed. And a moralizing, tittle-tattling so-and-so of a brat it was, too.

It scares him. There, he's admitted it. He – Herbert Wilkins, up-and-coming proprietor of Wilkins' Tool Manufacturers, owner of the finest tenor voice in South Wales, lover of the most beautiful woman in Llanfair – is terrified. Of a child.

He feels a sudden longing for his bed, for the familiar outline of Mairi's curler-studded head on the pillow next to his own. His hangover tomorrow will be of epic proportions, and Mairi will give him hell for it – faithful old Mairi with her cold-creamed face, Mairi with the rough red hands that cleaned and cooked and reeked of onion peelings and Lux soap flakes. Herbert shoots another look at Eleri, his head swimming with a queasy brew of whisky, guilt and revulsion. Thank Christ she's asleep, he tells himself. Thank Christ I don't have to attempt polite conversation, for what on earth would we talk about?

A clear stretch of road lies ahead of them now – the final one hundred yards or so of the A5876. In the valley below, Herbert can see the shadowy, haphazard sprawl of Llanfair, an occasional orange streetlamp or lit bedroom window winking reassuringly at him through the tangle of woodland. The night is so dark, visibility so poor, that you'd think you were in the middle of nowhere. But then the clouds part – the moonglow illuminating the hand-painted sign nailed, lopsidedly, to a tree trunk in the near distance:

Llanfair Quarry
Deep Water
Danger: Keep Out!

Herbert sees this burst of light from the heavens as a sign – divine permission to up his speed! – and he thrusts his foot down to the floor, cursing as he does so. For a small figure skitters out from the roadside into the pool of Herbert's headlights, launching itself directly into the path of his car: arms spread wide, Christ-like, the deep red hood of its overcoat completely obscuring its face.

Herbert swerves, propelling the car sideways. The cigar drops from his lips to his lap, and Herbert swears once more – glimpsing his smouldering thigh the instant his Morris Minor collides with the tree, dislodging the danger sign nailed to its trunk, shattering the Morris Minor's windscreen as it falls – the last thing Herbert sees.

His heart hurts. Everything hurts. Herbert can hear gurgling – his own, or Eleri's? He can't tell – can't see, can't move! But, by Christ, he can feel – pain, panic – and now the sensation of his handkerchief being drawn, slowly, from his trouser pocket, his wedding ring tugged from his finger, his jaw prised open by an unseen hand, a cold metal object forced into his throat, a familiar voice whispering, sibilantly, in his ear:

'Lust.'

Herbert Wilkins wants to shout.

Twenty Years Later

FRIDAY, 7 SEPTEMBER 1984

THE SOUTH WALES MORNING POST

Announcing the winner of this month's poetry competition – subject, The Miners' Strike Is Dividing Wales. Congratulations to Anonymous (full name and address withheld at entrant's request), who wins two tickets to see Wrong Jones (Tom Jones impersonator) at the Llanfair Arms on Wednesday, 12 September 1984.

A Tale of Two Villages
Two South Wales villages, one in mourning,
The other not knowing how lucky it is,
Divided by a mountain studded with sheep
And gorse and scudding shadow-cloud.
Barwood mourns the loss of its heart,
Ripped out by the National Coal Board,
Llanfair should lament the loss of its soul,
If only it had one to start with.
Instead, it bemoans the loss of a trophy
For Wales in Bloom, for the second year running,

Mourns the loss of a field
Sold to house the less fortunate.
Laments its 'doomed youth' not for sacrifice,
But for having opinions of their own,
Turning its fatuous face to the wall,
Weeping with righteous self-pity.
Blind to the hunger,
Blind to the fury,
Blind to the injustice on the other side.
Two South Wales villages, Barwood, Llanfair,
Three miles apart, as the crow flies,
Might just as well have three thousand miles between them
So deaf is one to the other man's cries.

Announcing next month's theme: Frankie Goes to Hollywood – political pundits, or poseur popstrels? Send your poems to the address on page 6 by Monday, 24 September.

1

Debbie

10.30 a.m., Dewi Sant Department of Child &
Adolescent Psychology, Cardiff

I should be at school today. I should be in class, flicking pencil shavings over Carrie-Anne Marston's pasta collage, until Mrs Bug-eyed Thomas hauls me off to the headmaster's office with the threat of a clout around the ear and a sore bum before bedtime.

But I'm not doing any of that. Instead, I'm kneeling in front of a cardboard box, and a lady with frizzy red hair and a great big mole on her chin. Mam's here, behind me, sitting with Nurse Rose Pugh, who looks a right state with her blonde helmet hairdo and tree-trunk calves in thick navy tights. Mam has an armchair to sit in, but Nurse Pugh has to make do with a plastic seat, like the ones we have in school. Carrie-Anne Marston once wrote *I do eggy farts* on the back of mine, and I'd check to see if someone's written the same on Nurse Pugh's if I didn't think I'd get a bloody good hiding for my trouble.

Pugh is the district nurse. She's very small and smiley, with a round pink face and soft white hands. But those hands are as strong as buggery – when she parts my hair to check for nits, it really hurts. She keeps smiling at me, which is nice of her, I suppose, because Mam isn't smiling at all – whenever I try to catch her eye, she stares out of the window at the cars parked outside. I didn't think she liked cars. Not like Dad. Dad loved cars – he used to joke that if he hadn't had to get married, he'd have bought himself a Lamborghini instead of a Datsun Cherry, the daft bugger.

The lady with the mole on her chin would be quite pretty if she wore some lipstick, but her dress sense is shocking. All khaki, baggy, shapeless stuff – like a walking Scout tent, she is, in Dr Scholl sandals.

'My name is Dr Vanessa Bridges,' she says. 'But you can call me Vanessa.'

'What if I don't want to call you Vanessa?' I reply. 'What if I want to call you Darren? Or Keith? Or Queen Le-Fou-Fou-Le-Fa-Fa?'

'You can call me whatever you like,' she smiles.

'All right. Keith.'

'Okay, Keith it is.' She flips open the cardboard box, takes out two dolls and puts them on the carpet in front of me. One is wearing a frilly pink princess dress; the other is dressed in a nurse's outfit – light blue, with a navy cape trimmed with bright red lining.

'I'm not sure I want to play,' I sniff. 'I'm not supposed to talk to strangers.'

'But I'm not a stranger. And your mum is here – and Nurse Pugh. They've joined us to see how our sessions will go, and to let you know that you're safe with me. Then it'll be just you and me, playing in my office two mornings a week. Won't that be fun?'

'No,' I say. 'Not really.'

'But before that, I'd like to chat about what happened in the summer. That's why I'm here, Debbie – to help you, so you can make better choices in the future. I'd like to talk about your feelings towards The Vicar, and why you tried to blackmail him. And then I'd like you to describe your relationships with Carrie-Anne and Lucy Marston, and why you felt the need to put bad things in their sandwiches . . .'

'Senna,' Mam sighs. 'Just crushed-up senna. A childish prank, gone wrong.'

'A childish prank,' Nurse Pugh says, 'that landed those poor little mites in hospital!'

Mam rolls her eyes. 'That wasn't the senna! That was the morphine the Marston girls took, stuff that had nothing at all to do with Debbie . . .'

I jam my fingers into my ears. I don't want to hear about the morphine, but it won't go away, the morphine stuff. The stuff I didn't see coming. I didn't see it coming, see, that the Marston girls would end up in hospital. That it wasn't the senna I'd put in the sandwiches that made them ill, but morphine. A dangerous drug, so Mam says. A drug that can *kill*.

I curl the rest of my fingers over the ones already stuck in my ears, but I can't blot it out – the sound of Mam thumping the arm of her chair with her fist. I pull out my fingers, and Mam's voice plugs my ears instead:

'Debbie is not to blame for the morphine! How on earth would an eleven-year-old child get her hands on such a thing? Can't people round here accept that? It's because she looks different, isn't it? Because she is – different. Oh, God!'

She looks dead panicky, Mam. I wonder if I should panic, too. 'The morphine could have come from anywhere!' She leaps up, waving her arms around like a lunatic windmill. 'An error at the hospital, or a tablet the girls found on the floor, thinking it was a sweetie. That daft mam of theirs, Blanche Marston! I bet she gave it to them, just to get attention!'

'No one blames Debbie for the morphine,' Mole Lady says. 'The police, I believe, are still looking into it . . .'

'When they're not in Barwood, persecuting the poor bloody miners! I will not have my daughter labelled a poisoner! I will not sit back and watch her hounded, persecuted . . .'

'Debbie's not labelled as anything,' Mole Lady says. 'Please sit down, Mrs Tunstall.'

'*Ms* Tunstall.' Mam flops into her chair. 'Debbie's dad buggered off five years ago. I'm nobody's missus, I'll have you know.'

'Apologies, *Ms* Tunstall. I'm just here to help Debbie. Her future at Llanfair Primary School depends, in part, on the success of our sessions together . . .'

'Debbie's future,' Mam groans. 'Oh, God. Debbie's future.'

Everyone goes all quiet, as though they've never imagined me having a future before. Mam sinks down with her head in her hands, her lank grey fringe hanging over her fingers. And when she looks up, which she does just now, you can see how lined and knackered she is; how very much older than Nurse Pugh she seems, even though they're the same age.

'I've not done nothing wrong!' I shout. 'And there's not even proof I put senna in those stupid sandwiches! I get blamed for everything round here, I do!'

Mole Lady rocks back on her knees and stares at me, taking

me in: my dirty hair, tatty skirt, my stained, greasy collar. I try to stare back, but I can't, because I know if my brain hears what her brain's thinking, I'll start bawling my eyes out. So, I look down at the carpet instead, at the two dollies she's laid on the square of sunlight in front of me.

'Perhaps you'd like to play with the dolls, Debbie?' she asks.

The nurse doll has such a nice outfit that I'm desperate to touch her cape. I reach out and stroke it, rolling the material between my fingers, pretending I can feel the heat of that deep red lining against my skin. It's much nicer than my nurse's outfit at home. Mam got it from the catalogue. It took ages to pay off.

Mole Lady is watching me. My nails are bloody filthy. I pull my hand away, lift up my bum, sit on my fingers. Nosy cow.

'I hate the doll,' I say. 'She has long brown hair, like the Marston girls. Mine is black and wiry. And she is slim. I'm built like a brick shit-house, so Blanche Marston says.'

'See?' Mam says. 'See what the poor kid has to put up with? You're Amazonian, Debbie, and don't let anyone tell you otherwise!'

Mole Lady ignores her. 'Do you want to play with the dolls, Debbie?' she asks.

'No,' I say. 'Not really.'

'Well, perhaps there's something else in my box . . .'

'Don't care,' I say. 'Not interested.'

'Gosh!' Mole Lady laughs. 'Well, what *do* you like to play with?'

Mam whispers, 'People.'

Mole Lady looks up with a frown. 'I'm sorry?' she says.

'People,' Mam says, almost with a shout. 'Deborah only likes to play with *people*.'

2

Barbara

3 p.m., Llanfair Village Square

Here comes Barbara Pritchard – stout-waisted, mackintoshed, wicker basket hooked over one arm – marching past the War Memorial, sagaciously surveying the village around her. She is accompanied by Utterson, her foul-smelling terrier, cursed with bad breath, an underbite and an insatiable fetish for upright objects.

Barbara prefers to walk Utterson during the school day, their progress unhindered by feral children and their equally undisciplined parents. She has never quite recovered from the fifteen years she endured as headteacher of Barwood Primary School, half joking upon her retirement – more than two decades ago – that she'd sell her soul to Satan himself if it meant she need never face a child or their ghastly parents ever again. But Deborah Tunstall (Barbara can never bring herself to use the diminutive form of anyone's name) is a different kettle of fish altogether. Yes, Barbara is happy to make an exception in such an exceptional case, for Deborah is a genius, and a most misunderstood one, at that.

God knows why Barbara taught primary-age children,

anyway. She's always preferred adolescents, cherishing that brief, brilliant time when a young person's mind is as unfettered as it is ever likely to be: unbound by the parental confines of the pre-pubescent years; unsullied by the rat-race awaiting every one of them. And Deborah Tunstall's mind is as free as any Barbara has ever encountered! Frank, fearless, feisty – Deborah is the child Barbara might wish she'd had, had she not spent her working life trying to civilize other people's.

'Stop that, Utterson!'

Untangling the dog's lead from the telegraph pole, Barbara looks up to see the names of The Fallen inscribed on the stone War Memorial in front of her. She recalls a recent letter in *The South Wales Morning Post*, berating the local youths for loitering around the memorial while wearing 'offensive' political T-shirts – *Frankie Say Relax* and *Arm the Unemployed* being two examples. She had no idea that Mr Sinatra was so sociologically minded, but had been delighted to read it, choosing to overlook the obvious grammatical error (surely Frankie *says?*), and resisting the urge to pen her own letter to the editor to point it out. She'd intended to bring the subject up with Robert during their next coffee together, but thought better of it – because how would she feel if he simply dismissed it? A letter like that would once have sparked a lively discussion between them. It's the lack of interest Robert shows in anything at all that worries Barbara sick.

Timothy Wilkins Albert Wilkins Arthur Wilkins

Three names inscribed on the War Memorial, all from the same family.

Barbara feels a surge of panic. She wants to race to the Llanfair Arms, scoop her nephew up from the crumpled, unwashed bedding where she'd left him dozing two days ago, where he'd murmured that yes, Auntie Barbara, he'd get up and wash himself today – maybe. She wants to rock him in her arms, like a baby. All six foot two and a half of him.

'I must say, Lynette,' she murmurs, lifting her face to the cloudless sky to address her late sister, 'you've caused a right to-do buggering off and leaving me and Robert and your grumpy-old-sod of a husband, Dai Hargreaves, like that. We all miss you, you darling old cow. We all miss you so very much.'

She's about to head towards the pub, but Utterson tugs impatiently on his lead in the direction of Llanfair Common, and Barbara Pritchard presses on.

Barbara sits on a bench with an *oof*, plucking a ham and egg sandwich from her basket, tearing off a chunk and chucking it down at her feet, where Utterson demolishes it noisily. Biting into the remainder, she is vaguely aware of the dog circling the bench with a petulant whine, but Barbara is distracted – as she often is on her jaunts to the common – by the startling clarity and variety of the scenery around her: Barwood Mountain looming behind to the north, the glinting industrial sprawls of Cwmbran and Newport colonizing the south, and the River Usk glittering through the green and golden valley beneath. Thank your lucky stars, she tells herself, that on a beautiful day such as this, you live on the right side of the mountain. That for all its flawed and frivolous inhabitants, Llanfair remains on the sunnier slope, its grassy outcrops unsullied by collieries and toppling slag-heaps, the demographic wealthy and healthy, not half-starved and held to ransom by the Westminster powers-that-be. For now, the sparkling streams of Llanfair flow free from pollution and waste.

Barbara loves water; had intended to spend her retirement taking luxury cruises – exploring the ancient world by day, dancing beneath the stars in the arms of someone she loved by night. But other things had got in the way. Robert – who'd promised he'd join her at some point – had been busy trying to build his music career, which had, like his father's, come to nothing, and she hadn't fancied travelling alone. But there is still time. Isn't there?

A Mediterranean cruise – that would be perfect! She will go by herself, while Robert cares for Utterson; she must stop relying on her thirty-one-year-old nephew for company. Robert is a grown man, though sadly showing every sign of being as much of a dreamer as his father, Dai, who'd only taken up pub-keeping – over thirty years ago, now – when Lynette insisted that skiffle bands and bowl-cut hairstyles would never take off. Yes, whether you believed in nature or nurture, it was hardly surprising that Robert was the way Robert was.

'What do you think, Utterson?' Barbara chucks another piece of bread to the ground. 'Robert is stuck. Has always been stuck. Is pre-determined to be stuck.' She reconsiders this for a moment. 'There are other factors,' she reminds herself.

For Robert had been bullied at Llanfair Primary School, the teachers doing sweet bugger-all until she intervened. Yes, when Lynette and Dai's pleas went unheard, she had stepped in – a revered headmistress, renowned for resurrecting a strug-gling primary on the other side of the mountain – threatening to phone the police, the inspectors, the Department of Education, whatever it took. With her intervention, the bullying stopped – but the damage was done. A part of Robert was frozen in time, forever a terrified ten-year-old boy.

And the perpetrator? The best-behaved girl in class. The butter-wouldn't-melt-in-her-mouth teacher's pet, complete with patent Mary-Jane shoes and pink NHS spectacles.

Wolves in sheep's clothing, bullies in pigtails. Tale as old as time.

And the tale hadn't changed in the years that had followed, as she'd witnessed herself one month ago at the Llanfair Summer Fete – the scene of the poisoned-sandwich affair. 'A fete worse than death,' Robert had joked at the time (he was going through one of his jollier phases). But the joke wore thin as the day wore on, and poor Deborah Tunstall was blamed for it all. Hung out to dry, along with her mother, by the Llanfair witchfinders general.

'It's all about survival of the fittest,' Barbara mutters. 'Darwin was right, we are all of us animals. Stop that, Utterson!'

She tugs at the lead to disengage the dog from the leg of the bench, intending to take one final loop of the common, delaying her return home. Because the cottage will be an absolute sight, with dirty dishes in toppling piles either side of the kitchen sink. And her heart will sink with the disappointment of it all – of a life done-and-dusted, spent bettering other people's children, nurturing other people's dreams, while always denying her own.

I prefer my own company. That's what she tells the village nosy-parkers, who enquire with a smile, heads slightly tilted, as to why she's never married. *I haven't met the right man,* she'll explain, when pressed even further. What else can she say? In a place like Llanfair, if she told them the truth – *there is no 'right' man because I prefer women, so stick that in your pipe and smoke it* – she'd be driven out with pitchforks and torches, condemned as a degenerate, a pervert, a witch. She's viewed with suspicion enough as it is – an elderly spinster, living alone with an old, smelly dog for company, surrounded by cobwebs and books and her own messy, incomprehensible paintings and sketches, her tumbledown garden crammed with strange flowers and herbs that no one else grew any more.

'This will not do,' she tells Utterson, rising from the bench, belting her mackintosh. 'Self-pity will not do. What do you say, old boy? That I should telephone Ingrid Tunstall to enquire after Deborah's meeting today with the child psychologist? I think you're right. And while I'm at it, I'll ask whether she can slot in an extra two hours of cleaning next Tuesday.'

But Utterson is distracted by something – his ears pinned back, body cowed, a low growl rumbling from his usually peppy underbite. A chilly unease pricks Barbara's neck, and she turns, fully expecting to discover that she has not been alone all this time.

But there is not a soul to be seen. The common is deserted. Even the playground – usually swarming with whirling, crazed pre-schoolers – is void of life.

Though some way off in the distance, Barbara spots a small, red-cardiganed figure dawdling along the pavement at the far edge of Llanfair Common; a child, it must be, weaving erratically in and out of the horse-chestnut trees, apparently without a care in the world.

'Should be at school,' Barbara murmurs, watching the diminutive figure diminishing further, until it rounds a bend in the road and finally vanishes out of sight.

3

Debbie

4.30 p.m., Flat 4B, Aneurin Bevan Estate

And now I'll have to keep my eyes open for evermore, because every time I shut them, I see the kids' faces; hear their stupid whiny voices chanting, *Debbie Bumstall stinks of poo, Debbie Bumstall, liar – that's you!* – and feel their stinky, snotty breath and spit and spite all over my face. One of them shouted, *Look! She's crying! She's seeing a shrink 'cos she's a fruitcake. You wanna kill yourself, Bumstall? Do it! Do it!*

And they all shouted *Do it! Do it!* until the bell went and it was time to line up, but no one wanted to stand next to me, because they all say that I'm evil. That I tried to poison Lucy and Carrie-Anne Marston. That I lied about The Vicar having it off with Brown Owl and Nurse Rose Pugh; that I should go to Broadmoor with the Ripper and all the other nutters. And I said to them, I did, I said: 'I didn't do nothing! I said lots of things and I wrote lots of things, but I never tried to kill no one, even though I really wanted to!'

I went to the toilet and cried for a bit. Mrs Bug-eyed Thomas came to find me. She knocked on the cubicle door and shouted, 'Debbie-Marie Tunstall, are you in there?'

'No,' I said.

'Well,' she huffed, 'you'd better come out, else you'll be off to the headteacher's office for the slipper, and you won't want that, will you?'

Actually, I wanted to say, I wouldn't mind, because at least Mr Griffiths is fair and only smacks the palm of my hand with his slipper if he has to. He always says, 'This is going to hurt me far more than it's going to hurt you, Debbie-Marie Tunstall', which isn't true, but it's his way of saying he's sorry, I suppose. And afterwards, he'll give me a biscuit.

But I didn't fancy a trip to Mr Griffiths' office today, because last time he didn't have any bourbon creams, and I think he's had his fill of me lately. So, I opened the toilet door, like Mrs Thomas told me to, and she was standing there glaring, all bulgy-eyed with her hands on her hips and her jaw sticking out, and I could see the grey bristles poking up all over her pink blancmange chin. Friday afternoon is painting time, and she was wearing her nylon overall, which always stinks of BO, so I thought I'd best do as I was told, else she'd put me in one of her headlocks between her armpit and ginormous boobs.

She calmed down a bit when she saw me. I think she could tell I'd been crying.

'You'd better sort yourself out before you go back to class,' she said, trying not to look at me. 'And for God's sake, wipe your nose. It's absolutely filthy.'

I walked home by myself, because everyone was going to Flicks N' Kicks' dance rehearsals at Carrie-Anne and Lucy Marston's house. Mam calls them the Toxic Twins. They're identical, though I reckon Carrie-Anne is a bit less stupid-looking.

Everyone thinks they're pretty, because they've got long brown hair that they tie up in ribbons, and they wear crop tops and stretchy shorts, like that singer Madonna, who's always shoving her belly button in everyone's faces. I overheard Lucy saying that they're going to re-do the dance that was meant to happen at the summer fete, the dance I wrecked because I put senna in their sandwiches.

I don't feel bad about what I did. I don't feel guilty at all, because they bullied me badly. Always have, always will. They leave me out of everything. Blanche Marston – their mam – looks down her nose at me. My mam says Blanche's head is stuck so far up her arse she can see out of her own navel, and I know she's right, but Blanche always makes me feel dirty, ugly and bad. The way she stares at me . . . like she'd wring my neck with her bare hands just to keep her precious girls away from a clumsy great monster like me.

Anyway, I didn't mind being on my own after school. It's conker season, so I went to the common where there are zillions of the things, freshly fallen, their spiky green shells just starting to split so you can see the brown jewel shining through the creamy pith. That's the best part of all, when you pick up the shell, and you catch it – the smell of fresh pulp, and the hope and the promise inside. You never can tell how big they'll be, until you rip the shell apart. Is it one huge conker, or two tiddly twins, nestling together side by side? Will it have sharp, killer wedges and edges, or be smooth and round, like a pebble?

I filled the pockets of my skirt until they were bulging, and that cheered me up, because I realized that with everyone wishing me dead and not wanting to play conkers at playtime,

I could keep them all to myself. I like lining them up on my windowsill, even when they go crinkly and wrinkly. They're my family and friends.

When I got home, the flat was empty. It always feels empty, anyway, because we don't have much furniture – just a couple of second-hand armchairs, with the stuffing falling out of their brown stretchy covers, and a blue plastic table Mam covered in flowery Fablon to cheer the place up. Mam was out cleaning, as usual. I used to go to Barbara's house straight after school, but Mam is worried that people will talk after everything I did in the summer. She thinks that Barbara is old and a 'target' and has enough on her plate as it is, what with her sister Lynette popping her clogs, and Dai and Robert falling to pieces all over the place.

I made myself a Marmite sandwich, then sat on the kitchen stool and ate it. But I didn't enjoy it much. The marge tasted off, the flat was dead quiet, and it felt very strange indeed, like the place belonged to somebody else, which it sort of does, because we rent from the council. Normally I don't mind that the flat isn't ours, it still feels like mine and Mam's, but today – I dunno. I was lonely and sad, and all I could hear was the sound of my chewing, and the clock on the cooker ticking away, in time with my heart, only weaker.

I went to my room, ripped the shells off my conkers and laid them out on my sill to dry out. The view from my window is really quite boring, just a lane and some garages and a few steel bins. I never see anyone out there, so I can play without having to worry that someone will look up and see me and think that I'm stupid, or *twp* as we say in these parts.

*   *   *

So here I am now, lining them up, my conkers, my people. Deciding who's who, and what will be what. The future that is in store for each of them.

This big, shiny one – the most beautiful of all – is Barbara Pritchard, my very best friend. This smaller one, but just as shiny, is Robert Hargreaves, her nephew. Everyone says that Rob is weird, because he wears leather trousers and ripped T-shirts, has mad curly hair and pudgy lips and looks like Bozo the Clown or Bob Geldof, depending on who you're talking to. Rob doesn't say much at all, even when he's pulling pints in the pub, but he's ever so smart – he did maths at uni – and he used to play in a band. He once dyed his hair bright yellow, but people said he looked like his mam's cockatoo and took the piss, so he let it grow out and went to work in insurance instead.

I like Rob. When I'm sat by myself outside the Llanfair Arms, he'll bring me a raspberry Panda Pop from the pub, and some pickled onion Monster Munch. He's been very sad since his mam died. Even sadder and quieter than before. Sometimes, when he brings me my pop, he'll sit with me for a bit. Not saying anything, mind. Just staring ahead and smoking a fag, lighting it with his hands cupped together, like he's telling it a secret.

Rob knows that I'm bullied. That the other kids hate me and won't let me play. Sometimes, if he sees that I've been crying, he'll say something like, 'Those Marston girls being little sods again, Debbie? I hate bullies, I really do. There's a special place in hell reserved for people like them.'

I don't take him on, though I want to say, 'So why are you shaggin' their mother, then?' but I don't. Because Rob's a friend of mine, and I don't have many left, let's face it.

He said something weird a few weeks ago, though.

I was sucking away on a Monster Munch, sitting on the wall outside the pub, kicking the heels of my trainers in time to Frankie's 'Two Tribes' blasting out from someone's car radio. It was late afternoon, and Mam was cleaning the lounge bar just before opening time, and Rob came and sat next to me – smoking, as per.

I noticed his eye twitching, like my kicking was getting on his very last nerve, which only made me kick even harder. There was a lovely smell wafting from the chippy across the road, and someone had just hosed down the big red flowers in the hanging baskets above my head. I could feel the soft plop plop of water on my shoulders, but I didn't mind because it had been hot that day and I'd had to wear my school jumper, even though it was still the holidays, because Mam couldn't be bothered with the washing that week. But then I looked up at the sky, and I saw that two white aeroplane trails had criss-crossed above my head, and I knew this was a lucky sign – really, I did – I often see signs that turn out to be right, because people say that I'm psychic, or psych-something. I can't remember what. Anyway, I thought to myself, this is a sign that my luck will change. The new school year will be much nicer for me, and I might even find a new friend!

But then Rob said, out of the blue, 'Llewelyn hasn't spoken a word since Mum died.'

I stopped kicking my heels and stared at him. It was such a peculiar thing to say.

'Well, that makes two of you,' I said, trying to make light of it all. 'You've barely opened your mouth, Robert Hargreaves, since your mam passed on. Anyway, just as well Llewelyn keeps his gob shut, because he talks absolute filth, that bird of yours. He kept asking Mam to show him her knickers whenever she dusted his cage. *Show us yer knickers*, he'd say. *Show us yer arse.* Where d'you think he learnt that, Rob?'

'Beats me.'

'Yeah, yeah.'

And he cracked a smile, before stubbing out his fag on the ground with the heel of his boot. 'You put that empty crisp packet and bottle of pop in the bin when you're finished, mind,' he called over his shoulder, his studded belt and buckled boots clanking like ghost chains as he stomped inside the pub.

I stared at his smouldering butt on the pavement. 'Hypocrite!' I cried.

Now this old conker – oven-baked in vinegar and hard as nails – is Blanche Marston. She's my number one enemy, or 'nemesis' as Barbara Pritchard puts it. Blanche has had it in for me and Mam ever since we moved from Barwood back to Llanfair after Dad left us, because Mam's on her own and we're common, I think, and Blanche doesn't like outsiders. Though Mam isn't an outsider at all. She grew up in Llanfair and only moved to Barwood when she fell in love with my dad. In fact, Mam and Blanche went to school together – they were in the same class as Nurse Rose Pugh – and Mam says she and Blanche have 'history'. I said, like Charles I and Oliver Cromwell? And Mam said, yes, a bit like that, and she'd certainly knock Blanche Marston's block off, given half a chance.

Barbara Pritchard doesn't like Blanche, either. She says that she's brash and as thick as a brick, but I don't think the last part is true. Blanche Marston is clever. There's a big, bad brain lurking under that bushy black hairdo of hers. She's as sharp as the white stilettos she wears, and as uptight as her spray-on jeans. She used to be a dancer, Mam says, but she always says 'dancer' with a wink.

I still can't decide which conkers are The Vicar or Nurse Rose Pugh, though.

That pair can keep.

I just hope The Vicar's learnt his lesson, and will lay off the ladies for a while.

It's all written down here, see, in my Kajagoogoo notebook.

And the stuff that's in there, you honestly wouldn't believe.

4

Robert

4.30 p.m., Llanfair Village Square

Robert mooches past Morris the Butcher's, trying not to look at the window display of miniature cows and sheep arranged in a field of plastic grass, and the platters of mottled pink sausages laid out in rows beside them. The smell of blood mixed with sawdust always makes him gag. He used to like the butchers when he was small, when Mum would take him shopping for the weekly meat, and Mr Morris would give him a sherbet lemon from the paper bag hidden under the counter – the sweeties reserved for the kids who were quiet and didn't run riot in his shop. Robert was such a good boy. Everybody said so.

No sign of Morris today. The butcher's counter is unmanned, the sawdust floor unsullied by customer footfall. Morris will be in his room in the back, a withered shadow of a man glimpsed through the clanking metal chains dividing shop-front from parlour, nursing his hungover head in his hands over a pot of industrial-strength tea. Morris has been going downhill for years, ever since the ring-road supermarket opened, under-cutting his prices and driving him to drink. Robert shakes his head as he passes. That's progress for you.

Llanfair is a village of thirds, each telling a tale of boom and bust. The thatched cottage to the east of the square, owned by Robert's Aunt Barbara, was built by a Tudor merchant when Llanfair was still a hamlet – the sole surviving dwelling after an outbreak of plague and witch-burning. The Victorian villas of Rowan Avenue, built for the emerging middle-class during South Wales's industrial heyday, fell into disrepair following the First World War, regaining favour in the 1960s and 70s among newly-wed couples keen to escape the paper-thin walls of eavesdropping in-laws.

Just now, Robert is strolling towards the red-brick parade of shops built for Llanfair's post-war expansion: Hoskins' Hardware, Lucky Suds Launderette, and Wilmslow's Chemist – every lease owned by Llanfair big-shot, Clive Marston, each one of them up for renewal.

Robert peers through the launderette window, wondering whether it's safe to go in. He and Dad have run out of kecks, he's down to his final pair of jeans, and he can't avoid this place for ever. No sign of human life – but then, these days, there rarely is. He rattles the door nervously in a bid to flush them out: the felines that have colonized this place of late – feeding on rats, getting fat, breeding and pissing all over the place; preventing people like Robert, who don't have a washing machine of their own, from getting their clothes clean.

On top of a dryer, two tabbies feign sleep, assessing Robert through half-closed amber eyes. Beneath them, in the open drum, three striped kittens tumble and playfight among a tangle of tights, while a thunder-thighed black Persian skitters towards him, tail fluffed up like a bog brush. Robert looks down. He can hear a low growl. On the other side of the glass door, a ginger tom is arching its back, baring its teeth, hissing and lifting its quivering tail in preparation for spraying the knees of Robert's trousers.

'Sod off, Mr Niblet,' he says.

Mr Niblet is Clive Marston's cat. There were rumours that Marston planted him here, along with a couple of female strays, intending to render the laundry unusable before turning it into a wine bar, thus avoiding public outcry and pesky legal fees.

'A standoff between two tomcats, eh?' says a female voice at Robert's side.

He turns to see WPC Jane Gill in full uniform, smirking at him from under the rim of her policewoman's hat. Olive of skin, doe of eye and honey-blonde of lustrous hair, Jane Gill might be considered an extraordinary beauty, were she not such an extraordinary thug.

'I could have you, Robbie Hargreaves,' she whispers. 'In more ways than one.'

'I really don't think so, Jane,' he sighs. 'I don't know where you've got the idea that I'm the village Casanova, but the joke is wearing rather thin. Didn't you have your fill of tormenting me when we were at school together?'

She touches the arm of his denim jacket, running her fingers up and down the bulge of his bicep. 'WPC Gill to you,' she breathes. 'And no . . . apparently not. Gosh, you're very muscular these days, Robert. Not at all the puny, undernourished runt from primary school. Those karate lessons your auntie forced you to take as a kid have really paid off.'

'They had to,' Robert replies. 'To protect me from the likes of you.'

She cocks her head to one side. 'What are you now, a green-belt?'

'Blackbelt,' he says stiffly, pulling his arm away.

She winks at him. 'Who's the lucky lady of the moment, then? Still having your wicked way with Blanche Marston? What would Clive do if he found out . . . Oh, bugger . . .'

Her radio crackles. A disembodied male voice cuts through the air with a tinny whine: 'Unit 24, are you out there? I need my dry-cleaning picked up ASAP. Are you there? Over.'

'See you around,' she calls over her shoulder, darting across the road to her waiting patrol car. The driver revs the engine, Jane hops in, and off they zoom – all flashing blue lights and screaming sirens, Jane blowing a kiss to Robert as the car sails past.

Robert drives down Llanfair Lane with something coiled inside him. Something like a snake – a hooded-eyed, vengeful viper, desperate to strike. Hardly surprising, given his encounter with Jane Gill just now. But his usual antidote to Jane's toxicity – driving far too fast in his yellow Ford estate – just isn't cutting it for Robert today. His head is in too bad a place.

Because it's nearly a year since the death of his mother – twelve months of, at times, unbearable grief – and so very much has passed Robert by. He's been aware of certain events, of course, because scandals are the lifeblood of a place like Llanfair, and dissected at length in his father's pub. But since his mum's death and losing his job, Robert has slipped, as though under water, while everyone else remains on dry land – their voices muffled above the surface, while he drifts aimlessly through the murk and weeds beneath.

Some things still penetrated, though.

Like the brouhaha over the Tunstall kid. Blanche always had it in for poor Debbie-Marie Tunstall. And the whispers over the various pies Clive Marston stuck his sausagey fingers into. Then there were the rumours of The Vicar shagging Nurse Rose Pugh, who'd moved back to Llanfair from Barwood following a swift and brutal widowhood.

'Married to a National Coal Board Area Manager,' according to Blanche. 'The richest man in Barwood – not that that's saying much – and a right shit to boot. I'd have happily danced on Phil Pugh's grave when I heard he'd finally snuffed it.'

She stubbed out her cigarette on the woodland floor (they were taking a break during one of their lengthier sessions) and rolled onto her side, plucking at the tufts of moss carpeting an oak-tree root. 'I *am* glad Rose is back,' she said. 'Honest, I am. What luck she was offered a job at the surgery, then little Susan getting that place at Llanfair Primary School – poor kid, losing her daddy like that . . .'

Robert, who was getting changed at the time, trying not to entangle his toes in his dress-suit trousers, smirked at her. 'Methinks the lady doth protest too much,' he said.

Blanche stood up quickly, plucking leaves and dirt from her backcombed raven hair. 'Yeah,' she muttered irritably. 'Perhaps I *doth*.'

Robert glances at his watch and stamps on the accelerator. He should be back at the pub by now. When he gets in, Dad will be vacuuming the lounge-bar carpet even more passive-aggressively than usual. *Look what you've made me do*, he'll say, all toothless, breathless and sweaty in his greying string vest, tracksuit bottoms hanging baggily around his arse. *You were meant to do the vacuuming, you lazy git!* And he'll toss a beer mat at Robert's head, then tell him to get his barman clothes on. 'Something respectable, mind,' he'll shout. 'Not that ripped T-shirt and those tartan trousers covered in safety pins, you ruddy great muppet!'

If he could drive all day long, Robert would. When he's not in bed, staring up at the ceiling, Robert needs to be moving – preferably on autopilot, not thinking or speaking, or registering anything around him. Even so, he can't help but notice the subtle changes in the trees leaning at awkward angles from either side of Llanfair Lane – meeting in the middle to form an arch, licks of golds just beginning to breach the leafy deep-green canopy. Dapples of sunlight filter through the gaps between the branches, marbling the tarmacked road ahead, and Robert notes – with some surprise – that he's feeling a little better. Autumn was Mum's favourite season. His, too, when he thinks about it.

He drives past Stockholm Villa – that showy great pile belonging to the stuck-up Bridges family, 'Built along Scandinavian lines,' his mum once said – ultra-modern and open-plan, all glass and black timber cladding the sprawling oblong exterior. Robert thinks it an ugly house, which is a shame, because his second-year housemate at uni had been a nice Swedish girl who did him the favour of taking his virginity, and Robert's dislike of Stockholm Villa always makes him feel rather disloyal to the lovely Gertrud, somehow.

Anyway, after Stockholm Villa, there's about half a mile of twists and turns, before the grey-stone vicarage and square-towered Norman church glide into view. There's another quick curve to the right before you arrive at the junction for Llanfair itself.

It still takes Robert by surprise, the sudden appearance of civilization. One minute you're on a single-track road, surrounded by birch trees and bugger-all else, the next you're at a crossroads with the War Memorial facing you, shops to the left and right, cars sailing past, and people going about their daily business. Sometimes, when Robert waits at the junction, he wants to jam his foot on the accelerator – ignoring the Give Way sign – and drive into the War Memorial, bellowing as he does so that he Gives Way to nothing and no one. But Robert knows he will never do this, because it would upset his Auntie Barbara.

Just now, Robert is approaching the vicarage, anticipating the sharp bend before Llanfair comes into view, when something explodes from the hedgerow – a blast of something black and woolly, with bright yellow eyes and a dribbling underbite, barking and bouncing directly into the path of Robert's car.

'Jesus Christ!' He slams his foot on the brake. 'Utterson – you absolute bastard!'

The car screeches to a standstill the instant his aunt's squat figure staggers into the road to stand astride Utterson, arms outstretched, wicker basket clutched in one hand.

'Halt!' she cries.

At the same moment, a silver Ford Escort XR3, travelling in the opposite direction, screams up behind Barbara. A young woman's head pokes through the driver's window.

'I nearly killed you!' the woman yells. 'And your bloody dog!'

Robert gets out of his car. The young woman emerges from

her XR3, looks up to see him staring, scowls, and turns her head away.

Robert recognizes her. The posh, sulky kid who no one ever spoke to, with the stuck-up, over-protective Lady Mayoress mother. The kid who was no longer a kid, who lived in Stockholm Villa. Vanessa Bridges. All grown up.

'What's up, Barbara?' Robert says. 'Are you hurt?'

Barbara shakes her head. 'I am not hurt,' she whimpers, 'but The Vicar – Lewis Morgan – is. He's . . . I'm afraid he's done something dreadfully stupid.'

A crowd has gathered outside the vicarage, watching a pair of inappropriately cheery ambulance drivers strap the great, holy man of Llanfair's terrifying six-foot frame to a stretcher. A red blanket swaddles The Vicar from the neck down, rendering him practically infantile – albeit an infant with a long grey beard. Hard to imagine this giant of a man towering over the edge of his pulpit, giving his congregation what-for with one of his hell-fire sermons, all spit and fury and laser eyes. He once made Robert wet himself. True, this wasn't a recent occurrence – Robert was only five years old at the time – but it was when The Vicar declared that God was all around them, and knew everything there was to know, and Robert felt deeply upset about that, because he'd forgotten to put on clean underpants that morning.

The crowd sighs audibly as The Vicar is lifted into the ambulance. Robert wipes away a tear. Not because he is particularly moved – upsetting though the situation is – but because he lost his footing on The Vicar's front path, steadying himself by gripping the gatepost, which happens to be covered in nettles.

The chemist Rachel Wilmslow, AKA Brown Owl of the 1st Llanfair Brownie Unit, touches his arm. 'Don't cry, Robbie,' she says. 'The Vicar's in safe hands.'

'But I'm not . . .'

'You know,' she stands on tip-toe, wiping the tears from Robert's face with the sleeve of her chemist's coat, 'I blame myself. I have to – I'm the one who supplies his insulin, after all. But I don't understand how it happened. He has a system – he keeps his short-acting insulin entirely separate from his long-acting medication, on different sides of the kitchen. If only I'd been here earlier and not at my Barwood store . . .'

Rachel is in her early thirties, and already owns several pharmacies around Uskshire – a fact she drops into conversation at every opportunity. She also confuses Robert. She appears to be single, sends signals she's single, yet Robert's spotted her pushbike hidden behind the vicarage bins on more than one occasion.

He looks over his shoulder, seeking out the woman from the XR3. Vanessa Bridges has set herself apart from the crowd, and is sitting, cross-legged, cross-armed and cross-faced on the wall in front of the Scout Hut, her mass of corkscrew auburn curls bristling with acrimony. Robert wonders if she ever smiles.

'Here you go, poppet. Dry your eyes.' Rose Pugh is smiling up at him, proffering a large white handkerchief. 'You've always been a sensitive one. You can keep the hanky until it's laundered. I do want it back, though, mind.' She waggles a finger.

'But I'm not . . .'

Rose isn't listening. 'What a stroke of luck,' she's saying, 'that your auntie was walking Utterson past the vicarage! Of course, that dog shouldn't have been off his lead on a road like this, but it was all thanks to Utterson that The Vicar was found in the first place.'

'Thanks to Utterson?' Rachel says. 'Why? What did he do?'

'Raised the alarm! Barbara heard barking and discovered Utterson sitting by The Vicar, who was flat-out on his front path, still in his pyjamas, clutching his insulin syringe in one hand – that's how we knew what he'd done to himself – but undressed in the afternoon? That's not like The Vicar at all. You never see him out of his vestments!'

Robert zones out for a moment, watching his aunt lean over The Vicar's stretcher, planting a very un-Barbara-like kiss on his deathly pale forehead.

'I was in the cemetery next door,' Rose is still yapping, 'putting flowers on Mammy's grave, when I heard Utterson barking and Barbara shrieking . . .'

'I did not shriek.' Barbara has joined them.

They watch the ambulance leave. Silence descends on the crowd for a moment.

Then – 'Where was I?' Rose says. 'Oh, yes, I was telling everyone, Barb, about Utterson finding Lewis – The Vicar – and I was just about to get to the bit where you rolled him into the recovery position, and I tried to call 999 from the phone in the hall. But the phone wasn't working, and I had to use the telephone box on the corner instead. An overdose.' Rose nods sagely. 'A lifelong diabetic, deliberately overdosing on insulin. Couldn't live with the shame, I'd imagine. The shame of that Polaroid photograph of him and me that Debbie-Marie Tunstall put on the village notice board . . . and I was only massaging his lumbar region at the time! Oh, God!' She buries her face in her hands.

'Buck up, Rose,' Barbara snaps. 'If it was intentional, then why was he lying on his front path with his door wide open? It looks like he was trying to get help when he realized his telephone wasn't working. An accidental overdose, I think.'

'Perhaps it was intentional, then he changed his mind?' Rachel suggests. 'What Debbie-Marie did to him . . . taking a photo when he was in such a vulnerable situation. So humiliating for such a proud man!'

'I dread to think what Ingrid will say about this apparent "overdose".' Barbara shakes her head. 'Though she'll find out soon enough. And when she does, heaven help poor Deborah.'

'That child needs a smacked bottom,' Rachel says.

'Violence is rarely the answer,' Rose adds, reprovingly.

Robert hears a car start. Rubbing his nettled hand, he turns, just as his eyes start smarting again, to meet Vanessa Bridges' cold-fish stare as she steers her silver XR3 through the thinning crowd.

Rachel tugs at his arm. 'Will you be serving in the pub tonight, Rob? Everyone who's anyone will be there. I'll be there,' she smiles, shyly. 'Rose is putting me up for the night. It's good I've got somewhere to stay – can't risk driving back to Barwood when I've had a drink or two. I bet you could do with a drink after this. You should join us, Rob.'

'She likes you,' Barbara observes slyly, as Rachel's slim, white-coated figure darts across the square towards Wilmslow's Pharmacy, Rose Pugh's shiny blonde bonce bobbing along beside her.

'Hmm? Oh. Right. Wasn't that Vanessa Bridges I just saw, from Stockholm Villa? The woman in the silver Ford Escort?'

'Possibly, Robert. I wasn't paying attention.'

Robert looks down at his aunt. She is frowning at the vicarage while chewing her thumbnail. She lightly touches his elbow. 'There is something I need to tell you. And show you,' she says.

From the pocket of her mackintosh, Barbara draws out a small red sachet with Durex Fetherlite printed on its front.

Robert raises an eyebrow. 'Now, Auntie Barbara,' he says mockingly, 'that's not a balloon in there, and it's not for playing with. Do we need to have a serious talk?'

'Don't be absurd. When I found The Vicar, I also found . . .' she waggles the sachet at him, clearly unable to utter its name, ' . . . *this* . . . *prophylactic* lying on the path next to him. I removed it before Rose Pugh saw, of course, because it seemed so, well – *grubby*.'

'Blimey.'

'Blimey indeed.' She stares at him. 'Most peculiar, no?'

'Well.' He thinks for a bit. 'Not necessarily. Perhaps a sex-addicted parishioner dropped it on their way to confessing their sins to him? Or it fell out of The Vicar's own dressing gown pocket while he stooped down to pick up his milk? He's a randy old goat, we all know that. Perhaps he was in the middle of getting down and dirty with someone, and the woman in question legged it when The Vicar collapsed? Or . . . I don't know,' Robert shrugs. 'Was it some sort of symbol? You know, wanting to kill himself after the shame of those photos of him and Rose Pugh, and leaving a Durex next to his body to prove a point? You know The Vicar far better than I do – he's one of your closest friends, after all. You should ask him.'

Barbara nods sadly. 'Yes, of course I'll ask him, Robert. Assuming he survives.'

5

Vanessa

5.30 p.m., Stockholm Villa, Llanfair Lane

Just who in their right mind would want to take on the Tunstall child? Not Dr Vanessa Bridges, that's for sure, who absolutely *is* in her right mind, has always been of sound mind, who understands that her fine mind is one of the few things going for her in a world minded to value platinum hair and 40G bosoms over an IQ of 138 and Grade 8 bassoon.

But child psychologist Dr Vanessa Bridges, rising star of kiddie forensics, has been given no choice in the matter – has been strongly advised that, if she refuses, she'll be looking for employment elsewhere. It's all her own fault, of course. Had she been less hubristic and more open-minded, Vanessa might still be stalking the oak-panelled halls of the Cardiff Institute of Psychology and rubbing shoulders with the shrink elite, not playing dollies with the gobby and grubby who just needed boundaries and a bloody good wash.

Vanessa considers all of this as she swerves her mother's XR3 into the gravel driveway of Stockholm Villa, stopping short of the garage door. She applies the handbrake with an almighty crunch, gazing forlornly at the palatial bungalow squaring up to her bug-spattered windscreen. A tribute to Scandinavian minimalism designed by her architect father, its glass and timber exterior has since been defiled by her mayoress mother: peach silk Venetian blinds sulk in folds at the living-room windows, while at the centre of the drive is a rococo-style pond housing several varieties of exotic carp, and a statue of a naked woman wrestling with some sort of sea-beast.

'The turning circle,' her mother calls it.

Her mother was nice and normal, once.

Vanessa idles the engine and waits, watching her mother's shadow faffing around behind the glazed front door. *Gwendoline Bridges, Lady Mayoress of Llanfair, straightens the skirt of her blue silk suit, pats her plumage into place, inserts a diamond earring into each earlobe, checks her handbag – navy snakeskin – for powder compact and priggishness (both essential items for the Uskshire Council AGM), before launching herself towards her XR3 in a noxious cloud of Rive Gauche . . .*

'Did you get the Ritz crackers?' her mother's yelling, propelling her court-heeled shoes along the gravel driveway. 'I'm on Light Refreshments, remember.'

Vanessa nudges her head at the back seat. 'No Ritz crackers I'm afraid. You'll have to make do with Iced Gems.'

'Iced Gems? *With cheese and wine?* Are you out of your bloody mind, Vanessa?'

'It would seem so, Mum.'

With any luck, Vanessa thinks, *Mum will be so distracted with Iced Gem angst, she'll forget her usual barrage of questions – did you have a good day? Any sign of getting your old job back? Has that nice Professor Murray been in touch?* To which Vanessa would like to reply: shit, not a chance, and mind your own bloody business.

Vanessa knows it is wrong to feel this way. That any decent, dutiful daughter would be grateful of her parents' welcome home when living alone in that flat of hers got too much in the end. And they'd been so nice about it all. Hadn't demanded to know why, hadn't even asked any awkward questions for a change – they'd known better than that, of course, having read all about the Robinson inquiry in *The South Wales Morning Post*. As it was, she had only to mention the silent midnight telephone calls at her Cardiff flat for her mother to cry: 'But you must come home at once! Your room is your room for ever, you know.'

Yes, she should feel guilty. For resenting her parents' kindness, for still needing their kindness at the age of twenty-six. For repaying that kindness by skulking off to her bedroom every evening like the moody thirteen-year-old she'd been half a lifetime ago.

I am a terrible person, Vanessa tells herself. *I deserve to be stuck in this purgatory.*

'Vanessa? *Vanessa?*'

'Hmm?'

'I said, did you have a good day? Any news on your job? And that Professor . . . what's his name . . .'

'Mark Murray.'

'Has he been in touch?'

'For Christ's sake, Mum!'

'Temper, Ness – we're not at home to Little Miss Moody. Now, out of the car you get, pronto – I'm going to be late.'

Vanessa realizes she's still gripping the handbrake, nails digging into the palm of her hand. She remembers the Tunstall girl's grubby fingers. Something in her chest constricts.

'Did you hear me, Vanessa?'

She edges the car door open. 'Receiving you loud and clear, Mum. Just give me a sec to pop my Dr Scholl's back on. There's a very good reason why I'm behind schedule, actually – an emergency on the way home. The Vicar – does anyone know his real name? – anyway, The Vicar's been carted off to hospital. Insulin overdose, so I heard.'

Gwendoline Bridges' over-plucked eyebrows shoot into her hairline. 'Good God! Lewis Morgan – that's his name. Horrid man. What a shame – I was planning to have his guts for garters at tonight's AGM.'

'Why? Whatever's the poor man done to you?'

'Backing Uskshire Council turning that field behind Stockholm Villa into social housing. I will not have it, Vanessa. I will not have problem families lolling on my doorstep.'

'Mum, you're a bugger. Has anyone told you you're turning into Margaret Thatcher?'

'We don't say bugger in this house, Ness. We say blighter, and only then under extreme provocation. And I hope you haven't been wearing my driving shoes, what with your verruca and all.' Her face brightens. 'Do I? Do I look like her, really?'

'Yes. Yes, you do. And you can rest assured that your driving shoes remain unsullied, fit to be worn by Thatcher herself, because I drove home barefoot.'

'Well, that's just disgusting and downright reckless. How on earth did you get any purchase on the brake pedal? You know how sweaty your soles get!'

'It would be easier for me to get out, Mum, if you just stepped aside . . . thank you . . . and thank you *very much* for the warm welcome home. I had a terrible day, thanks for asking. Oh, and your advice to camouflage the zit on my chin with eyeliner to turn it into a beauty-spot backfired spectacularly. My latest juvenile delinquent was transfixed by it, as was the dishy petrol-pump attendant on the way home.'

Vanessa's mother sighs, shimmies into the driver's seat, adjusts the rear-view mirror with a flourish, and slams the car door shut. She thrusts her head through the open window.

'There's a ham and egg salad in the fridge,' she bellows. 'Your dad's out at the pub tonight, so you'll be eating alone. Don't wait up, don't use all the hot water, and don't make a mess in the kitchen. And for heaven's sake, *do* something with your hair.' She blows Vanessa a kiss, skidding around the turning circle at alarming speed.

Vanessa looks down at her feet. Her mother has driven off with her sandals.

She must have fallen asleep. It's dark outside and her dinner plate has slipped off her lap, spewing lettuce leaves and a lone spring onion down the side of the cream leather sofa. On the TV, Geoff Hamilton from *Gardeners' World* is giving a demonstration on propagating pelargoniums, which must mean it's gone 8.30 p.m. – nearly time for bed.

Woozy of head and furry of mouth, Vanessa picks up the rogue pieces of salad, tosses them onto her plate, and staggers over the shagpile carpet into the kitchen. There, she feeds her uneaten dinner to the waste disposal unit, catching sight of her reflection in the window as she does so. Double-glazing distorts everyone's features, but Christ, she looks crap! So drawn, so pale, so hollowed-out under the eyes.

Well, what on earth does she expect? She's recovering from months of zero sleep – for a time, she thought she'd never sleep again. As it is, she can only let herself drift off when her bedroom light is on, and then for just two or three hours at a time.

She was never afraid of the dark before Isobel Robinson's accident. But now it's the unknown quality of darkness that gets to her. The not seeing, not knowing what's out there. Well, she sort of knows what's out there, of course. That on the other side of the kitchen window is the back garden – where elevated tiers of her mother's rockeries look down on her father's fat pink dahlias, the whole mismatched affair corralled by a high wooden fence. The garden felt exclusively hers as a kid, back in the days when she had her own swing and slide, and the occasional friend around to play with. The fence was ten feet high, and had no holes or gaps, so her parents never had to worry about people getting in. Or Vanessa getting out.

But on the other side of the fence lies the field. And Vanessa hates the field. Loathes it so much she's been praying for ever that it'll finally be sold for development. It's the field of doom, the field of the damned, overgrown with brambles and rye grass. The field owned by a weird old lady who still lives in a ramshackle house in the village, a witch-like woman who threatened to sell the field two decades ago, but then fell out with the builder and refused to go through with the sale after all. 'Let the children own the field instead!' she declared, proving her point by hosting a teddy bears' picnic for the local kiddies – a six-year-old Vanessa Bridges being one of them.

Vanessa hadn't hated the field back then. She'd initially loved every sun-dappled second of that August afternoon: galloping through the undergrowth, teddy bear in hand, a gaggle of giggling new-found friends tagging along behind her. The day was mellow, warm and golden; a dusty haze of humming bees, swaying grass and arched brambles laden with a bumper crop of glossy, swollen blackberries . . .

Oh, give yourself a kick up the backside! It wasn't like that at all. Stop telling yourself fairy stories, and face up to reality for a change!

'The truth,' Professor Murray had said to her, once the Robinson inquiry was over. 'You failed to acknowledge the reality of the matter, Dr Bridges, and therefore failed your patient. You have a lot to learn.'

All right. So, what was the truth of that afternoon, twenty years ago? Well, now, when Vanessa really thinks about it, it had been joyful for some of it, yes. But then one of the girls was left out of a game – possibly her, she can't remember. She recalls wandering off by herself to pick blackberries, scratching her fingers and staining her hands and her dress with juice the colour and texture of blood clots. And then (and she's never known why or how on earth she got there), she was hiding in a coppice at the edge of the field – a dark, dank tangle of a place, the cool air reeking of perfume and cigar smoke – peeking through branches as a very blonde woman with her eyes shut tight, mouth stretched into a glossy red 'O', was repeatedly shoved against a tree by a bare-bottomed man in a tweed sports jacket. The tableau was a matter of feet from her face, and Vanessa could clearly see the man's Paisley underpants bunched around his knees, a monogrammed handkerchief – the initials HW – sticking out of his trouser pocket.

When the man let out an almighty groan, Vanessa screamed, dropped her blackberries, and hurtled through the waist-high grass back to her friends and her mum and the weird old lady who owned the field. But when she tried to explain what she'd seen, everyone got terribly cross, and Vanessa cried. Two of the girls started to fight, and Vanessa knew it was all her fault, that the bad thing she'd witnessed that afternoon must never be spoken of ever again.

The front door slams. She jumps. 'Hello?'

'Hello, love!'

Her father. Standing in the kitchen doorway, swaying slightly, stinking of beer, cock-a-hoop with himself for being only slightly the worse for wear. Just look at him with his fuzzy grey sideburns, bright red face, golfing sweater and easy-fit slacks in complementary shades of charcoal and lemon. She loves the bones of the silly old sod, she really does.

'And what time do you call this?' she enquires, hands on hips, pretending to be all pissed off with him.

'I call it a great time!' he beams. 'Absolutely marvellous night at the Llanfair Arms. A few pints, a game of darts, a rousing chorus or two of "Arthur Scargill Walks on Water" . . .'

'Tra-la-la-la-la,' she trills in reply, slapping his thigh with a tea towel. 'You'd better not let Mum hear you singing that.'

'She's got delusions of grandeur, that one,' he laughs. 'I dunno. You take the girl out of Barwood, and thirty years later, she thinks she's the bloody Queen.'

'Or Margaret Thatcher.'

'Or Margaret Thatcher. God help us.' He rubs the stubble

speckling his chin. 'It's a bit much, though, isn't it? Your grandparents would turn in their graves at all this.'

'Turn in their graves over what, exactly?'

'The Miners' Strike. And they'd be on different sides – her mam and dad, mine too. Just as well they're all dead, and we got the hell out of Barwood years ago . . . but maybe that makes us worse than anyone. Worse traitors than the scabs themselves. Ah . . .' He waves a hand dismissively. 'Don't worry yourself about it, love. You've enough on your mind as it is.'

She nods. 'I do.'

'You did what you could. Stop blaming yourself.'

She twists the tea towel between her fingers. 'I did what I could, but not what I should. There's an important difference.'

'What happened to Isobel Robinson . . . none of that was your fault.'

'Well, whether it was or wasn't, I'm getting payback for it now. Because an extraordinary eleven-year-old girl is my latest charge. She's smart. Frighteningly smart. And she's created absolute mayhem – wrecked reputations, blackmailed a vicar, fed senna to her classmates . . . might even have given them morphine, too – who knows? In every way, she's the exact opposite of Isobel Robinson. Isn't that ironic?'

She closes her eyes, willing the tears that are welling to stop, but she just can't help herself; can't help wondering how Isobel Robinson's dad must be feeling tonight.

And then she remembers the Tunstall girl, who doesn't have a dad.

She feels her father's hands on her shoulders, propelling her towards him. She rests her head on the collar of his sweater, steadily breathing in his scent of tobacco, Brains beer and Old Spice aftershave.

'Listen, love,' he murmurs, 'everything will be fine, you'll see. You'll get your old job back, find a nice bloke . . . come on, give us a *cwtch*.'

'I wish I could believe you, Dad,' she says, *cwtching* him back with all her might. 'But I'm a little too old for bedtime stories, and I stopped believing in fairy tales a long, long time ago.'

MONDAY, 10 SEPTEMBER 1984

THE SOUTH WALES MORNING POST

Llanfair Plays While Barwood Pays

An opinion piece by Margaret Lawrence,
Welsh Affairs Correspondent

Clive Marston. Remember that name, then run for the hills should you ever hear him utter the words, 'May I interest you in taking out a financial loan?'

But before I explain why, let me tell you a tale of two villages. The first – Barwood – is living through the bitterest strike in industrial history; a dispute ripping communities apart, bleeding families dry of their savings, starving them into surrender. And yet, among the Barwood miners is the greatest solidarity I have ever witnessed – a profound loyalty bonding young and old, fit and infirm, man and woman, brother to brother, allowing this cynical hack to hope that in these godless times there might be a God, after all.

Now let me steer you three miles south, to the other side of Barwood Mountain, and the village of Llanfair – home to the most prosperous population in Uskshire. Here, houses sell for as much as £40,000, and its well-heeled inhabitants want for nothing. And yet, a visit to the local (and excellent) hostelry, the Llanfair Arms, and a discussion with some of the locals, reveals its inhabitants are very unhappy indeed with their lot. No Wales in Bloom trophy for the second year running. Youngsters loiter around the War Memorial while wearing Frankie Goes to Hollywood slogan T-shirts. Two girls suffered a tummy upset at a village fete, so a psychopath must be at large.

And now a field on the outskirts of Llanfair is about to be sold, to accommodate social housing tenants. A leaflet, sent to the offices of *The South Wales Morning Post*, was last week distributed to every house in Llanfair, encouraging its inhabitants to rise up and fight against this 'tragedy'.

Tragedy? I'll give you a tragedy.

Deirdre Crowdass of Hill Street, Barwood, took out a loan from Marston Accountancy and Tax Ltd to pay for her father's funeral, a funeral that could not be paid out of her husband's wages, as he is a striking miner at the local colliery. Deirdre only read the small print several weeks after taking out the loan. She was too distressed at the time of her father's death to focus on such details. The interest rate was 40 per cent. Repayments to start immediately.

Other, similar tragedies are playing out across Barwood: vulnerable, desperate people enduring the most despicable exploitation by Clive Marston, a name familiar with Barwood residents, who recall Mr Marston with fondness – making his recent financial activities hard to comprehend, let alone bear.

'He was one of us,' Deirdre Crowdass says. 'A Barwood boy, born and bred – a lovely lad, a friend of the family, until he moved to Llanfair! And now he's taking advantage of his connections here – it's disgusting. He should be thoroughly ashamed of himself!'

I attended last Friday night's Uskshire Council AGM, and asked Lady Mayoress of Llanfair, Gwendoline Bridges, for her comment on the matter. Her reply was as follows:

'We stand shoulder-to-shoulder with our dear friends in Barwood, and offer them our sincerest support. Where there is discord, may we bring harmony. Where there is error, may we bring truth. And where there is despair, may we bring hope.'

Mr Marston was unavailable for comment.

6

Robert

*10 a.m., somewhere between Llanfair Village Surgery and
the Village Square*

Robert is driving his Ford estate over the Llanfair railway
bridge, just as the Swansea to London Intercity 125 streaks
into view. He holds his breath, anticipating the train's thun-
derous passage under his wheels; recalling how, as a kid, he'd
lean over the bridge's flaking railings and watch the merry-go-
round coal train on its journey from Barwood to Cardiff,
counting the number of hopper wagons clattering beneath
him, praying for an even number because that sometimes
augured a good day. A day when Jane Gill and her cronies
might leave him the hell alone for once.

He turns left at the junction, following the curved incline
of Rowan Avenue, with its handsome red-brick Victorian villas,
trimmed front lawns and topiaries, past the mock-Tudor facade
of the Llanfair Arms, and on towards the village square. He
quickly finds a parking space, squeezing between a red Mini
and a white Vauxhall Astra, before turning off his engine,
slumping back in his seat and closing his eyes.

At this exact time, one year ago, Robert was holding his

mother's hand as she took her final breath. It was raining that day, the day that she died. Rainy and windy, not like today, which is all blue skies and no wind. Motionless, like him.

Robert is stuck. Stuck in his bed until noon most days; stuck in his head always. It took every last ounce of his energy to get to his doctor's appointment on time this morning. To sit in Dr Erasmus Jolly's surgery, plonk himself in the plastic chair opposite the portly, soon-to-retire GP with the Basset-hound jowls, to verbalize his misery: the constant gnawing in the pit of his belly; the lack of purpose or joy in his life. The endless, sleepless days and nights melding into an interminable chunk of . . . nothing. Did he have any interests, Dr Jolly asked. Anything he had to get up for – something or someone he needed to care for?

'Well, as you know, I help my dad in the pub. A bit of a comedown from my days in insurance, but beggars can't be choosers. And I have to look after Mum's bird, Llewelyn, of course.' And at that, he'd turned his head to the window, anticipating the lip twitch, the snigger that invariably followed whenever he let slip that one of the few things in his life worth getting up for was a foul-mouthed, sulphur-crested cockatoo.

But Jolly just stared at him for a moment, as though thinking, '*You're* depressed? Spend a day in *my* shoes!' before sighing heavily, and drawing out a packet of cigarettes from his breast pocket.

Jolly coughed. 'Do you mind if I . . . ?'

Robert shrugged. 'Go ahead.'

'Not a word to the wife, mind,' Jolly wheezed, jamming the cigarette between his lips with one hand, scribbling something in his prescription pad with the other. 'Here – one month's supply of amitriptyline, then book another appointment to let me know how you've got on. I mean, seriously – let me know if it works. I could do with some of this stuff myself.'

Robert opens his eyes, squinting through his dust-speckled windscreen into the morning sun, trying to focus on the timbered cottage directly across the road from his car, with its immaculately tended front garden of herbs and roses and trumpeted flowers he doesn't know the names of. He doesn't want Barbara to see him going into the chemist, to know that he's taking tablets. Again. Doesn't want her to worry, or ask awkward questions, or make any assumptions; doesn't want her to think he has any designs on the chemist, Rachel Wilmslow.

Even so, Robert sniffs under his armpits. Just to make sure they still bear the sweet, sharp fragrance of the Hai Karate deodorant spray he'd liberally applied that morning, before swiping his shirt from his bedroom floor – a garment that may or may not have been washed in the past few weeks. Even before Mr Niblet's laundry siege, Robert wasn't good with the washing – his responsibility, since Mum died. Dad does the cooking and shopping, while Robert does everything else, including the vacuuming on the days that Ingrid Tunstall can't make it in to clean. Though Dad often does the vacuuming anyway. He likes to be busy, does Dad. He's a live-wire, is Dai Hargreaves – a bald-headed, lanky-legged, toothless dynamo. He and Robert couldn't be more different. Two peas coexisting in entirely separate pods.

Robert strolls up to the pharmacy window, gazing past the display of deep-blue apothecary jars to the figure of Rachel

Wilmslow standing behind the counter. She has her back to him, her shiny dark bob skimming the crisp collar of her white chemist's coat. She is arranging packets of Durex in colour co-ordinated rows, and turns around and spots him. 'Robert!' she mouths, making beckoning motions. 'Come in! Come in!'

Robert goes in.

'Are you okay after last Friday?' she says. 'I'm still a bit shaken up, to be honest – I think The Vicar's doing all right, from what Nurse Pugh tells me, though he's likely to be kept in hospital for a while, under observation. Oh, and I completely forgot to thank you!'

'Thank me?' says Robert. 'For what?'

'Well, for how kind you were after my accident. You know, a couple of weeks ago. You wheeled my bike home, remember?'

She smiles at him. She's pretty. Not his type, but pleasant enough to look at. Even-featured. Nice straight teeth. Nothing jarring, challenging or in any way off-kilter.

Definitely not his type.

'It was nothing.' Robert smiles. 'I didn't do anything at all. It was Nurse Pugh who patched you up. Good job she was there when it happened. How's the bump on your head?'

She pats her hair self-consciously. 'Gone,' she says, with a grin. 'Took a few days to go down, though. Hoped it might knock some sense into me, but I'm still as daffy as ever.' She laughs, rolling her eyes. 'I mean, look at me – a woman in her thirties, still larking about with the Brownies and skipping around toadstools. I don't know why I bother, especially as it was probably one of the little darlings that cut the brakes on my bike in the first place.'

Their eyes meet. Robert senses she wants to say, *and we both know who that little darling might be*, but she seems to think better of it, because she'll know that Robert takes pity on Debbie-Marie Tunstall; that Robert will defend Debbie-Marie, no matter what mayhem that child might cause. Kindred souls and all that.

Robert fingers the crumpled prescription that feels like it's burning a hole in his pocket. 'For what it's worth,' he says, 'I think you're being hard on yourself. You do a really important job in this village – I mean, not just as a chemist, but as Brown Owl.'

She nods enthusiastically. 'I'm so happy to hear you say that! It's such wholesome fun for the girls. Much better than prancing around at that dancing club in mini-skirts – it's all so . . . precocious!' She over enunciates the 's', shaking her head. 'Flicks N' Kicks. I ask you! It'll be Strips for Kicks, once those girls get into their teens. Blanche Marston has a lot to answer for. Now, what can I do for you?'

Robert curls his fingers around the bottle in his right-hand pocket – the morphine that eased his mum's pain and, for a while, Robert believed, might ease his pain, too. Time to hand it in with a casual, *I found this in the bathroom – didn't think it was healthy having it in the house, especially after what happened to the Marston girls at the fete . . .*

But he pulls the prescription out of his left-hand pocket instead, sliding it over the counter. Rachel takes it, uncrumpling the ball of paper with a frown – a frown that, as she reads Dr Jolly's writing, relaxes into something altogether more tender.

'I'll sort this out for you straight away, Robert,' she says. 'Please, take a seat.'

7

Debbie

11 a.m., the library, Llanfair Village Primary School

I'm really getting under Mole Lady's skin. I can tell, because there's a nerve that keeps twitching under her left lower eyelid, but the mole has gone from her face, which is strange. Perhaps she had it taken off because people kept staring. I know I did, so I can't really blame her. But I'm cross, because she isn't Mole Lady any more. I don't like it when people change.

'Can I still call you Keith?' I ask, breaking off from the maths I've been doing – *if it takes two men three hours to dig a hole, how many hours will it take six men and a dog and a tin of spaghetti* – that sort of crap.

'I'll tell you what,' she says, sticking a pencil in the backside of one of those automatic sharpening thingies. 'I'll make a bargain with you, Debbie. You can carry on calling me Keith – you can call me whatever you like, within reason – as long as you promise to be totally honest with me. As long as you tell me the truth. That's one of the reasons you're here. Because you don't always tell the truth.'

'But I do! Brownie's honour.'

She sighs. 'Are you a Brownie, Debbie?'

'Yes!' I shout. 'I am!'

'Well, I heard that Brown Owl asked you to leave after the graffiti you wrote on the Scout Hut wall. The very rude things you wrote about her and The Vicar.' She narrows her eyes. 'Mr Griffiths told me about Brown Owl's bike. Are you sure you didn't cut the brakes?'

'I did not touch her stupid bike! Once a Brownie, always a Brownie. I swore an oath to the Queen, you know. And that graffiti was true. Or so I thought, at the time.'

Keith wants to 'observe' me at school today – to study me '*in situ*' – but Mrs Bug-eyed Thomas wouldn't let her in the classroom, because 'having a psychologist present might upset the other children.' So, we're stuck in the library, just us two, but I don't care. I like having someone all to myself, it makes a nice change. I don't even have Mam to myself, 'cos Mam's always somewhere else in her head, especially when she's stuck by herself with me.

Mam was dead weird all weekend. Ever since Barbara phoned last Friday about The Vicar's overdose – and I don't care what he did, I really don't, it wasn't my fault, it honestly wasn't. Though I fully expected a smacked arse, because Mam would blame me for what he did, just like every other bugger in Llanfair. But it didn't happen. She just came into my room and said – all robot-like – 'The Vicar tried to kill himself. Clean your teeth and go to bed.'

Then she took to her bed herself, and stayed there all weekend. I had to make my own breakfast and tea, and do my own washing – some pants and my shirt – in the kitchen sink. I passed the rest of the time watching telly and playing conkers, checking on Mam every hour or so. I didn't go into her room – I know better than that when she's in one of her states – but I looked through the crack in her bedroom door, just to make sure she'd moved since the last time I'd checked. A few times, she hadn't moved at all, so I waited, hardly daring to breathe, until I was certain her chest was still going up and down.

She must have got up to go to the toilet or drink something, but she'd have done that when I was asleep. She was staying out of my way. I'd hardly seen her all week, as it was – I haven't a clue where she is half the time, and she doesn't give a shit about what I'm getting up to. We're what Barbara would call *ships passing in the night*, though we don't see each other much then, either.

Anyway, Mam finally got up Sunday evening, when *Songs of Praise* was on the telly. The people in church were singing harvest songs – 'We Plough the Fields and Scatter', which is one of my favourites, but Mam hates it. She came flapping through in her housecoat and slippers, muttering something about me turning that God-bothering bollocks off.

I jumped up from my chair, and gave her a hug. 'Mam!' I said. 'I've missed you!'

She didn't reply or hug me back, just went all limp until I let go. Then she slumped in the chair I'd been sitting in, took a packet of fags out of her housecoat pocket, lit one and started puffing away, glaring at the telly.

'You hold your head high, Debbie-Marie Tunstall,' she said, sitting up very suddenly, peering into the washing basket I'd left at the side of the chair. The ash from the fag in her mouth fell onto my clean pants and shirt, but I didn't say anything.

'You keep your chin up, my girl,' she said, fag wobbling between her lips, 'and don't pay any attention to anyone who says that you're bad. Llanfair is full of absolute cocks.'

'So why do we live here?' I asked. 'Why can't we go back to Barwood?'

'Because.'

'Because of what?'

'Because Llanfair is the sort of place . . . well, it has high aspirations. And I want you to aim high, too. You know, do well in life and not end up like me.'

'But Mam,' I said, 'what's the point of living in a place with high aspirations when everyone here thinks that I'm a worm and should stay in the ground, where I belong?'

Mam put out her fag in my half-drunk cuppa so it hissed, then folded her arms and stared at me. She actually looks quite pretty when she doesn't have a cigarette dangling out of her mouth, and I very nearly told her so, but the *Songs of Praise* people had moved on to 'Come Ye Thankful People Come', and I was about to start singing along, when Mam said:

'Well, worms are wonderful. They're useful and beautiful, in their own way, and always make their way to the top of the soil.'

'Which means even when they get to the top, they're still on the ground,' I said.

She didn't have an answer for that.

'Debbie, are you paying attention?'

Keith's leaning over my desk, resting her chin on her hands, giving me a hard stare – trying to be top-dog, she is. 'Clearly, you weren't listening to a word I was saying!' she sighs. 'I was trying to explain that you have my full commitment and can always trust me, one hundred per cent. Everything you tell me in this room or in my office – our sacred space – is completely confidential, and . . .'

I can't help but laugh. 'Sacred space?'

Keith's twitching eyelid goes nineteen to the dozen. 'You are in serious trouble,' she says, sternly, 'and I am on your side, but in order for me to help you, you have to help me.' She swallows suddenly, not meaning to, tripping over her words.

Oh, she's taking the proverbial, she is. 'Help you?' I laugh. 'You don't need my help. Unless you're in trouble, too.'

She sits back in her chair, crossing her legs, trying to look all professional. 'I'm not in trouble at all, Debbie,' she says. 'I'm curious as to why you think I might be.'

'Well,' I say. 'You've got that look about you. You've gone bright red and don't know what to do with your fingers, like The Vicar when I saw him with his trousers down and Nurse Pugh's hands all over his bum.'

'Nurse Pugh was treating The Vicar's lumbago with a cold compress in the privacy of his living room,' Keith says, firmly. 'He did not expect an eleven-year-old child to be spying on him and taking Polaroid photographs. Actually, Debbie, this might be an opportunity for us to explore what happened that afternoon – what do you think?'

I shrug.

'Debbie, blackmail is a serious crime. It says here, in my notes, that you sent The Vicar an anonymous note, threatening to display the photograph on the village notice board unless he paid you five hundred pounds.' She takes a deep breath. 'You know, of course, that The Vicar was admitted to hospital last Friday after taking an overdose . . .'

'I thought I was safe in here,' I say quietly.

Keith nods. 'Yes, Debbie,' she says. 'You are. You are perfectly safe in here.'

'But you just made it sound like I was to blame for The Vicar trying to top himself. In our *Sacred Space*. And now I feel afraid, which means you're not very good at your job.'

Keith pretends to write something in her notes, but I can tell she wants to cry. I don't want to make her sad and not like me any more. I've been having too much fun for that. As it is, my sessions with Keith mean I'm getting a break from the bullies and Bug-eyed Thomas, who's the biggest bully in the whole bloody school, so I'd best be nice.

'Don't worry,' I say. 'I won't tell on you.' I cross my legs, so I look all grown up. 'You're only human, after all.'

Keith looks up from her notes. She's breathing very heavily. With gratitude, I think. She seems to appreciate my maturity.

'Thank you,' she says. 'Let's start again, shall we?'

'Yes,' I reply. 'I think that's for the best.'

'Thank you, Debbie.' She smiles. She's actually really pretty when she smiles. 'You know,' she says, 'it's just occurred to me that I don't know what *you* think about you.'

'You what?'

'Well, I know what other people think about you, but not what you think about yourself.'

I shrug. I mean, what do you say to something like that?

'So perhaps,' she says, 'before we continue discussing The Vicar, you can tell me a bit about yourself, and I'll tell you a bit about me. How does that sound?'

I chew the end of my pencil, wondering where to start. No one's ever asked me about myself. Well, they've asked me who the hell I think I am a few times, but never, you know, shown any actual *interest*. 'Okay.' I pretend I'm thinking for a bit, though I know exactly what I'm going to say, because I've rehearsed it often enough in front of the mirror for when I'm famous and Eamonn Andrews surprises me with his Big Red Book.

'Right,' I say, 'here goes. I was born on the seventh of April 1973, the day Anne-Marie David won the Eurovision Song Contest, and I'd have been christened Anne-Marie if Dad hadn't admitted to fancying her, so they called me Deborah-Marie instead. My early childhood was very happy. There were three of us, me, Mam and Dad, living off the land – that's what Mam called it – in a caravan at the bottom of Barwood Mountain on the Barwood side, of course. Dad always said that while we didn't have a pot to piss in, at least we had each other. But then, one day, he went off in his Datsun Cherry, and never came back – probably had another woman – and Mam went all funny, and said she was going back to the rat race after all. So, she moved us from Barwood to Llanfair, where she grew up, so I could have a decent start and she could make some money. I started school – a year after everyone else, because Mam and Dad taught me at home until I was six – so I've always been stuck in a class with kids a year or so younger than me, which makes me even more of a fish out of water, Barbara says. Anyway, Mam's a lone parent – she's been single since Dad buggered off – though she reckons she's fine with that because all men are bastards and she can do what she likes, which isn't strictly true, because to make ends meet, she has to clean people's bogs and she's always too knackered to talk to me.'

'I see.' Keith blinks. 'I'm so sorry, Debbie. That sounds like a tricky start.'

'A tricky start.' I think about this for a moment. 'No,' I say. 'Not really.'

'But that is a tricky start, Debbie. Perhaps you feel very cross about that, and that's why you feel the need to cause trouble . . .'

'I don't cause trouble, Keith. I record what I see in my Kajagoogoo notebook – it's got a lush photograph of Limahl on the front – do you want to see it?'

'I . . . no, thank you, Debbie.'

'And I take photographs, too, and I do what I can to make people pay.'

'But giving those poor girls all that senna . . .'

'Poor girls nothing. They're bullies. And anyway, there's no proof that I . . .'

'But The Vicar's not a bully, is he, Debbie? Are you able to tell me why you targeted him?'

'He's a hypocrite. I've sat through too many of his preachy sermons. Obsessed with the bloody Seven Deadly Sins, he is, even though he commits most of them himself. My mam says so. He asked for it.'

I pick up my pencil and open my book. I can't be doing with this any more.

'I'm struggling with this maths,' I say. 'I was never no good at solving problems.'

Keith stands up, pretending to stretch. 'Righto,' she says. 'Time for a break. I'll tell you what, why don't I get out my dolls? You know, the princess and nurse ones I showed you last Friday, and we can have a play together.'

'I'm not a child,' I say.

'But Debbie,' Keith laughs, 'that's exactly what you are!'

I put down my pencil and fold my arms. 'I. Am. Not. A. Child.'

'But you are a child! A child who deserves a fresh start. A second chance in life.'

'I don't want a fresh start. I'm perfectly happy with the start I've been given.'

'But, Debbie, how can you be? After all that's happened? You've lost all your friends!'

'I still have Barbara Pritchard. And Robert Hargreaves.'

She shakes her head. 'Who are they?'

'Mam cleans for Barbara – Barbara's ever so wise, and she's nearly eighty, but she's as sharp as a tack. And Rob's dad owns the pub in the village. He's dead cool, is Rob. He's got pierced ears, used to play in a band and looks like a friendly clown. You must know Rob and Barbara. They're the best people in Llanfair!'

Keith's eyes slide sideways – like she knows bloody well who I'm talking about. 'I don't know anyone in Llanfair,' she says. 'I live on the outskirts, a mile or so down Llanfair . . . well, never mind which road I live down. And my friends . . . well, they live elsewhere.'

'Have you lost all your friends, too, Keith?'

'Debbie,' she says, gently, 'we're not here to talk about me. We're here to talk about you, so you don't get into any more trouble. Perhaps we should take a breather? You can have a good think about how we'll get the most from today's session. And then, when you're ready to start again, let me know.'

We sit in silence for quite a long time. It feels dead awkward, so I twiddle the loose elastic on my daps for a bit, and then

I tell Keith that, yes, I'll start again. And Keith gives a little clap and a smile, and picks up the box at the side of her desk, pulling out the doll in the nurse's outfit and saying, look, let's just pretend, for a moment, that you are a child who likes to play with dolls. You never know, you might have some fun!

She kneels on the floor, smiling up at me. 'Come on, Debbie. I know you want to!'

'Well,' I say, 'I actually don't. And I feel very silly.'

'You feel silly?' she laughs. 'What about me? I'm on the wrong side of twenty-five! Look, humour me, won't you? Give me something to write in my notes and show Mr Griffiths later. Let's make the most of the time we have before lunch.'

I climb off my chair and kneel down beside her. She smells lovely and clean, close up. I wish Mam let me have a bath more than once a week.

'Where's the nurse doll going today, Debbie?'

'The hospital, I suppose.'

'Why?'

'Because she works there, of course!'

'Tell me more about the nurse doll, Debbie.'

'Not much to tell. Now – this princess doll.' I pick her up, smoothing down the frills on her pretty pink frock. 'I'll tell you all about her instead, shall I? On the outside, she's pretty. But on the inside . . .' I think for a bit. 'She's actually very sad. You see, everyone thinks that when you're pretty, life is easy. But this princess knows that it's not. Because of people like her husband. He's mean to her.'

'Mean to her? How?'

I mull this over, chewing on a loose bit of chapped skin on my lip. I think about Mam, mainly, and how she reckons Dad only married her because she was a right looker when she was younger, but he buggered off once her hair turned grey and she got her first wrinkle.

'Pretty women attract the wrong sort of man. That's what Mam always tells me, probably to make me feel better because I'm ugly.'

'Oh, Debbie! That's not true!'

I push the princess doll away. She reminds me of Carrie-Anne Marston, and what happened the last time I did PE with the other kids. When Gary White begged Carrie-Anne to be his country dancing partner instead of me, because I'm a freak, he said. An ugly ogre.

I clench my fist and sit on it. 'Don't want to play with the princess doll any more.'

'Okay. Tell me about the nurse instead. What kind of nurse is she, Debbie?'

'A good nurse,' I nod. 'A nurse that does good.'

'And how does she do that?'

'By fixing people. Broken people.'

'And why does she want to fix the broken people?'

'Because . . . I don't know. It's what she does.'

'Does she ever try fixing people that aren't hurt, Debbie?'

'Why,' I ask, 'would she want to do that?'

'I'm not sure. Why do you think some people might want to fix people that aren't actually broken?'

I shake my head. 'I don't know what you mean.'

'Well, I'll put it another way. Why might she want to make up stories or situations pretending people are broken when she knows that they're not?'

'Dunno. 'Cos she's bored and wants something to do?'

Keith nods. 'Anything else?'

'Well, people will notice her, I suppose.' I stroke the nurse's cape. 'They'll have to notice her, and then she'll feel important. She'll feel . . . not broken any more . . .'

I've said too much. I've lost myself, haven't I? Thrown me off my guard, she has! I'll teach her to mess with me.

'Sometimes,' I whisper, 'she takes it too far.'

'Takes it too far, Debbie? How?'

'She makes them ill. So that she can fix them. She's clever.' I'm talking very quietly now, so Keith has to lean in to hear me. 'But she's not as clever as she thinks she is.'

'How does she make them ill?'

'Poison,' I whisper. Keith leans in closer, her hair tickling the skin on my cheek. 'She puts bad things in their food. And sometimes she gives them the wrong medicine. Or far too much of it, because she's ever so bad. She's really bad. She's a *killer*.'

8

Vanessa

12.55 p.m., the staff office, Dewi Sant Department of Child & Adolescent Psychology

Vanessa is gearing herself up to telephone her supervisor, Professor Mark Murray, whom she fancies something rotten. Mark Murray is off limits because he's her boss, is several years older and a prize shit to boot. He also wears linen suits with the sleeves rolled up, has a floppy fringe, says 'cool' a lot and sits in the lotus position during consultations. Yet, despite his down-with-the-kids appearance, Mark Murray is a very powerful man indeed. Vanessa understands the primitive impulse at the root of her ardour, and loathes herself for it.

She, of all people, should know better.

She did know better, once.

And it was Mark bloody Murray who assigned Vanessa the Isobel Robinson case in the first place, providing inadequate supervision, then blaming her when it all went wrong. Mark bloody Murray, who'd banished her from the Institute of Psychology, dispatching her to the Dewi Sant Centre for 'correction', thereby lumbering her with the Tunstall kid and months and months of purgatory.

'You will report to me, Dr Bridges,' he'd snapped, 'by *tele-phone*, every Monday and Thursday. I want extensive notes on every patient that you see. By *telephone*,' he repeated. 'Not in person. You will not set foot in the Institute until I expressly permit you to do so.'

She's nervous as hell when she speaks to him. Not that she's spoken to him in weeks. Whenever she calls, his secretary – a woman with a high-pitched yowl called Sheri-Lee – puts her on hold while UB40's 'Red, Red Wine' plays down the receiver at her.

Three minutes to go.

She scans her office, searching for a distraction – if you can call it an office, that is. The Dewi Sant Department of Child & Adolescent Psychology is pretty much housed in a broom cupboard, shoehorned into the Dewi Sant Health Centre between the Genito-Urinary and Ulcer Dressing clinics. Not at all like the Institute offices, where you'd get a proper wooden desk and a big leather chair and a living, respiring plant in a proper porcelain pot next to a window with an actual view. No, in this room there really *is* a broom and a mop and bucket in the corner. The desk is Formica, the chairs plastic, the plant and view non-existent. There are several interesting NHS posters Blu-tacked to the walls, though – featuring cancerous lungs, pregnant teens and emaciated limbs mottled with lurid shades of purple and pink.

For a second, she feels a renewed spark of purpose. This is why she became a psychologist – to save kids like Debbie-Marie Tunstall from *this*: drugs, underage sex, disease – a perpetuating cycle that could end right here, in this building, thanks to *her* care.

Two minutes to go.

Oh, who is she kidding? What care had she given Isobel Robinson? Not a care in the world, at first. She'd diagnosed a cut-and-dried case of obsessive compulsive disorder, sadly not unheard of in a high-achieving child, presenting, in Isobel Robinson's case, with tics, repeated hand-washing and doing pretty much everything (touching door handles, light switches and so on) in multiples of three. So far, so textbook. And Vanessa had studied plenty of those. Pity she hadn't spent quite as much time with living, breathing patients.

Although, to be fair, at the Institute there hadn't been much call for that, unless one was writing an academic paper such as *Obsessive Compulsive Disorder in the Gifted Child* by Professor Mark Murray, Dr Vanessa Bridges *et al*, with Isobel Robinson (known as Miss X) at the centre of their study. The Cardiff Institute of Psychology was a bastion of world-class research, not face-to-face treatment. That was what clinics like the Dewi Sant Centre were for, and Vanessa had successfully swerved setting foot in such unsavoury places for years.

One minute to go.

Yes, Isobel was a typical case of OCD. But, it turned out, she was tortured by more than unwashed hands and touching objects in anything other than multiples of three.

'I'm ready for you, Isobel! Come in, don't be shy.'

But the brown-haired girl with the skinny olive face remained on the classroom threshold, assessing Vanessa through wide, suspicious eyes. Her small gloved hands were curled around the doorknob, as though she might shut the door any moment – though whether Isobel Robinson would be inside or outside the room was anybody's guess.

Just a matter of seconds into their first session together, and Isobel was already proving a challenging case, even though she was generally well-behaved, according to the headmistress of Barwood Primary School. And such a talented swimmer, the Head had enthused, during her preliminary chat with Vanessa. Isobel had been picked for the Welsh Junior Swimming Squad – there were high hopes of her becoming a future Olympian! But, the Head lowered her voice, the poor child suffered most terribly with *scrupulosity*.

And Vanessa said, 'Scrupulosity? Oh, we've changed the name for that! These days, we call it obsessive compulsive disorder.' And she went into full-on psychologist mode, asking questions, making risk assessments – was Isobel formally diagnosed? Was she receiving appropriate care? And the Head said, 'Oh, no, no – that's really not necessary. Isobel has excellent care from her general practitioner and the district nurse, and her parents are keen to not . . . you know, make a *thing* of it all. Just in case it affects her chances of being selected for future swimming competitions. So, we're keeping it all under wraps, for now – I trust you'll respect her anonymity, of course?'

'Well yes, of course. But I'm confused – if her parents don't want Isobel's case formally diagnosed, then why am I here? Why have they agreed to their daughter being used as a case study? Albeit an anonymous one?'

The headteacher shrugged. 'From what I've gleaned – which isn't much, to be honest with you – Professor Murray and Isobel's family already have a connection. Grew up together in Barwood, I gather. And I suspect,' she lowered her voice again, 'that Professor Murray may be treating the mother, who's a rather neurotic creature. Professor Murray is your superior, of course. Has he ever spoken of the family?'

'No, not at all.'

The silver-haired, yellow-toothed headmistress with the spider-veined nose was nearing retirement, and gave off the anaesthetized air of someone who no longer gave two hoots, which went some way, Vanessa supposed, to explain the lack of discretion and professionalism that followed:

'Well, I don't mean to speculate, of course,' the headmistress speculated. 'But I do wonder whether Professor Murray might be giving Isobel unofficial care in return for her being a case study, keeping everything off her medical notes. You know, Professor Murray scratches the Robinsons' backs, and they scratch his.'

Vanessa smiled stiffly. She wasn't prepared to agree openly with the headmistress – far more professional to say nothing at all. But she knew the headmistress was right, and the whole thing seemed . . . well, a bit stinky, frankly. Professor Mark Murray was seeing a patient privately, for free, off the record? And that patient – a child – was being forced, in return, to take part in academic research to further his reputation? And she – Dr Vanessa Bridges – was expected to ignore all of this? This lack of transparency, of basic ethics?

But ignore it she did. Of course she did. What choice did she have?

Well, she could have chosen to say 'no'. She could have told Prof Murray that she was far too busy with her own research, and encouraged him to collaborate with some other sucker instead. She could have walked away any moment leading up to that first meeting with Isobel; halted their session seconds before the child prised her white-gloved hands from the door-knob and shuffled across the classroom, reluctantly taking her seat at Vanessa's side.

'Do you know why you're here?' Vanessa asked kindly.

'Yes,' whispered Isobel. 'You've come to play.'

'That's right. Just for a couple of hours a week. Everyone thinks it might help you . . . relax. And I'll be making some notes for a paper I'm writing, but no one will know that the paper I'm writing is about you. Is that all right?'

Isobel nodded, crossed one leg over the other, right-angled at the knee – a curiously masculine pose completely at odds with her girlish clothing. For she was dressed like a five-year-old in a smocked floral pinafore, ankle socks, Mary Janes and a red crocheted hooded cardigan, tied at her neck in an over-sized bow.

'It says here, in Professor Murray's notes, that you like to wash your hands a lot.'

Isobel nodded.

'And why might that be?'

Isobel shook her head.

'I see. Okay. Well, I understand that your hands are terribly sore, which is why you wear gloves . . .'

'No, that's not the reason,' Isobel said. 'I just don't like touching. Anyone.'

'Oh.'

'Or anything. If I touch things without my gloves on, it has to be times three.'

'So, when your hands are bare, you can only touch things in multiples of three?'

Isobel nodded. 'That's right.'

'And why is that, do you think?'

Isobel chewed the inside of her cheek, mulling this over. 'Because three is the magic number,' she said. 'The Father, the Son and the Holy Ghost. The Lord is my redeemer, because I am a sinner.' And she burst into peals of laughter.

Vanessa takes a deep breath, picks up the receiver, dials Mark Murray's number.

'Yaaaas?' says a voice.

'Good afternoon, Sheri-Lee. It's Dr Bridges here. I have an appointment with Mark at 1 p.m.'

'*Professor Murray*,' the voice snaps, 'is rather busy at present, but I will check and see if he's free. I will just put you on hold.'

'Please,' Vanessa implores, 'no muzak. Or if you must play muzak, not UB40's 'Red, Red Wi—'

Too late.

9

Barbara

1 p.m., Hollyhock Cottage, Llanfair Village Square

Three days on, and it's torturing Barbara – the fact that she'd forgotten to have her usual Friday coffee with The Vicar. Damn and blast her useless memory! And now he's laid up in a hospital bed – at least, that's where Barbara assumes him to be, for no one has told her otherwise; she's not seen a soul all weekend. Lewis might be dead, for all she knows. And if he is, it's all her fault.

But something more is torturing Barbara. Something dark and troubling. She hadn't been entirely honest with Robert after discovering The Vicar's comatose body. For she'd not found the Durex at Lewis's side, on his front path, but in his *mouth*. He'd been drooling and gagging, so she'd prised open his jaw, seen the red packet between his teeth and whipped it out, concealing it in her mackintosh pocket, overcome with pity and rage and a desire to protect whatever was left of his dignity. What on earth was Lewis playing at? What bizarre sexual practices did he indulge in? And why was it anyone else's business – least of all hers?

She flicks through her diary. Yes, there it is – writ large in her spidery hand: *11 a.m., 7 September, coffee with Lewis. Take a Victoria sponge. Butter him up over planning permission. We need him on side at Uskshire Council AGM!*

While Barbara doesn't believe in God, she is nevertheless a regular churchgoer – it's somewhere to go on a Sunday morning, and a way to keep tabs on Llanfair's inhabitants without getting too close. For even now, after two decades of living here, the villagers remain a faceless, graceless mass to her – bleating sheep belonging to this society, that committee or some exclusive club or other, kissing the backsides of the Llanfair elite – namely the ghastly social-climbing Marston family.

Barbara taught Clive Marston at Barwood Primary School, many moons ago. A diminutive, ferret-faced boy he'd been back then, quietly if rather nasally spoken, thanks to his over-sized adenoids. Good at maths, but not much else. She would never, in a million years, have partnered him with Blanche – his glamorous polar opposite growing up on the other side of the mountain. Blanche Wilkins, as she was back then, the teen queen of Llanfair, all bee-hived hair and go-go boots. Blanche, who skittered off to London the day she turned sixteen – to join a modelling agency, so the gossips said – only to reappear, four years later, leaner, meaner and harder of nose than ever.

And Blanche's sidekick – the fragrant Rose – the smallest, kindest girl in Llanfair, obsessed with the nursing profession from the time she could walk and talk. Always wearing a nurse's uniform – a toy one as a child, the real thing as a teen – stethoscope draped around her neck, even on her days off. Rose was one of the first – and few – villagers Barbara got to know, not least because of the tragedies that blighted the poor girl's early life, leaving her orphaned aged just sixteen. Then history repeated itself, as history is wont to do; Rose was widowed a year ago – and poor little Susan half-orphaned at only ten years old.

'I'm gutted for Rose,' Ingrid told Barbara, taking a tea break during one of her weekly cleaning sessions. 'I mean, I hated her husband, but I daresay she loved him. And Rose, of all people, doesn't deserve the crap she's been dealt with over the years. We've never been close, but she's always been nice. Even at school, she was kind to me. Unlike Blanche and the other girls. They'd all take the piss because Mam was unmarried and drank all the time, and forced me to go to church and wear hand-me-downs. But when Rose told them to lay off me, they did. She's a goody-goody pain in the arse at times, but I've always been grateful to her for that.'

'Good for Rose,' Barbara replied. 'It baffles me, actually, the Rose and Blanche friendship. How two vastly different women remain on such close terms.'

'Opposites attract, though, don't they? Perhaps Rose is on a mission to save Blanche. Maybe she's on a mission to save bad people. Perhaps that's why she married that National Coal Board arsehole, Phil Pugh. Maybe that's why she lived and worked in Barwood for years, to help those less fortunate than herself. What do you think, Barb?'

'I think she's a dreadful judge of character,' Barbara replied. 'Some people are attracted to bad 'uns. Rose simply replaces one with another. When Blanche moved to London, Rose moved to Barwood and met and married Phil Pugh. On Phil Pugh's death, she immediately runs back to Llanfair and Blanche's open arms. Hardly surprising, really, when you consider the poor woman's history.'

'Poor *women's* history,' Ingrid corrected her. 'Whatever you and I think of Blanche, we can't ignore what she went through, too.'

'Well, yes. Perhaps you're on to something there. Blanche and Rose have a shared experience one can't even begin to fathom – each losing a parent in the most tragic of circumstances. That drunken buffoon, Herbert Wilkins, ruined so many lives that night. Childhood trauma can form the strangest of bonds. Cup of tea and a fig roll, Ingrid?'

Barbara drags herself back to the present, chiding herself for her wandering mind. She needs to control her brain, which has become rather unruly these last few weeks. Her memory has gone to the dogs, she has frequent headaches, her eyesight is dreadful . . . Her finger retraces the words in her diary – *The Vicar. Take a Victoria sponge.* The Vicar, the spiritual leader of Llanfair for as long as she can remember. The Vicar, who'd married Lynette and Dai, christened Robert, buried Lynette and held Barbara's hand while she ranted and raved and railed against the injustice of it all. The Vicar, who – two decades ago – had welcomed her to her new home with a bottle of Scotch and a sly-fox wink. She'd promptly put him straight on her sexual preferences, and he – to his credit – had kept schtum ever since, shielding her from the village witchfinders general, becoming a trusted ally. Yes, Lewis Morgan, Vicar of Llanfair, was a thoroughly decent chap, if you overlooked his hypocritical sermonizing. And Barbara is prepared to do that, because Lewis is remarkably tolerant of Utterson's – at times, quite literal – attachment to his trouser leg.

Yes, to forget their coffee morning was unforgivably rude. Barbara scans the rest of her diary for memory-jogs of other overlooked arrangements; folk she may have offended or abandoned to some similarly dreadful fate, but there is nothing. Just every Tuesday – *4 p.m. Ingrid.*

But, wait – there is one other entry for this coming Wednesday, printed – uncharacteristically for her – in spiked capital letters. *12 September, the Llanfair Arms, Wrong Jones.* She frowns. What on earth did she mean by that? Who is Jones, and why is he wrong? And what on earth is he doing in her diary?

She used to have such a firm grasp on dates, but she's failing fast. Far too fast. She slots her diary back in the drawer of her bureau, pursing her lips to whistle for Utterson who, she realizes, has been at her feet all along.

Barbara tries not to panic when she has these memory absences – she is seventy-nine years old, after all, and her 'senior moments', as Robert euphemistically calls them, are only to be expected. Expected and increasing, though. There are other things, too, that she dare not, will not, mention to Robert or Ingrid. And especially not to Dr Erasmus Jolly.

Barbara works her way through the usual sequence as she prepares to leave the house to walk Utterson. Whenever her brain has an 'off' day, she can rely on routine to carry her through: 'Mackintosh – belted,' she says to herself. 'Basket – looped, over one arm. Keys, spectacles, dog-lead. Come along, Utterson. Let us take the air together, and see what is what and who is who.'

But the moment she steps out of her door, Barbara senses it – *change.* The village is much busier than usual. There are several large vehicles parked outside the Llanfair Arms – BBC Wales emblazoned on their sides, and a growing crowd of agitated onlookers, whispering in huddled groups. Men in rumpled suits, sleeves rolled up, tail-end of their ties thrown over one shoulder, are unfurling coiled lengths of thick black cable from the back of their vans. The media are in town – but why? Barbara debates whether or not to call into the pub to ask Robert and Dai, but decides against it. She despises gossips – heaven forbid she become one herself! – and she steers Utterson to the right of her runner-bean wigwams, towards Llanfair Lane and the telephone box on the corner, which is empty – and ringing.

Barbara squeezes herself and Utterson into the booth, which smells of stale cigarette smoke. She picks up the phone. 'Hello?' she says.

'Is that Llanfair?' a male voice says.

'A resident of Llanfair, yes.'

'Good. Can you see the Llanfair Arms from there?'

'I can.'

'Is there a BBC Wales van parked outside?'

'Yes, there are several. To whom am I speaking?'

'Never mind *to whom* you are speaking. Just go over there and tell them to answer their fucking phone once in a while. And tell Barry Parry to put down his pint and pull his fucking finger out. I want that interview with Clive Marston recorded by end of play today.'

Barbara opens her mouth to reply, but the phone goes dead.

At the village end of Llanfair Lane is Llanfair Church – officially called St James the Lesser, the older and larger St James the Greater situated in Barwood. There was a campaign some years ago, run by Blanche Marston, to rename the Llanfair parish St James the Even Better.

'But the "greater" simply refers to one of the St Jameses

being taller or older,' Barbara tried to explain at the time. 'Not one of the St Jameses being superior in any way.'

In the end, Blanche abandoned her crusade, though never lost her resentment of Barbara for daring to challenge her. 'Bearing Blanche Marston's wrath is the price one must pay to preserve righteousness and sanity,' Barbara says to herself, side-stepping a lamppost. 'The only thing necessary for evil to triumph in the world is that good men do nothing. Edmund Burke, I believe. Stop that, Utterson!'

She turns as a battered white Ford Transit van thunders past, churning up mud as it does so, the identity of its driver's face obscured by a large plastic rain bonnet. Barbara considers shaking her fist, but the van disappears around a bend before she can do so. She has not walked this far along Llanfair Lane for quite some time. Prefers not to, just in case. 'You never know who you might bump into,' she muses, peeking through the iron gates of Stockholm Villa, curling her lip at Gwendoline Bridges' latest nouveau adornment – a ghastly statue of Amphitrite at the centre of her carp pond.

Barbara shakes her head. That poor Bridges child, who must be – what, in her mid or late twenties by now? Barbara caught glimpses of her over the years – a pasty, serious-faced little thing, gazing wistfully from the rear window of her mother's car, being driven to school, horse-riding lessons or the houses of carefully selected friends, no doubt. She'd made it to Cambridge University, which surprised Barbara, when she heard the news. The highly strung six-year-old she'd encountered two decades ago seemed unlikely to amount to anything much. Barbara has little to go on, though – just a few unfortunate hours at that bloody picnic she'd hosted with Lynette. A picnic party for the local kiddies in the field behind Stockholm Villa; a field – that for now, at least – remains in Barbara's possession.

But not for very much longer, she hopes.

'No good deed ever goes unpunished,' Barbara mutters to Utterson. 'And the picnic was all Lynette's stupid idea. She encouraged me to make a good impression, to ingratiate myself with the local families, after I fell out with the builder. But what a complete bloody disaster that turned out to be.'

Yes, Barbara is glad she is selling the field. It should have been sold years ago, would have been sold years ago had the prospective developer not turned out to be an absolute rogue. She'd bought it as a gift to herself for her fiftieth birthday, after a tip-off from Dai and Lynette. An investment, she believed at the time. Something for a rainy day.

Well, that rainy day is long overdue.

She needs the money – fast – however much Gwendoline Bridges objects to social housing on her doorstep. Well, that coiffured twit can object all she likes. She must be apoplectic with fury. Pole-axed with rage.

Good.

10

Robert

1.45 p.m., the Llanfair Arms

'Packet of NV Nuts, mate.'

He's going to be bloody late for her. She'll hate him, will never want to see him again . . .

'Did you hear me? I said, a packet of NV Nuts!'

'Sorry.' Robert turns to the panelled wall behind the bar, plucking the last-but-one packet of peanuts dangling by a hook from a poster featuring a blonde lady in a tight wet T-shirt. A cheer of 'wahey!' goes up from the tables behind him, and Robert yearns for the usual – albeit irritating – weekend punters: Queen Blanche and King Clive holding court over the Llanfair rabble, among whom there were one or two notable barflies – Morris the Butcher, with his smutty asides, and Myfanwy 'Bug-eyed' Thomas, chief persecutor of Debbie-Marie Tunstall, who invariably ended each Friday night by falling off her barstool.

But the atmosphere this lunchtime is different. Sweaty, besuited media types have invaded the Llanfair Arms, desperate to dig the dirt on Clive Marston: flouncing between the sticky oak tables, dropping their cigarette ash all over the red and gold Axminster. It was one of the things Mum insisted on: an upmarket pub needed an Axminster carpet, and what Mum wanted Mum always got – apart from a decent innings, that is. What would she make of all this, Robert wonders – the Llanfair Arms on the telly at last! But at what cost? It's full of wankers. It's full of wankers at other times, too, but at least at those times they're *local* wankers.

Robert slides the packet of nuts across the bar. He smiles at the man standing in front of him. 'Anything else?' he asks.

The punter – Barry Parry, ace reporter with BBC Wales – leans towards him, lacing his nicotine-stained fingers together, his broken-veined, pockmarked face assessing Robert with mock reverence from under a slick of oily fringe. The right elbow of Parry's grey suit rests in a puddle of beer, the tip of his pastel-blue tie is touching a smouldering butt in the overflowing ashtray, but Robert isn't going to tell him that. 'And a pint of Brains beer,' Parry smirks. 'You've got brains, haven't you?'

Robert grits his teeth and nods, turning to grab a glass from the shelf behind him. He's heard that 'joke' a hundred times, always uttered by absolute arseholes cock-a-hoop at their razor-sharp wit and repartee. Clive bloody Marston, for example, who'd made the exact same jibe last Friday evening. Manning the till for the night, Robert had had no choice but to witness Marston's usual weekend performance, silently seething as the rat-faced git pulled a giggling Rose Pugh onto his lap, and whispered hilarious nothings in the ear of a pissed-up Rachel Wilmslow.

It pained Robert to watch Blanche's purse-lipped tolerance of her weekly humiliation. But such was the price of remaining married to the richest man in Uskshire. Her only respite came when Marston finally rose from the table to order a belated round of drinks at the bar, rattling Llewelyn's cage as he passed. That stupid bird worships Marston, bouncing on his perch whenever Marston comes near; preening his sulphur plumage like a lovesick bloody schoolgirl.

Marston smirked at Robert across the bar. 'A pint of Brains, Hargreaves,' he'd droned. 'You've got brains, haven't you?'

I have indeed, Robert thought. *And a much bigger penis than yours, by all accounts.*

Robert places Parry's freshly poured pint on the bar between them.

'The head's too big,' Parry says with disdain.

'It certainly is,' Robert replies.

'I'll let it go, this time,' Parry grunts, taking a swig with a curled lip.

Robert glances at Llewelyn. The bird's head is cocked to one side, absorbing it all, and Robert thinks, again, of the previous Friday evening – of Marston holding court at his favourite table, next to Llewelyn's cage. Marston's flirty banter with Rachel Wilmslow, the murmuring between him and Rose Pugh as she sat on his lap in her nurse's uniform; his urgent, whispered exchanges with an agitated Blanche. And Llewelyn crouched on his perch at their side, watching and listening, mutely observing, taking everything in.

Thanks to a lull in lunchtime custom, Robert has made his escape. Dai will be livid when he finds out his only son-cum-barman's gone and done a runner again, but needs must and all that. Right now, in this moment, Blanche is the only thing in Robert's life that matters; the warmth of her powder-pink lambswool sweater tickling the nape of his neck, her soft whisper in his ear . . . *Are you ready, now, Robbie? Shall we begin?* Almost two hours of bliss ahead of him, before she has to pick her kids up from after-school knitting club.

Robert sidles along the edge of the car park, taking furtive puffs on his cigarette, slipping into the driver's side of his banana-yellow Ford estate. Hardly a suitable vehicle for an assignation, but there you go. He pulls on his baseball cap – didn't have a chance to wash his hair this morning – starts his engine, releases the handbrake, and glides out of his parking space, staring straight ahead in case anyone looking out of the window of the Llanfair Arms tries to catch his eye. He eases the car between a pair of TV vans flanking the car-park entrance, narrowly avoiding the corduroyed arse of a cameraman stooping to tie up his laces, performs a swift left and right, turns into Llanfair Lane, and prepares to put his foot down – if he gets a move on, he might just make it in time . . .

'Oh, shit!'

Robert's right foot sinks into the brake pedal. He winds down his window, acknowledging the elderly mackintoshed lady bustling towards him, dragging a snaggle-toothed terrier with one hand, brandishing a wicker basket with the other.

'Hello there,' he says.

Barbara leans breathlessly through Robert's window, peering at him over the top of her spectacles.

'Have you been drinking?' she gasps.

'No! I have not!'

'I'm very relieved to hear it, Robert. And I'm glad to see you out and about, though I do wonder why you're not helping

Dai in the pub? It looked unusually busy when I left the house. Are those men in suits still there?'

'They are.'

'And the television vans?'

'Yep.'

'And might I ask why?'

'Llanfair's in disgrace. Clive Marston's fleecing the striking Barwood miners, according to *The South Wales Morning Post*. Llanfair is full of self-serving bastards, apparently, and the local media hate our guts.'

'Fair enough.'

'I suppose it is.'

'I trust they don't know of The Vicar's situation?'

'If they do, they haven't let on.'

'Good. Let's keep it that way. Well, Robert, you seem a little brighter, if I may say so. There's a spark about you, I think.' Her eyes, boring over the rim of her specs, are in danger of nailing the back of his baseball cap to his headrest.

Robert nods stiffly. 'I do feel brighter,' he says.

A hint of a smile plays at the corners of Barbara's lips. Good God – the old bat never misses a beat. She knows he's up to something.

'I needed some fresh air and that,' Robert says, a little too quickly.

The smile playing around Barbara's lips widens. 'Fresh air *and that* in the woods, I presume?'

'Well, yes. I suppose.'

'And some solitude.'

'Of course.'

'I've just been up there, Robert. Not as quiet as you'd hoped,

I'm afraid. There's a white Ford Transit van parked in the layby just up from Stockholm Villa – nearly mowed me down in their zeal to get there. Didn't see who was in it, though I daresay they're out for a spot of fresh air *and that*, too.'

Robert frowns. Transit van? What the hell is that doing in his and Blanche's parking place? Blanche drives a Volvo estate – and she was meant to come alone!

The knot in his stomach tightens.

Something's not right, he can sense it.

11

Vanessa

*2 p.m., Outside Mr Griffiths' office, Llanfair Village
Primary School*

She's all over the place today, is Vanessa – at Llanfair Primary
one minute, the Dewi Sant Centre the next. Thanks to a
Barwood miners' protest and the police barricading the A5876,
her usual shortcuts have been off limits, and she's had to
negotiate the narrow roads surrounding the village square.
Annoying at the best of times, but especially with all those
television vans hogging the parking spaces outside the pub.
And she nearly collided with that fool from last Friday, driving
like a loon in his banana-coloured car. Showing off in front
of the TV crews, no doubt. Stupid sod.

Now she's back at Llanfair Primary, patiently waiting – for
what? For some recognition, that's all. *I've made a breakthrough,*
she wants to tell Mr Griffiths, wanted to tell Professor Mark
Murray, but Griffiths will have to do. *Debbie-Marie's opened
up! When she was playing with my nurse doll this morning, she
practically admitted she drugged the Marston girls – in a round-
about way, I'll admit it – but she's given a reason, too! She wants
to fix broken people, apparently. Wants them to notice her, poor*

kid. All she wants is to feel important and actually seen for a change . . .

She stares at Griffiths' door, willing it to open. Her stomach's churning, she's practically hyperventilating – why? For what? What on earth is she hoping to get from him? A pat on the head? A standing ovation? An Olympic gold medal?

She wants Griffiths to like her, that's all. But not in *that* way. She may have a yen for older men, but Huw Griffiths is twenty years her senior, has a monobrow and a taste for drip-dry suits and slip-on shoes. At least he's been civil and kind to her, though. Pity the same can't be said for the rest of the teachers. They're the old retainers, loathing the kids and any new blood, especially new blood with funny ideas that might interfere with their set-in-their-ways determination to do sweet bugger-all with the kids – measuring out their working lives in cups of strong coffee and Benson & Hedges smoked behind the staff room door, Radio 2 blaring out from a battered old transistor radio.

She's only been in the staff room once, when Griffiths showed her around the school during their introductory meeting. It was class time, and the staff room was empty of teachers, yet strangely full of their presence: the lingering smoke, the permanent, buttock-shaped dents in the worn upholstery of favourite chairs, the mugs holding half-full cold cups of tea, the sense of ennui contained, it felt, in the buckets of rainwater placed under broken ceiling tiles.

Griffiths must have noticed the look of distaste on her face, for he said:

'Sit down a minute, Dr Bridges. I have something to say to you.'

She did as she was told.

He stood in front of her, rising and falling on his toes, shoes squeaking as he lectured away: 'We may have a wealthy catchment in this school, Dr Bridges, but Llanfair Primary suffers from a dearth of young blood and ideas, and has been overtaken, shall we say, by a certain type of self-seeking parent who rather likes its teachers to be as lazy and pliant as possible. I was brought in two decades ago – the previous Head had been rather remiss in dealing with a particularly nasty case of bullying – and I dreamt of turning Llanfair Primary into an environment where any child, however different, might not just survive, but thrive. Alas – weak and feeble soul that I am – I have since given up the fight, and now see my role here as a damage-controller of sorts for the kiddies like poor Deborah Tunstall, whose faces don't fit. And while it might not be as cosy and community-minded as Barwood Primary, at least at Llanfair we don't hang our staff – or our educational psychologists, perhaps I should say – out to dry.'

He winked at her then, and her cheeks went bright red, and she felt herself shrink into her chair, wishing the buttock-worn brown woollen seat would cave in completely and swallow her whole.

'Isobel, whatever's the matter with you? Why are you shrinking into your chair like that?'

'I don't want to talk about it,' Isobel said.

'Talk about what?'

'The thing you keep asking me about.'

'The thing that makes you feel bad about yourself? The monster you claim has special powers over you . . .' Vanessa licked her finger and flicked through her notes. 'The monster you say has special powers over life and death.'

'Yes.'

It was their third session together, and Vanessa sensed she was making progress – Isobel was starting to trust her, was opening up bit by bit. Meanwhile, the child's fragility, her wide-eyed intelligence, the embarrassing clothes her out-of-touch parents forced her to wear, had ignited something in Vanessa. Something she'd never experienced before.

She was starting to feel maternal.

Which should, in hindsight, have raised alarm bells. Not least because her reaction to Isobel's 'monster' was that expected of a mother, not a psychologist.

'But Isobel,' she'd laughed, 'there's no such thing as monsters!'

Isobel spoke so quietly, Vanessa had to lean forward to hear her – 'Yes,' she whispered. 'There is.'

'Isobel, monsters are the stuff of fantasy. They only exist in our imaginations.'

'This monster is real. I see it most days.'

'Where do you see it?'

'Here.'

'In school?'

Isobel said nothing.

'Somewhere other than school?'

Isobel said nothing.

'Is this monster a person? Is that what you're trying to tell me?'

Isobel said nothing.

Vanessa tried again. 'Isobel, can I ask you whether you've spoken to anyone else about this monster? Your parents? A teacher?'

Isobel shook her head, her tiny frame shuddering beneath

her smocked dress and red crocheted cardigan. She reached the pincered fingers of one hand to touch her poker-straight hair and, taking a single strand, plucked it from her scalp without flinching.

Vanessa watched the hair drift down to the floor.

'Isobel, please tell me who this monster is – please, you can trust me.'

Isobel said nothing.

'Well, I need to tell someone. I can't keep this all to myself. We need to tell somebody about this monster, don't we? Someone who'll know what to do.'

Isobel solemnly shook her head. 'If you say anything to anyone, they'll make you regret it,' she whispered. 'They'll make you wish you had never been born.'

'Do they make you wish you had never been born?'

Isobel nodded. 'They say it would have been better if I hadn't been born.'

'Why?'

'I'm a terrible person.'

'Terrible? How?'

Isobel mouthed something. Vanessa leaned towards her. 'Please speak up, Isobel,' she said. 'I can't hear you.'

'Pride,' Isobel whispered.

'I'm sorry?'

'I'm prideful.' Isobel had tears in her eyes. 'I'm full of pride, and that's a sin, and there's no place on God's earth for sinners like me.'

*   *   *

The door of the staff room bursts open.

Mrs Myfanwy Bug-eyed Thomas appears at the end of the corridor, her cream cable-knit cardigan buttoned unevenly over her barrel-like chest. In one hand, she holds a plate of half-eaten mince, in the other, a copy of *The Racing Times*.

In the background, Vanessa can hear Stevie Wonder's 'I Just Called to Say I Love You' playing on the staff room radio.

'He's not here,' Myfanwy Thomas bellows.

'I'm sorry?'

'Huw Griffiths. Not here. Liquid lunch. At the Llanfair Arms.'

Myfanwy Thomas retreats backwards into the staff room, as though sucked in by the smoke and laughter and music and other mysterious social forces contained therein. The door slams shut. Someone guffaws.

Vanessa picks up her handbag. It smells sulphurous, of the egg mayonnaise and spring onion sandwiches her mother made for her that morning. And her Dr Scholl sandals squeak on the lino as she makes her way back down the corridor, to the car park and her mum's XR3, where she'll eat her packed lunch in the driver's seat, all by herself.

12

Debbie

2.15 p.m., Llanfair Lane

Rob freaked me out just now. I've never seen him drive so fast. Like a bat out of hell, he was, skidding around the War Memorial and into the pub car park – squealing brakes and all – like he was something out of *The Sweeney*. I nearly went into the Llanfair Arms to ask what the bloody hell he thought he was playing at, but I waited outside instead, because I'm underage and should be at school – Keith thinks I'm with Bug-eyed Thomas, and Bug-eyed Thomas thinks I'm with Keith, so it's a win-win for me.

I crouched down and spied through the lounge bar window, which was all steamed up because the pub was full of stupid Llanfairians with bugger all else to do with their lives, wanting to get on the telly. And then I peeked through the public bar window, 'cos I could hear Dai giving Rob a right bollocking. But that oily-haired git from BBC Wales appeared at my side, shovelling handfuls of nuts into his gob, glared at me, and said, 'Oi, kid, hoppit.'

So here I am on my tod, as per, on my way to the woods. I've just passed the telephone box on the corner, which was ringing – how weird is that? – and the church and the grave-yard with its toppling stones and statues of weeping angels covered in ivy and moss. But I'm keeping my eyes on the ground in case the weeping angels see my face and weep even more, because they'll know that I'm up to no good. I hug my bag to my chest to cover my heart, which is leaping about like a box of frogs – my bag, which holds my special stuff: my Kajagoogoo notebook, Mister-Man pencil, Polaroid camera and cola Spangles.

I plod on, still keeping my head down, because I don't want to look at the vicarage, either. It's a horrible, hundreds-of-years-old building, grey-stoned and flat – how I think Mam's moods would look if they were a thing you could see, not a thing in her head. The vicarage also has huge oblong windows that always look empty and dark, like Mam's eyes when she's lying in bed, staring up at the ceiling, not wanting to talk to me.

I've never been inside the vicarage, but Barbara has – loads of times. She says that it's nice, as is The Vicar, and I really shouldn't have blackmailed him.

But he creeps me out, he really does. He's so angry-looking and wears stupid long dresses and has the most ridiculous bushy beard – like, you know, *unnecessarily* bushy, like he's trying to prove something. 'He wants to look like God,' I explained to Barbara once, when she asked why I disliked him so. 'The angry God that throws bolts of lightning in those old-fashioned paintings from years ago. The God fawned over by chubby babies and naked ladies draped in sheets that don't cover their boobs and bums. He dresses the way some boys dress like their heroes – painting their faces like Adam Ant, or dyeing their hair red like David Bowie. Only those boys are stupid and don't know any better. The Vicar has no such excuse.'

The Vicar's back garden (if you can call it a garden; it's overgrown with brambles and weeds, lazy sod) backs on to the woods, and that's where I saw him that time – through what Barbara calls his French windows – getting his arse felt up by Nurse Rose Pugh.

Llanfair is a den of iniquity, that's what Mam says. She'd be dead proud if I caught someone out, like Rob Hargreaves and Blanche Marston. It would make Mam's year, it really would, if I grassed up Blanche Marston. I like Rob a lot, so I'd feel a bit bad about exposing his antics, but Blanche Marston deserves all she gets. And you can't make an omelette, Mam always says, without breaking eggs.

You see, Rob and Blanche meet in the woods every Monday. I'm earlier than usual today – I normally get here just before four, when they've finished whatever it is they've been up to. I know Rob was at the pub just now, but they never miss a session – so perhaps today I'll finally catch them at it!

My Monday afternoon routine is this: I get to the woods after school just in time to sneak into my hiding place, before Rob comes out of the trees, rummaging about in his trousers like he's checking his bits are still there. There's never anyone around, except me, though there's that funny house further down the road – Stockholm Villa, it's called – but I never see anyone coming or going from there. Anyway, out of the woods Rob comes, leaps into his car, and off he zooms – like a rat up a drainpipe.

Blanche follows five minutes later. She wears dead weird

clothes for the woods. High heels, a full, swishy skirt and her hair in a bun, and a tight pink cardigan buttoned up over her boobs. She looks like a film star from the 1950s, and I have to say it suits her. She always carries a plastic bag – it's got a name on it, Harvey Nichols, and I sometimes wonder if Mr Nichols minds Blanche Marston carrying his things around. Did she nick them, or did he give them to her willingly? There was one time when Blanche left the bag on the ground next to her car and drove off, forgetting it was there. I sneaked over and looked inside: there was a black tracksuit and trainers inside, which wasn't very exciting, and then I heard the car coming back – Blanche must have realized she'd left Mr Nichols' trainers and tracksuit behind – so I scarpered and hid until she'd gone.

I've never got here early enough to catch Rob and Blanche out. And in case today isn't the day I get to rumble the pair of them, I've brought Mam's tweezers for the other reason I love Llanfair Woods. I come here to collect owl pellets, so I can take them apart and see what's inside. It's something my dad taught me to do, one of the only things I remember about him, which is very sad, when I think about it. I wait until Rob and Blanche have left, then go to the thickest part of the woods where there are very old oak trees with holes in their trunks. And that's where the owls roost and leave their thick black pellets of vomited food.

Dad always said he found it relaxing, and I do, too – picking out tiny jawbones, fur, claws and teeth. I like to imagine what creature it was, how it died before the owl ate it up, how it felt when it died, how it feels just now as a ghost, watching me hold its tiny bones in the palm of my hand.

I keep all the bones in a jewellery box that Dad bought me

for my sixth birthday. It has a ballerina on a spring that twirls to the 'Dance of the Sugarplum Fairy' when you open it up; it's also where I keep a metal Mr Men charm that fell off the keyring Mam bought Dad for his last Father's Day.

She said she had to buy it, along with an extra two Mr Men charms, because the three of them reminded her of us: Mr Lazy – Dad, Mr Happy – Mam, because she was always smiling and laughing back then, and Mr Strong – that's me. Mam said she got Mr Happy for a knock-down price because he had a scratch mark under his mouth and it looked like he was sticking his tongue out, which really made her laugh.

But then Mr Strong fell off the keyring the very first time Dad used it. Which Mam always says, looking back, was a sign. A portent of doom.

As long as I've got my bag with me, I never feel scared in Llanfair Woods, even though it gets very dark the deeper you go. Some villagers say the bit by the quarry is where the Satanists meet and have blood-drinking parties when it's a full moon. They sacrifice animals on the rocky banks of the quarry lake, and prance around naked in the water wearing goat-headed masks. I once asked Barbara about it, and she said: 'Someone once found a headless rabbit floating on the surface of the lake – killed by a fox, no doubt – and the rumours of devil worshippers spiralled from there. I suggest you take it with a pinch of salt – the devils in Llanfair are mundane in appearance, but considerably more dangerous in their antics.'

I wasn't sure what she meant by that, and when I asked her, Barbara said: 'They walk among us, Deborah, taking the most benign of forms.'

'How do I know then,' I replied, 'that a nice old lady like you isn't a devil?'

'You don't,' she said. 'Trust no one. Especially someone you think of as *nice*.'

But I do trust Barbara. I do think she's nice. I trust her and love her more than anyone else in the world, even Mam. And if Barbara died – which one day she will, very soon probably, because she's so very old – I'll die along with her. Really, I will.

13

Robert

4 p.m., the Llanfair Arms

Rationalize, you idiot! Blanche got to the woods before you, saw the van, drove on and parked elsewhere, waiting until the coast was clear.

But Blanche would have had to have driven past Barbara to get to the woods. And if she had done so, Barbara would have said so to Robert, because that's what Barbara would do.

Blanche was in trouble. There was no other explanation. She'd expressed her fears to him often enough: that her clown of a husband and his double-dealings had exposed the Marston family to danger, and now . . . well, here we are.

Robert had driven back to the pub from the woods in a panic, nearly rear-ending several cars en route, barely registering Dad's bollocking on his return, before pulling dozens of pints for the media crew, making small talk with a few of the locals, and tossing a bag of pork scratchings at that garrulous pisshead Morris the Butcher to shut him up.

And now here he is, on the bog in the bathroom, having finally persuaded his father that yes, he really did need the toilet and no, he wasn't going to bugger off again.

Robert stares down at his trembling knees, trousers concertinaed around his ankles.

'Robert!'

Dad. Rapping on the bathroom door. 'Rob – what you doing in there? You've been bloody ages! We open again in an hour and a half and I need you – now!'

'I – I'm not feeling well,' Robert says. 'I'll be down in a minute.'

He can hear his father's laboured breathing rasping against the bathroom door. Dad will be waiting and wondering what to say next; will know something's up with Robert, but would sooner England beat Wales in the Five Nations' rugby than tackle it head-on. Dai Hargreaves will be wrestling with his conscience all right, knowing it's his fatherly duty to, at least, ask whether his only child is feeling okay. But Dai can't cope with the inconvenience of things not being okay. This Robert discovered during his mother's last illness, when he'd been left to deal with it all – the oncology appointments, the nurses, the drugs – while Dad dealt with running the Llanfair Arms. Which was fair enough, when Robert thought about it, because someone had to remain detached. Someone had to be practically minded, keeping food on the table, a roof over their heads. But the arrangement had formed a barrier between them; an unspoken agreement that Robert was soft in the head, and his father a hard-hearted bastard. And things between the pair of them just hadn't been the same since.

A heavy sigh erupts from the other side of the door. 'Do you need some more bog roll in there, or what?'

'No, Dad. I'm okay. I'll be down soon.'

Robert pulls up his trousers, flushes the toilet and waits. The rushing of water subsides with a gurgle, and he hears his father's slippers shuffling back down the staircase, to the now-silent bar. The media crew had packed up for the day, due to return tomorrow.

Robert washes his hands with cold water, staring at his pale, sweaty face in the mirror, preparing his barman mask – inscrutable, unflappable, hiding the fear.

Fear because Blanche hadn't been there, at their usual meeting place.

Blanche hadn't been there, but a Transit van *had*. A van that, when Robert finally plucked up the courage to park his car in the space beside it, get out and peer through its grimy windows, was empty. Yet he knew – with absolute certainty – that he wasn't alone. So he had a serious word with himself for letting his imagination run riot. It was only a van, for Christ's sake, but his guts kept on churning – the way they do when he's scared – so he decided to walk off his nerves, hoping Blanche's silver Volvo might glide into view. He got as far as the village outskirts, a ten-minute walk or so – for a while, the van and his car were completely out of sight – before turning back.

The walk back to the car seemed much longer than usual, which was odd, because Robert knows the woods like the back of his hand. Mum used to take him there as a boy, when the bullying got too much for him. She'd tell him about the village on the other side of the mountain – Barwood – where she and his Auntie Barbara were raised. Salt of the earth, the folk over there, she'd say – that's what most people are like, Robbie. Not like the self-serving gits over here who don't know they're bloody well born. They'll sell their grannies to get on in Llanfair, greedy social-climbers that they are. And he'd gaze up at the trees and the quarry beyond, up again at the heather-clad outcrops, and up to the sky, where God lived, apparently closer to Barwood than wicked Llanfair.

As he walked back to the car, Robert noted the strange lack of birdsong or breeze, and that the hazel saplings – planted the previous autumn in a side clearing – had developed a dreadful disease, their green-veined leaves mottled with some sort of blackspot. Finally, the layby came into view, but there was still no sign of life. There was, however, a wide, deep track that Robert could have sworn wasn't there before, sweeping from the van's rear doors. About two feet wide, as though something substantial had been dragged from the layby into the woodland, cutting a lengthy swathe through the red-brown mud.

A rolled-up carpet, perhaps.

Or a body.

14

Debbie

7 p.m., Flat 4B, Aneurin Bevan Estate

I'm pissed off, I am. No Rob, no Blanche, no nookie to photograph, and no bloody owl pellets, either. Someone had dumped a stupid white van where Rob and Blanche usually leave their cars, so maybe that was the problem – they knew they wouldn't be alone, so buggered off somewhere else instead. It'll be joyriders, I expect – that van would have been stolen and left there to rot. It's not from round here, I know that for sure. It had a Cardiff numberplate – CRD. Like Dad's Datsun Cherry. CRD 139J. I remember Dad's numberplate these days better than I remember his face. Sad, but true.

Mam's just come home from work. I can hear her in the kitchen, filling the kettle from the tap, lighting the stove with a match.

'Debbie-Marie?' she calls. 'You home?'

'In here,' I shout. 'Playing conkers.'

She pushes my bedroom door open, standing with her body half-in and half-out, one leg still in the hallway. I carry on lining my conkers up.

'You had any tea?' she says.

I don't look at her. 'I've been waiting for you to come home,' I reply. 'I couldn't eat until I knew you were safe. Where you been, anyway? You're normally home by six on a Monday.'

Out of the corner of my eye, I see her slump against the doorframe, hair all over the place. Her hair used to be a deep, dark brown, but now it's greying and crazy-lady looking. Her fringe is too long and hangs down like curtains, and her T-shirt and jeans are too big, because she's lost a ton of weight. I never see her eating. Or drinking. Or doing anything, really. Just working, smoking and sleeping.

Maybe she's sad because of me. Maybe she wishes I'd never been born.

Sometimes, I do.

'I had a lot of jobs on today,' she says, taking a drag on her cigarette. 'I told you I'd be late.'

She hadn't told me any such thing, but I didn't say so.

'Anyway.' She sighs. 'I just wanted to ask how it went with that psychologist of yours today, that Miss Bridges. That observing you *in situ* stuff she wanted to do. She seems nice.'

'It's *Doctor* Bridges, actually. Says she's a doctor in kids' psychology, or something like that. Yeah, she seems okay.'

'I still think I need to take you to a proper doctor. To get proper medical help. Someone who'd be able to refer us to the relevant people . . . it's not that I think you've done half the stuff that people accuse you of, but you do get angry, and you do make up stories, and you do find it hard to keep friends, and I just want you to be, well, *happy* . . . Debbie, can you stop playing for a minute and look at me when I'm talking to you?'

I don't want to do that because if I do, I'll cry. And whenever I cry, Mam does the same as Bug-eyed Thomas and looks away, embarrassed. And then she'll tell me to blow my nose and clean myself up, like Bug-eyed Thomas does – like they can't stand the sight of me as I am at that moment, as I really am, an eleven-year-old girl who's all upset, not the monster that everyone says I am. Then I want to curl up, ashamed of myself. Or ashamed of them. Maybe both.

The doorbell goes.

'Oh, bugger,' Mam says. 'I'll just go and get that. Stay where you are, I'm not done with you yet.'

The doorbell's been ringing on and off since I got home, but I haven't answered it, because I don't know who's there, and what they might want to do to me. I felt quite afraid walking home from the woods – the stares I got from some of the locals. Well, it just wasn't nice. Not that anyone would say or do anything outright, but it's written all over their stupid Llanfairian faces – they hate my guts, everyone does. Mam tries to tell me it's because I am special, and people will understand and like me when I am older. She says I'll have the world at my feet once I've grown into myself. She promises me that.

But perhaps she says it just to be kind. And she's saying it less and less these days. Like she can't be bothered to believe it herself. Like she knows she's talking bull.

I can hear people on the street outside – some of them, I recognize.

'You're all pissed!' Mam shouts. 'Bugger off home, the lot of you!'

And then the voices. Hate-filled, angry –

Little bitch deserves all she gets after what she did to The Vicar . . .

Llanfair's in disgrace because of you and what your daughter's been saying and doing!

You're absolute filth, the pair of you!

Go back to Barwood where you belong!

Scum scum scum!

And Mam's voice, getting louder and louder –

'It's not Debbie's fault Llanfair's on the news. It's all that shit-stirring the papers are doing between us and Barwood – she's the wrong target, you idiots! Picking on low-hanging fruit, you are, just because Debbie's different! If you had any sense, you'd be at Clive Marston's having a go at him – the real villain. But you've all got your noses so far up his arse you can't see it. Go home or I'll call the police!'

The door slams. I close my eyes. Minutes pass. The voices get fainter and further away.

And then I hear Mam's feet shuffling slowly towards my room.

I close my eyes, grit my teeth, wait for the slap I know will follow.

I sense her standing outside my room. I open my eyes and turn my head. She's in the doorway, arms stiff as a board.

'You've really done it this time,' she whispers. 'The whole village wants us out. You've ruined us. You've ruined *me*.'

I swallow hard. 'I thought you said I wasn't to blame for The Vicar . . . and you just said to the locals, you told them . . .'

'Thanks to your lies,' she says, lunging across the room at me, fist raised above her head, 'thanks to you and your stupid lies, The Vicar couldn't live with the shame . . . and you know what, Deborah? I can't live with the shame of *you* any more. How did I raise something so bad, so ungodly? How? How? *How?*'

She wails *how* over and over, like the howl of a wolf, and I duck, covering my face with my arms, waiting for the sting of her hand on my face.

But there is no slap, or blow or shake. Instead, she pushes past me, swiping my conkers to the floor, screeching at the top of her lungs:

'There! You and your stupid conkers . . . the only things you care about . . . you don't care about people, you don't give a shit . . . you're a psycho, you are! You're evil! Oh, God . . .'

She runs out of my room, slamming the door.

I sink down on my bed, my heart thud-thudding, making all wobbly fluttering feelings inside my chest.

I feel sick.

I want to run, run as far as I can – from the house, from Mam, from myself. From the school with its spiteful, spit-filled kids, from Llanfair with its hateful grown-ups. I want to run through the woods to the quarry, sliding down its slippery sides; wading into the deep, dark lake, sinking down to the very bottom until my feet touch the cool, sharp rocks on the floor, holding my breath, looking up at the sky through the weeds and the silt and the rippling water, so no one will see my stupid face ever, ever again.

But instead, I quietly pick up each of my conkers, and line them up on my windowsill.

And then I swipe them to the floor.

And I stamp on every one of my people, grinding my heel into their core. Grinding my heel 'til they're splattered and shattered; wanting so much to see for myself the messed-up pulp inside their heads.

TUESDAY, 11 SEPTEMBER 1984

THE SOUTH WALES MORNING POST

Villages at War!

By Margaret Lawrence,
Welsh Affairs Correspondent

The battle between Llanfair and Barwood continues apace, with Llanfair launching a counter-attack (or, as they'd no doubt rather call it, *defence*), via a *Spotlight Cymru* special to be screened later this week – *Llanfair Fights Back!* Fronted by veteran broadcaster Barry Parry, *Llanfair Fights Back!* promises a fascinating insight into the day-to-day agonies of Uskshire's wealthiest community. Parry exclusively revealed to *The South Wales Morning Post* that preliminary filming has already taken place, with further interviews planned with Clive Marston and Llanfair's Lady Mayoress, Gwendoline Bridges. Parry promises 'revelations, explanations, and live footage of a fundraiser to be held at the Llanfair Arms in aid of the Barwood Miners' Fund, featuring Flicks N' Kicks Dance Academy and

Uskshire's favourite impersonator, the magnificent Wrong Jones.'

Sounds an absolute blast. I can't wait for the fallout — can you?

15

Robert

7 a.m., the Llanfair Arms

He wakes with a thumping headache, stomach turning cart-wheels. He drank too much beer last night, again – albeit to cope with an even shittier bar-shift than usual. Some braying, chinless twit wearing a waxed green jacket asked for a white wine spritzer. You could have heard a pin drop. Robert's dad was having none of it. 'If you want a poncey drink like that, you can drink in Clive Marston's poncey wine bar when it opens,' Dai Hargreaves spat.

'If Marston gets planning permission,' Morris the Butcher slurred. 'The launderette is a public service and Marston's plans are a major concern.'

'So is your drinking, Mr Alcoholic-Not-So-Anonymous,' somebody said. And everyone – Robert included – laughed.

Robert's not laughing this morning, though. He needs some aspirin – pronto. He untangles himself from his candlewick bedspread, landing his size-ten feet squarely on the floorboards next to his single divan. His room has barely changed from his early teens, through his university years and beyond – posters of Bowie and Jagger still cover the space-age themed wallpaper. On the top shelf of his bookcase are two framed photographs – one of his mum, and one of him with a group of spiky-haired young men. Two of the men hold electric guitars, while he sits apart from them, gurning behind a drumkit bearing the legend 'The Slicks'. They'd had just one review, in the *NME*, of a gig they'd performed as students in Cardiff. 'The Sicks', the reviewer had called them. Stupid bastard.

Robert tip-toes along the landing in his Y-fronts, knowing he must look an absolute twit if Mum's looking down on him now, but he doesn't want Dad to know he's up and about, because that would be awkward. Talking to Dad is always awkward. Dai Hargreaves is a man of few words at the best of times (unless he's bollocking Robert, in which case he's alarmingly, swearily eloquent), but particularly so early on in the day, when he might not even have his teeth in. Robert can hear him downstairs in the bar, and in his mind's eye he sees Dai's wizened frame clattering between the tables in his threadbare dressing-gown, pushing the Hoover along the carpet, his balding noggin nodding to whatever tune is playing on his internal jukebox.

'Come on, boy!' he's yelling at the mute Llewelyn. 'Let me see you shake yer tail-feather!'

Robert goes into the bathroom, slams down the bog seat and sits on it, closing his eyes. What did he come in here for again? Aspirin, that's it. He gets up, shaking his fringe off his face, opens the bathroom cabinet, rifles around among the bottles of calamine lotion and half-used tubes of his father's haemorrhoid cream, and finds a strip of aspirin, popping two on his tongue, grimacing like a gargoyle as he chews and finally swallows.

Replacing the strip in the cabinet, his hand hovers a moment over Mum's bottle of morphine, next to his stash of amitriptyline and his father's packet of senna. He really needs to get rid of that morphine. Really, he does.

He returns to his room, sits on his bed, stares at his poster of Aladdin Sane for a bit.

So many things he should have done.

Too late now.

There's something more. Robert thinks hard. His brain is fuzzy, doesn't want to comply, but he knows there's more . . .

Oh, God. Blanche.

She's still not been in touch with him.

And that's why he's feeling so sick this morning. It's fear, not just beer.

16

Debbie

8 a.m., Flat 4B, Aneurin Bevan Estate

I didn't sleep very well last night. Every time I shut my eyes, a wolf with the longest, greyest face and blackest eyes and pointed teeth pounced on me, howling: *How? How? How?*

It took ages, but I finally did drop off. And then I had a dream.

I dreamt I was floating on my back with Dad in the lake at Llanfair Quarry. The sun was shining, the water so still and blue that it seemed we were actually gliding through the sky. We didn't say anything at all to each other – didn't need to, you see, because I knew exactly what Dad was thinking, because I was thinking it, too. *Peace.* One word, over and over, both of us thinking it. *Peace.*

When I turned my head to look at Dad properly, I realized with a rush of joy that I did remember his face after all, the bits I thought I'd forgotten: his dark brown eyes with crinkles around them, his thick black moustache and sideburns. And then, when he turned to me and said, 'Keep going, my girl. You're doing just fine,' my heart sang in a way it's not sung for a very long time. But then something gripped my ankle, yanking me down so I spluttered and choked; something hard and metal-like, tugging me down with sharp-edged fingers. I opened my mouth to scream *Dad!*, fighting like crazy to keep my mouth above water, to keep my eyes level with the tree-lined banks.

And that's when I saw Dad's Datsun Cherry driving away from the edge of the lake, when I realized that I was alone after all, that he'd gone and left me all over again. And I didn't want to fight any more. My body went limp, my sight went all black and my eyes filled up with water.

I woke up, then. Crying.

It was still quite early on in the night, because I could hear the boy racers speeding around the estate in the cars they'd nicked from the posh people's houses, and next-door's TV blaring out the bongs from *News at Ten*.

I tried to keep my eyes open after that, yanking my pillow around my ears to block out the noise. But I heard the blood in my ears instead, beating in time with the kids at school chanting, *die Debbie Tunstall die Debbie Tunstall die Debbie Tunstall die die die . . .*

By the early hours, all was quiet, so I got up and turned on my light. I looked out of the window at the lane and the bins. It looked strangely warm and beautiful, all lit up by the orange lamplight, and a ginger fox with white-tipped ears and a scabby tail limped past the overflowing bin-bags. Everyone hates foxes, but not me – I think they're wonderful, especially the scabby ones. Barbara says that they're misunderstood, and I wanted it to know that *I* understood, so I gently scratched at the windowpane, trying to get it to notice me. But it slunk off into the shadows, handsome head hanging down like its tail, looking dead mangy and ever so sad, like it was going off somewhere quiet to die.

I turned off my light and went back to bed, and lay in the dark for a very long time, waiting for the sun to come up. I thought I heard Mam in her bedroom, crying, but when I crept into the hall the sound stopped, and I wondered if I'd imagined it. Maybe I just wanted to think that Mam felt sad for the terrible things she'd said earlier. But she was probably fast asleep, like everyone else in Llanfair, like everyone else in the world, except me.

I lay there for what felt like for ever, staring up at the ceiling above my bed. Carrie-Anne Marston has glow-in-the-dark planets stuck on hers. She told the whole class that her dad put them there because, he says, she's the moon and the sun and the stars to him. And I started to cry all over again, because I'm nobody's moon, sun and stars, not at all.

My alarm went off at seven o'clock, and I waited for Mam to come in and tell me to get up for school, but she didn't.

I heard her in the bathroom, coughing, then flushing the bog, running the tap and cleaning her teeth. She usually comes in to check I've got up, but that didn't happen this morning. I lay there for ages, squeezing my eyes shut, praying to God for my door to open and the sound of her voice saying ever so softly, 'Come on, lovely girl, time to get up.'

But none of that happened. I just heard the door slam as she went off to her first cleaning job of the day. And that was that.

I got out of bed and got myself ready. No point in weeping and wailing. I knew what I had to do next.

After I'd got dressed, I went into the kitchen. Mam had left a loaf of bread out on the counter, and a note: 'Use two slices *only*. Bread is expensive. Mam.'

I wasn't hungry, so I left the bread. But I took the five quid Mam keeps in the kitchen drawer for emergencies, along with two first-class stamps and three envelopes. Not because I'm a thief, but because I'm leaving home.

So, here I am on the kitchen stool. Writing three letters in my best handwriting, with the *Oxford English Dictionary* that Barbara bought me open at my side. Barbara says my spelling is 'somewhat erratic', and she blames the education system for that. 'These new-fangled ideas that grammar and punctuation are somehow inhibitory to creative expression are nonsense, Deborah.' That's what she says. I'm not entirely sure what she means, but I don't want a ticking off from her when I get out of hiding, so *Oxford English Dictionary* it is.

Letter number one is addressed to Barbara Pritchard, Hollyhock Cottage, Llanfair.

Dear Barbara,

By the time you read this I will be far away. I am a bad person and you mustn't waste the rest of your life trying to be nice to me. I admit I put senna powder in the Nutella sandwiches, but it was only senna, I promise. I did not give the girls the other stuff that everyone says I gave them. I wouldn't even know how to get my hands on it, because I'm only a kid.

I didn't want The Vicar to top himself. I still think that he's a dirty old man, but he doesn't deserve to die and I am sorry if he felt that he wanted to die because of what I said and did.

If I could turn back time, I would. I'm sorry.

Thank you for being so kind and all.

Give Utterson a pat on the head from me.

Love, Deborah

xx

Letter number two is addressed to Dr Bridges at the Dewi Sant Centre.

Dear Dr Bridges,

I did poison Carrie-Anne and Lucy Marston with my mam's crushed up senna tablets (she takes senna because she's not as regular as she'd like to be), but I did not give them anything else. I wanted the girls in Flicks N' Kicks to shit themselves when they were doing their dance at the village fete because they never let me join in, and always made me feel like shit. I hope you can put this in your notes and people will think you're very good at your job because you helped me tell the truth and understand why I did what I did.

I did not mean to upset The Vicar as much as I did, though. I was angry at him, because I thought he was a hypocrite. I am still quite angry with him, actually, but I do not want him to die.

I am running away. I think it's for the best. I have also written a note to Mam, but I don't think she will be too sad and it will be a relief for her, to be fair. I do think my friend Barbara Pritchard will be very sad indeed, though, and she might need your help. We have been good friends for a long time and I tell her almost everything. She lives at Hollyhock Cottage in Llanfair. If you have time please go and see her. If you can help her nephew Rob be happy again, people will think you are even better at your job.

I'm sorry I was naughty when you were trying to help me.

Love, Debbie

Letter number three is for Mam. I will leave it on the kitchen counter, next to her bottle of Valium, so she'll definitely see it.

Dear Mam,

I am very sorry for what I've done. I just wanted the Marston girls to feel as bad as they sometimes made me feel, but now I know I made you feel the baddest of all.

I am also very sorry about The Vicar. I did not mean for him to get as upset as he did.

I am going away to start a new life. Dr Bridges says everyone deserves a fresh start. I'm not sure if I do, but I'm going to try. You deserve a fresh start, though, and I hope you'll be happy.

Love, Debbie xxxxxxxxx

I have packed my school bag with some pants, a jumper, my camera, my Kajagoogoo notebook and tweezers. I will start my travels in Llanfair Woods, up by the quarry. There's a hollowed-out tree up there, where I can sleep.

I'm going to live in the wilderness. If Jesus managed it for forty days and forty nights, then so can I. I just hope when I come out of hiding, I won't have to go through what he did.

17

Vanessa

8.30 a.m., Stockholm Villa, Llanfair Lane

'You seen *The South Wales Morning Post*, Ness? "Villages at War", I tell you! Bloody journalists, stoking things up. That flaming Clive Marston, bringing Llanfair into disrepute. I will never forgive Marston for this – him and his tart of a wife. Both gone to ground, refusing to answer the phone . . .'

'Tart is a derogatory term, Mum.'

'Well, Blanche Marston is a derogatory person.'

'That doesn't even make sense!'

Vanessa is at the kitchen sink, scraping the burnt bits off her toast, all the better to block out Mum's moaning and the background hiss of her father hosing down the XR3 on the driveway. Someone broke into the grounds of Stockholm Villa last night, and scrawled 'Tory Scum' on the boot in red marker pen. Vanessa found this funny at first, until she realized she needed the car for work. Did the person responsible know, she wonders, that it wasn't so much Gwendoline Bridges being punished, but *her*?

'And that bloody Blanche Marston is literally leading our youth astray.' Her mother shakes her head. 'I saw her a few weeks ago, at the Conservative Ladies' Summer Luncheon, marching that little girls' dance troupe of hers – Flicks N' Kicks – through the village, past the Llanfair Arms. *Little girls*, mind, dressed in those horrid little ra-ra skirts and crop tops showing their belly buttons. And as for *her* – wearing the most disgustingly tight jeans, she was. Left nothing to the imagination, *if you know what I mean.*'

'No, Mum, I don't know what you mean.'

'*Camel's toe*,' her mother mouths.

'Mum!'

'Not a sight for the weak of stomach, I can tell you.'

Vanessa slaps her toast onto her side-plate, thrusting her knife into the melting butter swimming in the saucer at her side.

'Oh, Ness, what an afternoon we had! And what a shame,' her mother shakes her head, 'it's come to this. Llanfair in disgrace. Although,' she muses, squashing a tea bag against the rim of a cup with the back of an apostle teaspoon, 'it could be worse, don't you think? At least it's only the South Wales press on our backs and not the nationals. I mean, *The Sun* could get wind of Marston's misdeeds, and we know what they're like – but *The Sun* likes entrepreneurs, and they don't like the miners, so I think we can safely discount *The Sun*. And *The Times*. And *The Daily Telegraph*. But *The Guardian* . . .' She sucks her teeth. 'And the *Mirror*. They'd crucify us, they really would. Which reminds me, I need to phone the hospital and find out how The Vicar is doing. Barry Parry's bound to bring it up when he interviews me later today, and we don't want to look like we don't care.'

'We?' Vanessa carefully slices her toast into four equally sized squares. 'Is that the Royal We?'

'Triangles, Ness. We cut toast into triangles in this house. Square toast is common. And we're not common.'

'Since when?' Vanessa asks with her mouth full.

'Since I said so. Now, I'm going to get showered, and I strongly suggest you get a move on, too, unless you want to be late. And when he comes in for his breakfast, tell your father he needs to phone the police. I am not having my worldly goods besmirched with political sloganeering.'

'Why can't *you* phone the police?'

'Too busy. I've a telephone interview with Sue MacGregor on *Woman's Hour*. Oh, and tell your father I've got a description of the little bugger that did it – saw them hanging around on the lane from the bathroom window when I was plucking my eyebrows.'

'That could have been anyone, Mum. The Tory Scum stuff . . . that probably happened hours ago!'

'She was dead suspicious, Ness. Staring in through the gates, like she was waiting for us, wanting to see our reaction. Funny-looking thing, too. Not quite a teenager – maybe eleven or twelve years old, with long dark hair and the skinniest face. Looked like butter wouldn't melt in her mouth when I opened the window and yelled at her, and off she scarpered, into the woods. Dressed ever so old-fashioned she was, in a little smocked dress and red crocheted cardigan tied in a ruddy great bow, just like you had when you were a little girl. You all right, Ness? You look like you've seen a ghost!'

*　　*　　*

And breathe.

Lots of girls wear smocked dresses and crocheted cardigans – not just Isobel Robinson. Pull yourself together! It wasn't Isobel Robinson. It couldn't be Isobel Robinson . . .

'Cheers, Ness.'

Vanessa offers her dad his mug of tea with slightly trembling fingers, cracking a smile as he takes it in his large, rough hands. She plonks herself down on the doorstep, lifting her own mug to her lips. He sits beside her with an oof, stretching out his legs. She shifts a little, to accommodate his stockiness.

'What sort of mood is your mother in now?' he asks, between slurps of tea. 'Do I need to don full body armour, complete with lead cod-piece?'

'Oh. She's okay, I think. But this Tory Scum on the car business and Clive Marston thing is getting to her. That said, I get the feeling she's enjoying the celebrity. She'll be on *Woman's Hour* this morning.'

He shakes his head. 'He's a prize shit, Clive Marston. Financial Advisor, my eye. He's nothing more than a loan shark, and it's bad enough he preys on the people of Llanfair, who've more money than sense. But targeting Barwood – the striking miners! Jesus, what a terrible man.' He rubs his chin vigorously. 'An utter disgrace, he is. And his wife isn't much better. Having it away with a local lad, who's still mourning his mam, poor sod. Or so I heard, down the Llanfair Arms last Friday. Quite a crowd that night, there was – that daft pair, Julie and Gary, from Love is in the Hair – always wearing matching Hawaiian shirts and white trousers, those two. And the chorus lines from the Opera

Society and Am Dram were having a sing-off, then the chemist woman and that funny little nurse were all over Clive Marston like a bloody rash . . .'

'I don't know any of these people,' Vanessa says irritably. 'I've absolutely no idea who on earth you're talking about.'

'Good. Let's keep it that way.'

There is something about this moment that Vanessa will later identify as a turning point: sitting with her dad on their doorstep on a chilly, overcast autumn morning, the smell of Swarfega and grease and oil, the sound of her father's slurping periodically drowning out the gentle warble of birdsong. For it suddenly occurs to her that half a mile down the road is a village of human beings whom she does not know. That, for reasons unknown, Vanessa's parents have kept her apart from these people for twenty-odd years.

'Dad,' she says, 'I don't know anyone in Llanfair, and that's really strange, don't you think? I have a handful of friends from school and university, people who live miles away, but that's it. Mum never let me mix with anyone here. Why is that, do you think?'

She looks sideways at him. He's staring into his tea with a look of surprise, eyebrows shooting upwards like he's never seen a hot beverage before in his life.

'I don't know, love,' he says finally, blowing on his tea with unnecessary force. 'I've never thought about it. You had friends enough, growing up, though, didn't you?' He shrugs. 'You still have friends . . .'

'I went to a private school five miles away. I went to university in Cambridge, the other side of the country. All of my life, I have lived in an ivory tower, and as a result, I know no one. Not really. My life is shrinking.' She shakes her head. 'I'm shrinking. I'm *stuck*.'

She looks away quickly, hoping he can't see her face slipping tearfully downwards, trembling lips curling around the rim of her mug. Inside the house, from the master bedroom, she can hear her mother trilling away – Gilbert and Sullivan's 'I Am the Very Model of a Modern Major General', followed by gargling and the soft, low vibration of an electric toothbrush buzzing away.

'Come on, Ness.' Her dad pats her knee. 'Let's get you into the garage. You can stick your hand in my Swarfega tin – you used to love that when you were a kiddie – before your mam comes and gives us what-for.'

18

Barbara

9.30 a.m., Hollyhock Cottage, Llanfair Village Square

Barbara Pritchard is drafting a letter to the editor of *The South Wales Morning Post*:

> *Dear Sir,*
>   *For several weeks, the signage of the Llanfair County Bowling Club has lacked an essential 'o' in 'county', removed by persons unknown. While many people – my own self included – may consider this revision fair and accurate, it is nevertheless criminal damage, and should be rectified immediately.*

Barbara rises from her chair with a sigh. There was a time when she'd have had a hearty laugh at that one, but Barbara is not in a jocular mood today. She peers through the gap in her curtains, willing Robert to appear on the front path: clean-shaven, hair brushed, clothes freshly pressed and not too outlandish, ready to take her and Utterson out for the day. To the Vale of Glamorgan and the seaside, perhaps, or a drive through the Brecon Beacons.

Fat chance of that.

For since Lynette's death and Robert's depression, every day is exactly the same, marked out by Utterson's periodic requirements: his feeding, his walks, his naps, his need to urinate and defecate. 'I might just as well have a husband after all,' Barbara mutters, pulling her curtains further apart, using the heel of one hand to rub condensation from the leaded pane. She wants to check whether Blanche Marston is there – unfolding her legs from her Volvo estate, which is always parked outside Love is in the Hair at this time on a Tuesday. Blanche has two hair appointments a week: Tuesday and Saturday mornings, when her raven plumage is backcombed and blasted into its customary bouffant style.

Barbara realizes that her other hand, gripping the curtain's fraying edge, is shaking. It always comes as a shock, the strength of her loathing for Blanche Marston. It's not just Blanche's status-seeking, her engineering of her unlovely daughters' social lives, or her penchant for too-tight trousers and layers of make-up that gets right up Barbara's nose. For such traits merely marked Blanche out as a stereotype – a cardboard cut-out of a person, and God knows life is full of such nitwits who should be pitied rather than despised. But there is something else about Blanche Marston that makes Barbara's blood run cold. Like the porcelain caps on Blanche's teeth, there are tiny cracks, if you look hard enough, revealing the rot that lies beneath, making Barbara's skin not just crawl but quiver, so much so that just now she tugs her cardigan tightly around her shoulders – her grey woollen armour – as she imagines Blanche springing from car to salon door in three stilettoed steps.

The steps would, of course, be perfectly timed, given that Blanche was a professional dancer. Three-times County Ballroom Champion in her twenties (a 'county' crying out for a missing 'o' if ever there was one), now proprietor of the Flicks N' Kicks Dance Academy, offering classes to the unfortunate souls with parents misguided enough to believe their inelegant offspring might be the next Margot Fonteyn.

'What a piece of work she is.' Barbara shakes her head. 'Poor, poor Deborah.'

And she thinks of Deborah – cloddish, plain, but with the most magnificent brain – another victim of Blanche Marston's spite. As Barbara herself has been – Ingrid, too – because anyone who has ever dared challenge Blanche's inflated view of herself must be a target, whether their challenge of her be intentional or otherwise.

'That's the chilling thing about her,' Barbara sighs. 'The fact that one might cross her simply for committing the sin of existing.'

She shudders again, aware that she cannot possibly wrap her cardigan more tightly around herself.

'Blanche is late.' Barbara looks down at her watch.

Blanche is never late.

And then Barbara realizes that instead of the Volvo estate, a tomato-red Mini is parked, skew-whiff, in Blanche's usual space outside Love is in the Hair. The diminutive, uniformed figure of Rose Pugh pops out, head first, from the driver's seat – page-boy hair lacquered firmly in place, her black district nurse's bag clutched firmly to her cardiganed breast, stethoscope dangling from her neck as she shoves her car door shut with a nudge from her backside.

A funny little woman, is Rose Pugh. Wherever you turn, she's always there – ubiquitous, yet overlooked. 'She's the human equivalent of grass,' Barbara mutters, realizing, with mounting alarm, that Rose is making her way across the village square towards her cottage.

The nurse's visits have become more frequent lately. Ostensibly to 'keep you company, Barb, especially with Robert being incapacitated an' all.'

But Barbara knows it is because Rose has noticed that things at Hollyhock Cottage are Not Quite Right. That Barbara is failing, falling apart – her mental and physical health declining day-by-day.

She quickly pulls her curtains closed, erasing the smiling nurse from sight.

19

Debbie

10 a.m., Llanfair Woods

Part of me's glad and another part sad that they haven't started looking for me yet. Perhaps it's because nobody's noticed I've gone. Or maybe they're just not looking hard enough, because no one actually gives a stuff. It's been hours since I left home, and I was expecting to hear a few sirens by now, or even a police helicopter circling in the sky, or someone shouting over a loudhailer – *Debbie-Marie, where are yooooou?*

I got my hopes up earlier, when I saw a police car outside Stockholm Villa. But it turned out they were visiting that mad mayoress woman, Gwen Bridges – I could hear her yelling merry hell, something about someone 'defiling her rear end with red marker pen'.

Anyway, it's nice and peaceful in Llanfair Woods – my favourite place in the whole wide world, apart from Barbara's chair in front of the fire, with Utterson up on my lap. I used to love it here in the autumn, because of the changing tree colours, but now I think when I'm older the reds and golds and the smell of blackberries will make me feel sad. They'll make me remember this time in a way that will hurt, the way only colours and smells and sounds can make your heart hurt.

But at least I won't go hungry. I bought loads of flying saucers and Caramac bars with the fiver I took from Mam, so I'll not starve. I bought them when Twp Lisa was behind the counter at Sandy's Newsagents – she's totally daft and easily fooled. I was wearing my very best disguise – Mam's plastic rain bonnet and reading glasses, with my Pac a Mac pulled around my chin, and a stick-on moustache from an old Christmas cracker; and as I left, Twp Lisa winked and said: 'Thank you very much, sir.'

I made my way to Llanfair Woods, keeping to the shadier pavement, hiding behind the church wall whenever a car went past. I saw Rob in his Ford estate, crawling along the lane like he was looking for someone, then Nurse Rose Pugh parking her Mini outside the Scout Hut for a couple of minutes, before driving back to the village square. It felt dead strange, watching all the comings and goings, people getting on with their business, when I was secretly getting on with the business of starting my brand-new life.

I wondered about going into the church to say goodbye and to pray to God for The Vicar. No matter what Mam says, I am not evil and I do feel bad about him taking an overdose because of what I said and did. The Vicar is a wicked man, but not as wicked as some, and I don't want God to be angry with me, even though I am often angry with him.

But I decided not to go inside the church after all. I thought someone might be in there praying, or arranging flowers or hiding from something or someone, too. They'd see me and ask what business did I have, visiting God, after I'd been so mean to The Vicar, who's one of God's best mates. I'd be livid if someone did something bad to Barbara, so I thought it best to keep out of God's way until he's had a chance to calm down a bit.

Besides, the church scares me. Even though it's supposed to be one of the prettiest churches in Uskshire, I don't find it nice at all. The air is damp and cold, and always smells of sadness, and that window over the altar – how can anyone call that beautiful? I think it's a bloody disgrace. It's got the Seven Deadly Sins – all grinning corpses in long, flowing robes – leering over Adam and Eve, who are holding hands next to a tree, with fig leaves stuck to their privates and a pit of fire under their feet. It's colourful enough, I suppose, and the purples and reds and greens and golds do look lovely when the sun shines through. But even that doesn't stop the awfulness and the absolute shudders it gives me. Perhaps it's because I'm bad and a sinner. Perhaps it's because it reminds me of hell. Perhaps it's because I know that's where I'm going, even though there are times when I think I'm in hell already.

I ran past The Vicar's house. I know he's not there – nobody's home – but it felt as though the house was alive anyway, watching me through its black oblong windows. And then I walked on to Stockholm Villa, before sloping off into the trees, creeping deeper through the undergrowth towards the quarry, until I was swallowed up whole.

And I'll live here, I will, in Llanfair Woods, for as long as I possibly can. And then I'll move on to somewhere else. I'll walk up Llanfair Lane until I get to the M4 and London. And then I'll have to get a job, because I'll have run out of flying saucers, and then I'll feel dead sad.

Flying saucers are still my favourite sweets, even though they're one of the reasons Susan Pugh grassed me up. I was sitting at the back of the Scout Hut when it happened, on the second day of the summer holidays. I felt so excited. Six weeks of fun ahead – anything could happen!

The Flicks N' Kicks girls were rehearsing their stupid dance for the Llanfair Summer Fete, and I'd snuck in to watch them. Blanche Marston might be able to ban me from her club, but she can't ban me from the Scout Hut because it's public property, so Barbara says.

Anyway, Susan came over and plonked herself on a chair next to me. I really do think she liked me back then. Or maybe she just wanted a flying saucer.

'They're shit, aren't they?' she said, sucking the sherbet out of a yellow one.

I remember thinking how big the flying saucer looked in her hand. She's only a year younger than me, but quite a bit smaller – most girls around my age are. She's prettier, too: blonde curly hair, light blue eyes, rose-pink skin. A proper little Tiny Tears. It was weird hearing her say shit, and I nearly told her so. You'd expect a word like that coming from someone like me, but not from her. And her mam's a nurse – practically a nun!

'Shit?' I said. 'What, the flying saucers?'

She laughed. 'No, you clown. Flicks N' Kicks. My old dance troupe in Barwood was so much better. We did *flips* and kicks. Pity we never got to perform.'

'Why not?'

Susan shrugged. 'Something always went wrong. We were doomed, Mammy said. Someone had it in for us. Odd things kept happening.'

'What sort of odd things?'

But she didn't seem to hear me. 'We'd have let you join,' she said. 'Even if you're too big and look a bit funny. Your hair is as dark as mine is fair, but I don't mind. I think it's shit the way they treat you.'

'I don't care,' I said.

'Bet you do.' She dipped her hand into the flying-saucer bag, and took out a pink one. 'Why can't you be in Flicks N' Kicks?'

'Dunno. I come to all the rehearsals; I even stand in some-times for the girls that can't make it. But Blanche – Mrs Marston – won't let me join. She says I'm a liability.'

Susan's eyes narrowed. 'What's she mean by that?'

'That I'll mess it all up. Because I'm big and clumsy, and I stand out too much, and I can't remember the moves.'

'Bet you can.'

I shrugged.

Truth be told, I *could* remember the moves – every single one of them. I just didn't always do them in the right order. My head, I wanted to tell her, was always a step or two ahead of my arms and legs, and it's hard when you have a head that doesn't work in time with everyone else's, especially when you're two stone heavier and your feet three sizes bigger.

Susan dipped her hand in the bag again. 'Blanche is a bitch,' she whispered.

'You can't say that!'

'I can,' she said. 'And anyway, it's true. She is a bitch. I hate her guts.'

'But her and your mam . . . they've been best friends for ever! At least, that's what my mam says. She was in school with them both, you know.'

'Mammy,' Susan said thoughtfully, taking a green saucer, 'always says, "keep your friends close, and your enemies closer"'.

'What's she mean by that?'

Susan nodded at the stage. 'Shhh,' she said. 'The first group are up again. I've got five more minutes 'til I'm on. Come on, give us another saucer.'

It was nice having someone to have a right laugh with, and that Flicks N' Kicks' dance had us practically wetting ourselves. They were dancing to Toto Coelo's 'I Eat Cannibals'. 'A shocking song,' Susan sniffed. 'Mammy says it's in very poor taste and she tried to tell Blanche that, but,' she sighed, 'you can't argue with stupid.'

Carrie-Anne and Lucy Marston had the main roles. They also had the best skirts – triple-layered ra-ra skirts with pink spots. All the other girls had only two layers, including Susan Pugh, though I noticed her mam had added a sneaky strip of white lace along the hem.

I was wearing trousers. Flared. Picked up from a jumble sale, too short for me. Sometimes, when I wear them out, I shuffle around with my legs close together so people will think that I'm wearing a dress.

'I'd look bloody stupid in one of them skirts anyway,' I muttered.

'Shhhh!' Susan nodded at the stage again. 'Watch this. Fucking ridiculous.'

I nearly fell off my chair at that. 'You can't say fucking!' I said. 'I fucking well can.'

The music started. Something about eating cannibals, about someone's love being so edible and cauldrons and stuff.

'What a load of bollocks,' Susan said.

'Bollocks,' I said. 'It is.'

Carrie-Anne pranced on stage first. She always gets the main roles. She had tinsel deely boppers on her head, and was clutching a huge pink papier mâché spoon, left over from Llanfair Panto Society's performance of *Jack and the Giant Beanstalk*. I watched her shimmy left and right, making stirring actions with the spoon with one hand, flicking her hair with the other, while the rest of the Flicks N' Kicks girls tap-danced behind her. Then Lucy bounded on from the left, joining in with the stirring actions, but without the spoon. Blanche waved her hand at Rose, who was in charge of the tape machine, and wearing enormous earphones.

'Rose, stop the music. Rose, stop the . . . *Rose*!'

Rose lifted one earphone. 'Pardon?' she said.

Blanche, wearing very tight jeans and red stiletto shoes, clickety-clacked across the wooden floor to Rose's side. 'Turn that racket off! And why are you wearing those ridiculous things over your ears?'

Rose smiled. 'So that I can't hear the music, Blanche. You know that I despise it.'

Susan sniggered. Blanche said nothing, but turned to face the stage. I couldn't see her face, but her shoulders were very stiff indeed and the backs of her arms had turned bright red.

'Lucy darling,' she said, trying to sound all posh, 'where is your spoon?'

Lucy shrugged. 'Dunno.'

'You don't know?'

Lucy shrugged again. 'I lost it.'

'You've lost the spoon?' Blanche said.

I could feel Susan next to me, holding her breath. I held mine, too.

Blanche finally exploded. 'How on earth could you *lose* the spoon?' she screamed. 'It's three feet tall and neon pink!'

Susan cracked up next to me, spitting bits of saucer all over her lap.

'If I may interject,' Rose touched Blanche's arm, 'we'll find the spoon, of course we will, because you really can't miss it, but we're a little tight for time, as the Junior Kickers football team have the Scout Hut in, oooh . . .' she checked her watch, 'an hour for their annual revels. So, let's press on, Blanche, my love, and we'll look for the spoon later.'

Blanche glared at her. 'Don't patronize me, Rose.'

Rose smiled back. 'I wasn't aware I was.'

Blanche fluffed up her hair with her hands, so it stood up in tufts from her head. Blanche's hair always gets bigger and bushier the angrier and madder she gets.

'Right,' Blanche said. 'From the middle section. Where the buccaneers tap-dance "lick it and stick it" around the totem pole, and Susan performs her backward flip.'

Rose touched Blanche's elbow. 'If I may?'

'What now, Rose?'

'Buccaneers?' said Rose. 'Where do buccaneers come in?'

'Costumes left over from Llanfair Opera's *The Pirates of Penzance*. Do you have a problem with that?'

'Well, no,' Rose said. 'Not with the costumes, exactly . . .'

'Then with what?'

'Well, given the nature of the song, which is – as you know – about cannibals and is utterly tasteless and I really don't agree with it . . . Would it not make more sense to have the buccaneers dancing around a cauldron rather than a totem pole so that the choreography actually matches the lyrics?'

Blanche glared at Rose. 'Does any of this make sense to you?' she said.

'Well.' Rose shuffled her feet awkwardly. 'We could make it make sense . . .'

'I have no budget, and this totem pole is the only suitable prop we have, left over from Llanfair Am Dram's production of *Calamity Jane*. It was either that, or the cross from Theatre Uskshire's *Jesus Christ Superstar*. If you've anything more appropriate up your sleeve, Rose, please – be my guest.'

'Bloody hell, how many different theatre groups are there in Llanfair?' Susan whispered.

'Four,' I whispered back. 'And they all hate each other's guts.'

Blanche turned to face us. Susan was swiping bits of flying saucer off her skirt.

'This is your cue, Susan,' she shouted. 'Tidy yourself up, and get into position!'

She didn't say a word to me.

And that's when it happened. When I lost Susan, when Susan went the same way as all the others. And I can't tell you why it happened. All I can tell you is that it's like a switch flicks somewhere in their heads; that there comes a time when they realize that it's better to be one of them than to be with me.

Susan got up and walked to the stage. I sat back to finish my flying saucers, only to find that Susan had taken the very last one. And I felt really sad about that, and was thinking about going back to Sandy's to get some more, hoping Twp Lisa was still on the till, because she always gives me extra, when I heard it – a horrible thump. I stood up, and someone – Rose, I think, was shouting –

'Oh. My. God. She's tripped!'

Susan was rolling around on the floor, holding her ankle, screaming in pain – 'She tripped me up! She tripped me up!' She was pointing at Rose or Blanche – I couldn't tell you who, and I couldn't tell why, because why on earth would either of them do such a thing? Then Blanche started screaming, 'Who tripped you up? It wasn't me, you little bitch!' And Rose knelt beside Susan, scooping her up in her arms, holding her tight while she squirmed like a fish, yelling, 'Let me go! Let me go!' Rose kept crying out, 'My poor, poor darling!' until Susan stopped wriggling and went all limp. Then Susan said, dead sulkily: 'I must have tripped.'

Then bloody Blanche Marston started it all. 'She was high on sugar,' Blanche said. 'Not paying attention, were you, Susan, but what do you expect when you've been eating flying saucers all morning?' She poked her long, bony finger at me. 'She's been giggling in the back with Debbie-Marie, gorging on sweets! And just before a performance, too!'

'Oh, Susan!' Rose cried. 'How could you?'

'But I didn't mean . . .' Susan wailed. 'It wasn't me!'

'Not you?' Blanche snarled. 'So, it was someone who looked like you?'

'No! No, I didn't mean . . . I didn't mean to eat them . . .'

'Well, no one forced you to eat them, did they?'

'Yes, yes!' Susan cried, sitting up, pointing at me, and she didn't look like Tiny Tears any more. No, she was Big Ugly Tears instead. '*She* made me eat them!' she roared, 'Debbie-Marie Tunstall! Said if I didn't eat all the flying saucers, she'd beat me up! She said shit and fuck, too!' (And everybody gasped). 'Oh, it was absolutely horrid, Mammy. I was so scared!'

I ran away then, like I've run away now, only back then I only hid for an hour or so. I laid low in Barbara Pritchard's front garden – she'd gone to the library, like she always does on a Wednesday – and I crouched behind her runner beans, all scrambling up wigwam canes in a race to get to the top. I saw the Flicks N' Kicks girls and Blanche Marston parading through the village together, and I'd have laughed my head off at how stupid they looked – the girls in matching ra-ra skirts with bloody great bows in their hair – if Rose and Susan Pugh hadn't been on the other side of the garden wall. I could hear Rose helping Susan into her Mini – Susan kept sniffing, and Rose said, 'We'll get this fixed – don't you worry.'

Then the boys – the Junior Kickers – appeared at the top of Rowan Avenue, walking in line, making their way through the village square to the Scout Hut in their red and white football shirts. Gary White looked stupidly smart and not that ugly in his, and as the boys and girls passed each other, the boys sniggered, and the girls giggled, and my heart twisted in a way I'd never known it twist before.

Then Blanche screeched, 'Time for an ice-cream, girls!' and Lucy said, 'Oh, I hope it's not the stuff we got from the van last week, 'cos it gave Carrie-Anne the runs, it did,' and everyone laughed, especially the boys, and I heard Carrie-Anne say, 'Shut up, stupid, you still wet your knickers, you stinking baby.'

On the other side of the garden wall, Rose and Susan were still talking. Susan was whining, and Rose kept saying – her voice all flat and matter-of-fact – 'Well, they can't do the show without you, Susan, so that's that.'

Then their voices went all muffled – they'd finally made it into the car, I suppose. I waited until Rose drove off, then got up and sat on the garden wall to wait for Barbara. A few cars went by. Brown Owl squeaked past on her pushbike, pretending she couldn't see me. And then, across the road, outside the pub, I saw a group of women eating at a table together, under a painted banner saying 'USKSHIRE LADIES' CONSERVATIVE SOCIETY SUMMER LUNCHEON'. They were old – not as old as Barbara – but looked so happy, like they really liked being with each other. And I thought, when I grow up, I hope the ladies I know are all happy and nice to each other like that.

All their heads turned 180 degrees as Blanche Marston marched past in her too-tight trousers, strutting down Rowan Avenue with the Flicks N' Kicks girls in tow. Then one of the women – that mad mayoress – said something about a tart, probably what she was having for afters, and then she mentioned a camel's toe, whatever that is, and all the other women laughed. And I thought, it must be great being a grown-up, when girls aren't mean to you any more, and you can laugh and laugh and laugh with your mates without a care in the world.

20

Barbara

10 a.m., Hollyhock Cottage,
Llanfair Village Square

'Would you care for another biscuit?'

Barbara prays the answer will be a brisk, 'No, ta, Barb – I must be on my merry way.' But Rose Pugh nods eagerly, extending a remarkably small, smooth hand with an, 'Ooh, don't mind if I do!' before posting a pink wafer sideways into her perpetually cheery mouth.

Yes, thinks Barbara, *I* do *mind, because you've already demol-ished two custard creams and three chocolate digestives.* She wills Utterson to disgrace himself; hoping his fetish might rear its ugly head and send Rose Pugh packing, since her legs – crossed at the ankles, encased in thick navy tights – are but a tantalizing two feet away from his nose. But Utterson, sprawled across Barbara's toes, merely raises his eyes heavenwards as the biscuit tin is passed over his head, emitting a sigh and full-bodied fart before settling back to sleep.

Barbara stares down at the rug, appalled. 'I'm so sorry about that,' she says.

'Oh, please don't apologize!' Rose carefully reunites her cup with its saucer. 'Happens to us all as we age. Anyway, Barb, as you were saying . . .'

'Was I?'

Was she? What was Barbara saying? She can't remember. Was Barbara actually saying anything at all?

'Yes! We were discussing Blanche and Clive and the girls! Whatever are we going to do? Should we call the police?'

A dull ache grips Barbara's chest – panic? Indigestion? She tries to think calmly. How did she get here? How did she get from watching Rose Pugh emerge from her car, to them both sitting here, cup of tea in hand, crunching their way through her Family Circle biscuit assortment? Barbara can't remember. She's having one of her absences, dammit, and her head is fuzzy, her chest hurts so much . . .

'Let me think,' she says, playing for time.

'Yes, of course.'

Rose frowns into her teacup, weaponizing her spoon to liberate a sodden lump of custard cream. She plops the sludge on her saucer, flashing Barbara a triumphant smile. 'Shall I pop into the kitchen and brew us both a top-up while you're ruminating, Barb?' she says.

'Yes please, Rose. That would be lovely.'

Jigsaw pieces of memory are starting to fuse in Barbara's head. She remembers hiding behind the curtain, ducking under her desk, knees giving way and cracking like fireworks as she sank down to the floor. And there she'd remained, anticipating the rap on her front door which, after several minutes, Barbara dared hope might not come after all.

For the pause was too long – Rose must have changed her

mind! Well, thank Christ for that, Barbara sighed, hauling herself up by the arm of her chair, rearranging the brushed-cotton petticoat that had rucked up under her tweed skirt. But then –

'Yoo-hoo!'

Rose Pugh. Rattling and cooing through Barbara's letterbox, sending Utterson bloody berserk.

When Barbara finally opened her door, Rose was standing on the front step, beaming expectantly, the early morning sunlight bouncing off her remarkably smooth blonde head.

'Yes?' Rose said.

'Yes, what?' Barbara snapped.

'Yes, how can I help?'

Barbara blinked. 'I didn't ask you to come here,' she said.

'Yes, you did.'

'No, I didn't.'

'Yes, you did.'

'No, I *didn't*.'

'But Barb, you did! You beckoned for me to come over, you stuck your hand through the curtains . . .'

'I was closing them, Rose.'

'Now, who closes their curtains on a weekday morning, hmm?'

'Well, me, evidently.'

'Don't be shy or embarrassed,' Rose said. 'No need to pretend you've changed your mind. Whatever you want to discuss, I've seen it all. How's the arthritis, Barb? Are you moving your bowels on a regular basis?'

Barbara opened her mouth to protest, but too late – the nurse, nimble and light on her feet, swerved around Barbara's sentry-like stance, and made her way down the hallway, glancing dismissively side to side at the amateur sketches and watercolours lining Barbara's walls. 'Now,' said Rose, 'let's pop the kettle on, and we'll have a lovely cuppa and chin-wag. I need your help, actually. The Marstons have gone AWOL, and I suspect foul play.'

'Here we are, Barb. A nice fresh cup of tea.'

'Thank you, Rose.'

The nurse sinks into the armchair opposite Barbara, hem rucking up around her thighs. Barbara can see the edge of her knickers, inexplicably worn over her navy tights – baggy white cotton and knee-length, trimmed with lace – the sort of undergarment Barbara's Edwardian mother might have worn if she was feeling frivolous.

'Have you had a chance to think?' Rose asks, lifting her cup of tea to her lips.

Barbara shakes her head. She is suddenly struck by Rose's smallness, her childlike mannerisms. The armchair practically swallows her whole; her legs – dangling free and uncrossed – are those of a little girl, and Barbara realizes there is something about Rose Pugh that brings out the latent headteacher in her. Something that makes her want to say, *you've had quite enough biscuits, now do some work, and sit up straight when you're talking to me!*

'You're a good woman, Barb.' Rose swipes a wafery crumb from her mouth with the back of her hand.

'Well.' Barbara forces a laugh. 'I'm not so sure about that.'

'A wise one, too.'

'Oh, pfft.'

'Which is why,' Rose leans forward, gripping Barbara's knee

with surprising fervour, 'I trust your opinion. What should we do, Barb? What on earth *can* we do?'

'Well, not a lot really.' Barbara shifts uneasily in her seat, but Rose's grip remains unabated. 'Blanche and Clive are grown adults,' she adds, uncomfortably. 'They can come and go as they please. The police wouldn't be remotely interested at this point, I think an adult needs to go missing for at least twenty-four hours before the police get involved, or the circumstances must be particularly suspicious.'

'Not true.' Rose sits back, releasing Barbara's knee. 'You don't have to leave it for twenty-four hours before contacting the police, and the circumstances *are* suspicious. Look, Blanche phoned me at work early yesterday morning – well, she didn't talk to me because I was doing my rounds, but she spoke to the receptionist and asked if she could get a message to Nurse Rose Pugh – that's me, by the way . . .'

'Yes, Rose. I know it's you.'

' . . . asking if I could pick the girls up from after-school knitting club and keep them overnight, because of a family emergency, and she and Clive would be indisposed for the next day or so.'

'I admit it's a bit odd, but there's nothing particularly suspicious about it.'

'But Clive doesn't speak to his mum and dad, or rather, they don't speak to him, and Blanche doesn't have any family. Both her parents are dead, and she hasn't any brothers or sisters, or aunties or uncles. She's completely alone in the world, like me. Well, I have Susan, of course, and Blanche has Clive *and* the girls, so technically, she's much better off than I am, what with my being recently widowed an' all . . .'

The nurse folds her arms, grim-faced. 'Clive's done away with her, that's what he's done. When I asked the receptionist how Blanche sounded, she said tense. Scared. Like she had the weight of the world on her shoulders.'

'Well, I daresay she will be tense. Being married to Clive would make anyone tense. I think, in the light of the media's efforts to stir things up between Llanfair and Barwood, that Blanche and Clive are lying low until things blow over.'

'And leave their girls to fend for themselves? Blanche would never allow such a thing – Carrie-Anne and Lucy are her world! And there's no change of clothing for them, either – Blanche would normally pack nighties and a change of pants and socks if they were staying over at mine, but they're having to share Susan's things. That's not like Blanche at all – she doesn't approve of sharing. Look, can't we just pop over to the Marstons' house and see if there's any sign of Clive – or Blanche, or,' Rose adds balefully, 'whatever's *left* of Blanche.'

'We can't just break in – that's breaking the law!'

'If we can't get the police involved, we *are* the law.' Rose tosses her head defiantly. 'And we won't be breaking in, because I have a key.'

'If you're entering the Marstons' house without their permission, you'll be doing so alone, Rose. I'm staying out of this. As, I think, should you.'

'You just won't get involved because you don't like Blanche,' Rose says, petulantly. 'If it was Ingrid Tunstall, you'd be there like a shot.'

'That's not fair!'

'Clive Marston is a dangerous man. If we don't act, there'll be blood on our hands, you mark my words.'

'Clive? Dangerous? Oh, come on! He mixes with some unsavoury characters, I grant you that, but he's never struck me as the violent type.'

'I know in my heart that you're a good person.' Rose's tone softens, her pale blue eyes meet Barbara's over the rim of her teacup. 'You always look out for people in need. You always looked out for *me*. I remember you standing at that very window, all those years ago, when I was a student nurse. Making sure I was all right while I waited at the bus stop. All those dark early mornings and evenings, you were always there for me, because my dear departed Mammy and Daddy couldn't be. I've never forgotten your kindness.'

Barbara stifles a yawn. It's so close in this room, so airless, so tiring. 'Stop trying to butter me up, Rose,' she says. 'I didn't come down with the last shower. I understand your concern for Blanche, but I do think it's premature. Now, if you don't mind, I need to press on. Ingrid Tunstall is coming to clean later today, and *I* need to clean before she arrives.'

'Apologies.' Rose drains her teacup in two large gulps. 'Oh,' she says. 'Just a little something else I wanted to discuss. And I do hope you don't think I'm speaking out of turn.'

Barbara narrows her eyes. 'That depends on what you have to say.'

'Well, it's about your friendship with Debbie-Marie Tunstall.'

'What of it?'

'I just don't want to see you being taken advantage of.' Rose carefully places her cup on the twist-leg oak table at her side. 'If I may speak plainly, I think Debbie is not just mischievous, but manipulative, too, and I believe that you are a nurturing, but lonely, person. This friendship between the two of you has disaster written all over it. Just think about what she's done to The Vicar! That could be you next, Barb.'

'Don't be ridiculous!'

'To an outsider, to someone who doesn't know you the way I know you, it all looks a bit peculiar, don't you think? A single, elderly lady, close friends with a child . . . well, who knows where it could end? I'm concerned for you, I am. And I am not the only one.'

Barbara opens her mouth to protest, then clamps it shut.

Her carriage clock, a retirement gift from the governing body at Barwood Primary School, ticks away on the mantelpiece at her side, mercilessly measuring out her mounting sense of exposure and panic –

I am not the only one.

And for a moment, Barbara sees herself the way Rose Pugh, the way everyone in Llanfair, must see her: at best, a fusty, feeble old woman, cobwebby-brained, living in a hovel, swamped by yellowing newspapers, out-of-print books and unfinished paintings and sketches, tottering towards oblivion with nothing but a farting dog for company. And at worst . . . well. They see her as, what?

A predator of children.

'I've said too much.' Rose, straightening her stethoscope, gathering the bag at her feet, rises from the hillocks of her badly sprung armchair. 'I'd best make tracks. Dolly Strange's leg-ulcer is grumbling again.'

She looks down on Barbara, who – suddenly feeling terribly small – remains sitting on the edge of her chair, chin resting in the palm of her hand.

'You look as though you're in pain, Barb. When did you last see Dr Jolly?'

'I avoid Dr Jolly at all costs,' Barbara mumbles, staring at Utterson's woolly head, studying the adorable thick black hairs curling around the edges of his tartan collar. When did his whiskers start turning white? Were they always white? How old is he now? 'I don't need to see a doctor, anyway.'

Rose pats Barbara's shoulder. 'Nobody has to live in pain,' she says. 'There's medication for that. No need to get up, Barb, I can see myself out.'

They both jump suddenly, alerted by a noise from Barbara's front garden – a dreadful high-pitched yowl, like an animal in pain.

'Oh, look!' Rose exclaims. 'It's Ingrid Tunstall, crying her eyes out, poor old soul! What on earth has that child of hers gone and done now?'

21

Vanessa

*11.30 a.m., the car park, Dewi Sant Department of
Child & Adolescent Psychology*

She sees them before they see her: two women, one elderly
and wearing a navy-blue mackintosh; the other in her thirties
or older, perhaps – it's hard to tell, because the hood of her
khaki snorkel jacket is pulled around her face like a funnel,
leaving only a pair of lips visible, puckered around the filter
of the final third of a cigarette.

It takes Vanessa a moment, but she *knows* these women. The
older one she nearly ran over outside The Vicar's house last
Friday; the other is Ingrid Tunstall – Debbie-Marie's mother –
apparently carrying the weight of the world on her already
rounded shoulders.

The mackintoshed woman has her dog with her: a scruffy
black terrier enthusiastically circling the bollard guarding one
of the few available parking spaces. The old woman doesn't
notice this, because she is too busy staring critically at the
concrete facade of the Dewi Sant Centre – a small but impres-
sively depressing example of 1950s Brutalist architecture.

Vanessa curses, turns the radio off, and rolls down her window.

'Excuse me,' she shouts. 'That's my parking space, and I'd wonder if you'd mind . . .'

The mackintoshed woman bustles towards her. 'Dr Bridges, I presume?'

She looks familiar, this elderly woman. Not just from last Friday, but from some time before. Vanessa can't quite place her. But there is something about the horn-rimmed spectacles, the voice – low and commanding – that is all at once comforting and disconcerting. A voice that addressed her sternly once, a long, long time ago. A time that reeked of overripe blackberries; when Vanessa spoke of something she shouldn't have seen, when salt tears burnt the back of her throat . . .

It's the old woman that hosted that bloody kiddies' picnic!

Ingrid Tunstall, slumped against the car-park fence, throws the butt of her cigarette to the floor as the old woman lifts the bollard, slips the dog's lead over one wrist, and motions with leather-gloved hands for Vanessa to position her car *just so*. She's a type, thinks Vanessa – stout, square-jawed, with cropped grey hair that does as it's told, and can't understand for the life of her why the rest of humanity can't do the same.

'Just a little further forward,' the old woman booms. 'Yes, a little further. No, not that far!'

Vanessa can't stop staring at Ingrid Tunstall, whose hood has slipped back off her furrowed grey face.

The poor woman looks broken. Absolutely broken.

'No,' Vanessa says, quietly. 'I haven't received a letter from Debbie, but she doesn't know where I live, so . . .'

She'd intended to be extra busy with admin this morning, but she won't be able to focus on anything now. Because

Debbie-Marie Tunstall has run away. Another young girl let down by *her*, another confused and vulnerable patient allowed to slip through Dr Vanessa Bridges' butter-fingers. To misquote Oscar Wilde: to lose one patient may be considered a misfortune, to lose two looks like a disciplinary hearing might be in order.

Vanessa wants to crawl under her desk and cry. In fact, when Ingrid Tunstall and the older woman, who's identified herself as Barbara Pritchard (headteacher, retired), leave her room, that's exactly what she'll do.

Barbara Pritchard shuffles impatiently in her blue plastic chair, tapping Vanessa's desk with irritated fingers and shooting the whining dog at her feet a cautionary glance. 'I haven't received a letter either,' she says, 'but I anticipate doing so tomorrow. Ingrid says that two first-class stamps and envelopes are missing, isn't that right, Ingrid?'

Ingrid nods.

'I think we can safely assume that you and I, Dr Bridges, will be the recipients of those letters. I doubt whether Deborah will reveal any more information than that already expressed in the note she left for her mother, but you never know. Did she give any hint during her last session with you that she was planning to run away?'

Vanessa shakes her head. 'None at all. I thought . . . I thought we were making progress. She was starting to open up to me.'

Oh, stupid, stupid, stupid! Has she learnt nothing about taking things at face value, of the convincing falsehoods children tell? 'Have you called the police?' she can hear herself saying, because she feels she must say something, however trite.

'Well, of course we've told the police,' Barbara Pritchard snaps. 'For all the good it will do us. She's only been gone a few hours. One would hope they'll start looking for her soon enough, but most of them are too busy policing the picket lines at Barwood Colliery, and I daresay we'll be left at the mercy of that piece of work, WPC Jane Gill.'

'What about community search parties?'

Ingrid shrugs. 'She's been gone for such a short time, the gossip hasn't spread yet. But I can't imagine . . .' Her eyes fill up. 'Let's face it – Debbie isn't liked in the village, after everything that's happened. She's not,' her voice falls to a whisper, 'the sort of child who attracts much in the way of sympathy in a place like Llanfair. I suppose the locals will just think it's one of her stunts. To get attention, you see.'

'And what do you think?' Vanessa asks gently. 'Do you think she's attention-seeking?'

'I think,' Ingrid says sadly, 'that this is all my fault. I walked out without saying goodbye this morning. We had a big row last night, and I said some dreadful things. I forget she's a child sometimes, because she's so big and mature-looking and talks like an adult, and I've come to rely on her more than I should since her father upped and left us . . .'

'Deborah is very articulate,' Barbara adds. 'As I'm sure you've noticed, Dr Bridges. She's highly intelligent. Unusually astute.'

' . . . and when I got to the pub this morning to clean,' Ingrid continues, 'I couldn't keep my mind on the job, I felt so guilty. So, I went back to tell Debbie how sorry I was, and that I really did love her. I really do love her,' her voice cracks, 'really and truly I do, but I was too late. She'd already gone. And she'd left that note. Oh, God . . .'

Barbara Pritchard rattles the dog's lead irritably. 'Buck up, Ingrid,' she says. She glares at Vanessa. 'You!'

Vanessa jumps. 'What?'

'We need your help. Where do you think she's gone? Time is of the essence!'

Vanessa scratches her head – classic displacement behaviour. This woman makes her feel like she's twelve years old all over again, caught napping in class with her tie undone and skirt rolled over at the waistband. 'I-I really don't know . . .'

'What do you mean, you don't know? Presumably you've spoken at length to Deborah? Tried to get to know her? Discussed her past, her hopes, her dreams, the places she feels safest?'

'I've only met her twice!'

Barbara Pritchard's eyes narrow. 'You are an academic by nature, I think, rather than a practitioner. You don't spend much time in the company of patients, do you, Dr Bridges?'

'I don't think that's any of your business!'

Barbara Pritchard nods. 'I thought as much. You're not comfortable with people. Textbooks, yes. People, no. You prefer to study humanity from a distance. Understandable, really, since most of humanity stinks. You remind me of how I was at your age.'

'Well, really!'

Barbara Pritchard rises. 'Ingrid and I have a bus to catch. Meanwhile, I'll leave you in peace to have a good think about where Deborah may have run off to. You're an intelligent woman, Dr Bridges, I'm sure you'll have some sensible ideas. Are you married?'

'What?!'

'No, I thought not. I live at Hollyhock Cottage, on the edge of Llanfair Village Square. Come over for tea when you're ready, and we'll discuss matters further.'

22

Robert

1.45 p.m., the Llanfair Arms

He's all fingers and thumbs, is Robert – trying to act dead casual as he removes the last packet of NV Nuts from the poster-lady's right breast – knowing he must look an absolute twit, like he's never seen a pair of boobs before in his life. He slides the packet over the bar, towards a smirking Barry Parry, for the second time in twenty-four hours.

'And a pint of Brains, mate,' Parry says. 'And one for yourself, of course.' He nods at the cage behind him. 'And one for your feathered friend.'

'No thanks. The bird's on the wagon, and I don't drink on duty,' Robert lies.

'Oi!' someone shouts. 'Parry, we need you, now!'

Parry turns to address the crowd – a motley crew of lunchtime punters: Griffiths from Llanfair Primary School, Morris the Butcher, Hoskins from the hardware store, each resting a sports-jacketed elbow on the edge of the bar, sipping their pints in unison, observing the chaos around them through frowning, tangled brows. In the far corner of the room, several floral-frocked representatives of Llanfair Ladies' Conservative

Association are enjoying a raucous game of darts with the chorus from Llanfair Opera Society, one of whom insists on singing the scores in an off-key mezzosoprano.

Parry holds his index finger aloft. 'Quiet, please,' he says. 'I'm about to record my exposé on Clive Marston, and would appreciate your silence. Watch and learn, my friends. Watch and learn.'

If Robert's quick, he can sneak out of the pub undetected while Parry's talking to the camera. He needs to get out, get away from all this – from the pub, the crowds, his father. From the pressure of playing the friendly barman, oozing merry quip and jest.

But Gwendoline bloody Bridges plonks her backside on a barstool directly in front of him. A camera homes in on her face, and someone shouts from behind a clipboard, 'Oi, you – barman – stay like that in the background, that's it. Pretend to look busy!'

Robert does as he's told, wiping the counter with a smelly bar towel, holding his breath against the ammoniacal stink as Gwendoline Bridges – clutching a pint of Brains bitter – grudgingly permits the wardrobe lady to rearrange the mayoral chain around her neck. Gwen looks baffled and frazzled, blinking repeatedly at the lighting equipment and cameras – a rabbit caught in the headlights, if ever there was one. There are beads of sweat glistening on her upper lip and, Robert notes with some surprise, tears in her eyes.

Parry begins by quizzing her over Clive Marston's misdeeds, then moves on to the social-housing proposal, with building to take place on a field just off Llanfair Lane, behind Stockholm Villa. Did she, Barry Parry enquires with a raised eyebrow, have some skin in the game, so to speak? Is the proposed building site literally a little too close to home?

'I am not here to discuss personal issues.' Gwendoline Bridges, dressed in a navy silk skirt suit and cream blouse, grins inanely at the camera, raising her beer glass aloft with a trembling hand. 'I am here,' she continues, 'to declare solidarity with our brothers and sisters in Barwood. We will be having a fundraiser for the miners at the Llanfair Arms tomorrow evening . . .' a feeble cheer and lone handclap goes up from one of the tables, ' . . . where there will be dancing with Blanche Marston's Flicks N' Kicks girls, and a singalong with Wrong Jones – Llanfair's very own tribute to the one and only Tom!'

'I see,' Parry says with a smirk. 'So, you're using the miners' plight to promote Llanfair businesses and artistes. Is that not ill-advised, given Clive Marston's exploitation of Barwood residents? Do you not think donations – money, food, toys and clothes – might be more useful? Or standing shoulder-to-shoulder with the miners on the colliery picket lines? Isn't using the miners' dire situation for self-promotion in rather poor taste, Lady Mayoress?'

Gwen's mouth opens and closes like a dying fish.

'Well?' says Parry. 'Isn't that the case? Llanfair is riding on the back of Barwood's misfortune?'

Robert senses a steely resolve grip Gwendoline Bridges. She sits up, ramrod straight, rolling back her shoulders, lifting her chin, fixing Parry with an icy stare. 'Aren't you doing exactly the same, Mr Parry?' she archly enquires. 'Like all journalists, you feed off misfortune. Bad news is your bread and butter.'

Touché, thinks Robert. Nice one, Gwen.

Parry doesn't miss a beat. 'But we're not here to talk about me.'

'We're not here to talk about me, either.' Gwendoline Bridges, equilibrium restored, swivels on her barstool, beaming at the camera full-on. 'All are welcome tomorrow evening,' she trills. 'Llanfair will really go to town! We'll have a Welsh-themed buffet, and our Welsh hags flung out . . .'

A groan goes up from the pub. Parry buries his head in his hands. 'Christ's sake,' he mutters. '*Cut!*' He glares at Gwen. 'Welsh. Flags. Hung. Out.'

'That's what I said!'

'Really, it wasn't.'

Parry turns to address the man in corduroy trousers, whose backside Robert nearly sliced off with his car the day before. 'Blanche Marston's Flicks N' Kicks girls – she'd be Clive's missus, yes? Any sign of him yet?'

Corduroy-arse shakes his head. 'We've tried everywhere. His home, his office, his secretary's house and various other ladies' homes he, er, apparently frequented. But no one's seen him. Looks like he's done a runner.'

'His wife?'

'What about her?'

'Well, if Marston can't speak for himself, isn't she the next best thing?'

Corduroy-arse shakes his head again. 'There was no one home when we knocked, but a neighbour said she'd heard a rumour that Blanche Marston spoke to someone at the GP surgery yesterday morning.' He looks down at his notes, scribbled on the back of an empty fag packet. 'The receptionist said Blanche Marston asked her to pass on a message to the district nurse, asking if the nurse – a close friend, apparently – could have the kids overnight, because of a family emergency. Not a sign of either of the adult Marstons since.'

Robert bolts from the pub, not giving a monkey's who sees him. Something bad has happened to Blanche, he's absolutely sure of it.

He hops into his car, speeds through the village and over the railway bridge, past Aneurin Bevan Estate, crunching into second gear and crawling up the newly tarmacked road towards Llanfair Heights. He cranes his head, praying for a glimpse of drainpipe-trousered thigh sashaying along the white, dog-shit-free pavements, knowing, with a heavy heart, that he's almost certainly craning in vain.

He pulls up outside Blanche Marston's house, with its mani-cured lawn and mock-Georgian facade. Her Volvo is parked askew on the driveway, as though dumped in a hurry, but Clive's Jag is nowhere to be seen.

She'd been so scared of late. She knew something bad was brewing. That's why she'd needed Robert so badly – she'd made her panic perfectly clear.

Blanche, Blanche. Where the hell are you?

'Robert! Robbie Hargreaves!'

WPC Jane Gill. Marching across the road towards him. 'What are you doing here, Hargreaves?' she shouts. 'Are you looking for the Marstons?'

She's looking unusually ruffled, thinks Robert – there are strands of honey-blonde hair sticking out at stiff angles from under her hat. She's flushed of face, her top button's undone, and her uniform looks rumpled.

She sticks her head through Robert's window. 'Is your car tax up-to-date?' she pants.

'You can see perfectly well that it is,' Robert replies. 'And why would I be looking for the Marstons?'

'Well,' Jane tucks a strand of hair behind her ear, 'you're pretty close to Blanche these days, if you know what I mean . . .'

'No, Jane, I don't know what you mean. I just fancied a drive, that's all.' He struggles to keep his voice even. 'Why are *you* here? Have Blanche and Clive been formally classified as missing persons, then?'

'Can't tell you, mate,' she says, furtively glancing over her shoulder. Robert follows her gaze, seeing nothing of interest – just a turning circle at the top of the road, colonized by spikes of coneflowers and pampas grass tufts, with a police patrol car just visible behind it. The driver – a bum-fluffed rookie PC with cropped hair – stares back at him, red-faced.

Robert feels scrutinized – out of place and guilty of some unspecified crime. His banana-yellow car and unkempt hair and leather trousers feel illegal here, at Llanfair Heights, where everything is tasteful and neatly aligned. Even Mother Nature knows her place – lawns freshly mown, neatly clipped evergreen shrubs marking out boundaries between the identical properties. Everything just so.

'You'd best be on your way,' Jane Gill says, evidently making the same observation. 'You're loitering in a suspicious manner and making the place look untidy. Oh, and just to let you know, that kid you're always hanging around with – Debbie-Marie Tunstall. Run away, she has. Left her mum a letter. You sure you don't have anything to do with her disappearance, Robbie?'

'Don't be ridiculous,' he growls. 'The poor kid probably needs some time to herself, away from her bloody persecutors. Do you have any idea the effect people like you have on people like Debbie-Marie? And on people like *me*? I have to ask you, Jane,' he says, shaking his head. 'For years, I've wanted to know, just why did you bully me so badly in primary school? What did I do to deserve it?'

For a moment, Jane's face softens. She speaks so quietly, Robert has to lean out of his window to hear her:

'Because you had a mum who thought you were the bee's knees, Robbie,' she says. 'A mum who believed you could do no wrong, even though you were an absolute loser. I was never good enough for my mum, see. And I hated you for that.'

'You were jealous? You made my life absolute hell, because my mother was *nice* to me?'

Before Jane can reply, he slams his foot on the accelerator, and doesn't look back.

His return journey to the Llanfair Arms is deliberately slow and circuitous. Now Robert is keeping his eyes peeled for Blanche Marston *and* Debbie-Marie; he's also avoiding his dad and those berks from BBC Wales. He doesn't want to speak to a soul right now. Well, except perhaps to that stuck-up woman who nearly ran Barbara over last Friday. Vanessa Bridges, from Stockholm Villa, with her porcelain skin and bonkers hair. He wonders what she smells like, then wonders whether wondering what she smells like makes him a pervert. He'd bet his last fiver that she smells of flowers and herbs, not of the inside of pubs, like him.

He'd like to ask what it's like being her. What goes through her head at night, when she's lying in bed, unable to sleep. He'd like to know her hopes and fears, her likes, dislikes, her favourite colour, and whether she'd order chips or rice if they ever went out for a curry together – or would she go for a half-and-half? That's what he'd do – half chips, half rice. He's always been crap at decisions.

And after their curry and one or two pints, he'd ask her about her childhood, or what she remembers of it. And whether she recalls that teddy bears' picnic, twenty years ago now, when she – a tiny six-year-old girl – had tried to kill Blanche Marston.

23

Debbie

4 p.m., Llanfair Woods

Now, here's something I never thought I'd hear myself say –
I'm bored as buggery of Llanfair Woods.

I've done everything, I have – found some owl pellets, torn
them to pieces, and pulled out two jawbones and several claws.
I've eaten two Caramacs, climbed a tree and walked to the
edge of the lane and back. I tried to nap, but the ground was
damp and smelt of something dead, then a midge got up my
trouser leg and bit me on the knee.

And I was really, really missing Mam. And Barbara. Even
Bug-eyed Thomas.

I've talked to the birds and I've talked to the trees. I've laid
on my back and stared up at the sky through the branches,
seeing faces and shapes and whole cities carved out of the
clouds. I've looked down at the earth, at the molehills and
anthills, and imagined the countries down there, underground,
and the millions and zillions of creepy-crawlies scurrying about
in their caverns below, going round and round making tracks
in the dirt without knowing why.

I keep telling myself I'm not really alone. I can't be alone in Llanfair Woods, with all these worlds above and below me. But I've never felt more alone in my life.

I don't know what to do. Go back, get a hiding from Mam for running away? Face the music tomorrow at school, let the kids take the piss out of me even more?

Or stay here and tough it out.

I should give it a night. Build a fire, like Brown Owl tried to teach me in Brownies, before I messed everything up and she booted me out with a flea in my ear. I should have listened; I should have done as I was told for once in my miserable life – that's what Brown Owl said to me.

Anyway, no point in moping. I'm supposed to rub two sticks together, so I need to find some dry enough to get a spark going. There are twigs all around me, but they're all too damp, so I have to go somewhere that's open and dry – like the banks of the quarry.

I take a path that snakes steeply upwards, between the oldest oak trees in Llanfair Woods. I don't think there's a full moon tonight, so the quarry should be safe from the Satanists. But I'm still bloody scared of what I might find. A goat's head, perhaps, or a sacrificed squirrel or chicken entrails or suchlike; and as I crack on, the path trails off into nothing – overgrown with brambles and nettles, and I have to lift up my knees to push through, like I'm marching with an invisible army. I know these woods like the back of my hand, but I could still get lost – anyone could – because when the trees are so tall that you can't see the sun, you don't know which way is east or west. And then you'll go round in circles for ever, and never see daylight again.

But, scrambling down this muddy mound, I can see a break

through the trees ahead – a flash of silver and light bright blue coming from the quarry lake. That lake should be drained, Barbara says, because it's 'a magnet for tragedy'. But I find it peaceful and beautiful, the water so calm and clear and clean, even though I know there's a ton of crap down there – cars and fridges and all manner of shit left to rot at the bottom.

Speaking of stuff left to rot, some filthy sod's left a rolled-up rug here – one of those old-fashioned flying carpets, heavily patterned in dark jewel colours. Probably worth a fortune, I bet, and makes a nice change from the usual stuff that gets dumped in Llanfair Woods. I've found a piss-stained mattress before, a baby's buggy and a cot, and a bag of ladies' under-wear and mucky magazines. But I've not found a rug, and it'll look dead lush on the floor of my den, if I ever get round to building it. I can drag it all by myself, too, if I tug on the edge, but it's heavy, so heavy, and . . .

Oh.

The earth spins, then stops with a shudder.

All I can hear is my quick, sharp breaths, cutting through the quiet.

I want to scream, but I can't.

Because it's horrid, it is – seeing Clive Marston's body, roly-polying out of the rug, flopping lifelessly down the dirt slope, ending up flat on his back in the hollow, arms open wide, like he wants a hug, eyes staring up from under the big black bullet hole in the middle of his head. Such a nice suit he's wearing, too – grey with a pinstripe, a light blue tie and a matching hanky folded into a triangle and popped in his right breast pocket.

Poor Clive.

He'd have been getting dressed the day that he died, not knowing this was the day that he'd cop it: whistling a tune, folding his hanky, knotting his tie, greasing his hair, admiring his ratty face in the mirror, kidding himself he looked handsome. I never liked Clive, I won't lie, but just now I pity him so very much. He looks lost and naked, somehow, in spite of his fancy-pants suit.

I should go and get help, but I want, I need, a closer look.

I creep towards him, whispering a prayer: *Dear God, this is Clive. He wasn't that bad, well, maybe he was, but he didn't deserve this, and I hope you can find a place in heaven for him.*

I've never seen a dead body before, never mind a murdered one, but I am not afraid – I feel more sad than anything. Sad for Clive, who's not Clive any more, but a tailor's dummy with pale, waxy skin, his face all starey and empty-looking, like he can't understand what's happened to him. I crouch down to look at him closer. It's such a clean hole, the wound in his head, a hole that's black and deep, like a well. Straight in and out, that bullet had gone, through his brain and out the back of his skull. Which part of his brain did it smash through, I wonder. The part that loved Carrie-Anne, and gave her the stars and the moon on her ceiling? Or the part that was greedy and bad and did all it could to screw over the miners? Or the part that helped his hands tie his tie, pull on his socks and brush his hair?

He's missing his shoes, which is very strange. Did the murderer kill Clive for his shoes? I doubt it. He wore shiny black loafers with built-up heels – that's what Mam always said. Who in their right mind would want to murder a man to steal a pair of shoes like that? Maybe the shoes were a souvenir. Maybe the killer took something from Clive that they knew really mattered to him, just out of spite. But Clive's still wearing his lovely gold watch, and that would have mattered much more to him than his built-up loafers. It's worth a few bob, too, that lovely gold watch. Why take Clive's shoes, and not his watch? It doesn't make any sense.

A crow caws, but I don't flinch. We're too busy locking eyes, me and Clive Marston. And all the while, I'm listening. For the sound of a car, for the snapping of twigs, for a sign that there's someone here with me, the person who rolled Clive's body up in a rug and dumped it here in a hollow. But everything's silent – just the trees, watching, waiting and whispering. And they won't tell, the trees won't tell, or the ants or the moles or the worms in the ground, none of them will say a word about what I'm about to do next.

Because I take it, I do – Clive Marston's gold watch. I take it and put it into my bag next to my Kajagoogoo notebook and my Polaroid camera and my Caramac bars, and I say to Clive Marston inside my head, I say: *Mr Marston, I'm ever so sorry, but this will help me more than it will help you. Because you are dead, and nothing can help you now. And I can't go for help, anyway – there's no point, and I'd only get blamed for whatever it was that happened to you, because I get blamed for everything around here . . .*

And that's when I see something between Clive's lips, which are at a strange angle – his jaw all twisted, as though someone clamped his mouth shut after he died so he wouldn't tell tales on them. It's the papery edge of something rolled up, shoved between his teeth, and what I do next is disgusting, I know, but I can't help it, I really can't help it, because I'm

Debbie-Marie Tunstall and I'm bad. I'm a psycho. That's what everyone calls me.

I draw it out of his mouth.

And unroll –

A fifty-pound note!

There's a sharp snap of twig behind me. A soft thud-thud of footsteps on mud. My heart skips a beat and my head starts to swim as I spin round and look up the walls of the hollow to see a flash of red darting from tree to tree.

And I run. I run for my life, I do – racing towards the light of the lake, where I floated last night in my dreams with my dad; but at the last minute, I swerve, tripping over the jaggedy limestone rocks. I take a right turn, back into the trees, sprinting past brambles and red-berried hawthorns 'til my lungs feel on fire and my guts want to heave, knowing that if I stop or look back, I'll end up just like Clive Marston – no shoes on my feet and a hole through the part of my brain that loves Mam and Barbara and Utterson. And I want my brain to be whole, not a hole where the people I love used to be.

So, I keep on running. Tripping over my feet, picking my knees up, swiping low-hanging branches out of my face and my tangled-up hair. I run and I run, without looking back, praying to God that I won't die of fright.

24

Vanessa

7.30 p.m., Stockholm Villa, Llanfair Lane

Vanessa's room hasn't felt like hers in a long time. Her child-hood bedroom was very different – all psychedelic patterns and hues of lime, turquoise and tangerine. The chaos was soothing, although being soothed wasn't important to Vanessa back then, because life was good. It was easy.

At secondary school she'd been liked, if a loner. But being an outsider hadn't bothered her then. She'd liked her own company, wasn't interested in the Osmonds, or roller-ball lip-gloss and clodhopper shoes. She'd liked Bowie, Biology and Emily Brontë, and being with her dad, who helped design houses that wouldn't fall down, because he was good at maths, and so was she, because it was easy.

Then life stopped being easy.

When did that happen? When was Vanessa's room taken over by someone less happy, less free? It seems the more tasteful the décor became, the more chaotic her life and relationships. Now everything in the bedroom matches: the Laura Ashley rose-sprigged duvet, the curtains, the lampshade, the rug. But Vanessa doesn't match, she doesn't fit in. Doesn't fit in anywhere any more.

Briefly, at Cambridge, she'd managed to wing it – observing and aping the people around her, moulding herself to be the right peg in the right-shaped hole. And she'd played the part ever so well: drifting in kaftans from lover to lecture; dawn, drunken flits through spire-flanked lanes; sprawling in buttercup-spangled meadows reading Proust, never daring to admit that she loathed it. But her Cambridge years were a vacuum of sorts, sucking all sense of reality out of her; persuading Vanessa that life would continue that way indefinitely. And, when it didn't, when her days as a student finally came to an end, it had come as a shock, as a terrible grief, from which she'd still not recovered.

Even so, she'd remained in a bubble of sorts. Given a job at the Cardiff Institute of Psychology, with very few patients to see (thank God), then renting a flat that was close – but not *too* close – to her parents. One-bedroomed, in a Victorian villa in an upwardly mobile part of the city, her two upstairs neighbours female professionals with whom she'd discussed throwing parties and swapping the names and numbers of handsome young men.

Life after Cambridge, she'd started to hope, might not be so bad after all.

Then Isobel Robinson fell under a bus, and Vanessa began to unravel. First, the enquiry finding her wanting. Then the silent phone calls – made by Isobel's family, or the child herself? What did it matter, the result was the same. She couldn't sleep, could barely eat, and had to move back with her mum and dad.

Vanessa closes her eyes. She ought to be tearing her hair out. She should be climbing the walls. She remembers Ingrid Tunstall's face. *The poor woman looks broken. Absolutely broken . . .*

'I've already lost one patient,' she explains to the teddy bear that is lying, spreadeagled, next to her head on her rose-sprigged pillow. 'I can't lose another. But I'm numb, you see, from the neck up, because that's what losing a patient does to you. You have to be numb – it helps you survive, because if you took on everyone's pain, you'd lose your mind, you really would.'

Vanessa's mother owns a cookery book penned by Elizabeth David, which she refers to as her '*livre de cuisine*'. This evening, she is serving *Tomates Provençales en Salade* with griddled *pain*.

'Tomatoes on toast,' Vanessa observes. 'Tinned tomatoes with a sprinkling of dried parsley on grilled Mother's Pride.' She lifts the bread, examines its underside. 'Is there any meat to be had, Mum? Anywhere at all?'

'For your main course,' her mother says with a heavy sigh, 'we will be having *coq au vin*.'

Gwendoline Bridges has selected loungewear for this relaxed night *en famille*: a lilac velour leisure suit teamed with titanium earrings and fur mule slippers, which slap fiercely against the soles of her feet as she steers her squeaking hostess trolley into the dining room.

'It'll be all *coq* and no *vin*,' Vanessa's father guffaws from the head of the table, jutting his thumb at the trolley hotplate. His dining chair has carved oak arms, while all the others are armless. Vanessa's chair not only lacks arms, but also its original salmon-pink Dralon upholstery – testament to an incident involving her Auntie Dilys, a lit cigarette and a disastrous game of Monopoly last New Year's Eve. 'There was no Blue Nun at the Co-op,' he chuckles, 'so it's chicken in gravy with mashed spuds.'

Her mother sits down, shaking her napkin, placing it onto her lap. 'Shut up and eat your tomatoes,' she snaps.

'Don't tell me to shut up, Gwen.'

'I will if you insult my cooking!'

Vanessa prods her *tomate* with her fork. *Here we bloody go again.* 'Dad wasn't being insulting, Mum,' she says. 'He was just trying to be funny. And there's nothing wrong with chicken in gravy.'

'It's not chicken in gravy, young lady. It's *coq au vin*. And if you think you can do any better, John, be my guest. Do the shopping. Do the cooking. Do the bloody washing and ironing and cleaning day after day, week after week, when you're also picking Clive Marston's metaphorical dirty under-pants off the floor and being interrogated by *Woman's Hour* and BBC Wales for the sins that bloody man has committed, because, as the Lady Mayoress of Llanfair . . .'

'Well, I can't do any of that, Gwen, love, because I'm too busy designing buildings so you can swan around in your XR3 *being* the Lady Mayoress of Llanfair. Behind every great woman, and all that.'

He sits back in his chair with a self-satisfied smirk.

'*For your bloody benefit!*' Vanessa's mother explodes. 'I gave up a promising sales career for you and Ness, and I try to be a good wife, a decent mother, a pillar of the community . . .'

'I never asked you to stop being an Avon Lady,' Vanessa says quietly. 'But rest assured, Mum, you are an excellent wife and mother and Lady Mayoress of Llanfair. And Dad, you are an excellent father and provider. You're both excellent people. Truly excellent in all that you do.' She tries to lift her *tomate* to her mouth; bright red juice spills over her dress.

Something passes between her parents: a look of concern and self-reproach, reproach of each other, then panic.

'Oh love,' her father says. 'Take no notice . . . we're being silly billies, that's all.'

'Having the regular weekly row,' her mother adds with a tinkly laugh.

'It's not funny though, is it?' Vanessa replies.

Her parents shrug at each other.

'It's not funny,' Vanessa continues. 'It's actually very damaging for a child to . . .'

'Vanessa love,' her mother says gently, 'you're not a child. You're twenty-six years old.'

'Twenty-six and a half,' her father adds, dabbing at his mouth with the corner of his napkin.

Vanessa prods her *tomate* again. Now they'll end up eating in silence, save for the sound of her father's jaw clicking whenever he takes a bite of his *pain*.

'My patient's gone missing,' she blurts.

'You what?' says her mother.

'My patient's vanished. Run away.'

'Well, well.' Her father shakes his head. 'That's not good, Ness. Any idea what happened? Are the police involved?'

'The police have been notified, yes. For all the good they'll do. In fairness, Uskshire Constabulary are pretty stretched at the moment, given that most have been redeployed to Barwood . . .'

' . . . Bullying the striking miners,' her father snorts.

'Protecting the working miners,' her mother retorts.

'The poor kid left a note for her mum, saying she was running away. There are two envelopes and stamps missing, so we're assuming that she's written to me and a woman she's made friends with in the village. An older woman – in her late seventies or early eighties, I'd guess. An ex-headteacher. Funny old soul. A bit of a Margaret Rutherford type.'

Vanessa's mother looks up from her plate. 'Retired head-teacher, you say? Living in Llanfair? What's her name?'

'Barbara Pritchard.'

Her mother drops her fork to her plate with a clunk. 'Good God.'

'You remember her?'

'Well yes, of course! Though we've not spoken in years. She's that retired headteacher who fell out with some of the villagers twenty years ago. First, she had a row with a builder over the field behind this house. And then she had a picnic for the local kiddies, and squabbled with some of the parents after an incident with a child. All water under the bridge now, of course.'

'Gwen . . .'

'What, John?'

Her father shakes his head. 'Not now.'

'What?' says Vanessa. 'What child? What happened? I have such odd memories . . . I was very upset about something I'd seen . . .'

'Oh,' her mother says breezily. 'You weren't upset! You had the most wonderful afternoon. I made sure of that.'

'But I saw something I shouldn't . . .'

Her mother frowns. 'No, you didn't, Ness. I was with you the whole time. If you'd seen something you shouldn't have, well then. So would I.'

The pretty lady with the white-blonde hair, mouth formed into an 'O'; the thrusting man; the dank air heavy with stale cigar smoke – I can still feel the ache in my calves as I hurtle through the long grass to safety, but instead of safety there was shouting, screaming, a violent altercation . . .

Vanessa shakes her head. 'Okay. So, if it wasn't me, who was upset? And why? What happened?'

'Well, it was all gossip and hearsay, and nothing was ever proved . . .'

'What was never proved?'

'Gwen . . .' her father raises one eyebrow, fork poised mid-air.

'Mum?'

Her mother glances furtively around the room, as though expecting an invisible entity to scold her for saying too much. She looks down at her *pain* and shrugs at it. 'Well. Like I said, it was all gossip and hearsay and nobody saw what actually happened. But Barbara Pritchard was new here. Fresh from Barwood, where she'd been a headteacher of great renown. She moved into that old cottage on the village square, and it turned out she'd bought the field behind this house years before, and there was a bit of a stinker about both of those things – you know, an outsider buying the prettiest house in the village owning a field she intended to sell to a builder. And there were whispers, too – her being an older, unmarried woman. You know.'

'No,' says Vanessa. 'I don't know.'

'Well, anyway. She and her sister Lynette from the Llanfair Arms cooked up this idea of holding a picnic in the field for the local kiddies. We parents weren't stupid, we knew she wanted to curry favour with the locals but we went along with it anyway. And it was all very silly, looking back, but there was an argument between the girls, not that I saw what happened, because I was too busy running around after you. Anyway, Barbara Pritchard intervened, and was accused of hurting one of them. Not that I believed a word of it. The end.'

'And something happened in the wood at the far edge of the field . . . I saw two people, a man and a woman . . .'

Her mum shakes her head. 'No, you didn't, Ness. As I said, you were with me, the whole time.'

Her father sits back in his chair with a sigh.

'Well, that's what happened, John!'

'I wasn't there, Gwen, love. But it was what happened, if you say so.'

'Well, I do say so. That's what happened. And you got upset, Ness, because you were only six years old at the time and it was all very unpleasant. We learnt our lesson from that little taster of letting you mix with the local kiddies, didn't we, John?'

'We certainly did, Gwen.'

'And the girl . . . the girl that got hurt,' says Vanessa. 'Who was she?'

'Oh.' Her mother waves a dismissive arm. 'A proper little madam. Ordering around the other girls, threatening if they didn't do what she liked there'd be hell to pay. You know the type. Then she claimed that Barbara Pritchard, who was only wanting to help, tried to strangle her. Admittedly, there was a red mark on the girl's neck, and that had to come from some-where. Barbara insisted it was an accident – that she ended up in a ruckus with the girl while trying to protect one of the younger children. But everyone turned against her – a proper witch-hunt, it was – until a few weeks later, when there was that terrible car accident up by the quarry. Two of the girls involved in the spat – little Rose Ellis and Blanche Wilkins, as they were back then – lost a mother and father. Barbara was very kind to both families – paid for the dead woman's funeral, because the Ellis family didn't have a pot to piss in, and all was forgiven. She was left alone after that.'

'Left alone,' Vanessa says slowly, 'to befriend a young girl twenty years later. A lonely, vulnerable girl who's apparently run away.'

She looks down at her tomato-strained dress.

Vanessa suddenly doesn't feel quite so hungry any more.

25

Debbie

I hid in The Vicar's back garden for ages, waiting for bloody Little Red Riding Hood to come out of the woods and slaughter me. But I ended up feeling quite bored, to be honest, because the more I thought about it, the more I realized that even if the red thing found the vicarage, it wouldn't necessarily find *me*, because I was hiding in The Vicar's brambles – my tried-and-trusted spying point. There's a space big enough in the middle of the bushes to sit up straight, but I'm surrounded by masses of blackberry boughs reaching and arching over each other from all different directions, and all those branches end up crossing me out.

Though I did spend the first few hours crapping myself, my heart doing cartwheels in my chest – I was knackered after all that running, and felt a bit sick after what I'd just seen. So, I cried for a bit, ate a Caramac bar, then took Clive's watch out of my pocket to see what time it was.

It had stopped at twelve thirty – the time that Clive died? At night, or early afternoon? I don't have a watch of my own with me, so didn't have any way of knowing what time of day it was. But by then, the light had completely changed. The earth had kept turning while my heart was turning cart-wheels, and by the time my heart completely calmed down, the sky had moved on from a soft grey-pink to a deep inky-black.

I hadn't noticed it happening, but now it was night-time, and my heart sank. I'd nowhere to go, nowhere to sleep, nowhere to keep warm and stay safe in the dark.

And then I remembered. The Vicar – daft beggar – keeps his French windows unlocked! It was how Nurse Pugh got into the vicarage the day I took my Polaroid photo – the day I tried to blackmail The Vicar, one week after Susan Pugh twisted her ankle and seven long days of being Nobby-no-mates with no one to talk to and nothing to do. There were still five and a half weeks of the summer holidays left. I was already off my nut with boredom, and screaming inside for excitement.

So, I spent that morning behind the Scout Hut during Flicks N' Kicks' rehearsals, hiding under the toilet window, where I could eavesdrop on lots of things – mainly the Marston girls squealing and shouting and talking absolute bull. But there was interesting stuff, too, like Blanche Marston taking a tinkle, and telling Rose Pugh who was in the next stall that The Vicar was a filthy old gripper who was having it away with Brown Owl. And when I heard that, I was *livid*, I was – that dirty, hypocritical pair – and I wrote on the Scout Hut wall in marker pen to say as much.

And then I thought, why not go even further? Why not be like a private detective, and take a photo to grass them up? I didn't feel bad about my plan. Brown Owl was always so mean to me, kicking me out of the Brownies, saying that my life was miserable – which it is, but who was she to say so?

So, that afternoon, I set myself up here in the vicarage brambles, hoping and praying that Brown Owl would turn up and I'd catch the pair of them at it. But it wasn't Brown Owl who turned up that day. It was Nurse Rose Pugh, bustling round the side of the vicarage in her uniform, opening The Vicar's French windows and calling, 'Yoo-hoo! Leeeeeeeewissss!'

And The Vicar came into his lounge dressed in jeans and a manky old tank top, with his dog collar hanging around his neck, and he was absolutely *tamping*, he was – shouting and waving his arms around, telling Nurse Pugh to bugger off. But Pugh just laughed, and touched his arm, and said something that seemed to calm him down. Then he nodded, undid his jeans, lay flat on his front on the settee, and Nurse Pugh got to work on his bum.

And that's when I did it – took my Polaroid picture – forgetting the flash would go off.

The Vicar leapt up, Rose Pugh shot into the garden, and I scooted backwards into the brambles, holding my breath, my heart thud-thudding in my throat. I could see her neat black lace-up shoes shining through the cobwebby branches, and hear her saying: *Did you see that, Lewis? Looked like a camera flash, or was it lightning? What do you think?*

And The Vicar said something I couldn't make out; then he yelled, so loudly that most of Llanfair and half of Barwood could probably hear him – *I think you should just piss off! I don't need a massage; I don't have lumbago. I don't need anything from you, Rose Pugh*, which I thought was quite funny because the last bit rhymed, even though I knew that what I'd just seen wasn't funny at all, not really. It was adult stuff, or rather the sort of stuff that would lead to adult stuff, if you know what I mean. Then I heard Rose shout, *Suit yourself!* and a few minutes later a car started up. And I stayed in the brambles until it got dark and it was safe to come out without being seen.

I admit I was a bit naughty with what I did next – the blackmailing note, then Blu-tacking the Polaroid of The Vicar with his trousers down to the village notice board. But The Vicar is rich, and wouldn't have missed a few bob, and I nearly said that in my letter to him. Mam needs that cash more than he does.

Anyway, back to this evening. Remembering the Polaroid incident made my mind up for me: I'd sneak in through The Vicar's unlocked French windows, and set up camp in his spare room. He'd be in hospital for a while yet, and I wouldn't be scared, being alone in an old man's house. It was the only sensible thing to do.

I crawled along the lawn like a fox, praying I didn't put my hands in any actual fox poo. Close up, the grass smelt mouldy and rotten, and that made me think of Clive Marston and what will become of his body before very long. And that made my heart flip cartwheels again, so I told myself that God was in heaven and all was right with the world – that's what Mam used to say when I was scared of the dark, back in the days when she could be bothered with me, and I'd pretend to believe her, even though I know things are not right with the world, not at all.

When I reached the vicarage, I waited for a cloud to pass

over the moon, so it was safe to stand up without being seen; then I reached out my hand, gave the French windows a shove, and – lo and behold – they opened!

So, here I am, inside the vicarage, and I've had an all-right few hours, all things considered. I'm not too frightened, because the moon has been glowing through the windows, guiding me, and I don't think The Vicar is dead yet, so there'll be no ghosts in this house tonight. Then again, Clive Marston's ghost might track me down and demand revenge for nicking his watch, but I'll cross that bridge when I come to it.

I went into the kitchen first, fumbled around in the drawers and cupboards – which were rammed with all sorts of rubbish, like twine and elastic bands and used batteries and boxes of medicine and needles and stuff – until I found a torch, and then I did a bit of exploring. The kitchen smelt of stale fat, and everything felt greasy against my fingers – the cupboard door handles and counter tops. I don't know why The Vicar doesn't get Mam to clean for him, but he'll be too much of a tight-arse to pay her, I'll bet.

There was still some washing-up in the sink – a plate and a pan, with crusted baked beans stuck to the bottom, and two mugs upside down on the draining board. One of the mugs had 'Jesus Saves' printed on it, and the other had 'With the Halifax'. I shone my torch into the kitchen corners, just to make sure no one was hiding there. Two of the corners were empty, but in one there was a mop and a bucket and, in the other, a big steel bin. I lifted the lid and looked inside: there was an empty baked-bean can and egg shells, and a copy of *Kerrang!* – that heavy-metal magazine – and *Cage and Aviary*

Bird, and a comic or something The Vicar had torn into tiny pieces.

I left the kitchen, taking the mop, in case I needed to wallop Clive Marston's ghost with it, and I crept through the hall, shining my torch at the floor – black and white tiles, like a chess board. I had a sudden pang for Barbara, who taught me to play chess last Christmas, and I moved down the tiles like a knight, like she showed me – one, two, and a leap across; then diagonally, like the bishop. The Vicar's lounge was to the right of me, but I'd come in through there and knew it was safe, so I shuffled sideways to the left, like the castle, and into a room with rough, bare floorboards that could really do with a rug.

It was a big room – as big as the lounge – with a massive oak desk in the middle of it, and all the walls lined with shelves of very old books with brown leather covers. I had a good search of The Vicar's desk, in case I discovered something interesting, but all I found was a framed drawing of the baby Jesus sitting on his mam's lap, a pile of blank paper, a type-writer and a telephone and something that looked like a tape recorder with a flashing red light.

I didn't like the room that much. I felt like Jesus's mam kept giving me filthy looks. So, I went back to the hall and climbed the stairs, which are covered in an old-fashioned swirly carpet that doesn't quite reach the walls, and is kept in place on each step with a black metal rod.

I found The Vicar's bedroom first. The bed was unmade – all blankets and sheets rucked up in a pile – and I screamed, because the heap looked just like a body. But I was dead brave and poked at it with my mop, and the heap collapsed and fell apart. I might have laughed, I was that relieved, and then I tip-toed around the bed, opened the wardrobe and shone my torch inside.

Nothing much to report in there. Just the long dresses The Vicar wears to church, a couple of suits and a pair of jeans (they were dead trendy Wrangler, too!). Folded up on the shelves were his pants and socks – big, baggy underpants, mainly white, black socks, probably wool. On the big upper shelf was a folded eiderdown, and a cuddly toy – a felt sausage dog – and a teasmade, still in its box.

I went to his window and held back the curtain, peeking through the gap. I had a good view of the woods and the garden – like a black and white photo, it was, with the trees and grass and brambles so still and all lit up by the silvery moon. But then an owl hooted, the wind got up, and the rain that was just beginning to fall got battered against the window-pane, scattering drops like diamonds. I let the curtain fall again, feeling ever so sorry for Clive out there in that awful weather; his designer suit getting all ruined, his mouth and eyes filling with water.

Once I'd pulled myself together, I poked my head into the box-room – packed to the rafters with trunks and crates and old leather suitcases. There was a brightly painted wooden rocking horse against the far wall, which must have belonged to The Vicar when he was small. It's strange to think of The Vicar as a child. I can't imagine him being anything less than seventy years old.

I've set myself up here in the spare room. It has a bare mattress, which I've made up with sheets I found folded in an old wooden chest. The chest is lined with yellowing news-papers that absolutely stink of mothballs. I might read them later – old copies of *The South Wales Morning Post*. Should be good for a laugh, I reckon.

Truth be told, I'm quite disappointed. I was expecting The Vicar's house to be . . . I dunno. Something more exciting than this. Because it's as close as you can get to God's own house, but the vicarage is dull, old-fashioned and dirty, and frankly quite stinky in parts. The bathroom is clean enough, and the bog and the sink and the bath are a lovely dark green colour, with fluffy mats on the floor and the bog lid, and one of those dollies in a ballet skirt covering The Vicar's Andrex. There's a bar of soap on the edge of the sink – Imperial Leather, which is ever so posh. We only ever have Imperial Leather in our house at Christmas. It'll be The Vicar's one luxury, the stingy old git.

Barbara once told me that very rich people don't like to look too rich at all. That they live 'very shabbily', so she said, because 'conspicuous consumption is vulgar.' I said to her, 'That's because when you're poor you're invisible, and you want to buy nice things, to be seen for a change.'

'Deborah,' she said, 'you are quite correct.' And she gave Mam two quid extra when she did her next clean.

The house is much smaller inside than I imagined. It's the opposite of Doctor Who's Tardis. It looks bloody huge from the outside, but it's actually wide and not very deep – just four rooms up and three rooms down. I've searched every one of those rooms, and it's taken me less than an hour.

Anyway, I've had my tea. The Vicar had a packet of Smash at the back of one of his kitchen cupboards – it's my lucky day after all! – and there was some bread in the larder, too, and a jar of pickled onions, so I've had my daily veg. I ate my tea on my lap in the lounge, sitting on the red velvet settee – the one The Vicar was lying on when Rose Pugh massaged his bum. And I tried very hard not to think about that, though the more I tried, the more I did. Funny old thing, the human brain. But eventually, my brain moved on to something else, and I realized that The Vicar's lounge was not quite how I expected a vicar's lounge to be.

For a start, there was a dark wooden sideboard, with two brass candlesticks either end, like an altar, but in the middle of that there were bottles and bottles of booze – gin and whisky and brandy and suchlike – and a box of All Gold chocolates with the lid left open. I snuck a look, and the greedy old goat had eaten all the soft centres, but he'd left a pack of Benson & Hedges, so I thought I'd have a puff on one before I went to bed. There's a ginormous painting of Jesus on the wall above the sideboard, too, rising up to heaven in his toga, glaring down on the evidence of The Vicar's worldly excesses. And I said out loud: 'Jesus might be raising his hand to bless you, Mr Vicar, but you're running the risk of pissing him off and not getting into heaven at all, thanks to your boozing and smoking and chocolate guzzling and carryings-on with the ladies.'

I shone my torch around the room, just to make sure I'd not missed anything important, and that's when I saw it – a small chest of drawers pushed against the wall next to the fireplace. A chest of drawers with a record player on top, and a pile of LPs on the floor at its side. And that was the next big surprise. I mean, ABBA's *Arrival* I understand – everyone likes ABBA. But The Sex Pistols' *Never Mind the Bollocks?* And *Radio 1's Funkiest Disco Hits?* Not that I was complaining – I love disco, I do, so I made sure the curtains were closed, and put on the record player – ever so quietly, so the red thing in the woods wouldn't hear me – and I danced round the room in the dark, pretending I was on stage with Flicks N' Kicks. I was wearing a ra-ra skirt, had my own pink spoon, and I was getting a standing ovation!

I did 'Dancing Queen', with a three-point hustle, then 'Disco Duck', which I did the Funky Chicken to. And the audience was clapping along, and Mam was in the front row, all dressed up in her one posh frock – up on her feet she was, wiping her eyes, looking so proud of her little girl. Blanche Marston was sitting next to her with a face like a smacked arse. I flicked her the V-sign as I turned a pirouette, but lost my footing and smashed into the sideboard, up-ending the chocolates and ashtray and hitting my arm as I fell.

As I lay on the floor, she came and stood over me – bitch-faced Blanche Marston – kicking me with her stiletto and shouting, *That's what happens to stupid girls who get too big for their boots. They end up flat on their arses. Now pick up those chocolates and fag butts, and get your sorry backside off to bed. You've been* twp *enough for one day.*

The audience started to slow-clap. And Mam sank down in her chair with her head in her hands, and she wasn't wearing a frock any more, she was wearing her snorkel coat with the hood pulled up. Then everyone – Blanche Marston included – faded into the wallpaper, and I picked up the crap from the carpet and tried to make the room tidy again. The record stopped playing and started crackling, I could hear heavy breathing and started to freak – until I realized the breathing was mine. And then I started to cry.

I pulled myself together after a fashion, turned off the record player and took my plate to the sink, and left it there with the others. I crept up the stairs to the spare bedroom, shining my torch around the floor in case of spiders; then I got into bed in my clothes, and had a Curly Wurly as my bedtime snack.

And that's where I am now. Listening to the rain rattling on the vicarage roof, and the wind rushing through the trees in the woods, trying not to think of Clive Marston's dead-fish eyes, filling up with water. It's ever so cold in this room, and the mattress is hard and lumpy and smells of the dust made by all the people who've slept here. I wish I was home in my own bed, with my conkers lined up on the windowsill, like they were before I smashed them all up. My people, my beautiful people, all watching over me through the night.

I get up, open the wooden chest, pull out a pink woollen blanket, drape it around my shoulders. Then I gather up all the old yellow newspapers lining the bottom, put them in a pile on my pillow, and I lie on my front, wrapping the blanket around me, turning myself into a fat pink worm, using the torch so I can read without anyone seeing a light from outside.

Barbara says that words give you power. Words can transport and transform you, she says. And Barbara's never wrong.

I flick through every one of the newspapers. And as I read, I realize each has a news story or reader's letter circled in red marker pen:

Story one, taken from *The South Wales Morning Post*, 9 September 1964:

Llanfair Businessman and Passenger
Killed in Car Crash

Police are investigating the tragic death of Mr Herbert Wilkins, aged 42, owner of Wilkins' Tool Manufacturers and husband of Mrs Mairi Wilkins of Dove House, Llanfair, and Mrs Eleri Ellis, 32, wife of Mr Huw Ellis, a labourer, of 26a Bryn Lane, Llanfair. Both were killed instantly in the early hours of 7 September, after Mr Wilkins' Morris Minor collided with a tree on the A5876, at the turning for Llanfair Quarry. The pair were returning from a choir competition held in nearby Barwood.

Police are unable to establish the cause of the crash. 'It was a clear night, with no precipitation,' PC Mervyn Watkins said. 'Tests show that the car had no issues with its brakes or steering. The cause of the crash remains a mystery. However, there is evidence to suggest that Mr Wilkins had been drinking heavily, and may have been indulging in some tomfoolery prior to the incident. His wedding ring was found lodged in his throat. The significance of this is not clear, but may have contributed to his losing control of his vehicle.'

The Vicar has circled this story, and written in very large letters: *Wedding ring in mouth. LUST*

Story two, taken from *The South Wales Morning Post*, 1 September 1969:

Local Builder Dies in Choking Tragedy

An inquest was held on Monday into the sudden death of Llanfair resident Mr Brian Musgrove, proprietor of

Musgrove Builders, after his body was discovered in the vicinity of the children's playground on Llanfair Common in the early hours of the morning of 6 August. A post-mortem revealed that Mr Musgrove died from choking on a piece of sausage. Tests also revealed significant levels of alcohol in his blood. Witnesses confirmed that Mr Musgrove had spent much of the previous evening drinking heavily in the lounge bar of the Llanfair Arms. He left the public house shortly after 10 p.m., the last time he was seen alive.

Mr Musgrove was a controversial figure in Llanfair, following his attempted purchase of a field on Llanfair Lane some five years previously. An unnamed source told *The South Wales Morning Post*, 'He tried to undercut the owner – a local woman – by several thousand pounds, and was viewed rather dimly for that. His reputation and business never recovered, and he finally took to drink.'

Verdict: accidental death.

The Vicar has circled this story, too, and written in very large letters: *sausage (pig) forced down throat. GREED*

Number three, taken from *The South Wales Morning Post*, 14 July 1974:

Letters to the Editor

A Plea – and an Apology

Dear Sir,

I am writing to complain about antisocial behaviour in Llanfair village – specifically damage to my personal property – while also offering an apology for an unfortunate misunderstanding regarding my own behaviour.

For several weeks, my house has been targeted by person or persons unknown, intent on painting it green. My garden fence and front gates have been defiled, as has the outer rim of my carp pond. Somebody daubed 'I will make you eat your words' in green paint on my Austin Mini. This is criminal behaviour, and the police have been informed.

However, I have the unsettling suspicion that these attacks are connected to a complaint I made regarding the Best Domestic Garden Award for Wales in Bloom. I raised a concern that Miss Barbara Pritchard's garden (which took first prize) was not eligible for entry, as it was largely stocked and planted by the previous owner of Hollyhock Cottage, while my own – albeit simpler – effort was planted by myself.

I wish to make it clear that I accept the judges' view that Miss Pritchard has not only maintained her garden single-handedly over the past decade, but has also restocked and redesigned most of her borders. She is, therefore, a worthy winner, and I deeply regret questioning the judges' decision.

Yours sincerely,
Gwendoline Bridges,
Stockholm Villa,
Llanfair

The Vicar has circled this letter, and scrawled in very large writing: *GREEN WITH ENVY.* Then, in smaller print: *publicly apologized – so therefore GB spared??*

Story four, taken from *The South Wales Morning Post*, dated 7 August 1984:

Girls Poisoned at Village Fete

Two ten-year-old girls are recovering in hospital following a poisoning incident believed to have taken place at Llanfair Summer Fete on 1 August.

The girls, principal dancers with Flicks N' Kicks, headed by three-times County Ballroom Champion, Blanche Marston, fell ill after eating a buffet prepared by local residents. 'It's such a shame,' one witness said. 'The girls had waited all day long to perform, only to collapse just before their performance with nausea, confusion and severe stomach pains. They are such talented girls, too – born performers, and an absolute credit to their mother.'

Hospital tests revealed the girls had ingested a combination of laxatives and opioids. Police are investigating.

The Vicar has circled this story, and scrawled: Pride. *Targeted girls rather than mother with Mother's Pride bread?*

And then, under that final story, The Vicar has written in the same red pen:

Proverbs 6: 16–19
There are six things the Lord hates, seven that are detestable to

him. Haughty eyes, a lying tongue, hands that shed innocent blood, a heart that devises wicked schemes, feet that are quick to rush into evil, a false witness who pours out lies, and a person who stirs up conflict in the community.

My heart is leaping all over the place. What the flipping flip is The Vicar up to? My fingers curl under my pillow, searching for where I've hidden Clive Marston's fifty-pound note and his gold watch.

Greed.

Clive Marston was a greedy pig, and had a fifty-pound note shoved into his gob.

I can hear a car engine outside, the crunch of gears as it pulls into The Vicar's driveway, headlamps flashing two silver beams over the spare-room ceiling and walls.

Two doors open, then slam shut.

Then The Vicar's deep growl:

'Thank Christ. I'm home.'

WEDNESDAY, 12 SEPTEMBER 1984

THE SOUTH WALES MORNING POST

Mystery Woman Discovered Unconscious in Barwood Car Park

By Paul Powell,
Crime Correspondent

A woman was found unconscious in the car park of the Barwood branch of Texas Homecare shortly after 10 p.m. yesterday evening (Tuesday, 11 September). The discovery was made by a courting couple, who immediately contacted the emergency services.

The mystery female, believed to be in her thirties, is described as slender and well-dressed with black shoulder-length hair. She was wearing a heavily embroidered denim jacket, jeans and white high-heeled shoes.

'A woman was taken to hospital with concussion and minor cuts and bruises,' a police spokesman said. 'We are trying to locate her next of kin. If anyone has any information as to her identity, or saw anything suspicious yesterday evening in the vicinity of Texas Homecare, please can they contact Uskshire Police as soon as possible.'

The courting couple recalled seeing a white Ford Transit van behaving suspiciously shortly before their discovery. The man, who wishes to remain anonymous, said, 'The van was already in the car park when we arrived – we assumed it was another couple enjoying the night air. But after several minutes, it sped off, leaving behind what we initially thought was a pile of old clothes. On closer inspection, we discovered an injured woman, unconscious but breathing. I pray the police catch the animal that did this. It's not safe to go out at night any more!'

26

Barbara

9.30 a.m., Hollyhock Cottage, Llanfair Village Square

Barbara has barely moved from the sofa this morning. She has fed Utterson, but not fed herself; has let Utterson into the back garden to do his business, but has not changed out of her nightwear, washed her face or cleaned her teeth. Instead, she has stared at the cracks and dents scarring her limewash living-room walls, chewing her thumbnail and thinking – of what? Of who she once was, of what she's become and the husk of a thing she'll turn into next. Her memory absences are becoming more frequent, lapses that started – when? Days or weeks ago? She can't remember. And her head always hurts. Her eyesight is failing. She's coming apart at the seams, like one of her moth-eaten twinsets.

Only Nurse Rose Pugh appears to have twigged that something is up with Barbara – her visits becoming more frequent these last few weeks, for 'a quick cuppa and a catch-up, Barb'. But Barbara knows it is because Rose Pugh realizes she's going doolally. Nobody else has – not even Robert, though he does have other fish to fry. Barbara can tell he's up to something; the boy's been downright shifty of late. But why? Barbara wishes she had the mental energy to tackle him over it, but her mind is too cobwebby; her fears over Deborah Tunstall's fate an additional drain on her once razor-sharp mind.

A whole day has passed, and still no news. Barbara's initial confidence that Deborah was safe – just having a little adventure, would come home once she got tired, bored or hungry – is starting to slip. No, worse than that. Has already slipped and smashed to pieces, each shard piercing her conscience more deeply with every passing hour.

Just yesterday morning – in this very room – Rose Pugh had suggested that Barbara should be cautious of her friendship with Deborah Tunstall. Well, it turns out that Deborah Tunstall should be equally wary of Barbara. For without Barbara's interference in the little girl's life – her championing the child's 'specialness' – events may have taken a different turn. Perhaps Deborah would have been less emboldened, less prone to stirring up trouble. No wonder Barbara feels sick to her stomach. Guilt does that to a person; it eats them up inside.

She shuffles to the window in her slippered feet, tutting at the horticultural devastation that was, until last night's downpour, her immaculate front garden – her herbaceous borders are decimated; the late-flowering perennial spears that once flanked her front path lie sodden and battered, their last hurrah routed by the previous evening's torrential rain.

There is a sudden commotion upstairs – it's Robert, thundering onto the landing! She'd forgotten he was there. He'd hammered on her front door earlier, demanding to use her shower because Dai was using the bathroom at the Llanfair Arms to give Llewelyn his weekly clean. She hadn't thought to ask why he wanted to shower so early in the day, when he'd barely been up before noon for months, or why a cockatoo trumped a human when it came to matters of personal hygiene.

'No bloody hot water!' he shouts.

'This is not a hotel,' Barbara yells back. 'I daresay the boiler is on the blink again. Perhaps you could take a look at it for me, Robert.'

He says something in reply, but Barbara doesn't register. She is distracted by a waifish young woman with long red hair making her way up Barbara's front path, picking her way through the toppled perennials in pixie-booted feet. It's Dr Vanessa Bridges, slipping and mouthing a four-letter word as her heel swivels on a hollyhock stem.

Barbara feels a tingle of something – excitement and antici-pation! She's come. Dr Bridges has actually come!

Barbara shuffles to the foot of the stairs. 'Robert!' she cries.

No answer. Try again. 'Robert?'

A muffled, 'Yes?'

'Put some clothes on!'

'What?'

'Put some . . .' The doorbell rings, and she speaks more quietly, 'clothes on!'

'Clothes on what?'

Barbara opens the door.

'Hello,' says Dr Bridges, with an uncertain smile. 'I'm here, as instructed. Rather early for tea, I realize, but I received my letter from Deborah this morning.' She pulls a white envelope out of her handbag and waves it at Barbara, to prove her point. 'I just wanted to talk to you.' The uncertain smile inverts itself, and Dr Bridges bites her lip. Much like she did as a six-year-old child, thinks Barbara.

'Of course,' Dr Bridges continues, 'my visit here is highly irregular, and I don't know why I've agreed to it. In fact, I shouldn't be here at all, I should have stayed at work, and I'd get into even more trouble than I'm already in if my supervisor knew I was discussing a patient with you. But there is something that concerns me about you, Miss Pritchard, and I daresay that when you discover my past, you'll be just as concerned about me. Oh, I'm gabbling. What a mess this is.'

Barbara ushers Dr Bridges into the hall with a waft of her dressing-gown sleeve. 'Come in, come in!' she says. 'Allow me a few minutes to wash and get dressed, and then we can share our distrust of each other over a biscuit and a cup of tea.'

27

Vanessa

She's smart, this Barbara Pritchard woman, Vanessa concludes, nibbling her way around the chocolate edge of a Mint Club biscuit. So far, she's managed to dodge every single question I've asked about *that* picnic and the child she assaulted. There is something not right about her, something squashed and suppressed, like her hair. She'll be full of secrets, probably lugs them around in that bloody great wicker basket of hers.

'And that,' Barbara Pritchard is saying, 'was the last I saw of Deborah – when she came with her mother last Tuesday to clean my house. Of course, Deborah doesn't help with the cleaning – she's only a child, after all – but Ingrid and I have an understanding. She cleans for a reduced fee, while I give Deborah an hour's free tuition. Deborah is extraordinarily bright, is already tackling secondary-school-standard maths questions, and has just finished reading *Lord of the Flies*, which is an O-level text. She fully appreciates Golding's exploration of innate evil and the degradation of civilization . . . in fact, I have an essay somewhere she wrote recently, let me see if I can find it . . .'

'Miss Pritchard . . .'

'But of course, you'll know all that. You, of all people, would have recognized Deborah's precocious intelligence, which has rattled quite a few cages around here, I can tell you. She's rather outspoken, of course, but really is the most delightful child. Funny, loving, insightful . . . Now, did I leave her essay inside this copy of *The Radio Times* . . .'

'Miss Pritchard . . .'

'I suppose she also reminds me of me. An outsider and misunderstood. Ah, here it is. The spelling leaves a lot to be desired, but the arguments Deborah makes are quite compelling, don't you think?'

Barbara Pritchard thrusts a piece of A4 paper towards Vanessa, who declines it with a polite shake of her head. The black woolly terrier curled at her feet looks up, stretches and yawns. Vanessa tickles the back of his ear until he settles back down again. 'Look,' she says, 'I really do need to discuss the picnic and the girl you attacked. I know it must make you uncomfortable, but given that Debbie's run away, I wouldn't be a responsible adult if I . . .'

Barbara Pritchard slaps the rejected paper down on her lap with a sigh. She removes her glasses, wipes them with her handkerchief and pops them back on the bridge of her nose. 'You're not going to let this lie, are you?' she says. 'All right. There was a bit of a bust-up, I admit it. A silly disagreement between two girls, I tried to separate them, and one of them – Blanche Marston, or Wilkins as she was back then – ended up with a red mark on her neck. Though I swear I didn't lay a finger on that child.'

'Well, that's what my mum thinks, too.'

'I am very happy to hear it.'

'I was there, too, of course, though I was only six years old at the time, so my memories are a bit disjointed and sketchy.' Vanessa laughs nervously. 'My recall is all over the place – one minute I'm in the field behind my house, the next I'm in a small wooded area, then there's a lot of shouting . . .' She pauses, uncomfortably aware of Barbara Pritchard's questioning stare.

'It was a long time ago, Dr Bridges,' Barbara Pritchard says, finally breaking eye-contact. 'I daresay neither of our memories are as sharp as they were. And I'd hold my cup a little more steadily, if I were you – you're in danger of spilling Earl Grey over that lovely brown tunic of yours.'

Vanessa looks down at herself. She hadn't realized her hand was trembling, but her saucer is full of tea. 'Were you given a very hard time?' she tries to ask casually, carefully reuniting the spilt Earl Grey with the rest of her cup. 'Mum says that the villagers weren't very nice to you.'

'Oh, only for a short time. Always desperate for someone to burn, the village witchfinder generals. But they soon moved on to persecute some other poor soul – the local builder, Brian Musgrove. Came to a rather nasty end. Most unpleasant business. Now, let us return to discussing Deborah Tunstall. Do you have a diagnosis? I suspect some sort of attachment disorder. Her father left home when Deborah was six – took off one night, and that was the last anyone saw of him. He was a bit of a rogue, though lovable, from what I understand. Bit of a mystery man, actually. He certainly didn't come from around these parts – no one quite knew where he came from. Not even Ingrid.'

'Well, Debbie did mention her parents' estrangement, but I didn't realize it was all so final. She and her father have no contact at all? No one's heard anything from him since?'

'Not a dicky bird. Poor Ingrid took it very badly. She had

a difficult upbringing of her own – her mother reared Ingrid alone, you see, after Ingrid's father passed away, and she became depressed and drank too much, before dying young from cirrhosis of the liver. I'm afraid history might be repeating itself. Custard cream, Dr Bridges?'

'No, thank you.'

'Well, whatever your diagnosis, I can assure you Deborah is no psychopath.'

'I don't think I've suggested . . .'

'You may not have suggested anything of the sort, but that's how she is seen by the villagers, and once people put you in a certain kind of box, it can be impossible to break free. It was only senna Deborah put in the sandwiches at the village fete, Dr Bridges, I am certain of that. A childish prank gone wrong. A mischievous child Deborah may be, but a dangerous one she is not.'

'What about the morphine found in the Marston girls' blood samples?'

'Could have come from anywhere. Anyone could have added a sprinkling of morphine to the chocolate spread sandwiches – the whole village was involved in preparing that buffet, including me. How on earth would a child come across morphine – let alone know what it was? And how has the village come to this – blaming young Deborah, when there are far more likely contenders? The pharmacist Rachel Wilmslow, or Nurse Rose Pugh for example – both medical people. I daresay Clive Marston could get his hands on anything he wanted. My late sister, Lynette, took oral morphine in her final weeks. Perhaps a half-used bottle has been rattling around the Llanfair Arms all this time? Dai and

Robert Hargreaves live there; Ingrid Tunstall cleans for them, and there are frequent lock-ins – anyone could gain access to the upstairs rooms when Dai and Robert's backs are turned. And how do you know the culprit wasn't me? I still have several morphine tablets left over from the surgical procedure I had on my hip two years ago. I keep meaning to return the bottle to the chemist, of course.'

Vanessa's cup rattles in her saucer. '*Was* it you?'

'No,' Barbara Pritchard smiles. 'It was not. Though you'd be a fool to believe me, of course. So, that is my story, Dr Bridges. Now it is time to talk about *you*. I'm aware of your name and reputation, of course, because of that patient of yours falling under a bus and sustaining serious injuries. Very sad business, for all concerned – including you. The enquiry was most unfair. I would even go as far as to say you have been scapegoated. And whatever did the patient's father mean when he accused the "medical professional" of abandoning his injured daughter? You are a psychologist, not a psychiatrist, and therefore not medically trained. Though all I know is what I've read in the newspapers, and they can be guilty of misre-porting at the best of times.'

'I'd rather not discuss it, if you don't mind.'

'Well, we've discussed my murky past, so why not yours? If we're going to team up together to find Deborah, we need to be open with one another, don't you think?'

'Team up together? Are we?'

'I think that's what Deborah would like us to do, hence the letters she's sent us.' Barbara Pritchard picks up an envelope from the table at her side. 'Mine arrived, too,' she says. 'First post, this morning.'

'We're being manipulated!'

Barbara Pritchard grins. 'Clever little darling, isn't she? Shall I make us another pot of tea?'

That was the part of the enquiry that hurt Vanessa the most – the accusation, by Isobel's family, that Vanessa had been negligent. The 'medical professional' part confused her at the time, but had not angered her so much until now, when Barbara Pritchard brought it up all over again.

But *how* had the misunderstanding come about? Vanessa considers this while Barbara Pritchard clatters about in the kitchen. She remembers Mr and Mrs Robinson's letter of complaint to the enquiry – stating that, 'according to several witnesses, the medical professional present at the accident was neglectful, failing to treat or comfort our daughter, and instead fled the scene . . .' Well, she hadn't fled the scene. She'd comforted Isobel, then run to a shop to phone for an ambulance. How dare they! How bloody dare they?

Barbara bustles into the room. 'The tea is brewing,' she says.

'I was there,' Vanessa says slowly. 'My office – at the Institute of Psychology – was just around the corner from where the accident happened. My patient – I can't tell you her name . . .'

'Of course not. Confidentiality.'

'Yes. Well, she had her appointment with me after lunch. It was the half-term holiday, and we'd agreed that she'd travel to my office for a change. I thought she'd come with her mother or father, but it turned out she'd made the journey to Cardiff alone – wanted to take the opportunity to buy a gift for her father's birthday. We'd made so much progress, you see, that she felt able to step out by herself for once. She was no longer afraid of "the monster" – that's what she called her biggest fear – finding and punishing her. Anyway, she'd decided to buy a record for her dad, a song he'd heard on the radio that he liked, and she went to Spillers on The Hayes – the record shop where all the teens hang out. And that's when I saw her – from a distance. Her style of dress was so distinctive, I recognized her immediately. I had just come out of Habitat, and was getting into my car to drive back to the office, when she ran out of Spillers, looking distraught, and the bus swung around the corner and hit her, and I remember screaming, "That's my patient!" Oh . . .'

She buries her face in her hands.

Barbara Pritchard gently touches her arm. 'I'm so sorry,' she murmurs. 'Truly, I am.'

A male voice interrupts from the doorway –

'If it's any consolation, I screwed up at work, too.'

28

Robert

10.30 a.m., Hollyhock Cottage,
Llanfair Village Square

He moves from the doorway, plonking himself on Barbara's sofa, next to Vanessa Bridges, telling her that his name is Robert. Robert Hargreaves, Barbara's nephew. Lives at the Llanfair Arms with his dad, studied maths at Cardiff Uni, then worked for Hippo Insurance, until it all went wrong. It all went wrong when he acquired a new boss, a man called Mason Priestly. Priestly had a Rolodex, a Rolex and a Filofax.

'That's a lot of Xs,' Robert had joked, offering Priestly his hand to shake as they stood, sizing each other up, in the photocopying room. But Priestly rejected the proffered hand with a grin as sharp as his pin-striped trousers. 'Exes, yes,' he'd sneered at Robert. 'I've a lot of those, too.'

Three months later, Robert was jobless. 'The official story is I resigned,' he shrugs at Vanessa. Barbara, clutching a teapot dressed in a crinoline tea cosy, gives a derisory snort. 'But it was really constructive dismissal. Priestly hated my guts on sight, and wanted one of his old school chums to take my place. I never stood a chance. I was set up to fail. Given underfunded projects to manage, kept out of meetings, the wrong figures to crunch, that sort of thing. So here I am, thirty-one years old, living with my dad, and hanging out with my aunt and her sex-mad dog.'

Utterson, asleep at his feet, emits a low moan.

'All a bit shit, really,' Robert adds.

'Language,' Barbara snaps.

Vanessa Bridges says nothing, but Robert clocks her eyes flitting over his suit jacket and black leather trousers that squeak whenever he moves his legs. Which happens to be most of the time just now, because his knee is jiggling with nerves. She puts him on edge, Vanessa Bridges, with her cat-like eyes and smooth, pale skin and oh-so-superior air.

Robert knows what she's thinking. That he looks like the bastard love-child of Bob Geldof and Bozo the Clown. Not that there'd been too many laughs to be had in his company so far.

'I'm low on clothes,' he explains, nervously. 'I've two T-shirts, a jumper and jeans in the wash – all still at the launderette, I'm afraid. I abandoned them after Mr Niblet bit my hand when I reached past his head for the Bold Automatic.' He's gabbling, he knows he is. *Shut the hell up, you idiot!* 'I never realized how much time I spent wearing a suit at Hippo Insurance,' he continues. 'Until you lose the suit, you don't realize how much you depend on it. It's like a second skin.'

'It was certainly starting to smell like a second skin,' Barbara says. 'And you left that job well over a year ago. I've no idea why you haven't bought yourself some decent clothes yet.'

'Because I can't afford to,' Robert says. 'Anyway, that's my story.'

'Yes, I suppose it is.' Vanessa Bridges starts gathering her things together, much to Robert's dismay. 'Well, I'd better be going.'

'Already?' Barbara exclaims. 'But you and Robert have only just met! And we need to find young Deborah!'

'Miss Pritchard, I came here to discuss Debbie-Marie, and we've done that, so . . .'

'But we don't have a *plan*,' Barbara says emphatically. 'And you're going nowhere until we have a plan. Robert, budge up, and do stop jiggling. Now, tell me, Dr Bridges, where do you think Deborah is hiding?'

'I think we can safely discount the woods.' Vanessa Bridges shifts obediently, making room for Barbara's backside. 'A kid that age wouldn't cope with the woods, not in the dark. She'd be too frightened. And it was pouring with rain last night.'

'Fair point.'

'Maybe she's in the Scout Hut?' Robert suggests.

Barbara shakes her head. 'Constantly in use – nursery mornings, whist drives, Flicks N' Kicks rehearsals.'

'She could be miles away by now,' Vanessa Bridges muses. 'We know that she took money with her.'

Barbara nods. 'Excellent point. She's not one to do anything by halves, our Deborah. If she's run away, she's run *away*. Barwood – that's where she's gone! She's returned to the place of her birth, Dr Bridges. I wonder if she still has family or friends living there? I'll phone Ingrid and check.'

Barbara disappears into the hall, the phone pinging as she lifts the receiver. A thick, uneasy silence descends on the living room in her absence, broken only by the tick of the carriage clock on the mantelpiece at Robert's side. He closes his eyes. He needs to say something, anything at all, to plug the gap widening between his leathered knees and the Titian goddess perched on the other side of the sofa.

'Redeem yourself with Debbie-Marie Tunstall,' he hears himself saying – the words sounding like they're coming from someone else entirely – 'and you'll vanquish the guilt of letting down your previous patient. The one I overheard you discussing with Barbara just now.'

Robert is rather taken aback by his insight and eloquence. It's all he can do not to give himself an actual pat on the back.

Vanessa Bridges glares at him. 'I don't think that's any of your business,' she snaps.

'It absolutely is my business.'

'No, it's not.'

'But it is. If you're involving my aunt in your quest to find Deborah Tunstall, you're putting her at risk. She's not as fit as she was – she's eighty in six weeks' time.' It's a fair point, Robert realizes, but a point that'll piss Vanessa Bridges right off. Not least because he must sound a censorious arse, and he really doesn't mean to. He needs to soften the blow a bit. *Tell her it's because she's a nice girl, Rob – that you know she only means well.*

'You like to save people, don't you?' he says. 'Can't live with yourself if you let someone down. It's quite uncanny, actually, how like my aunt you are.'

Vanessa Bridges stands up, furiously massaging her knuckles like she's preparing to punch his lights out.

'You patronizing dickhead!' She slings her handbag over her shoulder, nearly knocking Robert's block off. 'I can do without the armchair analysis. And by the way, you're flying low. Try learning to dress yourself properly before addressing me with your cod psychology.'

His hand jolts down to his fully zipped fly, and he starts to protest that he's not flying low at all and that really was a cheap shot, when a commotion from Barbara's front garden distracts them both, rousing Utterson from his sleep with a sharp, quizzical bark.

Rose Pugh – ashen of face, helmeted hair unusually ruffled and hatless this morning – is skipping up Barbara's front path, arms and stethoscope windmilling wildly.

'Barbara!' she's yelling. 'They've found Blanche Marston! Alive, in a car park in Barwood!'

29

Debbie

10.30 a.m., the vicarage, Llanfair Lane

'And what, I repeat, is the meaning of this, young lady?'

My throat is sore from screeching so much. 'You scared the shit out of me!' I cry.

'*I* scared the shit out of *you*?' The Vicar explodes in a red-faced fountain of fury. 'You're the intruder I've just discovered in my bloody spare room! You, of all people – fast asleep on my guest bed like fucking Goldilocks!' He jabs a finger in my face. 'It was you, wasn't it? You, who ate my last packet of Smash. I'd been looking forward to that for days! And where's my rug? The one in my study? What have you done with my fucking rug?'

'You said the eff word,' I gasp. 'Twice! You're a horrible old man! And I haven't seen your stupid old rug!'

'I can say worse than that,' he growls.

'Really?' I ask, impressed.

That throws him. He stares at me for a moment.

'What,' he says, more gently now, 'are you doing here, Deborah? Why are you in my spare room? Why aren't you at home?'

'Home.' I shake my head. 'But I don't think I have a home.'
And then I start to cry.

I didn't mean for The Vicar to find me. I meant to creep out of his house once he'd fallen asleep. But I was so tired, and he stayed up so late jabbering away to Brown Owl – that's who brought him home last night – and I kept saying to myself, *just hang on a bit longer and keep your eyes open, Debbie-Marie Tunstall. Brown Owl will be gone very soon, and then The Vicar will go to bed and you can make your escape . . .*
Stupid Brown Owl. It's all her fault.

And I could tell that she was *loving* it, absolutely relishing being the one to bring The Vicar home – she'll be bragging about it, I'll bet, to her cronies at the Llanfair Arms next time there's a lock-in. 'Home sweet home!' I heard her coo from the hallway. 'Shall I pop the kettle on?'

Then The Vicar's deep, gravelly boom: 'Ta, love. I'd murder a cuppa. I've been living on NHS gnat's piss for the past few days. Worse than the bloody insulin overdose itself, that was.'

I could hear Brown Owl tittering away. 'You're a marvel,' she said. 'I can't believe how strong you are. No one would know you were at death's door only five days ago. Bet you were their star patient.'

'I doubt it. Couldn't wait to get me out of that ward fast enough. I'm a belligerent old bastard, apparently. That's what I overheard Sister saying.'

'Nonsense!' Brown Owl cried. 'You're not belligerent at all!'

'But I am an old bastard.'

Brown Owl tittered again. Then they must have gone into the kitchen, because I couldn't hear what they were saying.

So, I got off the bed and opened the door very carefully, and crept out onto the landing, my breathing so loud I had to cover my mouth in case they heard it. I crouched at the top of the stairs, sticking my ear through the banisters.

'Still no sign of the Tunstall kid?' I heard The Vicar saying. 'What if she's not run away? What if she's hurt?'

'There's enough who'd want to hurt her,' Brown Owl said darkly.

'Aw, come on, love, she's not that bad.'

'Well, what about what she did to the Marston girls!'

'Rumour and speculation. Anyone could have put morphine in those sandwiches – if, indeed, the morphine the girls ingested *was* in the sandwiches. It's all too convenient, methinks, pinning everything on poor Deborah Tunstall.'

'Poor Deborah Tunstall? That child's a menace! Good God, before she had a go at you, she tried to blackmail *me*! She strutted into the Scout Hut, proclaiming: "I know what you and the old man are getting up to!" She was talking about you, of course, and she started making all sorts of accusations and threats unless I reinstated her into the Brownies, *and* made her a Sixer. Then the little bitch kicked over my toadstool – the one that the Gnomes, Sprites and Pixies dance around at the start of our sessions – and I said, "You be careful, young lady, that's papier mâché, that is!" And she said, "Crapier mâché, more like!" And now you're laughing. It's not funny!'

'But it is, love. Come on, admit it. She's a spirited one.'

'Deborah Tunstall tried to blackmail you, the shame of which nearly killed you.'

'An accidental insulin overdose nearly killed me. I've very

broad shoulders, Rachel. I'd hardly try to top myself because of village gossip.'

'But what about your reputation? A man in your position . . .'

'I'm a village vicar, Rachel. Not the bloody Pope. And reputation is vastly overrated, in my opinion. Besides, I think reputation-wise, it's Nurse Rose Pugh who'll come out of this worse than me. People always turn on the woman in these situations. I don't want to be seen as a victim in this, because it's not the case.'

'Well, I don't see you as a victim. You're far too strong for that.'

Everything went quiet for a moment – they were probably kissing – bleugh! Then Brown Owl again:

'But the villagers haven't had a go at Pugh, and I doubt they will, anyway. She's only recently lost her husband, a fact she parades for sympathy at every opportunity. *Ooooh, you have to be nice to me, I'm a widow. And you have to let my daughter get away with being a right little bitch, because she's lost her daddy . . .*'

'Harsh!'

'But fair.'

'Look, all Rose Pugh did was massage my lower lumbar region.'

'Oh, come on! She was planning on massaging more than that. You're quite a catch, you are.'

'Rubbish.'

'Think about it. You told me she's been banging on for weeks about you needing a live-in housekeeper. I reckon it's only a matter of time before she suggests herself. She's on the make, you mark my words. If you're not careful, she'll have her feet under your table by Christmas and her slippers under your bed by Easter. She's a taste for wealthy old men. Phil Pugh was at least twenty years older than her.'

I gasped out loud at that, and missed the next thing Brown Owl said, then –

'All right, so if you weren't trying to kill yourself, there's only one other explanation – someone tampered with your medication. You've been injecting yourself for years, and never made any mistakes. Gosh, do you think someone's got it in for us both? You know, with the brakes on my bike being cut – is someone on to us? Are these "accidents" actually someone sending us a message?'

'I don't see why,' The Vicar said. 'Sending us a message about what? How could they possibly know about . . .' He paused for a moment, then said very quietly, 'The sin.'

'I just have a bad feeling,' Brown Owl said, 'that something terrible is going to happen. And don't you think it's a very odd coincidence, your phone being out of order the day you were taken ill? Here . . .' I heard her shuffle through the hall and into the study, then the ping of the receiver being picked up. 'It's working again!' she cried. 'What on earth do you make of that? Do you think someone unplugged it so you couldn't call for help?'

'Now, that I do put down to a coincidence,' The Vicar said. 'My phone's been temperamental for months, ever since Thatcher said she was privatizing British Telecom. But,' he added, ever so softly, 'if you're so worried, why don't you move in with me? We could pretend that you're my lodger . . .'

'It would raise too many eyebrows,' Brown Owl replied. 'If anything, we need to keep a lower profile. I should probably stay away from you for a while.'

And then she said something else I couldn't quite hear, then they went into the lounge and shut the door behind them.

I crawled back into the spare room and onto the bed, where I curled into a ball, like I've seen Utterson do when he's frightened by a thunderstorm or people letting off fireworks. I didn't like what I'd just heard. And I liked even less what I'd just read in the old copies of the *Morning Post*. What on earth was The Vicar up to?

I tried to stay awake for as long as I could, until the coast was clear, but the voices downstairs got fainter and fainter and drifted in and out of my head, and the next thing I knew, The Vicar was standing over me, barking his bloody head off.

But now the wrinkles on his big red face have settled into something gentler, so he's not so scary any more. He looks like a bearded bulldog in a green knitted tank top. God alone knows what Brown Owl and Rose Pugh see in him.

'Running away is not the answer, Deborah,' he says. 'You need to be brave and accept your fate. You have a lot to learn.'

'I've learnt to trust no one in this village!'

'You can trust me,' he says. 'You can trust me to do the right thing. Which right now is to phone your mam and the police. Everyone's worried sick about you. Even I know you're missing, and I've been in hospital for the past five days.'

'No! I'll kill myself if you do!'

'Deborah, I have to do what is right. And right now, it's the right thing to lock this door, so you can't run away again, or do something silly.'

Before I can get off the bed and stop him, he leaves the

room, shuts the door, and turns the key in the lock. I rattle the handle.

'Pervert!' I yell. 'Holding an eleven-year-old girl against her will!'

'You'll be let out soon enough,' he says. 'The key is safely in my pocket. And I am not a pervert.'

I hear him limp across the landing. *Pervert!* I'm screaming. *Pervert! Pervert! I hope you rot in hell, you perv!*

And then it comes – the trip, the yelp. The sickening thud, thud, thud down the stairs. The terrible silence that follows.

'Mr Vicar?' I whimper. 'Mr Vicar? *Mr Vicar?*'

30

Vanessa

11.30 a.m., the car park, Dewi Sant Department of Child & Adolescent Psychology

Vanessa opens the passenger door of the XR3, tripping over her pixie-booted feet in a bid to avoid the wet black snout of the terrier circling eagerly at Barbara Pritchard's side.

'Right,' Vanessa says. 'Back in the car with you both. We can start our search at Llanfair Heights. I've made my excuses to my receptionist, but might just as well have signed my own letter of dismissal, because if my boss finds out about this . . .'

'Finds out about what?' Barbara Pritchard asks. 'You are trying to locate a vulnerable patient. What else did you have to do this morning?'

Vanessa shrugs. 'A report or two to write.'

'Any patients to see?'

'Not today. Not any day, really. It's all very odd. I only have one patient at the moment, and she's gone AWOL, as we both know.'

'Well then, what are we waiting for? Off to Barwood we go!'

'But you told me that when you phoned Ingrid Tunstall earlier, she said that Debbie has no connections in Barwood –

no relatives, no friends. She doesn't think Debbie's there. Does it not make more sense to search Llanfair instead? The common, people's sheds . . .'

Barbara Pritchard shakes her head. 'I'm not sure Ingrid really knew what she was saying. She is, shall we say, a little away with the fairies at present . . .' Barbara lowers her voice. 'That quack, Dr Jolly, has upped her Valium to help her cope with the stress of Deborah running away – highly irregular, if you ask me, because she was on a very high dose to start with. I advised her to take to her bed. Ingrid always takes to her bed in a crisis, anyway, so didn't need much persuasion.'

'Poor Ingrid.'

'Poor Ingrid indeed. But falling apart isn't going to bring her daughter back safely, so it's down to us, Dr Bridges, to keep our minds sharp, our powder dry and our peckers up. Now, I put it to you that Barwood is in a current state of disarray, and no one in their right mind would choose to go there. Which means Deborah knows it's the last place on earth we'd look for her, so that's where she'll be.'

'Oh, but I really don't think . . .'

'Good lord, Dr Bridges, do you have no idea the way a devious child's mind works?'

'But I don't want to go to Barwood!' Vanessa protests. 'I've not set foot in the place for a year; haven't dared show my face since the enquiry. They hate me there, I know they do.'

'I daresay they hate me, too,' Barbara says. 'I turned my back on Barwood two decades ago. Took my retirement carriage clock and buggered off to Llanfair with my pension.' She gives Vanessa's shoulder a hearty thump. 'Come on, buck up. Your fear of the reception you'll get gives us even more reason to go. Kill two birds with one stone. Revisit your demons and quash them, and perhaps we'll find Deborah at the same time. And some clues about Blanche Marston! Found in a car park, can you believe it? I daresay Robert will do what he can to find out what happened. He was extremely energized just now – tearing off in his car with Rose Pugh. It's the most animated I've seen him in months.'

Vanessa remembers something. Her father telling her about Blanche Marston having it away with a man in the village who'd recently lost his mum. That would be Robert Hargreaves. She opens her mouth to say, and why do you think he's so energized, Barbara? But then wonders why she feels such regret. Such disappointment in the messy-haired, stubble-chinned, not-entirely-unattractive man for his dire taste in women.

Barbara Pritchard is staring at her. 'Whatever's the matter?' she says.

'I don't want to do this. I don't want to go!'

Barbara narrows her eyes. 'But you're curious, aren't you? To see how you'll feel about the place, and how the people will feel about you?'

'In a warped way, yes. I suppose I am.'

'Twenty years ago, I had no choice but to face the people who accused me of assaulting a child, because they lived in Llanfair and so did I. It's oddly empowering, Dr Bridges, facing those who dislike and distrust you. But I don't need to tell you, a psychologist, that.' She clambers into the car, hauling a grumbling Utterson onto her lap.

'Actually,' Vanessa says, climbing into the car beside her, 'I *do* need to be told. I needed that reminder.' She smiles. 'Okay, let's get going. Has your dog done his business this morning? I don't want any accidents on the way.'

'He is fully trained,' Barbara Pritchard says with a sniff. 'You and I are more likely to disgrace ourselves en route, Dr Bridges, than dear old Utterson here.'

31

Robert

11.30 a.m., Prince of Wales Hospital, Cardiff North

Tomato soup and boiled cabbage – that's what hospitals smell like to Robert. That, and bodily fluids. However Herculean the effort we humans make at cleaning and disinfecting, we're no match for nature's pungent reminders that everything must rot and die, or at least spend some of its life in incontinence pants, or hooked up to a catheter.

He'd been desperate to get here – fleeing Hollyhock Cottage, leaping into his car the second Rose told him that Blanche had been found and hospitalized. But his churning belly just now reminds Robert how much he despises hospitals. Ever since he was circumcised at nine years old because his foreskin was too tight, and his mum and dad didn't warn him – just brought him to the ward, and his dad coughed and said, 'They know what they're doing, son. Be brave.'

He hates them even more since Mum died. She came in for a 'rest' after her chemo, and never made it out. But Blanche is alive, she's come back from the dead – or rather, from Robert's presumption that she was dead. It could almost be a fairy tale. If only the same could be true for his mum.

The soles of Robert's trainers squeak on the tiles of the polished corridor – that's another thing he hates about hospitals; everything gets so amplified. The sounds, the smells, the fluorescent lighting, which is giving him the mother of all headaches. He thrusts his nose into the white chrysanthemums he's holding, inhaling their earthy, menthol scent, his eyes tracking the signs for Ward 5A, General Women.

There is nothing, Robert wants to shout, 'general' about Blanche Marston.

'And she's alive,' he says out loud. 'She's actually alive!'

'Not just alive,' Rose Pugh trills at his side, 'but giving them absolute bloody hell. I know the Sister on the ward, and when I phoned for an update, she said, "For Christ's sake, Rose, take her away – she's a bloody nightmare, she is."'

Robert laughs. 'That's our Blanche. She's back – thank Christ, she's back!'

They hear Blanche before they see her – the familiar lilt rising shrilly with increasing frustration at not getting her own way (Blanche always gets her own way).

'I am discharging myself,' she's shrieking. 'I must see my girls – my beautiful angels! Oh, Rose, there you are! And dear, darling Robbie!'

Blanche is berating a tiny nurse – who looks twelve years old and about to cry – and raises her arms in salutation, hospital gown flapping open at the rear to reveal a pert derrière encased in NHS paper pants.

'Oh, God,' she cries. 'I must look a sight!'

Which she does, Robert inwardly concedes. Her unwashed hair stands up in tufts, above her eye is a six-inch cut, apparently stitched by Dr Frankenstein himself, her cheek is bruised, her lip encrusted with dried black-red blood. And still she looks amazing, the coolest woman alive.

Robert takes a step forward, offering Blanche a hesitant hug. Her scent is different, somehow. Not of her usual perfume, but of stale sweat and . . . *something*. A smell Robert's encountered many times on himself, but never on Blanche Marston.

Fear.

He pulls away.

'What bastard did this to you?' he says, searching her face for clues. 'I'll kill him. I'll fucking kill him!'

Over Blanche's shoulder, Robert sees the young nurse fiddling with the starched hat perched atop her demi-wave with fun-size, trembling fingers. 'You can't say words like that in here,' she whispers. 'Matron will go ape, she will!'

'Matron can go boil her head,' Blanche snaps. 'Now, leave me alone with my friends and get my clothes for me, will you?'

'I told you, Mrs Marston, I can't . . . you're still under observation, and your clothes are filthy, they need to be . . .'

'Then I'll discharge myself and go home in this backless nightgown, arse on full view. I've had my fill of it here, I have. First bloody WPC Jane Gill and her bum-fluff-faced sidekick PC Plod, or whatever his name is, grilling me, then you acting like my prison guard. Go on, eff off, and torment some other poor bugger!'

'But you're concussed . . .'

'I'm bloody fine!' Blanche screeches. 'Completely compos mentis; one hundred per cent my normal self!' She gesticulates in the nurse's face. 'Here,' she says, 'how many fingers am I holding up? One, that's right. My middle digit. Now fetch my clothes!'

The nurse hurries out of the room.

'Harsh.' Rose stands on tip-toe, pecks Blanche's cheek. 'Poor kid. She'll tell on you now, you'll see, and they'll give you merry hell. Ice-cold blanket baths, the works.'

'They won't have a chance to do anything of the sort, because you're getting me out of here.'

Rose raises an eyebrow. 'I am?'

'Yes, you are. I'm perfectly fine.'

'Are you?' says Rose. 'Are you really?'

'Well,' Blanche says archly, 'you should know. You being a nurse, and all that. And, if I'm not, *you* can keep me under observation, because I'll be staying with *you*. You're going to take care of me and my girls, until Clive comes back. That's right, isn't it?'

Blanche and Rose eyeball each other, unspoken words ricocheting back and forth between them. There's an atmosphere you could cut with a knife; an uncomfortably familiar undercurrent that takes Robert right back to his childhood, and the occasions his mum and Barbara had A Difference of Opinion.

'What if Clive doesn't come back?' Robert suggests, keen to break the standoff.

Rose and Blanche turn to stare at him. 'What do you mean, *if Clive doesn't come back?*' they ask in unison.

'Well, what if – whoever did this to you has hurt Clive, too – killed him, even?'

Blanche slumps down on the bed. 'I can't begin to think about that,' she says, shakily. 'It won't come to that. Clive's had his ups and downs with a few dodgy characters in the past, and they've done stuff to scare him – you know, chaining him to a radiator for twenty-four hours, that sort of thing.

But they'd never actually harm him.' She looks up at Rose. 'Would they?'

Rose shrugs. 'They harmed *you*, didn't they? What happened, Blanche? You must remember something!'

Blanche bows her head, folding her arms defensively over her chest. 'I honestly don't,' she says. 'Well, I do remember dropping the girls off at school, getting into the car, and driving to Clive's offices, because we needed to talk about . . .' She lifts her head, catches Rose's eye. 'Stuff.' She takes a deep breath. 'I wanted to leave him, though you both already know that. And I decided to tell him at his office, because there'd be plenty of staff around and he'd be less likely to . . . well, get nasty. But when I arrived, there was no one there. Not even Clive. Not his secretary, not the typists – no one, like he'd given them all the morning off. So, I sat in his chair for a while and waited, and then I phoned the surgery to ask Rose to pick the girls up from school and have them overnight, because I knew I wouldn't be in a fit state to deal with them once I'd told Clive I wanted a divorce, but I ended up talking to the receptionist, who was her usual snooty self, and I clammed up and said something about there being a family emergency. I waited a little longer, and then I thought – well, stuff this, I've a manicurist's appointment at noon, and I got up to leave, got to the top of the stairs, heard a noise behind me . . . and that's it. That's all I remember, until I woke up here. I try to remember, but I can't. I just can't!'

Rose rests a small pink hand on Blanche's shoulder. 'It wouldn't surprise me if Clive was behind this – setting you up, having you beaten, and doing a vanishing act to punish you. He'd have got wind you were leaving him. He always was a poor loser.'

Blanche's slender fingers pluck at the bedsheets. She's avoiding Robert's eye – she's keeping something from him, he can tell. And for the first time since they became close, he suspects that he doesn't actually know Blanche Marston at all. The floor beneath him seems to give way. *Just when I finally thought I had something, someone to hold on to . . .*

'No,' Blanche says finally. 'This is gangland business, nothing to do with me. Clive would never do something like this to me.' She looks up at Rose. 'Would he?'

'I don't know,' Rose replies. 'Is there anything else you remember?'

'A white Transit van parked outside Clive's offices that morning, with nobody in it, and I remember thinking, well, that's strange, because I'd seen it before. Driving up and down outside our house a few days earlier. And the couple that found me told the police they saw a white Transit van acting suspiciously in the Texas Homecare car park.'

'How do you know it's the same one?' Rose asks.

'Well, I don't. But it's a hell of a coincidence, don't you think?'

Robert's mind is whirling. *White Ford Transit van.*

There was a white Ford Transit van in Llanfair Woods two days ago!

'Robbie? *Robert?*'

An NHS pillow narrowly misses his head. Blanche is standing with her hands on her hips, raven plumage ruffled with pique. 'Earth calling Robert Hargreaves,' she's saying. 'Stop gawping like you're *twp* and get me home, back to my girls. Clive is the least of my worries right now. It's the charity do tonight at the pub, and Flicks N' Kicks need me. My baby girls need me!'

'It's being filmed as well,' Rose Pugh says. 'For a *Spotlight Cymru* special! Oh, Blanche – so much has happened in the past two days, I hardly know where to start . . .'

She's interrupted by a cough from the doorway.

Roberts turns to see a grinning man in his late thirties or thereabouts, leaning against the architrave – tall, dark and annoyingly handsome, wearing a relaxed linen suit, sleeves concertinaed up to his elbows; all white teeth, tanned skin and crows-feet-crinkled eyes twinkling wickedly at the three of them from beneath a Bryan-Ferryesque fringe.

'Mark!' Blanche cries. 'Look, it's Mark!'

The man hastens towards her, opening his arms. Blanche crumples into them, weeping noisily.

'Oh goody,' says Robert. 'It's Mark.' He turns to Rose. 'Who the hell is Mark?'

The man is murmuring *poor baby, poor baby* into Blanche's hairdo – which is bouffant enough, to be fair, for an actual baby to be hiding inside it.

'Her psychologist, Professor Mark Murray,' Rose whispers. 'Blanche suffers so much, as you know, with her nerves.'

Robert shuffles uneasily. The man is now stroking Blanche's spine through the gap in her vented hospital gown. 'I can only stay a moment,' he says tenderly, holding her at arms' length, giving her face the once-over. 'I've a clinic to get to. But I had to see you, had to know that you were okay . . .'

'Isn't this all a bit unprofessional?' Robert hisses to Rose. 'And why has Blanche never mentioned this Mark person to *me*?'

Rose raises an eyebrow. 'Now, why on earth would she want to do that?'

Robert looks away, embarrassed. As he does so, his eye is caught by something white and shiny on the hospital bed. His chrysanthemums – still wrapped in a protective layer of cellophane – have been tossed aside on the sheets; the fragrant, pure-white blooms crushed by Blanche Marston's backside.

32

Debbie

11.30 a.m., the vicarage, Llanfair Lane

I should be relieved The Vicar's alive, but he hasn't shut the bloody hell up for the past fifteen minutes, and I'm starting to lose patience.

'Well, I daresay we'll make the best of things until someone comes to find us,' he shouts, 'which I suppose they will in due course. I shall be relying on you to bang on the window and get the attention of passers-by, Deborah. Christ knows what I've done to my back, but I can't move!'

'If Christ did know, would he find a way to tell you? You being one of his mates, and all. Would he tell you if you'd broken it? And if you have broken it, does that mean you'll die?'

'Thank you, Deborah. That's very reassuring. No, I don't think I've broken it. I can still wriggle my fingers and toes. I just can't turn over . . . I can't . . . I mean, I can slide along the carpet on my back, but that's no use when the phone's on my desk in the study, the lock on the front door is four feet above my head, and . . . well, this is a right to-do, isn't it? Ah, of course! There's an extra key to your spare room in the drawer next to the bed. Thank God for that! Can you find it, Deborah?'

I open the drawer, look inside. The key is there all right.

'I said, can you see it, Deborah?'

I think about this for a bit. If I unlock the door and go to get help, I'll be found and in for a rollicking. Besides, what if The Vicar's a weirdo killer? Those newspaper stories he'd circled in pen – what if he was the person behind the crimes, and he keeps the articles as a sick reminder? What if he's really cross that I've found them, and he's locked me up not so he can call the police, but to think about how he will kill me – and he's faking his fall, playing for time?

'I can't find it!' I shout.

'You *what*?'

'It's not here.'

'But that can't be right – I left it . . .' His voice trails away.

'Not here,' I repeat. 'Perhaps someone nicked it. Anyone can get into your house, you know. Like I did. You really shouldn't leave your French windows unlocked.'

'Thank you, Deborah. Very useful advice, if a little late in the day.'

'No need to be sarky.'

He goes quiet for a bit. Then, 'Deborah?'

'Yes?'

'It takes three days for someone to die from dehydration. We don't want that to happen, do we?'

I think about this for a moment. I should bide my time, wait for Mam to get worried sick, so she'll be more relieved than angry when I come home. And I need to make sure that The Vicar's not a nutcase.

'Three days?' I yell. 'Don't worry. It won't take that long.'

33

Barbara

12 p.m., somewhere between the Dewi Sant Centre and Barwood

'You looked away and touched your mouth several times just now, when I asked whether everything was all right, and you replied that it was,' Barbara says. 'All signs of lying. Really, Dr Bridges, I would have thought someone in your position would be more *au fait* with rudimentary body language. And, might I add, if you rolled your eyes any further into the back of your head, they'd be rattling around with Utterson on the rear seat of your car.'

'I turned my head away from you to look at the road because I am driving,' Dr Bridges replies.

They continue their journey in silence for several minutes.

'All right,' Dr Bridges sighs. 'You may have a point. Things are not All Right. Before we left the Dewi Sant Centre just now, I tried to telephone Professor Mark Murray.'

Barbara winces at the pain in her head – bloody migraine brewing again. 'Who is Professor Mark Murray?' she asks through gritted teeth. 'You know, I taught a Mark Murray at Barwood Primary School. A remarkably confident boy, highly intelligent and charismatic. Always wore the sleeves of his blazer rolled up. Quite the alpha male.'

'Sounds familiar.'

Utterson squeezes his grizzled chops through the gap between Barbara's and Dr Bridges' seats, muzzle quivering and dribbling with adoration. 'Well, well, well,' Barbara says. 'Mark Murray a professor, no less. And making your life miserable, Dr Bridges. You don't have to tell me about it if you don't want to, of course.' She ruffles the dog's head. 'If it causes you distress.'

'He was my boss – my supervisor. Still is, sort of. We were working together on some academic research when my patient had her accident. The research was about her, actually. He was furious with me after the enquiry – I was found wanting, as you know – and he demoted me to the Dewi Sant Centre. So, now I have to check in with him every Monday and Thursday, to let him know my progress.'

'Today is Wednesday, Dr Bridges.'

The good doctor's fingers drum irritably on her steering wheel. 'I know it's Wednesday,' she snaps. 'But Mark – Professor Murray – has not been around for the past few weeks, so I hoped to catch him this morning.'

'Mark?' Barbara raises an eyebrow. 'How very familiar of you. I suspect you have feelings for this man.'

'I do not have *feelings for this man* at all. But I have been badly let down. And I feel upset.'

'I wouldn't say upset. Not exactly. You seem more angry than upset. I wonder what Professor Murray said to you this morning that disturbed you so?'

'Well, nothing at all, because he didn't speak to me. He

wasn't there. He's never there. I'm always put on hold, always forced to listen to UB-bloody-40's "Red, Red Wine" playing down the phone at me, although today I was treated to Stevie Wonder's "I Just Called to Say I Love You". Which I did not, because I do not love Mark Murray.'

'I am very relieved to hear it. He sounds most unsupportive. And a song about alcohol . . . what an inappropriate choice of on-hold music for a psychological institution. I would have thought something more soothing and instrumental would be better suited, such as Mantovani's orchestra . . . Ah, look! To the left of you, Dr Bridges. Castell Coch. A magnificent building, don't you think?'

'I can't look, Miss Pritchard. I have a double-decker bus in front of me and a ten-ton truck up my arse.'

'Complete phoney, of course.' Barbara grips her seat with her one free hand – bloody pain in her head feels like a drill boring a hole above her left eye, and she can barely make out the castle's Disneyesque turrets thanks to her blurred vision. 'Built in the nineteenth century to satisfy the ego of the richest man in Wales. The Marquess of Bute. Though the uneducated would swear it was built in the thirteenth century for Sleeping Beauty herself.'

'The uneducated and underage,' Dr Bridges corrects her. 'I believed it belonged to a beautiful princess until I was eleven years old. Wouldn't listen to anyone who tried to tell me otherwise. I didn't want to believe otherwise.'

'What made you stop believing?'

Dr Bridges shrugs. 'Maturity. Eleven years old is a funny stage. You're not a little child any more, but you've not fully hit puberty, either. Though to be fair, I was a late developer.'

She smiles. 'Over-protective parents, you see. Eleven was my least favourite age to be, mostly because I finally stopped believing in Father Christmas and fairy tales.'

'Some never stop believing in fairy tales – grown women telling themselves that one day their prince will come; grown men viewing women as either unsullied virgins or pox-riddled hags. Everyone wants to believe that good trumps evil, that the bad fairy is always found out, the wicked goblin gets his comeuppance, while in reality . . .'

But Dr Bridges isn't listening. 'It's funny,' she muses, 'that while eleven years old was my least favourite age to be, it's my favourite age patient-wise. It's a crucial stage. A crossroads age. A period in one's life when taking the wrong path . . .'

'You're veering into the outside lane, Dr Bridges.'

'Oh! Bloody hell, sorry.' Dr Bridges corrects her positioning, swivelling her eyes from the road to the wing mirror at Barbara's side. 'Gosh, are you okay?' she says. 'You look like death!'

'A headache,' Barbara grimaces. 'All the worry over Deborah. I don't suppose you have . . .'

Dr Bridges nods at the brown leather satchel in Barbara's footwell. 'In my bag,' she says. 'There's some aspirin. Is your pain very bad?'

'It is rather,' Barbara admits. 'But this should help.'

'There's a bottle of water in the glove compartment. Take the tablets with that. If your headaches are frequent, perhaps you should see a doctor?'

'I am under the doctor,' Barbara gabbles, between gulps of water and painkiller. 'Dr Jolly. A misnomer, if ever there was one. I don't like him, and he can't stand me. We nearly came to blows in his surgery once. I said I wanted to try acupuncture for my arthritis; Dr Jolly said I was wasting my time with "that woo-woo nonsense" and I might just as well stick needles in Utterson for all the good it would do me. So, I allowed Utterson to . . . well. Take *a vigorous interest*, shall we say, in Dr Jolly's surgical trolley. He wasn't too happy with either of us.'

Barbara can feel the driver's seat rocking at her side. She turns to see Dr Bridges creased over the steering wheel, laughing her socks off.

She closes her eyes and smiles. Barbara likes Vanessa Bridges. Very much. What a difference two decades can make, since she last knew her as a child! And the pain in her head is easing – a placebo effect, perhaps, as it's far too soon for the painkillers to take action, but welcome relief nevertheless.

And then she remembers.

'Dr Bridges, I saw something rather odd when you were trying to telephone Mark Murray . . .'

But Dr Bridges is hooting her horn and flicking a V-sign at a lorry that's cut in front of them, and Barbara decides that now is not the time to distract her driver further. To mention the teenage girl lurking behind a lamppost across the road from the Dewi Sant Centre. A solemn-faced girl dressed rather childishly in a floral dress, knee-high socks and a red hooded cardigan, plucking at strands of her poker-straight hair as she waited, watching the centre's comings and goings with the widest brown eyes Barbara had ever seen.

34

Debbie

12.30 p.m., the vicarage, Llanfair Lane

'Has it ever occurred to you, Deborah, that you don't make it easy for people to like you?'

He's still banging on, The Vicar is. Hasn't stopped yapping since he fell down the stairs, and he's spent the past five minutes trying to persuade me to shin down the drainpipe outside. 'Have you considered being a little kinder, Deborah?' he's saying. 'Have you considered putting yourself in someone else's shoes for a change? It's called empathy, Deborah. You should try it once in a while.'

'I'm not shinning down no drainpipe for no one,' I say. 'So, you can stop the emotional blackmail. You can hate my guts for all I care, but I'm not doing that for no one.'

'I'm not trying to get you to do anything, and I don't hate your guts. I just wish . . .' His voice wobbles a bit. I think he's tired. He's very old, after all, and if he hasn't faked it, he's taken one hell of a tumble. And it must take a lot of energy, shouting up the stairs like that, especially when he's flat on his back and in pain.

I pop a flying saucer into my mouth. 'And just how,' I yell, crouching next to the door so he can hear me better, 'do I not make it easy for people to like me? I always say hello. I'm always polite. I mind my Ps and Qs. The Marston girls are rude little bitches – that's what Mam says, but everyone likes them. No one likes me, because I'm not pretty. It's that simple.'

'No, Deborah, it's not. You cause trouble. Tell tales. And that makes it easy for people to tell tales about *you*. And, for what it's worth, that's what I think happened at the fete – with the poisoning of the Marston girls, who people don't like as much as you think. You'd be surprised, actually. Are you eating something up there?'

I swallow hard, the flying saucer sherbet tickling the back of my throat. 'No,' I cough. 'Not really. So, I got what I deserved, that's what you're saying? That people say I gave the girls morphine not because they really think I did it, but because they don't like me and I'm easy to accuse. That's not kind. Or fair.'

'Please, Deborah, just think about what you've done over the past few months – the rumours you've spread, the evidence you've based your rumours on, or lack thereof, and now you're on the receiving end of it all.'

'So, I *am* getting what I deserve!'

'I am a man of the cloth, Deborah. In the absence of evidence, I try very hard not to make any judgements at all – only God can do that.'

'Is that why you've kept all those newspapers in your blanket box, then? All that stuff circled in red marker pen? Are you collecting evidence?'

He goes all quiet.

'Well?' I say. 'Is it? It looks dead suspicious to me. How do

I know you're not the person behind all those dead people? How do I know I'm not going to be your next victim?'

'You won't be my next victim, Deborah, because I have no previous ones. I have held on to those newspapers because . . . well, yes. I am collecting evidence.'

'Evidence against who?'

'For your own good, Deborah, I don't think we should discuss this any further.'

'Well, on the subject of collecting evidence, I have lots of it, actually – here, in my Kajagoogoo notebook. I'll go through it, and you can tell me whether I deserved the treatment I got.'

'Deborah, I don't think I'm up to listening.'

'If you listen, I'll shin down the drainpipe and go and get help. Before your three days are up. Fair?'

His voice sounds weaker and quite far away. 'Do I have any choice?' he asks.

'No.' I say. 'Not really.'

35

Vanessa

12.30 p.m., somewhere in Barwood

Standing shoulder-to-shoulder, the net-curtained Barwood terraces are silent and brooding this afternoon, their grey stone facades squaring up to a mountain bruised with mining scars and heather. The shops are all shuttered up for the day: Mario's Hairdresser's overhead dryers stand, hoods bowed, over empty black chairs, mourning their usual gossiping clients clutching teacups to plastic-caped breasts. A typed sign dangles by a chain from the door handle:

Set and blow-dry for wives of striking miners – 50p each

And under that –

Wives of scabs – go to hell

Vanessa realizes they'll all be at the pit – men, women, children – picketing. Which means she'll be spared. This time.

Her hands relax on the steering wheel.

'I think our chances of bumping into someone we know are

negligible,' Barbara Pritchard says, apparently able to read minds. 'Much to our mutual relief, I suspect.'

'And guilt,' Vanessa adds. 'I don't like myself for feeling relieved. Those poor people, being starved into submission . . . shit!'

She slams on the brakes, stalling the car as a girl, aged eight or nine or so – a skinny little thing with a tangle of mouse-blonde hair – leaps from an alleyway between two end of terraces, a huge sack of coal slung over one shoulder. She yells at the younger boy tagging behind her to *run*, you twerp, *run*!

She staggers past Vanessa, coal flying from her sack, dragging her haul towards the main road – one free hand clutching the waist of her skirt, because it's so big and baggy it's slipped down to her hips.

But if Barbara's noticed Vanessa's emergency stop, she's not letting on. Apparently recovered from her migraine, she's yakking away about Barwood Colliery – how her uncle had been a miner; how fascinated she'd been as a child by the black marks criss-crossing his forearms. 'They're known as Blue Scars,' she's explaining, 'or the Miner's Tattoo. If the skin is cut or grazed in the pit, the coal dust gets in and stays there for life. Are you all right, Dr Bridges? You look rattled.'

'I'm fine.' Vanessa restarts the car. 'I stalled, that's all. Your head seems better.'

'Fresh air and distraction. Do you have connections in Barwood, too?'

'I did.' Vanessa drives on, eyes narrowed, primed for more coal-picking whippersnappers. 'My grandad worked down the Barwood pit. He died when I was little – emphysema.'

'Then you'll understand . . .'

'I understand very little about Barwood,' Vanessa says. 'We hardly ever visited. I didn't really know my grandparents at all.'

With a lump in her throat, Vanessa watches the pitifully thin girl, with the bouncing coal sack and tiny sidekick, turn a corner in the distance.

'Well,' Barbara Pritchard continues, oblivious, 'having worked in Barwood until relatively recently, you'll be more up-to-date with the place than I am.'

'I'm ashamed to say that I'm not. I'd drive to the primary school, spend an hour with my case study, then drive straight back to Cardiff. I spent as little time here as I possibly could. Couldn't wait to get away. Just like my mum and dad. And no, I'm not proud of myself. My dad's not proud of himself, either. He says we're worse than the scabs themselves. And you know what? I think he's right, so judge away . . .'

'No judgement from me. I turned my back on Barwood as well, remember? Oh look, The Red Lion pub!'

'The pub? Isn't it a bit early in the day to start drinking?'

'Pubs are hotbeds of gossip. If anyone's seen a little girl that doesn't belong to anyone here, they'll talk about it in The Red Lion pub. Of course they will! And I daresay, Dr Bridges, that you'll be desperate for the lavatory, by now?'

'I'm bloody bursting, Miss Pritchard.'

But the pub isn't open. Shuttered up, 'Closed for business until further notice, due to unforeseen circumstances', according to the hastily written sign propped against the padlocked door.

Vanessa lets the car engine idle, and makes a quick assessment of the boxy, grey-stone, four-up-four-down-windowed exterior of The Red Lion pub, its dangling sign bearing a rough hand-painted beast standing on one hind foot, forefeet in the air. Someone, at some point, had written the word DISCO in large white letters on a ground-floor window, followed by a downwards arrow, apparently pointing nowhere.

'I'll park up anyway,' Vanessa says. 'If all else fails, I'll just have to squat behind the car.'

'You'll do no such thing,' Barbara snorts. 'Have some restraint and self-respect. There's a library across the road. They're bound to have a lavatory.'

The library – a new-build prefabricated monstrosity clad in yellow panels – is open, thank God. Vanessa races ahead, sweet-talking the librarian – a slightly younger version of Barbara Pritchard, complete with tamed grey hair and twinset – into letting her use the loo.

She returns to an unsettling tableau: Actual Barbara and Spare Barbara sitting side-by-side on matching mini plastic chairs in the kiddies' story-time section – a carpeted corner corralled by walls covered in finger paintings of Barwood Mountain basking beneath a perpetually sunny blue sky. Utterson is sprawled at their identically shod feet, gazing from woman to woman in bafflement and wonder.

'Deborah isn't in Barwood,' Barbara announces. 'Pull up a chair and sit down.'

'Oh!' Vanessa does as she's told. 'And you know this, because . . . ?'

'Because Celia here says so.' Barbara nods at the woman at

her side. 'Celia and I worked together, many moons ago. She helped run the library at Barwood Primary when the librarian was on maternity leave.'

'I see everything,' Spare Barbara smiles. 'I hear everything, too.'

'Gosh,' says Vanessa. 'That's quite a superpower you have there.'

'Less of the sarcasm, Dr Bridges. Celia hears and sees everything because this library is probably the only public facility open in Barwood at present. And it's not just a library, either. It's a soup kitchen, charity shop, community centre, toy depository . . .'

'We're collecting toys for Christmas,' Spare Barbara beams, nodding at the tsunami of brightly coloured plastic objects toppling out of the cupboard behind her. 'No child of a striking miner will go without. We'll make sure of that.'

'The library is,' Barbara adds, 'the beating heart of a community that is currently having its vitals ripped out.'

Spare Barbara winces. 'An unpleasant analogy, Barbara, but an unhappily accurate one.'

Jesus Christ, Vanessa thinks. *They even speak alike!*

'You see,' Spare Barbara continues, 'if Deborah was in the village, we'd know all about it. She'd have been seen getting off the train, for a start – a girl that age all by herself! And some people would certainly recognize her – she may have been gone for five years, but she was the image of her father. Still is, I presume?'

'I'd imagine so,' Barbara says. 'Her mother says she's a Tunstall, through and through.'

'He was a nice man, Anthony Tunstall,' Spare Barbara muses. 'If rather unconventional. He was what you and I might call a hippie, Barbara. He and Ingrid lived hand-to-mouth, wanting to give little Deborah an alternative, simpler upbringing, living in a caravan at the foot of the mountain and taking on casual, seasonal work. Some people called him a layabout, but I rather liked him. And the three of them seemed such a happy, loving family, which made his leaving poor Ingrid and Deborah so very shocking and surprising. He worshipped that little girl, you know. Home-schooled her, all by himself, taught her to read and write – she really was forward in so many ways. I daresay she's changed quite a bit in five years, but we'd recognize her, I'm sure of it. Tall for her age, dark, like her father, rather outspoken . . .'

Barbara smiles fondly. 'That's our Deborah.'

'Well.' Vanessa shuffles impatiently in her seat. 'We should probably go, if Debbie's not here. If we leave now, we'll have plenty of time to have a look around Llanfair . . .'

'Not so fast.' Barbara holds up her hand. 'Celia may have other information.'

Spare Barbara shoots her doppelgänger a look of surprise. 'I do?'

'Yes,' says Barbara. 'About Blanche Marston. Wife of ex-Barwood-resident Clive. Found in the car park of Texas Homecare yesterday evening.'

'Well, I know as much as you do about that one. And,' Spare Barbara visibly bristles, 'I'd rather you didn't mention Clive Marston's name in my company, avaricious piece of shit that he is.' She peers at Vanessa over the top of her spectacles. 'Should he show his face in this village again, I would happily force-feed him his own testicles, and I say that as someone who babysat him while he was still in very short trousers.' Her face brightens. 'Now, shall I make us all a nice pot of tea?'

36

Debbie

1 p.m., the vicarage, Llanfair Lane

'It was most peculiar, Deborah, my insulin overdose, because I was as sharp as anything mentally that morning. I'd just done the crossword in *The South Wales Morning Post* in a record time of thirty-eight minutes and fifteen seconds, and was about to phone that dizzy lisping blonde at Sandy's Newsagents . . .'

'Twp Lisa.'

' . . . Twp Lisa, yes, that's the one. Well, Twp Lisa had forgotten to include my usual Friday copy of *The Radio Times*, and had given the paperboy copies of *Kerrang!* and *Cage and Aviary Bird* and that pornographic magazine for women, *Venus Blue*, to deliver to me instead, which was most unfortunate, because I don't like heavy metal music, and I don't own a bird, and I don't care to look at photographs of naked men in cowboy hats. I tried to telephone Sandy's to complain, but my telephone wasn't working – it was completely dead. So, I went through my usual steps with my medication: measuring things out just so, being extremely careful. I have different sides of the kitchen for the two different types of insulin I use, because the diabetes has damaged my eyesight, and if I mistake one for the other, I might overdose. Anyway, after injecting myself with what I assumed was my long-acting medication, I intended to go straight to the telephone box on the corner, to tell British Telecom about my phone, and that's all I remember before waking up in hospital . . .'

I yawn loudly on purpose, but he doesn't take the hint.

'Are you still with me, Deborah?'

'Yeah,' I shout. 'But can you get to the point?'

'Well, the point is, I overdosed by taking my short-acting medication, but I had absolutely no intention of killing myself and I can't see how the overdose was accidental, either, because I was so with-it that morning. I admit I was still rather displeased about the Polaroid incident, but I wasn't the least suicidal.'

Christ on a bike, this man likes the sound of his own voice – no wonder his sermons last for hours. 'Yes, yes,' I shout, 'I believe you. But we were talking about me and the day of the fete, and the evidence I'd collected. What was going on around me when the Marston girls got poisoned.'

'Well then, look at your notes from the day of the fete, Deborah. Read out everything you've written.'

I open my Kajagoogoo notebook.

'*The day,*' I read out loud, '*1 August 1984, was hot.*'

'For God's sake, nobody cares what the weather was like!' The Vicar shouts.

He's getting impatient. He's desperate for me to shin down that bloody drainpipe.

'Do you need the toilet?' I ask.

'Just get a move on, Deborah. Keep to the stuff that's relevant.'

I pop another flying saucer into my mouth. 'But,' I reply,

'the weather *is* relevant. Especially the fact that the day was hot, because there was a lot of chat about whether or not it was safe to leave the buffet out in the heat for hours. All the helpers were handling the food and putting it into cool boxes, which meant lots of chances for someone to do something bad to the sandwiches. Can I carry on reading my notes now?'

'Oh!' he says. 'I didn't know that. Yes, you can carry on reading.'

'*The day was hot – the day of the village fete, in aid of the Miners' Strike, with Flicks N' Kicks the highlight. That's what Blanche Marston said – that Flicks N' Kicks would be the focus of the day, the cherry on the cupcake, the stars of the show . . .*'

'She really said that?'

'Yes, she did.'

'She didn't mention the miners, then, or their families? That sounds about right for Blanche Marston.'

'*But I am not included. I have been banned. I'm in the dog house. I'm the bad penny. I'm the . . .*'

'Bad fairy?' The Vicar interrupts.

'Yes. Something like that.'

'And do you know what the bad fairy did? As revenge, when she wasn't invited to Sleeping Beauty's christening?'

'She cast a spell.'

'What sort of spell?'

'That Sleeping Beauty would prick her finger and die.'

'She'd be poisoned.'

'Yes.'

'Continue.'

'*Even though the day was hot, I was cold. I felt cold and hard as I watched the council putting up road blocks around the village square. I felt even colder as I watched Rob Hargreaves fixing big wooden boxes together to make a stage in front of the War Memorial. Blanche Marston was prancing around the place, all silly big hair and high-heeled trotters, squealing, Ooh . . . do be careful, mind your fingers, Robbie! Your sensitive fingers!*

I could see and hear her, but she couldn't see me, because I was hiding behind Barbara's runner-bean canes. I'd turned up early to watch them set it all up . . .'

'Why?' asks Mr Vicar. 'Why torture yourself like that, when you'd been excluded and treated so shabbily? Why not keep a dignified distance?'

'Because I'm an eleven-year-old kid,' I reply. 'And sometimes I can't help myself. Could you help yourself when you were eleven years old, Mr Vicar?'

'Well, it was a very long time ago,' he says. 'I can't think back that far. Continue.'

'*Barbara was out walking Utterson. Before she left, she asked if I wanted to come with her. I said no, that I wanted to sit in her front garden instead, in the sun. She looked at me in a funny way and said, Don't give the enemy ammunition, Deborah. Keep your head down, your spirits up and yourself out of mischief. Not necessarily* your *mischief, but* theirs. *Do you understand?*

I said I did, even though I didn't really. Then Rose Pugh turned up, with Susan, whose ankle was out of its bandage after she twisted it during rehearsals, and Rose said that Susan could do her solo after all, because her ankle had healed. And Blanche shouted No way, she's not rehearsed, and Rose said No, no, not the solo to 'I Eat Cannibals', which I despise, but the one she's been learning for over a year. The Flashdance *solo.'*

'You've lost me,' Mr Vicar says. 'What is a *Flashdance* solo?'

'"What A Feeling",' I reply.

'I beg your pardon?'

'That's the song the girl in the film *Flashdance* does her audition for ballet school to. She's called Alex something-or-other. Welder by day, dancer by night. And all her dreams come true, they do, when she skips about in front of some people in suits, and spins around the floor on her arse.'

'Good God,' says The Vicar. 'What has the world come to? Continue.'

'I'd never heard Blanche so angry. Over my dead body, she said. My girls have rehearsed their little backsides off, and they're not being upstaged by Susan and her Flashdance *solo! And then she called some other women over, who'd been helping Rob, and they must have backed Blanche up, because there was loads of shouting and pointing of fingers, and Rose backed away and looked really upset. End of Part One.'*

'What do you mean, end of Part One?'

'I needed a poo before I started Part Two.'

'And how long were you on the toilet for?'

'Dunno. About an hour, maybe?'

'An *hour*?'

'I do all my thinking when I'm on the bog!'

I hear him sigh. 'Continue.'

'When I went back outside, Brown Owl was up a stepladder in her uniform, stringing up bunting. Rob was holding the ladder, pretending not to stare at her legs. Blanche Marston trotted over and said, Union Jack bunting, Rachel? Isn't that

rather inappropriate? Should it not be the Welsh flag, on account of the Westminster government shafting our miners?

Which was a fair point, I have to admit, and Rob nodded, and Brown Owl saw this – I think she fancies Rob as well as The Vicar; she fancies anything that moves – and she got very angry and stomped down the ladder onto Rob's hand. Rob said shit very loudly, and Brown Owl turned to Blanche Marston and shouted, Union Jack is all we've got, but you just can't help yourself, can you? Always having to get one over me. Always having to keep Bozo the Clown here all to yourself!'

'Bozo the Clown!' The Vicar chuckles. 'I like that.'

'You won't like the next bit as much.' I take a breath before carrying on. '*Then Blanche Marston said, Better Bozo the Clown than the dirty old man you're having it away with, and Brown Owl burst into tears and ran off.*'

'Ah.'

'I'm sorry,' I say. 'But I think the dirty old man she mentioned was you.'

'Yes, thank you, Deborah. I get the picture. Was there anyone Blanche didn't offend that morning? Anyone at all? Well, I suppose you'd better continue.'

'*Then Barbara turned up with Utterson, dragging him away from the telegraph pole, and Blanche said, Have you made the sandwiches, Barb? And Barbara said, really grumpily, What flaming sandwiches? And Blanche said, All the village residents – you included, Barbara – agreed to make refreshments for the girls today, who'll be dancing their little hearts out later. And Barbara said, I agreed to no such thing, especially after the dreadful way you've treated Deborah Tunstall. And Blanche said, really nastily, Don't you think that your obsession with that little girl has gone too far?*

And Barbara pretended not to hear her, but I know that she did, because as she came through the garden gate there were tears in her eyes and her face looked a lot like Utterson's when he can't find his favourite bone. So, I went inside to give her a hug, but she wouldn't let me and went upstairs. She must have told Rob, who was using her toilet, because when he came down to the kitchen, I'd never seen him look so cross. He went over the road to Blanche Marston, and I couldn't hear what he was saying, but he was really tearing a strip off her . . .'

'Was Barbara all right in the end?'

'I think so. She said she was. Said the tears in her eyes were hay fever, but I knew she was very upset. What Blanche said stank. She's trying to make out that Barbara's, you know, into kids. But she's not. She's the best person I know.'

'I agree. Continue.'

'Later, when I was sitting on Barbara's stairs, Brown Owl and Nurse Pugh came to Barbara's front door. Brown Owl said, Oh, Barb, since you live so close to the stage, can you put some of the food for the Flicks N' Kicks girls in your fridge? We've run out of cool boxes for the sandwiches, and need some extra space. And Barbara said, Why on earth should I help after the way Blanche Marston spoke to me? And Brown Owl said, She's spoken badly to all of us, she's under a lot of strain, I think, but please, please think of the children. We've some Nutella sandwiches here and sausage rolls and Scotch eggs, and Barbara got rather huffy and said, Well, I suppose I'd better say yes.'

'So, the sandwiches were in Barbara's house for quite some time?'

'For a couple of hours I suppose, yes.'

'And what did you do in that time, Deborah?'

'I went back home and got my mum's senna. And then I went back to Barbara's.'

'And you crushed up the senna and sprinkled it in the sandwiches?'

'When Barbara and Rob were out of the kitchen and Utterson was in his basket. Yes.'

'But why, if the sandwiches were in Barbara's house for so long, does everyone assume it was you, and not Barbara or Robert or anyone else, who contaminated them?'

'Because I was the one who carried the sandwiches out to the girls, pretending I wanted to help. And because I took the ones I'd sprinkled senna on straight over to Carrie-Anne and Lucy, and lied that those particular sandwiches were the only ones Utterson hadn't licked, because he'd got his greedy snout in the fridge when the door was open. They didn't thank me. Just scoffed the lot and laughed at the other girls, who went without.'

'And plenty of people saw you offering Lucy and Carrie-Anne those particular sandwiches?'

'I put them on different coloured plates. Red for the Marston girls, blue for everyone else. I went out of my way to make sure they ate the right ones. Or wrong ones. Depending on how you look at it.'

'Continue.'

But I can't continue. Because a short while later, just before their performance, the Marston girls started wailing, clutching their bellies and throwing up. Blanche was shouting and screaming at me – *What was in those sandwiches? What have you done, you crazy bitch?* Even Barbara was looking quite stern. Rose Pugh put the girls into the recovery position, Brown Owl was crying in Rob's arms, then Mam ran up to me, shook my shoulders, screaming in my face: *What the hell have you done, Debbie-Marie Tunstall? What have you done, you stupid child? You're just like your father, you are. Just like your father after all!*

'Deborah,' The Vicar says gently, 'would it help if I told you I believed you? At first, I thought my overdose was an accident. But a . . . friend suggested my medication may have been tampered with.'

'Brown Owl?'

'Never mind who, Deborah. Let's just say I now strongly suspect that someone moved my fast-acting insulin to my slow-acting insulin kitchen cupboard, and vice versa. They're back in their original positions now, of course – I checked last night. But I do believe my medication must have been tampered with. Do you think that's plausible?'

I think about this for a moment. 'No.' I say. 'Not really.'

'Well, what if I were to tell you that I believe I am one of several victims of a serial killer?'

I dab at my eyes with the back of my sleeve. 'How can you be?' I sniff. 'You're not dead.'

'All right, the intended victim of a serial killer.'

'All that weird stuff in your blanket box. All those newspaper cuttings. You think there's a murderer on the loose.'

'I shouldn't really be telling you this, but yes – I do.'

I don't want to go along with his serial killer story yet – I'm still not sure I can trust him. I'm going to play for time, I think, and play dumb, instead.

'Okay,' I say, 'so over the past twenty years, someone's died in a car crash with their wedding ring in their mouth. A drunk builder chokes on a sausage. That mad mayoress woman's carp pond gets painted green. The Marston girls eat some sand-wiches and get sick. All a bit strange, but it doesn't strike me a nutter's on the loose in Llanfair. I'd say you've got a bigger imagination than I have. And, if there was a serial killer, why would they target *you*? You're a dirty old man, but you've not done anything to deserve getting murdered.'

'Deborah,' The Vicar says. 'Are you familiar with the Seven Deadly Sins? And I am not a dirty old man.'

'Course I am,' I say. 'I've been accused of most of them.'

'You are what is known as a scapegoat, Deborah. Some families have one; most communities, too. Especially communities in crisis. You see, when a group of people are under threat, everyone wants to prove how pure they are, that way they won't get singled out and blamed for whatever's going wrong. So, they find an easy target . . .'

'But Llanfair's not under threat! Llanfair wouldn't know a threat if it bit them on the bum.'

'*Au contraire*, Deborah. Llanfair is a hotbed of one-upmanship. Everyone desperate to outdo everyone else. A social crisis on a daily basis – survival of the fittest. Of course, that is an insult to the folk of Barwood, who are trying to survive in the most basic of ways. But Llanfair is entering an even greater period of crisis, a state of danger threatening its very high opinion of itself, thanks to Clive Marston giving Llanfair a dreadful reputation . . .'

Clive Marston lying dead in the woods. Should I tell The Vicar what I saw? I finger the gold watch in my pocket.

Not yet. Still not sure I can trust him.

'So, what's all this got to do with you and your insulin injection, the Seven Deadly Sins, and me being a scapegoat?'

'The people who have been targeted in the past have sinned against the good name of Llanfair. Everyone knew that Herbert Wilkins and Eleri Ellis were having an affair. *Lust.* That builder fellow tried to defraud Barbara Pritchard. *Greed.* Gwendoline Bridges was jealous of Barbara Pritchard's gardening award. Green with *envy*, you might say. And Blanche Marston with her dance troupe and being terribly precious about her girls – *pride.* Think about it. Herbert Wilkins had his ring lodged in his throat. The builder fellow a piece of sausage. Gwendoline Bridges had the decency to apologize, so saved herself from death by "green" for "green with envy". God knows what the killer had in store for her.'

'A frog in her throat?' I suggest.

'Very funny, Deborah.'

'But what about the Marston girls? Nothing was found in *their* throats.'

'Well, what sort of bread were the sandwiches made of?'

'White?'

'What else? What brand?'

'I dunno. What everyone uses, I suppose. Mother's . . . Oh, blimey!'

'Quite so. Mother's Pride. The girls were going to suffer for their mother's sin of *pride*. And not necessarily just the Marston girls – they were the only ones who ate the sandwiches, after all. The whole troupe might have been targeted because of their *mothers'* pride.'

'It's all a bit of a stretch,' I scoff. 'And like I said, what does this have to do with you and me?'

'I believe I was targeted because of what you wrote about me and Brown Owl on the Scout Hut wall, and the photograph of me and Rose Pugh – *lust*, I suppose – though I do not believe anything suggesting lust was lodged in my throat, so the killer's modus operandi is beginning to change. Or perhaps they were disturbed before they had a chance to leave their usual calling card? Anyway, thanks to Clive Marston and *The South Wales Morning Post* stirring up tensions between Llanfair and Barwood – Brown Owl's been filling me in . . .'

'I bet she has,' I mutter.

' . . . Llanfair's reputation is in tatters. We're in the midst of another crisis, and my money's on another dead body turning up anytime soon. Incidentally, Brown Owl told me the Marstons are both miss—'

'Mr Vicar,' I shout, 'there's something I need to tell you.'

'Please don't interrupt me, Deborah. What I have to say next is important. Blanche and Clive Marston have, according to Brown Owl, done a runner, as they say.'

'Mr Vicar, about Cl—'

'Now, Deborah. With the Marstons out of the picture, you are now the most obvious village scapegoat. Because you have played a part in bringing the village into disrepute.'

My heart flip-flops into my mouth. I feel sick. The sherbet from the flying saucers rises into my chest, burning the back of my throat. 'Does that mean I'll be next?' I whimper. 'Why? What sin have I committed?' I start counting them on my fingers. I hate the Marston girls. *Envy.* I fancy Gary White. *Lust.*

I shout again. 'What sin, Mr Vicar?'

Silence.

My fingers curl around the gold watch in my pocket. A voice inside my head says *greed*.

'*Please?*' I shout again. 'Please, tell me, apart from telling tales, what else have I done wrong?'

No answer.

'Mr Vicar? *Mr Vicar?*'

37

Barbara

1 p.m., Barwood Community Library

Barbara is battling to stay awake, to focus on Celia Owen. There had been a frisson between them once, over a quarter of a century ago, with an unspoken agreement that said attraction must never be acknowledged. Or perhaps it had all been in Barbara's head. Her head. Her once sharp-as-a-tack head, now woollier than Utterson's. She must pull herself together, for Deborah's sake, for Utterson and Robert's sake. Barbara is even beginning to feel responsible for Dr Bridges, too.

So much responsibility, so little time.

She'd zoned out of Celia's ranting and raving over Clive Marston's dirty dealings, but Dr Bridges has been listening keenly, leaning forward in her chair and asking all the right questions at the right time, intense interest etched on that lovely elfin face of hers. Barbara feels a pang of something. Envy? That she will never be so young or vibrant again? That Celia appears to be mesmerized by Dr Bridges – and rightly so?

She zones back in, realizing that the conversation has moved on.

'So, you're saying that Rose Pugh was a battered wife?' Dr Bridges looks at Barbara, aghast. 'Miss Pritchard, did you know this?'

'I had no idea,' Barbara replies. 'I had nothing to do with Rose during the years she lived in Barwood.'

'You've had nothing to do with any of us since you stopped living in Barwood,' Celia says, not unkindly. 'But yes,' she continues, 'I can assure you it's true. Phil Pugh was a dreadful man!' She shudders. 'Rose was a frequent visitor to the Uskshire Women's Sanctuary – I was a volunteer there. Sadly, the pattern was always the same – she'd move in for a few days with her daughter, Susan, then *he'd* turn up, playing merry hell. Shouting about how it was all her fault – how she'd "done this to herself" – blaming the victim, as always.' Celia raises her palms in despair. 'God knows why, but Rose always went back to him. Maybe she loved him. Maybe she pitied him. Who knows, and what can you do?' She smiles. 'The things we do for love, Barbara. Or the things, perhaps, we didn't do that we bitterly regret.'

Barbara reaches down, pats Utterson's head, avoiding Celia's eye. 'Good boy,' she says.

'The whole town breathed a sigh of relief when Phil Pugh died,' Celia continues. 'The most successful man in Barwood – Area Manager of the National Coal Board – and the cruellest, too. He was a bully. The mining community hated him. There were even rumours he had underworld connections. Some people said he kept a gun under his pillow. Nonsense, of course – Rose would never have allowed such a thing. Not with a child in the house.'

'How did he die?' asks Dr Bridges. 'Given his connections, were there any signs of foul play?'

'Oh no.' Celia shakes her head. 'Nothing like that. It was death by natural causes – heart attack, I believe, brought on by a rage when Rose didn't have his dinner on the table on time. Rose ran into the street, screaming blue murder, and Rachel Wilmslow was first on the scene – her chemist shop is across the road. She has one in Llanfair as well, I understand? Such a successful young lady. Anyway, Rachel tried to resuscitate Phil – Rose would have known first aid, of course, but was in no fit state to carry it out. But Rachel's efforts were all in vain, and well . . . that was that.'

Dr Bridges shakes her head. 'Poor Rose!'

'Well, yes, but not poor for very long. I wouldn't go as far as to say that Rose was dancing on her husband's grave, but the transformation in her after his passing really was remarkable. Almost overnight, the little village mouse became the life and soul of the party! She even took over that ridiculous dancing school for a couple of months, but gave it all up when she moved back to Llanfair.'

'Ridiculous dancing school?' Barbara says. 'No such thing existed when I lived in Barwood!'

'Lucky you.' Celia raises her eyes heavenwards. 'Another pie the Marstons stuck their grubby fingers into. Blanche ran a dance school here in Barwood similar to the one she owns in Llanfair. What's it called again?'

'Flicks N' Kicks,' Barbara and Dr Bridges say in unison.

'Well, of course, Blanche became far too busy and important to run the Barwood school properly – kept cancelling lessons, but still charged the full fees. Naturally, the parents were angry and threated to pull their daughters out. That's when Rose stepped in and offered to manage the Barwood branch, and

Blanche agreed. And you know, Rose made a terrific job of it. Renamed the school Little Flickers – said she didn't want it overshadowed by Flicks N' Kicks, and then she made Blanche agree to offer concessions for the daughters of miners. God knows how she pulled that one off, but pull it off she did! Sadly, something always went wrong for poor Little Flickers. Some of us even joked it was the ghost of Phil Pugh, wreaking revenge on his merry-widow wife. And after just a few months, the whole thing fell apart.'

'What sort of things went wrong?' asks Barbara.

'Well, Rose would try to put on a show, only for the venue to get flooded just before, or the electrics would blow. Small wonder she was happy to give it all up when she moved back to Llanfair. Can't blame her. Oh!' Celia claps her hands together, making Barbara jump. 'I've just remembered! Rose had two dozen T-shirts printed for the girls, but she left for Llanfair before they could use them. Adorable little tops with *Little Flickers* embroidered across the chest. We still have them, taking up valuable space in my Christmas toy depository. Why don't you take them with you? They might prove useful.'

'Don't you want to hang on to them?' Barbara asks. 'Surely the Barwood children need clothing?'

'It turns out Rose had them printed,' Celia says with curled lip, 'with funds from the National Coal Board. Relations between Us and Them are extremely tense at present, for obvious reasons, and they have form for trying to bribe the children of miners with gifts. None of the young ladies of Barwood would be seen dead wearing such a garment in the current climate. Quite surprising, actually, that someone as community-minded as Rose could agree to getting into bed with the Coal Board in the first place, even if she had been sharing a marital bed with their Area Manager for more than a decade. Nevertheless, I would hate to see the T-shirts go to waste.' She stares intently at Barbara. 'I do hate waste,' she says, gently. 'Don't you?'

38

Vanessa

3 p.m., Hollyhock Cottage,
Llanfair Village Square

Vanessa, performing a perfect example of parallel parking, slots her mother's XR3 into a space directly in front of Barbara Pritchard's cottage. 'A wasted journey I'm afraid,' she sighs, cranking the handbrake into place. 'I hoped we might return with Debbie-Marie on the back seat. Instead, we've got twenty-four Little Flickers T-shirts crammed inside two Kwik Save bags, and what the hell are we meant to do with them? That's what I'd like to know.'

'I think they might prove rather useful,' Barbara says, wearily unbuckling her seatbelt. 'I'd like to see Rose and Blanche's reactions when we hand them over. It might trigger a little tension between them, jog an underlying grudge or two. One can only hope. I suppose you'll be wanting a cup of tea. I'll go and put the kettle on.'

Vanessa shakes her head. 'I need to get back to work.'

'You *are* at work.'

'I need to check in at the Dewi Sant Centre. See if there are any messages for me. I'll be back in a couple of hours anyway, for the miners' fundraiser at the pub this evening.' She nods at the Llanfair Arms. 'I see the BBC vans are back – it'll be the team from *Spotlight Cymru*. They'll be desperate for Clive Marston to show up at tonight's Flicks N' Kicks performance, though that's looking increasingly unlikely, given the fact that his wife showed up in a Barwood car park battered and bruised and out for the count – I'm assuming that what Rose told us this morning is true and not just hearsay. Either way, surely the police must have Clive Marston listed as a missing person by now?'

'I don't know,' Barbara says breathlessly. 'At this precise moment, I really don't have the energy to care . . .'

Vanessa turns to look at Barbara – really, properly look at her. 'Oh, God!' she cries. 'You're not well!'

'Get Robert,' Barbara grunts. 'The Llanfair Arms. Be quick.'

Robert Hargreaves tenderly removes his aunt's nut-brown brogues from her feet, before chucking them unceremoniously to the floor, narrowly missing Vanessa's head.

Vanessa, perched on the edge of the bed, is mesmerized by Barbara's legs. So thin, so painfully fragile, so heartbreakingly breakable-looking. *Why* hadn't she noticed how frail the old woman was? Because Barbara Pritchard hides it so well: padding her frame with woollen layers, cunningly cultivating the image of a strong, stout figure – not just through the power of dress, but the power of suggestion.

But now, laid out on her bed, Barbara Pritchard was just a little old lady after all, engulfed by the undulating mounds of a sage-green satin eiderdown. If Robert were to scoop his aunt up in his arms, Vanessa would not be at all surprised if there were no body-shaped indentations on the bedding beneath her, such was the old woman's lightness of being.

She starts to say, 'I'm so sorry, Miss Pritchard, I didn't realize you were so . . .' but Robert raises an eyebrow.

'Don't give the old bat any attention,' he says. 'You'll only get a flea in your ear for your trouble.'

Barbara closes her eyes and smiles.

'You're a good boy, Robert,' she whispers. 'Now kindly bugger off.'

Downstairs in the kitchen, Vanessa tries to act casually, leaning against the cooker top – an old Baby Belling, in mint condition – while waiting for the kettle to boil, hoping her hair doesn't catch fire on the hob. Robert is on his hands and knees, pretending to find Utterson's bone in the heap of canine detritus spewing forth from the cupboard under the sink. The dog is curled up in his basket, ears drooped. All three of them know the lost bone is not the cause of Utterson's depression.

'She's not a well woman,' says Robert's muffled voice. 'Don't ask me what's wrong – I don't know, and she won't tell me. But I do know that over the past few weeks, she's let the house and garden go a bit, and she takes a while to get dressed in the mornings. She's made a few jokes about losing her marbles, and her usefulness. About becoming a sloth.'

'But she's an old lady – she's bound to be slowing down a bit!'

Robert, head still stuck in the cupboard, apparently doesn't hear her. 'And her memory's not what it used to be, her appetite's up and down, and she often complains of migraines and stomach upsets. I reckon it's this house. There's weird energy in this place. I often feel under the weather when I'm here.'

Come to think of it, Vanessa does have a bit of a dull ache at the back of her head. 'Robert,' she says, 'could you please come out of the cupboard? I can't talk to you properly when you're in there.'

'I'm looking for Utterson's bone.'

'No, you're not.'

'Yes, I am.'

'No, you're not. You're being avoidant. We got off to a bad start this morning, and now you don't want to face me . . .'

'Found it – here it is!'

He backs out of the cupboard, brandishing a femur. 'Sheep,' he declares with a grin. 'Not human.'

'I'm very glad to hear it.'

He tosses the bone at Utterson, who studiously ignores it. 'No luck finding Debbie-Marie, then?' he says.

'Sadly not.'

'Shame. She's a nice kid, not the psycho the locals make her out to be.'

'I know.'

'And Barbara loves her to pieces. Gives her extra tuition, when Ingrid – her mum – cleans the cottage. Debbie needs extra tuition, and . . .'

'Needs extra tuition? I thought she was a child genius! That's what your aunt thinks.'

Robert stares at her thoughtfully. 'Yes,' he says. 'I still can't quite work that one out.'

'Debbie's not a child genius?'

Robert smiles enigmatically, beckoning with his index finger. 'Come with me, Dr Bridges,' he says. 'I have something to show you.'

She follows him into Barbara's living room, where he picks up a sheet of folded A4 paper from the coffee table. He unfolds it. 'Look at this,' he says.

'Your aunt tried to get me to read this earlier – she said it was an essay on *Lord of the Flies*.'

'Well, it isn't. Read it and see.'

In handwritten script – presumably Debbie's – is line after line of carefully printed letters in bright red marker pen:

The fat cat sat on the mat
The fat cat sat on the mat
The fat cat sat on the mat
And so on, and so on.

39

Debbie

3.30 p.m., The Vicar's spare room, the vicarage, Llanfair Lane

The Vicar stopped talking yonks ago, and I'm crapping myself, I am.

Because he might be dead, or *playing* dead. The first scenario's bad enough, but the second's even worse. Because what if he's the Llanfair serial killer? What if he's out in the hallway, waiting to catch me off guard, ready to pounce and kill me and shove something nasty in my gob, because now I know what he's been up to?

'Mr Vicar!' I try again. 'Mr Vicar . . . Stop messing about! It's not funny!'

Still no answer.

What would Barbara Pritchard do?

That's what I always ask myself whenever I'm in a pickle. What would my best friend Barbara do? Not that she's ever landed herself in anything like the trouble I end up in, but she's dealt with enough crap over the years to give advice that's worth listening to.

Well, she'd tell me to buck my ideas up. And then she'd tell me to make a plan.

Which I've tried doing, but so far, no good.

Plan number one was to open the window and shout at passers-by. But not one person has passed by here all day long.

So that's plan number one buggered.

Plan number two – jump from the window. The stupidest plan of all. If I did that, I'd break my legs or my back, or both, which at first seemed like a good idea, because everyone would feel dead sorry for me, *and* I'd get to go to hospital. They give you ice-cream to eat in hospital, though that might just be when they take your tonsils out, and I'd probably get given tripe and onions, knowing my luck. And anyway, jumping from a height – I could die.

So that's plan number two buggered.

Plan number three is to get down the stairs armed with my mop, ready to bash The Vicar's head in if he's not already dead. It's a scary prospect and one I don't relish, I can't lie. But I've got no choice. Not least because I really, really need the toilet.

40

Vanessa

*4.30 p.m., Hollyhock Cottage,
Llanfair Village Square*

She's stuck in a limbo within a limbo, waiting for Robert Hargreaves to return from wherever it is he's gone off to. He vanished half an hour ago, plonking a copy of *The Radio Times* on her lap, absent-mindedly muttering, 'Here, have something to do until I come back. Do you like Clive Doig's Trackword on the back page? Bloody impossible most of the time, but you're much cleverer than I am. I'll be back in a few minutes.' And she'd opened her mouth to say, 'I need to get back to work!' But too late. Moments later, the front door slammed, followed by a quizzical bark from the kitchen.

She should check on Barbara, but it wasn't how she was brought up at all – going upstairs alone in a stranger's house. 'Not the done thing,' her mother would say, 'invading someone's privacy. It would serve you right if you took a wrong turn and saw something you shouldn't.'

But she's spent her whole life trying to do the right thing, and look where that's got her.

She gets up from the sofa, straightens her skirt. Something outside has caught her eye.

Through Barbara's leaded window, Vanessa can see at least a dozen Llanfairians hard at work outside the pub, while a woman with violently backcombed black hair, a cut on her face and a swollen lip, is having a heated discussion with Nurse Rose Pugh. Blanche Marston, it has to be! But what is she doing out and about? She's been beaten up, her husband's missing, yet there she is, pouting and preening, while Robert and an older, balding man stagger past, grappling with a towering wooden object carved with leering animal faces.

'A totem pole?' Vanessa gasps. 'What on earth is going on here?'

Meanwhile, several women in tunics and jeans are shinning up stepladders in front of the pub, stringing Welsh flags and fairy lights between the hanging baskets, barking an occasional warning at the dozens of primary-school-aged girls skipping and darting between them.

It takes a few minutes, but Vanessa eventually realizes she is witnessing the time-honoured hive-mind dance: the favoured girls linking arms, turning their backs on the lesser mortals, subconsciously forming a beeline leading to a striking young girl with long brown hair tied in ribbons and rags, and dressed fashionably in a cropped pink top with matching leggings. She is holding court from a deckchair, sucking on a lolly and scowling at her minions, and has a bowl of sweets on her lap, which she doles out to The Chosen Ones.

'It never changes,' says a voice from the door.

'Barbara, you're awake! And looking very much better, if you don't mind me saying.'

Barbara Pritchard shuffles forward, Utterson at her side. 'You called me Barbara, not Miss Pritchard,' she says.

'I'm sorry – I didn't mean to be disrespectful.'

'I'm glad,' Barbara smiles, linking her arm through Vanessa's. 'I'm glad you feel you're able to.'

Barbara nods at the scene playing out in front of them: the Queen Bee gesturing for a pretty blonde girl to unlink arms with her less fashionably dressed friend, entreating her to sit on the empty deckchair at her side. The pretty girl obliges with a whoop and a skip, cosying up to the Queen Bee, cupping her hand and whispering. The Queen Bee giggles and hands her a sweet; the plainer friend slinks off, dejected. Nobody runs after her.

'Carrie-Anne Marston,' Barbara says. 'The girl with the lollipop and bowl of sweets. Poor Deborah's nemesis. Little girls can be brutal.'

'Big girls, too,' Vanessa murmurs, watching Blanche Marston brush something off Robert Hargreaves' chest. Robert tenderly touches the cut on her face in return, and Blanche casts a triumphant look at the chemist, Rachel Wilmslow – AKA Brown Owl.

'For someone who's been kidnapped, beaten up and left for dead in a Texas Homecare car park, and whose husband is missing, Blanche Marston seems remarkably chipper this evening,' Vanessa muses.

'She's not like us,' Barbara replies. 'I'm not even sure she's the same species.' She smiles up at Vanessa. 'I really wouldn't worry too much, Dr Bridges.'

'Hmm?'

Barbara pats Vanessa's arm. 'Robert might be a bit of an

idiot, but he's not an outright fool. He knows if he went anywhere near Blanche Marston, I'd cut him out of my will. Now, why don't we go out and join them? As good a time as any to hand over the Little Flickers T-shirts to Blanche and Rose, don't you think?'

'All right – on one condition.'

'And what might that be?'

'No more Dr Bridges, please. Just call me Vanessa.'

41

Debbie

5 p.m., behind the runner-bean canes in Barbara Pritchard's front garden

Sooner or later, I'll have to come out of hiding, and then *I'll* be in for a hiding. My crimes are stacking up by the hour: I've gone AWOL, nicked money from Mam, bought a shit-ton of sweets, taken a watch and a fifty-pound note from the mouth of a dead man, broken into a vicarage, stolen a packet of Smash, smoked two Benson & Hedges and nicked a nut caramel from The Vicar's box of All Gold, then left him unconscious at the foot of his stairs.

That's really, really naughty. Even for me.

And poor Mr Vicar's completely knackered. After I let myself out of the spare room and went to the bog for a tinkle, I tip-toed down the stairs and very nearly fell over him, making him grunt, so at least I know he's alive. I kept my eyes shut the whole time – I've seen one dead body too many this week – and then I made a run for it, dropping my mop, which is made of light plastic, so not much of a weapon at all, because what if The Vicar – all six-foot-plus of him – was faking his fall after all, and tried to attack me? What would I do with it? Clean him to death?

I couldn't sprint from the vicarage fast enough. And now here I am, in Barbara's front garden. Nobody's clocked me so far; everyone's too busy. There's so much going on that I was able to scramble from Llanfair Lane into Barbara's front garden and vegetable beds like I was in the SAS. And now, peeking through the runner-bean wigwams, I can see Barbara and that nice Dr Bridges, standing outside the pub together, watching Dai and Robert Hargreaves struggling with the Flicks N' Kicks totem pole. Barbara has Utterson on a lead, and he keeps looking over to where I'm hiding, maybe because he can smell me. I haven't washed properly in days and days, and more than likely stink.

No sign of Mam. I hope she's all right. I hope she's working and not worrying about me. She'll be enjoying the break, I hope. If I was her, I would be.

It looks dead pretty, the village square, with its fairy lights and bunting – a bit how it looked back in August, but better, because the sun's going down earlier now, and everything's nicer just before dusk. The light is much softer, blurring the bits that don't look as good when it's really bright. Dr Bridges and Robert keep taking sneaky peeks at each other. Dr Bridges is pretending to be interested in whatever it is that Barbara is saying, but every so often she glances over at Robert, who's arguing with his dad. I think it's over the totem pole, which won't fit through the pub door. Dai has just poked Robert's chest with his finger. Every so often, I catch Robert staring at Dr Bridge's backside when he thinks no one is looking.

A crowd has gathered around that absolute twit who told me to 'hoppit' two days ago. He's dressed in the same slimy grey suit, with his oil-slick hair hanging over his face, and is shaking hands with a man in tight black trousers, an unbuttoned shirt and stick-on sideburns. Wrong Jones, it has to be.

All of Llanfair is out here this evening, all wanting to get their mugs on the telly. The men are wearing their best Sunday suits, the women their flowery two-pieces. WPC Jane Gill is here – Brown Owl, too – and Nurse Rose Pugh, in her uniform, with that stethoscope draped round her neck like a bloody boa constrictor. Blanche Marston elbows Julie and Gary from Love is in the Hair out of the way, so a couple of blokes wheeling cameras on stands can push past them. Someone shouts, 'That totem pole's blocking a right of way!' And Dai shouts back, 'The totem pole won't fit in the pub, you muppet, so the girls are dancing outside on the pavement instead.'

There's no sign of the Flicks N' Kicks kids yet. They'll be inside the pub, I expect, getting changed. I'm dead jealous, I really am. I wish it was me dancing tonight. I wish it was me that the grown-ups would look at. I wish it was Mam who'd have all the praise – all the, *Oooooh! Hasn't your little girl grown up! And isn't she pretty and talented, too?* I wish it was me, that I wasn't me. I wish it was me, I wish . . .

I can hear voices. Bloody Blanche Marston and Nurse Rose Pugh have moved across the road, and they're standing by Barbara's garden wall, just a few feet away from me. Having a right up-and-downer, too, by the sounds of it.

'Look,' Blanche is saying, 'you had no damn right, agreeing to let the girls wear those Little Flickers T-shirts tonight. No right at all! I didn't order them – you did, over a year ago. I haven't sanctioned them, haven't even seen them – Barbara

Pritchard didn't show them to me, she went completely over my head!'

And Rose says, very gently, like she's trying to soothe an angry horse, 'Well, I would have shown you them, Blanche, my love, but you were too busy flirting with Barry Parry. And anyway, it's a lovely touch – a way of bringing the Llanfair girls and the daughters of the striking miners together without actually bringing them together, if you know what I mean. A show of solidarity! The T-shirts are lovely, as I recall – Little Flickers embroidered in pink. It will break the girls' little hearts if they're not allowed to wear them.'

And then they cross back over the road, and I watch Rose hurry into the pub while Blanche struts over to the man in the shiny grey suit, to straighten his tie and neaten his hair, because apparently he can't do those things for himself. She doesn't know she's a widow yet, but she's acting like she's been widowed for years.

Dai Hargreaves climbs up one of the stepladders, holding a loudhailer. He's a lanky-limbed, bald-headed bloke who always looks like he's about to snuff it, but he's scrubbed up nicely this evening. He's wearing a suit, but it's far too big, so he has to keep hitching his trousers up.

'Ladies and gents!' he hollers. 'Welcome to the long-awaited . . .'

'Show us your cockatoo!' a red-faced bloke in the crowd shouts – Morris the butcher, reeling around, spilling his pint of beer over the front of his tank top.

Dai tries again. 'Ladies and gentlemen, welcome to the Llanfair Arms' special fundraiser for the Barwood miners.

Wrong Jones will be performing inside the pub from 7 p.m. onwards, but meanwhile, our very own Flicks N' Kicks girls will entertain you with their dress rehearsal, before the *Spotlight Cymru* cameras roll at 6 p.m. . . . '

He climbs down the stepladder, switches on the ghetto blaster at his feet, leaps up and pumps the air with his fist, roaring: 'The miners!'

Stupid sod.

The music starts thumping, the crowd claps in time, swaying together, becoming as one – a giant, swishing, lizard-tailed monster made up of flowery two-pieces and Sunday-best suits, waving its arms, stamping its feet, screeching and squawking along to 'I Eat Cannibals'.

And then the singing stops.

The Flicks N' Kicks girls, led by Rose Pugh, start trooping out of the pub in pairs. The crowd parts as they take their places on the pavement. They're wearing ra-ra skirts and T-shirts I haven't seen before.

Someone laughs nervously. Other people join in. The titters get louder and louder. A woman shouts, 'My God!'

I can't believe my eyes.

The T-shirts, with Little Flickers embroidered on the chest, aren't saying Little Flickers at all. The embroidery is in joined-up writing; the L and the I of 'Flickers' spelling out . . .

'Little Fuckers!' Dai Hargreaves shouts, not realizing he's still holding his loudhailer.

'Oh, my eyes,' Blanche Marston cries. 'Rose, what on earth have you done?'

Then Carrie-Anne Marston faints. Then Lucy. Then Susan Pugh. Then another Flicks N' Kicks girl, and another and another. Every single one of them toppling over, like dominoes.

'It's happening again!' Blanche Marston shrieks. 'The girls have been poisoned! Call an ambulance! Call the police!'

And I see my chance – I can clear my name! Because if the girls have been poisoned again, it can't have been me this time, because I've not been here. Which means there's a nutter on the loose in Llanfair, some other nutter who poisoned them the day of the village fete!

I run up to the crowd, waving and shouting: 'Here I am, here I am!'

Blanche stops cradling Carrie-Anne, leaps to her feet and grabs my throat.

'You bitch!' she screams. 'You've done it again!'

Then Barbara's voice. 'Deborah! You're back!'

The crowd closes in, Blanche's face spits in mine:

'You've done it again, you murderous cow!'

Then Robert – 'Leave her alone, for Christ's sake!'

'Slap her face!' a woman shouts.

The monster-crowd falls in on me, its hundreds of faces gnashing their teeth. I know all the faces, I know that I know them, but can't place them, because they all look the same. The faces of hate all look the same – covered in spittle, crooked with spite.

A slap's too good for her – she needs a good beating . . .

Let's knock some bloody sense into the little cow!

Then a kick and a punch to my stomach and back. I scream at the top of my lungs:

'It's not me! I've done nothing wrong! I've been locked in a room – I was kidnapped, I was!'

The monster-crowd sways backwards and gasps. I take a deep breath.

'I've only just escaped!' I wail.

Dr Bridges crouches beside me, taking my hand in hers. She examines my knees. They are covered in scratches and bruises from scrambling through brambles and runner-bean canes.

'Locked up in a room by who?' she asks gently.

'Mr Vicar,' I whisper.

'Liar!' Blanche cries. 'He's in hospital, stupid! Look what you've done, you horrible child!' She points at the girls, all rolling around, moaning and groaning and wailing and weeping – hamming it up, the lot of them. They're not ill this time, I want to scream. They're not ill at all, can't you see? They were embarrassed, because everyone laughed at the T-shirts they're wearing! Pretending they're ill is their only way out.

'Debbie's right. The Vicar *is* out of hospital,' Brown Owl says quietly. 'They discharged him yesterday evening. Oh, God, I can't believe he'd . . .'

Dr Bridges strokes my face. 'What did he do to you? Are you able to tell me, Debbie?'

The monster-crowd's face is changing: from hate to shame, from shame to concern. Something warm and fuzzy is growing inside me.

'He did lots of things,' I whisper. 'And he threatened me, if I told. I've been so frightened and hungry and cold . . .'

'Bastard,' I hear a man mutter. 'Sick bastard. I knew he liked ladies, but little girls?'

'Let's go get him!' another man yells.

The Marston girls stop rolling around and get up, looking

really pissed off. The warm and fuzzy thing inside me grows even bigger.

'It's been awful,' I whimper. 'Really awful.'

Dr Bridges hugs me so close I can bury my face in her lush-smelling hair. *It's okay,* she's saying. *You're safe with me, now. Let's take you to Barbara's, and we'll phone for your mum . . .*

Robert Hargreaves scoops me up in his arms, and carries me through the crowd, like a trophy. 'Make way,' he shouts. 'Coming through.' And the crowd parts, like the Red Sea did for Moses, and I close my eyes. I'm in heaven, I am.

Robert whispers in my ear, but his voice gets caught up in the mayhem around us –

The monster-crowd chanting, 'The Vicar's a perv!'

Blanche Marston shrieking, 'Dial 999!'

Dai Hargreaves and the butcher are having a fist fight. 'Show us yer cockatoo!' the butcher keeps shouting.

BBC Wales are filming it all.

As Robert carts me away, the last thing I see is a cameraman pointing his lens at the totem pole, which is rocking madly back and forth, ready to fall any second. And Barbara, yelling at the top of her lungs:

'Stop that, Utterson!'

One week later
WEDNESDAY, 19 SEPTEMBER 1984

THE SOUTH WALES MORNING POST

The Hate Must Stop!
Comment by Margaret Lawrence,
Welsh Affairs Correspondent

One week on from the discovery of businessman Clive Marston's body in Llanfair Woods, shot through the head at point-blank range. One day on from the news that three Barwood miners have been arrested on suspicion of his murder, and of abducting and assaulting his wife. And one hour on from my witnessing a baying crowd, chanting: 'Free the Barwood Three!' outside Barwood police station, while throwing missiles, breaking windows and overturning parked cars.

A statement from one Barwood resident, who wishes to remain anonymous, reads: 'The Barwood Three have been arrested on suspicion of murder with no concrete evidence, simply because they contacted *The South Wales Morning Post* some weeks ago, raising concerns over Clive Marston's financial exploitation of the miners and their families. Consequently, three innocent men have been arrested and face life imprisonment. We believe these men are scapegoats, whose families are suffering quite enough hardship and heartbreak as it is.'

As I write this, I gather that a further five arrests have been made, following a police chase along the A5876 in the early hours of this morning. 'We received a tip-off that a group of young Barwood males were travelling to Llanfair to exact revenge,' a police spokeswoman tells me. 'Several weapons were recovered from the boot of the vehicle, including hammers and cricket bats.'

One week on from the discovery of a brutal murder, and the aftershocks continue. Barwood and Llanfair, we implore you – the hate must stop!

42

Debbie

10.30 a.m., Dewi Sant Department of Child &
Adolescent Psychology

I should be at school today. I should be in assembly, taking my harvest basket up to Bug-eyed Thomas, so she can curl her hairy lip at it. Later, she'll take all our baskets to the old people's home, so they can tell her what lovely Christian children she's teaching, and that she's a good Christian, too.

Every year, for Harvest Assembly, Mam packs me off with a basket holding two potatoes and a tin of spaghetti. Every year, the other kids laugh at me. Their harvest baskets are packed to the brim with bread, apples, pears and pasta – the dried sort you get in a pack, not a tin. Bug-eyed Thomas smiles at their baskets, but always scowls at mine. It's crap being poor, because it gives people like her good reason to think that Mam's just being tight.

So, I'm half relieved that I'm back in Dr Bridges' office, with Mam and Nurse Pugh on their plastic chairs. But the other half is crapping itself, because I'm in for another bollocking – this time, from Dr Bridges. And I deserve it, I know I do. I've done some terrible things – failing to report a dead body being the worst thing of all. Poor Clive. I shouldn't have left him there, all cold and wet and lonely like that. I know how it feels to be left all alone, how scary it is and how much it hurts, and I've gone and done it to somebody else – to a dead man, in fact, whose wife and kids had no idea where he was.

No wonder Dr Bridges can't look me in the eye.

I've been forced to stand this time. No kneeling on the brown fuzzy carpet for me. I'm to stand and feel ashamed of myself while everyone sits on their backsides and glares. If Barbara was here, she'd let me sit down. She'd pop me on a chair next to her, and she'd say, Now, Deborah – what a to-do this is! What a pickle you've found yourself in!

But Barbara's not well. She's very unwell, so Mam says, and it's all my fault.

And the less said about The Vicar, the better.

'Do you know why you're in trouble?' Dr Bridges asks.

I nod.

'Then perhaps you could tell us, Deborah. I'd like to hear your view of the situation.'

'I lied,' I whisper.

'You're a born liar,' Mam snaps. 'I've run out of patience, I really have – I was worried sick about you; we all were . . .'

Dr Bridges holds up the palm of her hand, stopping Mam in her tracks. Dr Bridges means business this morning. She's got her hair pinned up in a bun, and she's wearing brown woollen trousers and a smart cream blouse. It suits her, dressing like a grown-up for once, and I'd tell her so if I didn't think I'd get a bloody good hiding for my trouble.

'What did you lie about?' Dr Bridges asks.

'About Mr Vicar kidnapping me.'

Dr Bridges nods. 'What else?'

'I – I found a dead body. And I didn't tell anyone straight away.'

Rose Pugh shakes her head. 'Poor Clive Marston! Left out in the woods for days to rot. So little left of him, too, once the foxes had had their way with him . . .'

'I was scared!' I start to cry.

'Failing to report a death is a crime, Debbie,' Dr Bridges says gently.

'That was the worst thing of all that you did,' Mam says, shaking her head. 'I despair, I really do.'

'I was scared,' I whisper.

Dr Bridges nods. 'How do you feel now about what you've done?'

I think about this, but there's no easy answer.

'Do you feel bad?'

I want to say, No, not really. I'm not sure I feel anything at all any more, but if I do that, I'll run the risk of a smacked bum. So, I nod. 'I do,' I say. 'I feel bad. Really, really bad.'

But I don't feel bad. Not one little bit. I don't feel good either, though. I just feel numb. Floppy and funny and wobbly inside, like when I've had a tummy bug and I can't keep my food down.

Dr Bridges starts scribbling in her notepad. I look out of the window and, inside my head, start counting the cars I can see parked up. A Ford Fiesta. A Mini. A Metro. A Datsun Cherry – what Dad used to have – and I remember the keyring that Mam and I bought him for his very last Father's Day, and Mr Strong falling off the fob. And I wonder if Dad still has that keyring, whether he ever looks at Mr Lazy and Mr

Happy, with the scratched face that looks like a sticking-out tongue, and wishes, with all his heart, that he could turn back time. I know I do.

If I could, I'd go back five years, back to when Mam was happy. Before Dad buggered off, because I never saw her smile again after that.

Standing next to the Datsun Cherry, looking like she knows she shouldn't be there, is a girl, a little bit older than me, wearing weird clothes – even weirder than mine, and that's really saying something. Funny smocked dress, knee-high socks and a red hooded cardigan. Poor little cow. She's pretty though, much prettier than I am, with long dark hair that's poker straight, brown skin and great big starey eyes.

I blink, and she's gone.

'Can I sit down now? I'm tired,' I say.

'No,' Mam snaps. 'You can't.'

43

Robert

11.55 a.m., Dewi Sant Department of Child &
Adolescent Psychology

He's been peering through the gap in Vanessa Bridges' office door for fifteen minutes now, like a filthy-dirty peeping Tom. Too much of a coward to make himself known, knowing he's done something wrong, but not knowing what that something is.

What a hell of a week it's been.

And it had all started so well. Catching Vanessa Bridges' eye as he carted Debbie-Marie to safety – elbowing his way through the baying mob, side-stepping a toppling totem pole, ducking to avoid the flying fists of his father and Morris the Butcher – he'd have sworn at the time that the chemistry between them was tantalizingly tangible. But then the vicarage went up in flames, and Barbara collapsed with chest pains, and Vanessa Bridges stopped speaking to him – just like that. As though everything that happened last Wednesday evening was all his fault!

For the past seven days, it would seem that Dr Vanessa Bridges has found Robert repulsive. Which has only served to make him like her even more. Why? Because he's a professional victim, let's face it, and maybe it's time he moved on from that. Maybe that's what she senses – that Robert wallows too much, finds comfort in his own misery, and that's not attractive in a man, at least not to any woman *he'd* find attractive.

Robert opens the plastic bag he's been carting around for the past few hours, and gazes longingly at the two Pot Noodles he's brought along as a peace offering. Sweet & Sour flavour, his favourite. Robert doesn't even know whether Vanessa Bridges likes Pot Noodles. Still doesn't know her favourite colour, or whether she'd order chips or rice or a half-and-half with her curry. Doesn't know much about her at all. Only that, at six years old, she was nuts, and that she has hair that smells of violets, and lovely eyes and smooth, pale skin, and occasionally smiles in a way that has helped him believe that life might be worth living, after all – so much so that this morning, he actually left Mum's bottle of morphine pills on the Llanfair Pharmacy counter when Rachel Wilmslow was busy with a shop full of customers. He's been hanging on to the pills for a year, in case the desire to end it all should finally overcome him. But that desire has faded of late. In fact, he's hardly thought about Mum for the past week or so.

He peers through the gap in the door again.

Vanessa looks different today – wearing a blouse and smart trousers, hair pinned up in a bun, all sleek and neat and business-like. Far too lovely for the likes of him. What on earth was he thinking?

Pull yourself together, you coward! Take a deep breath, open your gob and . . .

But she's still on the bloody phone, on hold – he can just about make out the muzak playing down the receiver –

UB40's bloody 'Red, Red Wine' . . .

Robert hates that song. Reminds him of last year, when Mum was dying. It was number one in the charts at the time.

Scrap that, stop thinking about me, Rob, it'll only depress you – that's what Mum would say. *Think about something constructive instead. Ask yourself why Vanessa Bridges went cold on you. Think back to last Wednesday, when everything seemed so right, then went so wrong.*

He remembers the ugly scenes outside the pub, scooping a terrified Debbie-Marie in his arms, and carrying her back to Barbara's, catching Vanessa Bridges' eye as he muscled his way through the crowd. He'd sensed something, he really had – something actually fizzing between them. She fancies me back, he told himself. She actually finds me attractive!

And then, a little while later, when they were standing together in Barbara's kitchen, and he accused her of catastrophizing (steady on, Robert, he'd cautioned himself. That's a five-syllable word you're dealing with there).

'Catastrophizing?' she'd replied.

He was spooning a stinking pile of meat chunks into Utterson's bowl at the time, the dog gnawing hungrily at his toes, while Vanessa Bridges leaned against the stove, looking pensive and rather sad. He could hear Ingrid Tunstall's sobs of delight and relief coming from Barbara's living room, and couldn't help but feel choked up. Reunions between mums and their kids . . . well. All a bit too close to home.

'What's with the face?' he'd asked her. 'I thought you'd be thrilled Debbie was safe and sound, and back with her mum.'

'Well, of course I am,' she'd said, flatly. 'But my job was on the line as it was, and now I'm well and truly stuffed. My vulnerable patient ended up in the hands of a child abductor. Not looking good for me, is it?'

'You're a psychologist. Not a fortune teller. Or a mind-reader, for that matter.'

'As a psychologist, I'm expected to be both of those things.'

'Nonsense! You're catastrophizing.'

And he'd winced, waiting for the rebuke that would surely come, because she'd see straight through him all over again; she'd already called him out over his armchair analysis and cod psychology, after all.

He discreetly checked his flies, just to be on the safe side.

But she just carried on talking. 'I wish I had a normal job,' she sighed. 'Something nice and not too taxing, where I don't feel I'm always playing a role. You know, trying to be what I'm expected to be, rather than who I actually am. All my life, I've had Mum and Dad's expectations shaping everything I do. Who I was friends with, where I went to university, what I did for a living. The joys,' she smiled stiffly, 'of being an only child.'

'I'm an only child, too.'

'Then you'll know what it's like, having everyone pinning their hopes and ambitions on you.'

He shook his head. 'No,' he said. 'Not really.'

'Now you're sounding like Debbie-Marie Tunstall!' she laughed. And he'd laughed, too, nervously brushing her shoulder with his own as he reached to get the tea bags out of the cupboard above her head.

'Do you know,' she said, shifting ever-so-slightly out of his way, 'that we've just witnessed a fascinating example of mass hysteria?'

He plopped a bag in each of their mugs. Their elbows were touching. 'Have we?' he said.

'Yes! All the Flicks N' Kicks girls fainting just now, then making a miraculous recovery as soon as Debbie-Marie appeared. Social contagion.' She smiled at him, and he was struck by how utterly lovely she looked at that moment, talking so animatedly about her work, and he wanted to say – stay just as you are. You're not playing a role, being a psychologist. You're just being you. Please don't change.

'Social contagion?' he'd asked.

'Yes! In this case, an inverse version of the Dancing Plague.'

'Dancing Plague? You've lost me.'

'Of 1518. Hundreds of people in Strasbourg danced for weeks on end, many of them died. Might have been caused by an extreme stress reaction to famine and disease.'

'And now we have the great Non-dancing Plague of 1984, caused by an extreme stress reaction to striking miners' fund-raisers and sweary sequin T-shirts,' he said, chuffed at his cleverness.

And to his delight, she laughed out loud, and he took a deep breath and said, 'There's a packet of Orange Club biscuits in the cupboard above your rather lovely head, Dr Bridges. Would you mind passing them down to me?'

The air was static. He could feel the electricity flowing between them. Could actually hear something buzzing – a high-pitched whirring sound – before realizing it was coming from the boiler next to his head, which was probably on the blink. Again.

Then they heard the sirens off in the distance, and the spell – already hanging by a thread – was broken.

Barbara bustled into the kitchen, red-cheeked and puffing. 'Three police cars, an ambulance and two fire engines just sped past, on their way to Llanfair Lane,' she said, breathlessly. 'The vicarage, Robert – can you smell smoke?'

'Jesus!' he cried. 'Those mad village bastards – what the hell have they gone and done now?'

She must have still liked him at that point, when they raced down Barbara's front path together, passing a pissed-up Morris the Butcher urinating in the telephone box, opening the door of the booth to yell: 'Got another girl running after you, Robert? Screwing Blanche Marston not enough for you, boyo? I've seen you, I have, going into the woods. What you offering the ladies, eh? What you got under your counter that I haven't got, 'cos I've got a sherbet lemon to suck on!'

Robert was about to stop and defend himself, to tell Morris to eff off, to plead with Vanessa not to believe a word of Morris's pissed-up nonsense, when there was an explosion from the vicarage, and the pair of them sprinted towards it . . .

Ah, right. That explains it.

In the commotion that had followed, he'd completely forgotten to put her right on Morris's vile accusations. And now, of course, she believed the worst of him.

Vanessa Bridges slams down the phone, slumps back in her chair, puts her head in her hands, taking a sharp intake of breath.

Robert knocks gingerly at the door.

'Yes?' she says.

He shuffles into the room. 'I have two Pot Noodles,' he announces, holding the plastic bag aloft.

'I want to be alone.'

'Look, Greta Garbo, I've already been in the staff kitchen and put the kettle on. There's no getting rid of me now.'

'I don't want to eat,' she says.

'You need to eat.'

'Can't you just bugger off?'

'No,' he says. 'I will not bugger off. I think you need someone to talk to, and I've tried – I really have. I've phoned you here, at work, waved at you in the car, and you've ignored me, not allowed me to explain . . .'

'I barely know you, so I don't understand why you suddenly expect my attention. And for your information, I don't *need* to talk to anyone.'

'Well, *I* need someone to talk to, actually, after everything that happened last Wednesday.'

'Go and talk to Blanche Marston, then.'

'I don't want to talk to Blanche Marston. I want to talk to you. A hell of a lot's happened, and I'm worried about Auntie Barbara.'

Robert knows he's resorting to emotional blackmail, and he's not proud of himself for that. But needs must. If he tries to explain the truth behind Morris's outburst, Vanessa Bridges won't believe him – that ship has well and truly sailed. *It's been a week, Robert*, she'll say. *Surely enough time's gone by for you to come up with a better explanation?*

She sighs. 'All right,' she says. 'Give me an update. How is Barbara doing?'

'She's okay. A little brighter, perhaps. When I phoned this

morning, the staff nurse said she'd still be in for another few days, though. I'm visiting her later, if you fancy . . .'

'I'm busy,' she snaps.

His eye catches hers. Their eyes move jointly to the empty surface of her desk.

'Are you?' he says.

'No,' she replies. 'I'm not. My days here are numbered, thanks to Debbie-Marie Tunstall. No new referrals, and no word from my boss, though he's bound to know everything by now. He'll be biding his time, the bastard, before firing me in the most humiliating way. There'll be some sort of summons winging its way to me in the internal post as we speak, I just know it.'

She points at a chair for him to sit down. He obeys.

'What flavour are they?' she asks.

'What flavour are what?'

'The Pot Noodles. Hope it's Chicken Chow Mein. I hate Sweet & Sour, though that's probably all you've got, knowing my bloody luck at the moment.'

44

Barbara

*12 p.m., Ward H (Geriatrics), Prince of Wales Hospital,
Cardiff North*

It's the intensity that stays with you, she'll tell anyone who'll listen. *The pitiless savagery of the flames.* The choking smoke, the crackling timber, the chanting crowd left an impression, of course, but it was the searing heat that haunted Barbara most of all. Extreme, even from where she was standing; then the mounting horror as she realized that no one, but no one inside that house, could possibly survive such appalling conditions.

But, somehow, survive them The Vicar had. Lewis Morgan had, in fact, survived a fall down the stairs, several hours in the company of Deborah Tunstall, not to mention the arson attack on his home. Apparently, he'd passed out some time earlier, when Deborah was 'locked' in his spare room, stirring only when the mob descended, screaming for his blood. When a lit firework was pushed through his letterbox, igniting the vicarage doormat, primal fear finally spurred Lewis Morgan into action. He propelled himself on his back through the hall, pushing through the pain in his spine and the fear he may have broken it, then across his living-room floor towards his unlocked French windows.

The fire brigade found him at the bottom of his garden, splayed on his back like an inverted crab, gawping in horror and whimpering 'Shit!' as his kitchen window exploded.

And now, as a fellow inpatient at the Prince of Wales hospital, The Vicar is a constant presence at Barbara Pritchard's bedside, zooming into the ward in his wheelchair every visiting hour. He's got a broken wrist, a cracked coccyx and is in severe pain, but that doesn't stop him from gobbling Barbara's grapes at every opportunity.

'Are you sure you don't want one, Barb?' he says, dangling the bunch in her face.

Barbara shakes her head. 'Your house has been gutted,' she replies. 'I don't see how you can have an appetite at a time like this.'

'The downstairs of the vicarage is damaged, Barbara, but I am still alive. And most of the building remains intact. It can and will be rebuilt.'

'Unlike me.' Barbara smiles sadly, wishing she had the energy to raise her head from the pillow. But she's too sick at heart.

'Don't be so hard on yourself,' Lewis says.

'I've been blinded by my arrogance,' Barbara replies. 'I've been an absolute fool.'

'No, you haven't. You took a lonely little girl under your wing. You tried to make her feel better. She said something stupid . . .'

'She accused you of abducting her. You could have been killed!'

'By all accounts, she was terrified. The local busybodies had her surrounded – what else was she supposed to do?'

'Tell the truth, not tales!'

'She's only eleven years old.'

'Humph.'

They sit in silence, Lewis biting down on a particularly crunchy grape, and Barbara turns her head to the wall. She's done rather a lot of turning her head to the wall over the past few days.

She has frequent flashbacks – she's having one now: standing outside the burning vicarage while a rookie policeman with scant facial hair announces through his shaking loudhailer that: 'The Vicar was released from hospital less than twenty-four hours ago, while Deborah Tunstall had been missing for almost two days. Therefore, The Vicar could not have abducted her!'

'Bollocks,' someone yells.

'And Twp Lisa served Debbie-Marie the day she went missing,' the policeman continues. 'With enough Caramac bars and flying saucers to sink a ruddy battleship. The kid was clearly running away!'

'Why didn't Twp Lisa say so before?' someone mutters.

''Cos she's *twp*,' adds another.

'Because nobody asked me,' Twp Lisa replies, stepping out from the crowd, wearing a yellow sou'wester, yeti boots and an oversized towelling bathrobe. 'I've not seen a soul since yesterday morning. I've been stuck indoors, finishing my PhD on black hole growth through cosmic time. I'd be working on it now if those bloody sirens hadn't disturbed me.'

Everyone stares at Twp Lisa.

'Have none of you got homes to go to?' she says. 'Or some other poor sod you can persecute? And for the record, I am not "*twp*". Just because some daft bastard equates blonde hair, blue eyes, a charming lisp and eclectic dress sense with *twp*ness doesn't mean the rest of you sheep have to play follow-my-ruddy-leader.'

A wave of awkward mumbling ripples through the crowd.

Then – 'That lying bitch Tunstall!' Blanche Marston cries.

'Get her!' someone shouts.

'No one's going to get anyone!' WPC Jane Gill has emerged from the side of the vicarage, and is gliding, apparition-like, through the swirling smoke and dust, yelling through her own loudhailer. 'You're all going home and you'll leave this to us!'

'You've done bugger all so far!' someone says.

'We're overstretched and underpaid,' the rookie policeman replies.

'And underage!' someone else quips, and the crowd laughs.

'Go on,' yells WPC Jane Gill, 'go home. There's nothing to see here.'

But there's plenty to see here, Barbara remembers thinking. The destruction of the vicarage, the near destruction of The Vicar's reputation and The Vicar himself, not to mention the destruction of her faith in basic human decency.

She'd limped home, Robert and Vanessa each taking an arm to hold her upright, guiding her gently into the living room, where Deborah and Ingrid were waiting for news.

Robert gently confronted the child, while Barbara held on to his arm for support, turning her face to stare at the wall – anywhere other than Deborah's face.

And the crushing pain she'd felt in her chest at the time, she'd thought, was heartbreak.

45

Vanessa

12.30 p.m., Dewi Sant Department of Child &
Adolescent Psychology

'Do you know, I foresee a Brave New World where anything can be reconstituted. Food, money, love. Just open the packet, put on the kettle and add boiling water.' Robert Hargreaves twirls the last strands of his Pot Noodle around his plastic fork. 'Still not hungry?'

Vanessa shakes her head.

'Shame,' he says. 'And to think I brought the Pot Noodles all the way from Llanfair, which was an adventure and a half, I can tell you. I stopped at a petrol station, and the attendant claimed he had David Hasselhoff's KITT computer implanted in his brain. The Milk Tray man has nothing on me.'

Vanessa tries to smile. 'I've hardly eaten all week,' she says. 'Mum's tearing her hair out trying to find something to tempt me. She's worked her way through Elizabeth David, and now we've moved on to Marguerite Patten's *One Thousand Favourite Recipes*.'

'Impressive. My dad cooks fry-ups. Barbara gives me biscuits, like I'm ten years old all over again.'

'We're always ten years old to them. Or five years old. Always their baby.'

'Poor baby, poor baby,' Robert mutters.

'What?'

'Oh, sorry. Just the mention of babies – reminds me of something peculiar I saw a few days ago in a hospital side-room. You're a shrink – does the name Mark Murray mean anything to you?'

It's all Vanessa can do to stop herself spontaneously combusting with ire. *Mean something to me?* He's my bloody boss! Blames me for an ex-patient falling under a bus – she survived, just – and he's punished me for it ever since! How do you know him?'

'Well, I don't. Just his name – it cropped up recently. Rose Pugh and Blanche Marston both seem to know him well.' He slides Vanessa's rejected Pot Noodle over the desk towards him. 'May I?' he says.

'Fill your boots.'

'Well, not my boots.' He points at the pining terrier slumped at his feet. 'It's for Utterson. Missing his mum, aren't you, son?' He offers the dog a forkful of noodles, which the dog ignores.

'Poor Utterson,' says Vanessa with feeling.

'Poor Barbara. Poor Ingrid. Poor Clive Marston. Poor bloody Lewis Morgan. Do you know, the villagers have completely closed ranks? No one's admitted to shoving that firework through his letterbox – he could have been killed! Oh, and poor the Barwood Three. Let's not forget about those poor sods. I trust you've seen this morning's paper?'

'I have,' says Vanessa. 'That journalist – Margaret

Whatsername – what a hypocrite! *The hate must stop.* Demanding a halt to hostilities, when she stirred stuff up between Llanfair and Barwood in the first place with her stupid opinion pieces!'

'I saw the vehicle driven by Marston's murderer,' Robert says. 'At least, I think I did. There was a white van parked in the layby in the woods early in the afternoon the day the Marstons disappeared. It might have been the same van as the one in the Texas Homecare car park, where Blanche was dumped. It might even be the same one Blanche told me she saw driving around Llanfair Heights, then parked outside Clive's offices the morning she and Marston disappeared . . .'

'Did you get the registration number?'

He shakes his head. 'Sadly not.'

'No way of proving anything, then. And what's the point, if the police believe they've got their men?'

'Do you believe they've got their men?'

Vanessa recalls the heated discussion she'd had with her mother that morning, just before leaving the house for work. Mum was flapping about in her peignoir and curlers, muttering what a disgrace they were, the miners of Barwood – killing Clive Marston, beating his wife, and after all the money Llanfair had raised for them! But what do you expect from Barwood, she'd scoffed. Animals, they were.

And that was when Vanessa lost the plot.

'You're born-and-bred Barwood yourself!' she'd screamed. 'How dare you, how fucking dare you? You're a disgrace, Mum. I'm ashamed of you!'

Her mother stared open-mouthed for a moment, then

stormed to the front door, flinging it open. 'Leave, then!' she shrieked. 'Go! If I'm such a disgrace, how can you bear living here? Get out of my house!'

Vanessa did as she was told, and . . . well, here we are.

They'd never spoken like that to each other before. Vanessa still feels sick.

'I think it's all too convenient,' she says, quietly. 'I think the miners have been stitched up. Are the arrests actually based on any real evidence?'

Robert shrugs. 'Not a clue. And I daresay the police will refuse to tell us. Tell you who might know, though. Barry Parry, at BBC Wales. That oily git knows everything.'

An idea is beginning to form in Vanessa's head – a way she and Robert might uncover some evidence. A way of proving her mother wrong. Or right. Of clearing innocent men. Or not. Either way, she has to do *something*, otherwise she'll go mad.

'When did the *Spotlight Cymru* filming start in your dad's pub?' she asks.

'Late last Monday morning.'

'Just as I thought. The day that Clive and Blanche Marston went missing. The afternoon you saw the white van in Llanfair Woods. The day before Debbie-Marie found Clive Marston's body. Was there any filming going on *outside* the pub?'

'Well yes, loads – at first. They were trying to get shots of the village . . .'

'There's a slim chance that they may have filmed the white van driving to Llanfair Woods. There might be footage of the person driving it, or the registration number!'

'But the van probably approached the woods from the north

end of the village, from the A5876 and Llanfair Lane – that's the most direct route. It wouldn't have had to drive past the pub at all.'

Vanessa shakes her head. 'The approach from Llanfair Lane and the A5876 was shut all day, because of a miners' protest and police barricade. I was driving between the school and the Dewi Sant Centre, and it added a good thirty minutes to each of my journeys, because I had to drive through the village and past the pub – I couldn't take my usual shortcut. There was no exit or entry point from Llanfair Lane, other than through the village. The van would have had to have driven past your pub to get to the woods – there's no other way! It's a long shot, but it might be worth giving BBC Wales a visit, and asking Barry Parry to look through his footage? Of course, there's no guarantee he'll put himself out for us.'

'He'll put himself out if there's something in it for him – like getting one over on *The South Wales Morning Post*. If Parry and his team identify the registration number from their own film footage, then hand it over to the police, maybe the police will locate it, find evidence that Clive and Blanche were kept in that van, *and* that it's not registered to any of the Barwood Three! What a scoop that would be.'

'So many ifs and maybes.' Vanessa slumps back in her seat. Stupid, stupid idea! 'I don't know what I was thinking.'

'At least you were thinking, which is more than can be said for me. But it's worth a shot, isn't it?'

'Oh, I don't know,' she says wearily. 'I'm not sure I've got the energy.'

'Did you have other plans for today?'

She shrugs. 'Just sitting here, waiting to be sacked.'

'Get your coat, Dr Bridges. I'll drive; you hold Utterson. We've got some scapegoats to free.'

46

Barbara

1.30 p.m., Ward H (Geriatrics), Prince of Wales Hospital, Cardiff North

She must have dropped off for a bit, but Lewis is still at her bedside, flicking through a copy of *Titbits Summer Special*.

'You've eaten all my grapes,' Barbara says, eyeing the empty stalks splayed on her bedside table. 'They were seedless, too.'

'I was hungry.' Lewis doesn't look up. 'There's a story in here about an Austrian aristocrat who claims he was kidnapped by little green men.'

'I suppose I don't really mind that much,' Barbara muses. 'I'm not at all hungry. My appetite's gone. To be expected, I suppose, after a heart attack.'

'A minor heart attack.' Lewis slaps *Titbits* shut, regarding Barbara sternly over the steel rim of his spectacles. 'From which, your nephew assures me, you are expected to make a full recovery.' He picks something out of his teeth. 'And you can tell him from me that these grapes are not seedless.'

'I'm dying,' says Barbara. 'You know it, I know it, Robert knows it, we all know it. My feeble heart or bonkers brain will get me sooner rather than later. There's no point in pretending any more.'

'Balls,' Lewis says. 'Nothing's going to get a tough old bird like you.'

'This tough old bird's had her wings badly burnt.'

'Well, this old rooster's had his home burnt down, but you don't hear me complaining.'

'Sorry. That was insensitive of me.'

Lewis shrugs. 'Oh, don't worry about it. I'm just glad I have someone sane to talk to. Rachel's constant whinging about Deborah Tunstall being the spawn of Satan is getting on my last nerve. I love her, really I do, but by God she's trying at times.'

Barbara feels a brief spark of her old energy returning. 'And when,' she says, turning her head from the wall to glare at him, 'are you and Brown Owl planning on coming clean? I can't keep your secret for ever, you know. People are beginning to talk.'

He grins. 'Let them,' he says. 'If they're making up stories about us, they're leaving some other poor sod alone.'

'It's not fair on Rachel.' Barbara speaks reprovingly. 'People put two and two together, making five. Our own Deborah, for example. One of the reasons she turned against you was because she believed the gossips, and came to the wrong conclusion. You have responsibilities. You both have reputations to uphold. And I don't understand why you can't just be honest. In this day and age, people are more open-minded. They *will* understand.'

Lewis holds up his bandaged arm. 'I am not ready, and neither is she. We've only just found each other, and for now we want to keep it between ourselves. You're the only other person who knows about it, so keep a lid on it, will you? For me?'

'I'm tired of dishonesty. Is anyone in this village of ours ever honest about anything?'

'Afraid not. Not me, not even you. In fact, I'd say you're the most dishonest of all.'

'I beg your pardon!'

'Well, if people will be so open-minded and understanding about my situation, what about yours? What's stopping you from admitting you fancy women?'

'They'll crucify me, Lewis – spread all sorts of stories.'

'They do that anyway. And it might not be so bad. Remember that tennis woman, Navratilova . . .'

'Given a terrible time by the newspapers! Whatever wasn't factual, they simply made up.'

'But she wasn't given a terrible time by the *people*. After she came out, Navratilova got a standing ovation at the American Open – and that was after she'd lost!'

'This is Llanfair, Lewis. Not New York.'

'Look, I'll strike a deal with you. You and I are getting on. And it's time you stood up for yourself, and stopped obsessing over other people as a distraction.'

'I'm not obsessed with anyone!'

'You're obsessed with the belief that Deborah Tunstall is a closet genius, and it's your job to reveal that genius to a cruel, misguided world. Ask yourself – what are you trying to conceal with that "reveal", Barbara? What are you trying to avoid?'

'Humph.'

'Look, I'll make a bargain with you. If Rachel agrees, I'll let my skeleton out of my closet, if you let your skeleton out of yours.'

'Rachel Wilmslow is your daughter,' Barbara sniffs. 'And she'll do as she's bloody well told.'

47

Vanessa

*1.30 p.m., inside Robert's yellow Ford estate, the car park
outside BBC Wales*

She hadn't intended to use his car as a confessional box on
wheels, but Robert Hargreaves has one of those faces that
invites people to divulge their life stories. Besides, he knew
something was up. No sooner had she buckled up in the
passenger seat than he turned to her and said:

'You've crossed your arms, you're scowling, and your hair's
more fluffed up than usual. Would you like to tell me about
it?'

He didn't need to ask her twice. It all came tumbling
out – every last bit of it – during their drive to BBC Wales.
She told him again about Miss X falling under a bus, Mark
Murray blaming her for it, then the decidedly dodgy relationship Murray appeared to have with Miss X's family (at
which point Robert chipped in that Mark Bloody Murray
seemed to have a dodgy relationship with everyone). And
then, she took a deep breath, and told him about the other
stuff – the anonymous phone calls she'd received at her
flat, and her mother mentioning a girl fitting Patient X's

description loitering outside Stockholm Villa the day the family car was vandalized.

She finishes speaking just as Robert reverses into a parking space. He turns off the engine, fumbles around in his pocket, and pulls out a packet of fags and a brass Zippo lighter.

'You mind?' he says.

She shakes her head.

'Okay,' he says, sparking up. 'So, you've just asked if I think your ex-patient was responsible for making funny phone calls, and has now tracked you down to your parents' home, and started stalking you.' He inhales deeply, and Vanessa wishes she was able to smoke without throwing up, turning green or passing out. 'Well, I very much doubt it.' He exhales. 'From what you've told me, she's twelve years old, would have to travel from Barwood by herself, and after the accident she was involved in, I can't imagine her parents letting her out of their sight for a moment, can you?'

'You're right. I'm nuts.'

'No.' He swivels in his seat to look at her square on. 'No, I don't think you're nuts at all. But you've had a really crap time, made even worse by the fact that Debbie-Marie went missing, and you'll be – well, really sensitive, watchful, alert . . .'

'Hypervigilant.'

'Yep, that too.'

She smiles at Robert. 'Thank you,' she says. 'The mind plays cruel games under stress. I'm a psychologist – I should remember these things.'

'You're also a human being. And it's not easy being object-ive when you're going through shit.'

She nods and ruffles Utterson's head. The dog had perked

up during their journey, slobbering affectionately over Vanessa's hand as she told her story. She's never thought of herself as a dog person, or an animal person, full stop. She wasn't allowed a pet as a child. Too noisy, too dirty, her mum always said. 'And your father's a handful enough as it is.'

'Did I touch a nerve?' Robert asks.

'Hmm?'

'You look like you're about to cry.'

'Oh . . . I was just thinking about my mum. We had a blazing row this morning.'

'I can't imagine the Lady Mayoress of Llanfair is an easy person to live with.'

'Well, I daresay, neither am I. I do love her, but she's a terrible snob. Forgotten who she is, where she comes from. Lives in a bubble of her own making.'

'Kept you in a bubble, too.'

'What do you mean by that?'

'Sent you to a different school. Never let you mix with anyone from the village.' He winds down his window, flicks his fag butt onto the BBC Wales car park.

She glares at him. 'Litter lout.'

'Although, there was one occasion,' he says, slowly, 'when you were allowed to mix with the likes of me. A picnic in the field behind your house, hosted by my aunt. Twenty years ago. You were six, I was eleven, as was Jane Gill. Blanche, Rose and Ingrid Tunstall were all thirteen. You were the youngest one there by a long way. You had a teddy clutched under your arm the whole time. I remember it, clear as anything.'

'Oh, God.' She rolls her eyes. 'Well, I don't remember much at all, but I know there was some drama.' She bites her lip.

'I'm sure it was after that afternoon that Mum and Dad became ridiculously protective of me. Something happened that made them think that there was some sort of threat or danger.'

Robert raises an eyebrow. 'A danger to *you*?'

'Well, yes. It would hardly be the other way around.'

'Dr Bridges,' he says, cautiously, 'do you really not remember anything about that afternoon? Anything at all?'

'Well.' She frowns. 'There was a row. A terrible row. And I think it was because I saw something I wasn't supposed to see and I opened my big mouth, but it's all so hazy and I don't know how much I've made up in my head. Besides, Mum swears I didn't see a man and a woman . . . oh, never mind.'

'There certainly was a row,' Robert says. 'I was there when it happened, hiding up a tree, keeping out of the way of Jane Gill, who was determined to kick the crap out of me. Blanche Marston – Blanche Wilkins as she was back then, and Rose Pugh, née Ellis, were at the bottom of the tree trunk, standing guard. Not because they felt any loyalty to me, you understand. Blanche just hated Jane Gill. Hated most of the other girls, in fact.'

'No change there, then.'

'Blanche is okay,' Robert says briskly. 'She's misunderstood, that's all.'

'But you understand her, of course.'

He frowns. 'What's that supposed to mean?'

'Nothing. It doesn't mean anything. Look, we were talking about the picnic.'

'Yes, we were.'

'You were up a tree.'

'Yes, I was. And then all hell broke loose.'

'I know that. But why?'

He gives her an odd look. 'No one's ever told you?'

'No!'

'Okay.' He opens his door. 'Well, let's go and see Barry Parry. We've got just enough time to . . .'

She grips his arm. 'Not so fast! Told me what, Robert? Tell me, please!'

He slumps back in his seat. 'Okay,' he says at last, nodding his head. 'So, you'd buggered off by yourself during a game of hide and seek, and no one knew where you were. Then you burst through the brambles – like a bat out of hell – under the tree I was hiding in. You'd been picking blackberries – loads of the things – and eaten them, too. Covered from head to foot, you were, in blackberry juice – an absolute mess – screaming and crying about a man with a bare bottom doing something terrible with a beautiful lady who had a dead fox around her neck. You kept shouting: *The naughty man was pushing his willy against the pretty lady; I could see his hanky sticking out of his pocket – his hanky had his name on it . . .* But before you could say anything more, Blanche yelled at you to shut up, that you were a baby talking rubbish, that nobody wanted you there at the picnic, because you were such a pain in the arse. That even your own mother couldn't stand you, and that was why she'd left you and your dad. And that was when you went for her.'

'*I* went for *her*?'

'Tried to strangle her. I'd never seen anything like it. You were like a wild animal. It took two of us – me and Rose – to pull you off. For a six-year-old kid, you were bloody strong. Blanche may have been seven years older than you, but there were red fingerprint marks on her neck. Everyone was shaken up – Rose in particular. White as a sheet, she was. Couldn't stop shaking, she even threw up.'

'My God! But . . . let's go back a minute. What did Blanche mean about my mum leaving me and Dad? My mother has never done any such thing! My mother was there the whole afternoon – she told me so!'

He shrugs. 'Well, if that's what your mother says, maybe she was at the picnic. Somewhere. Anyway, Barbara came over, and I told her what happened. But she wasn't cross with you. She was furious with Blanche, because Blanche was so much older and should have known better than to goad you like that. And that was when Blanche turned on Barbara, claiming that she was the one who'd attacked her. All out of spite, because Barbara had crossed her. You were off the hook, all but forgotten in the aftermath . . .'

'Didn't you or Rose stand up for Barbara? You saw what really happened!'

He shrugs. 'Rose was in no state to say anything. She was really rattled by what you'd done – couldn't stop shaking and retching for the rest of the afternoon. And Barbara gave me a funny look – like she wanted me to go along with it all. She was prepared to take the rap, I think, to protect you and, perhaps, the identity of the couple you'd seen, though we all knew who you were talking about . . .'

'But why did your aunt protect *me*? She barely knew me! Oh, God – no wonder Mum and Dad kept me apart from you all after that. All my playdates were supervised, my friends vetted because my own mother thought I was a psychopath. And what about poor Barbara! All the villagers turning on her . . .'

'Well, not for that long, as it happened. A few weeks later, Blanche's dad and Rose's mum – the couple you'd seen *in flagrante*, by the sounds of it – were killed in a car accident. My aunt helped pay for Rose's mum's funeral because the family was skint, and all was forgiven.' He shakes his head. 'Like a stack of dominoes it was, after that. One thing after another for Blanche and Rose.'

'What do you mean?'

'Both were only children; both had one parent left. Both lost that remaining parent three years later. Blanche's mother died of a broken heart when Blanche was sixteen. Rose's dad dropped dead from a stroke around the same time.'

'Blimey! Something similar happened to her husband, too. Poor Rose!'

'Yep, poor Rose. All very tragic, but life goes on. Llanfair,' Robert adds with feeling, 'moves on from grief very quickly.'

'All very tragic,' Vanessa echoes. 'Yes.'

'Are you all right, Dr Bridges?'

She nods. 'I needed to know. I've been living a lie. That's also tragic, don't you think? And Robert, for goodness' sake, can you drop the Dr Bridges crap and just call me Vanessa?'

48

Debbie

4 p.m., Flat 4B, Aneurin Bevan Estate

That girl I saw this morning – the one in the smocked dress standing outside the Dewi Sant Centre. I can't stop thinking about her. Maybe it's so I'll stop thinking about myself and the terrible things I've done and the bloody awful mess I've got myself into. But I'm not sure it's that. She unnerved me, she did. She looked . . . angry and lost, like how I feel inside but even worse, if that's possible.

Nobody else saw her. Mam was too busy sucking her teeth, Rose Pugh was busy being all forgiving, and Dr Bridges kept writing pages of stuff about me in her notepad. Bad stuff, I'll bet. Which made me wonder whether Dr Bridges had written bad stuff about that girl in the past.

Anyway, when Mam dragged me back outside (she's dragging me everywhere at the moment) the girl was nowhere to be seen.

'Where's she gone?' I asked.

Mam stared at me. 'Who?'

'The girl who was outside in the car park just now. The one that kept staring at me and Dr Bridges. You must have seen her!'

Mam yanked me to her side by the elbow, so hard it made

my shoulder hurt. 'Stop it!' she hissed in my face. 'Just stop it! You and your lies! I don't know what to do with you any more, Debbie! I give up,' she wailed. 'I completely give up!'

Mam never used to use the eff word at me, however angry I'd make her. But she's said it to me a lot these last few days. She's furious – angrier than I've ever seen her, and I know that I disgust her, because she can't look me in the eye. Like she doesn't want to admit I exist. Like she wishes I'd never been born.

So, I'm back in the house all alone in my room, playing with some conkers I found on the common, to replace the ones I stamped on. Mam's out cleaning, so she says, so I can make as much mess and noise as I like. I want to make lots of mess and noise. I want to smash everything up. I looked in the tool drawer in the kitchen, and found a hammer that Mam uses when she has to fix something, because she hasn't a man to do it since Dad ran away, and there's always something to fix in our house. Always something that needs a damn good thump.

So here I am THUMP bashing the brains out of conker number one THUMP and seeing its creamy brains ooze out of its shiny shell and I'm thinking THUMP of Blanche and Carrie-Anne THUMP THUMP and Lucy THUMP and Susan THUMP THUMP THUMP and that I have to go back to school next Monday and face Mr Griffiths and Bug-eyed Thomas, and I have to be taught by myself, Mam says, because none of the mams want their kids stuck with me THUMP because I'm bad, because I'm bad THUMP THUMP, because I'm bad I'm a psycho I am a psycho psycho psycho . . .

And worst of all, I've lost Barbara's trust. And The Vicar

will hate my guts as well. And I care more than I imagined about that, which makes me hate myself even more.

THUMP.

I wish I was dead.

SATURDAY, 22 SEPTEMBER 1984

THE SOUTH WALES MORNING POST

Barwood Three Released

By Margaret Lawrence,
Welsh Affairs Correspondent

In a dramatic development late last night, Uskshire Police released the three men arrested on suspicion of Clive Marston's murder without charge, citing new evidence from television footage filmed on the day of Marston's disappearance.

WPC Jane Gill, a resident of Llanfair and close friend of the Marston family, said: 'Thanks to tireless investigative work by Uskshire Police, and a tip-off by BBC Wales's Barry Parry, the three men previously arrested on suspicion of Mr Marston's disappearance and murder, and Mrs Marston's abduction and assault, have been released without charge. At this delicate stage of our investigations, we ask the public to avoid unhelpful speculation, and to respect the privacy of Mr Marston's widow and children. As our investigations continue, and out of respect for the Marston family, BBC Wales have kindly agreed to postpone the screening of their *Spotlight Cymru* special, *Villages at War!* indefinitely.

Mr Barry Parry commented: 'I simply did what any responsible journalist would do – fought tooth and nail for the truth. The miners of Barwood and their families have suffered quite enough as it is, without a potential miscarriage of justice adding to their nightmare.'

Barwood resident Deirdre Crowdass told *The South Wales Morning Post*, 'Thank the lord for Barry Parry. The residents of Llanfair have a lot to answer for, stoking up hysteria with their false accusations. They can shove their dancing girls and Tom Jones impersonators where the sun don't shine. We don't need charity – we just need justice and common sense to prevail!'

Lady Mayoress of Llanfair, Gwendoline Bridges, was unavailable for comment.

49

Robert

7 a.m., the Llanfair Arms

Barry Bastard Parry.

Robert stares up at his bedroom ceiling. If he disliked Parry before, he loathes the tosser now. Taking all the credit for freeing the Barwood Three, when it was Vanessa Bridges who'd done all the work, all the thinking, the putting two and two together, actually making four. And Parry hadn't been remotely responsive at first. 'What can I do for you two losers?' he'd sneered, as Robert and Vanessa were ushered into BBC Wales's newsroom by Parry's PA.

'You should listen to what they have to say,' the PA stage-whispered to Parry, whose shiny-suited, slippery arse was perched on the edge of his news desk. He was holding court with two younger males, equally slippery-suited and sneery, one of them wearing sunglasses. 'There must be a factory churning these arseholes out,' Robert said a little too loudly, but Vanessa – who must have heard him – didn't crack a smile. She was too busy staring at Parry, who gave her a quick once over in return, clearly deciding she wasn't his type, before turning his attention to his PA – a good-looking woman in her mid-thirties, skirt-suited and designer-spectacled, with a sleek blonde ponytail and patent stilettoes that clip-clopped when she walked.

Parry looked the PA up and down, eyes lingering on her cleavage. The PA was having none of it. 'The Genito-Urinary clinic phoned, the prescription's ready,' she said. 'You need to use the ointment twice a day, and no sexual intercourse in the meantime.'

The younger men sniggered.

'Thank you, Janet,' Parry replied, not missing a beat. 'You'll need to use the ointment as well, of course.'

'Of course,' the PA smiled amiably. 'Well, I'll leave you to it.' And she clip-clopped out of the newsroom, whispering 'wanker' under her breath. Parry responded with an equine whinny. The younger men sniggered again.

Parry cast his lizard eyes over Robert's leather trousers. 'This had better be worth it,' he said. 'I'm a busy man, and I daresay,' a smirk played on the edge of his lips, 'you've important business pulling pints. And you . . .' He waved dismissively at Vanessa. 'Who the hell are you?'

'I'm a psychologist,' Vanessa replied. 'I treat the mentally ill and personality-disordered.'

'Fascinating,' Parry said with a smile, but his smile didn't reach his eyes. 'You're a shrink, no less.' He leaned back, folding his arms behind his head. 'Have you come to analyse me?'

'No,' Vanessa replied. 'I have neither the time nor inclination. We're here to ask whether you have any footage from last Monday's filming. Any footage from outside the Llanfair Arms.'

'I might,' Parry replied. 'But I'm not sure I've the time or inclination to share it with you.'

'If you help us,' Robert chipped in, 'you could have one hell of a scoop on your hands. You might even free three innocent men!'

'What if I don't give a toss about freeing three innocent men?'

'You will when I tell you that Margaret Lawrence from *The South Wales Morning Post* has wind of this,' Vanessa lied, 'and you don't want her getting an exclusive before you, do you?'

Parry sat up, meerkat-like. 'Wind of what?'

'The case of the white Ford Transit van,' Robert said. 'The van we believe may have been involved in the kidnapping of Blanche and Clive Marston, and of transporting Marston's body to Llanfair Woods. The van that may save three innocent men from a dreadful miscarriage of justice.'

Or prove them guilty, depending on whether the van turned out to be registered to one of the men in custody or a connection of theirs. But it was worth the risk, surely?

'Margaret Lawrence – wasn't she the winner of last year's Welsh Investigative Journalist of the Year Award?' Vanessa mused, stroking her chin.

'That's right!' Robert replied, giving his thigh a hearty slap. 'And Barry Parry was runner-up, if I remember correctly. That must have been very disappointing for you . . .'

But Parry was already on the move, barking orders to the young men in slippery suits. 'All the footage from *Spotlight Cymru* – I need it. Now! And for Christ's sake, Gavin, take those bloody sunglasses off, you absolute bell end.'

Vanessa's hunch proved correct. Hours after their visit to the BBC newsroom, Parry burst into the Llanfair Arms to tell them that not only had footage of the van been located on the *Spotlight Cymru* recording, the van itself had been reported, abandoned, outside a Cardiff kebab shop, a pair of men's tasselled loafers inside. Parry's anonymous source at Uskshire Constabulary (Jane Gill – Robert would bet his life on it) also let slip that the loafers had been identified by Blanche Marston as those belonging to Clive. The shoes were unique, Blanche had explained, thanks to their built-up insoles. And by the way, she was certain the van was the same as the one she'd seen parked outside Clive's office, and the one cruising up and down Llanfair Heights the days before he went missing – driven by a man with wild, curly hair sticking out from under some sort of hat. There was something about his mannerisms that seemed oddly familiar, though.

Why, Robert fleetingly wondered, had Blanche not mentioned those extra details before?

But, crucially for the Barwood Three, the van was filmed gliding past the Llanfair Arms in the direction of Llanfair Woods at 12.50 p.m. on Monday, 10 September, fake numberplates in full view. The day Clive disappeared, the day before Debbie-Marie discovered his body – a date when the three falsely accused men were picketing outside the Barwood Colliery, with legions of witnesses (including police) to vouch for them. The driver of the van, frustratingly, was unidentifiable – their face and hair obscured by a large plastic rain bonnet. But at least three innocent men had been reunited with their families; a dreadful miscarriage of justice avoided.

When Parry burst into the pub with his news, Vanessa was sipping a shandy. She'd popped into the Llanfair Arms to see whether Robert had an update on Barbara's progress. Robert offered her a drink on the house, but she insisted on paying anyway. He ushered her to the best table in the pub – Clive Marston's favourite, naturally – and sat on a stool opposite, trying to summon the courage to ask her out. Then Parry whirled in with his big swinging dick of an ego, and the moment was lost. Vanessa kept her head down and sat in silence, until Parry departed in a fug of Drakkar Noir and Marlboro Red.

After he'd gone, Robert turned to Llewelyn's cage at his side. 'Say "wanker",' he said.

Vanessa laughed. 'Does he speak?'

'Used to. Hasn't since Mum died. Used to copy everything people said – you had to be careful around Llewelyn. Anyway, congratulations on your hunch – you've saved three innocent men, so if you fancy celebrating . . .'

But she was already standing up, slinging her bag over her shoulder. 'I need to go,' she said. 'See you around, Robert.'

He frantically fumbled for the words to explain his relationship with Blanche Marston, that it wasn't at all how it seemed. But too late. She'd gone, leaving the faint aroma of violets behind her.

'Yeah,' Robert mumbled into his pint. 'See you around.'

Robert stumbles into the bathroom. It's an ungodly hour, 7.15 a.m. – far too early for him, but he'd promised Dai that he'd help get the pub ready for the Saturday lunchtime punters. He cleans his teeth, rinses his mouth and spits, assessing himself in the mirror. Bloody wreck of a man, he is. No wonder Vanessa Bridges wants nothing to do with him, after having to look at his stupid clown face across that table yesterday evening . . .

That table. Clive Marston's favoured haunt.

The last time he'd seen Marston at *that table* was Friday, 7

September, the day Barbara found The Vicar unconscious on the vicarage front path. The pub that night was buzzing with gossip, especially at *that table*, where the Marstons were sitting with Nurse Rose Pugh and Rachel Wilmslow.

'If I'd not been at my Barwood shop at lunchtime, none of this would have happened!' Rachel Wilmslow whined for the umpteenth time.

'I saw him just hours before.' Blanche shook her head. 'He was picking up his newspaper delivery from his front path. I pulled up outside the vicarage, and he told me to piss off and park my Volvo up my greedy husband's arse.'

Everyone, apart from Clive Marston, laughed. 'You've got to love the miserable old bugger,' Blanche said.

'I was putting flowers on Mammy's grave when Utterson started barking,' Rose added wistfully. 'Just a stone's throw away from that poor, poor man.'

'Can we move on?' Clive droned. 'You donuts are doing my head in.'

They all looked up at Robert. He was collecting their glasses, taking his time, listening in.

'Same again,' Marston barked.

'You can come up to the bar and order like everyone else,' Robert replied.

'I'm not everyone else, though, am I? God,' he said, loud enough to be heard throughout the pub, 'we need a wine bar in Llanfair. A classy boozer, with table service and continental beverages.'

The Llanfair Arms fell silent. Dai, polishing a pint glass behind the bar, audibly growled.

'Don't be an arse, Clive,' Blanche hissed. She turned to

Robert. 'I'll come to the bar and order now.' She glared at her husband. 'Behave!' she barked.

'Ooooh!' Marston draped an arm around his wife's shoulders, hand creeping stealthily towards her left breast. 'Being quite the dominatrix, aren't we, Blanche? My lucky night tonight, eh?'

She shook him off. 'Stop being a twat,' she said. 'Same again, everyone?'

The night wore on. And on. The pub became drunker and darker. Robert watched the table dynamics changing – Rose Pugh in deep conversation with Clive Marston; Clive sidling up to Blanche, Blanche giving Clive short shrift; then Clive with his arms around Rachel Wilmslow, pinching her backside when Blanche wasn't looking, and Rachel whispering in his ear. And Robert picking up their empty glasses – dozens and dozens of empty glasses – wandering through the aimless chit-chat, the cigarette smoke and pffut pffut pffut of darts lobbed at corkboard, wondering: *Is this it? Is this my life? Is this the life my mother wanted for me?*

'Robert!'

He's roused from his ruminations by Dai – downstairs in the bar, yelling blue murder. Robert dries his hands on his underpants and hurtles down the stairs.

'Robert!'

'I'm coming! What's up?'

Dai, standing in the middle of the lounge, Hoover hose coiled around his feet, is toothlessly mouthing, 'He speaks! He speaks!', and pointing, with a trembling hand, at Llewelyn's cage.

'Listen!' Dai says in awe. 'Robert, listen!'

Robert listens.

Silence.

'Come on!' Dai shouts. 'Come on, you daft bird! I heard you! I heard you talk!'

'Dad . . .'

'I'm not hearing things!' Dai points at Robert's nether regions, shaking his head. 'What the bloody hell are you doing, Rob, walking around like that? And why is the arse of your underpants wet?'

'Well, I came downstairs in a hurry,' Robert replies. 'I thought you were ill. I thought you'd collapsed, or something.' He turns to make his way back upstairs. 'I'll go put some clothes on . . .'

'Clive!'

That squawk, that unmistakable, beautiful squawk that Robert hasn't heard in a year, has missed so much at times it's hurt, is uttering Clive Marston's name. Not his, not Dai's, not his mother's, but Clive bloody Marston's.

'Clive! Let's be naughty, Clive! Let's be naughty at your office, Clive! Monday morning, Clive, Clive, Clive, Clive, Clive!'

50

Debbie

8 a.m., Church of St James the Lesser, Llanfair Lane

I'm having a serious chat with God, because no other bugger's talking to me. It's not much fun being an outcast. And I'm cast out from everything, I am. I'm suspended from school until Monday, and then I'll be taught all by myself until Mr Griffiths decides what to do with me. Whatever he does, I daresay I won't be given a biscuit this time. Mam reckons he'll expel me, and that will mean I'll be sent to a school for very naughty girls. A boarding school. That might be fun. Or it might be hell. Either way, it'll be better than staying here.

Earlier this morning, I took a look at the vicarage, or rather what's left of it. The downstairs is black with soot, but the shell of the house is stone, and stone is strong, so maybe that means it can be rebuilt. I wish Barbara was here, so that I could ask her. But Barbara's still ill, and I don't think she's too happy with me at the moment.

I shuddered as I walked through the graveyard. Too close for comfort. It could have been The Vicar or Barbara being laid to rest in the newly dug grave by the wall, with the jackdaws picking worms and stones from the mound of soil next to it. But it's there for Clive Marston, poor sod, once what's left of his body is buried. And I still have his watch and his fifty-pound note. I know I should give them back to Blanche Marston, 'cos, strictly speaking, they belong to her. But I'm keeping them for a rainy day. I'll have plenty of those in the future, I know – far, far more than Blanche ever will. So, I've squirrelled the watch and the money away in my ballerina jewellery box, along with my owl pellet bones and Utterson's whisker and the Mr Strong charm from Dad's keyring.

I wish Dad would come home. Mam will really need the company, once I'm gone.

When I went inside the church, it was packed with flowers – the altar vases were full of them, and someone had hung garlands of red and white roses along the back of each pew. There'll be a wedding later I expect, though the place was empty when I arrived. I walked up the aisle and curtsied. I felt a bit of a twit, truth be told, and didn't know what to say. I just waved at the ceiling and shouted, 'All right up there, God?'

My voice bounced back, and I seemed very small and alone in that big stone space, with its hundreds of years of comings and goings: of births, deaths and marriages, of happiness, sadness, wailing babies and weeping widows, and all the stuff of life that happens in between. Someone had lit lots of candles, which I thought was a very nice touch, though the flames all flickered and sputtered whenever a draft rattled the battered oak door.

Then Rose Pugh burst in. I turned with a jump at the noise,

to see that Brown Owl was already there – she must have crept in when my back was turned – and was sitting on the very back pew, head bowed, deep in prayer. Rose shuffled past, ignoring her, then marched down the aisle before making a spectacular curtsy when she got to the altar. She turned, gave a nod to Brown Owl, and made a beeline for me.

'Hello, Debbie,' she said with a smile. 'Been here long?'

I stared at her, open-mouthed. 'You're talking to me!'

She frowned. 'Well, why on earth wouldn't I be talking to you?'

'Because of what I've done. Because you're Blanche Marston's best mate, and I didn't tell the police about Clive being dead in the woods.'

'Of course I'm talking to you, Debbie!' She laughed. 'To err is human, to forgive is divine. Alexander Pope, I believe.'

'Is he a mate of yours?' I asked.

She shook her head. 'Not exactly. Can I sit with you for a bit? It would have been my mammy's birthday today. She was fifteen days away from being thirty-three years old when she died. The same age I am now. I could do with some company, to be honest. A nice, friendly face to talk to.'

I slid along the pew I was sitting on to make room for her. She sat next to me, folding her neat pink hands in her lap. She was wearing her nurse's uniform with her stethoscope around her neck – even on a Saturday. She must be a very good nurse. Always on duty, even when she's not.

'I'm sorry,' I said. 'That must have very been hard, losing your mam so young.'

'Yes, it was.'

'Do you miss her?'

'I miss her every single day. Do you know why she died, Debbie?'

Well, I did. Of course I did. Everyone in Llanfair knows why Eleri Ellis and Herbert Wilkins died that night.

'Because Herbert Wilkins was drunk and driving too fast, and he killed himself and your mam when he skidded around a corner and crashed into a tree. They'd been celebrating winning a choir competition. It's Llanfair folklore, that's what it is. The greatest tragedy the village has ever known, my mam says, because two families were left half-orphaned . . .'

'Mine and Blanche's,' Rose says, sadly. 'But you're from a single-parent family too, aren't you, Debbie?'

'You know I am.'

'And so was your mum.'

'Yes, she was.'

'Her own mother drank herself to death.'

I blinked at her. 'Is this meant to be making me feel better?' I said. 'Because I'm sorry to say, it's not working.'

But Rose didn't seem to hear me. She just carried on staring ahead. A funny little smile crossed her lips. 'Then you know how I feel, perhaps. You've had a less than perfect childhood. You and I have something in common, after all.'

'Yes, I suppose we do.'

'Even before Mammy was killed, I used to come here most days. I liked to sit and look up at the altar window. It gave me comfort. Do you have a special place that gives you comfort, Debbie?'

I didn't have to think about it. 'Barbara Pritchard's house,' I said. 'Her lounge, to be exact. On the settee, with Utterson curled up on my lap. But you – how can you feel comforted here? That's such a gruesome window! And why did you need comfort even before you lost your mam?'

'In truth, Debbie, I had already lost her. She'd been lost a long time before she died.'

'Lost? How?'

But Rose didn't answer. Just pointed at the window, and said, 'Do you know what that's all about?'

'The Seven Deadly Sins,' I replied with a shudder. 'Gives me the willies, it does, all that hellfire and tortured sinners writhing around in the flames, and Adam and Eve standing naked above them in the Garden of Eden, and the angels looking dead smug as they fly around heaven, looking down on it all, and that great big tree growing up through the middle . . .'

'The tree from which the apple fell. The apple that Eve gave to Adam. The apple that made all of us sinners. Can you name each of the Seven Deadly Sins, Debbie?'

I nodded. I wanted to say: *Not you, too! The bloody Vicar kept banging on about that when he was lying at the bottom of his stairs.*

'Pride, greed, wrath, envy, lust, gluttony and sloth,' I said. 'Which one's your favourite?'

But Rose didn't reply. 'Such a beautiful window,' she said, in such a quiet voice that I had to lean in to hear her. 'Look at it closely, Debbie. In all the chaos, there's an order of sorts. The red, orange and yellow of hellfire below, reaching up to the green grass in the garden of Eden, which in turn reaches up to the blue, indigo and violet of heaven above, and all us sinners at various stages of our journey, the tree of life running through the centre of it all . . .' She suddenly grabbed my hand. 'Your thumb!' she cried. 'It's swollen and red!'

'I hit it,' I said. 'With a hammer.' I bit my lip. 'An accident,' I lied.

'But it might be broken! Does it hurt? Can it bend? Let me . . .'

'No!' I said, pulling my hand away.

'Your mammy should take you to hospital! Promise me you'll get her to do that?'

'Yes,' I mumbled.

'It's a nasty injury.'

'It's fine. I'm fine.'

Rose narrowed her eyes. 'Well, you're not really, arc you?'

I gulped a little, tried to speak, but swallowed the words down with my tears. Rose patted my hand. 'It'll all be all right,' she said. 'You'll see. You remind me of me at your age, Debbie. You should come here more often, you know. I came here a lot when I was young, not just looking for comfort, but answers, too.'

'Answers to what?'

'Oh,' she shrugged. 'About life. You know, the way young people try to work out how the world works. Why humans are the way they are, and what should be done about it.'

I liked Rose more than ever, now. She made me feel all tingly inside, a bit like Barbara does. Safe and important, listened to. Liked.

'I'd sit here,' she said, 'often on this very pew, and I'd look up at that window and think to myself, well, for as long as someone can create something as beautiful and meaningful as this out of all of that evil, the world can't be such a bad place after all.' She cleared her throat. '"A wholesome tongue is a tree of life, but perverseness in it crushes the spirit." Proverbs 15:4.'

I groaned inside. Another bloody quote. 'Which old man said that?'

'God,' she replied. 'Lovely words, don't you think?'

I didn't, but didn't want to say so. 'I don't understand what they mean,' I shrugged, taking a Caramac bar out of my pocket and starting to unwrap it.

She snatched it out of my hand. 'Oh, Debbie,' she cried, shaking her head. 'Can't you get through a few hours of the day without eating? And sit up straight when I'm talking to you. Slouching around like that! You'll end up an absolute layabout, just like your father.'

'My father? You knew him?'

'Well, yes, when I lived in Barwood, of course! I was the district nurse there and I knew you, too, but you'd have been too young to remember.'

'Did you like him?'

She thought for a while. 'Yes, Debbie, I did. Even though,' she chuckled, 'he was a lazy old so-and-so. All that business about wanting to live off the land – he just wanted an easy life and to live off the public purse. That said, he had a kind heart, just like yours, and we were all shocked when he upped and left you and your poor old mammy.'

And then she slipped my Caramac bar into her pocket. To give to bloody Susan later, I'll bet.

Things got a bit awkward after that. We sat in silence for quite a long time, until Nurse Pugh knelt down and said, 'Well, I'd better say a prayer for poor Mammy.' And she patted my arm and said, 'Look after yourself, Debbie. I'm always here, if you need a friendly shoulder to cry on.'

I took the hint and shifted myself to another pew, to give her some privacy. So here I am, trying to pray to God. But I can't, because Brown Owl and Nurse Rose Pugh are making it impossible to concentrate, what with their muttering all manner of weird stuff under their breath.

I'll just have to slip out, as quiet as a mouse, my own prayers going unheard.

51

Vanessa

9 a.m., Stockholm Villa, Llanfair Lane

Vanessa is at the kitchen sink, scraping burnt bits off her toast, trying to ignore the slap-slap-slap of her mother's mule slippers. Gwendoline Bridges is in full force this morning: strutting from breakfast bar to butler sink to cafetière and back again, banging down crockery, rattling cutlery – pointedly ignoring her daughter, as she has for the past three days.

'Clive bloody Marston!' she barks, wafting the sleeves of her silk peignoir in a fit of pique. Vanessa's father, perched on a stool, hiding behind *The South Wales Morning Post*, emits an affirming grunt. 'Even in death,' Gwen Bridges continues, 'that beast wrecks *everything*.' She tenderly touches her husband's back. 'More coffee, John?' she enquires, tilting her head coquettishly.

'No ta, love.'

'Actually, I'd like a coffee,' Vanessa says. 'Why don't you sit down, Mum, and I'll make one for both of us?'

'I was talking to your father. I don't recall addressing you.'

'Mum, you've ignored me for three days solid. Isn't it time . . .'

'We are not at home to Little Miss Sweary, Vanessa. I have never, ever been spoken to like that in my entire life. Using the eff word – and under my own roof!'

'*Our* own roof,' her father adds, lowering his paper. 'Not your finest hour, Ness. Your mother was very upset by your language. True, she's a bloody awful snob at times, but even she doesn't deserve to be spoken to like that.'

'Thank you, John. Now, would you like me to butter your baps for you?'

'No ta, love, I can butter my own.'

Vanessa closes her eyes.

'No cutting your bap with a knife, John! We break bread rolls with our fingers in this house. Using a knife is common, and we're not common.'

'Right you are, love.'

'*But we are common!*' Vanessa explodes. 'Look, what I said three days ago was out of order, I admit it, but can we stop pretending to be people we're not? You're both Barwood, born and bred. Nothing to be ashamed of. And I'm . . . well, we all know what I am. And that *is* something to be ashamed of.'

Her father carefully folds his paper, places it on the breakfast bar at his side. 'What do you mean, Ness?' he asks.

'What happened at that picnic, twenty years ago. And there I was, thinking you and Mum were being over-protective, trying to keep me away from the local riff-raff, when it turns out that *I* was the riff-raff, and you were trying to keep the other kids away from *me*.'

'Ness,' says her father, 'you're not making sense.'

'I tried to strangle Blanche Marston. Or Blanche Wilkins,

as she was back then. It took two other kids – Robert Hargreaves and Rose Ellis – to pull me off.'

Her father nods his head. 'That's right.'

'And Barbara Pritchard took the blame for it all.'

'And so she should!' her mother cries. 'She was meant to be keeping an eye on you!'

'What about *you*? You were there! Weren't you supposed to be keeping an eye on me? My own bloody mother?'

'Language, Vanessa! I will not engage with . . .'

'Ness,' her father interrupts, gently touching Vanessa's arm. 'Sit down, love, there's a good girl. And Gwen, we need to stop the pretence. For everyone's sake. Vanessa, your mother was not at that ruddy picnic. She was . . . indisposed.'

'Because she'd left us both, isn't that right, Dad? That's what Blanche said to me the afternoon of the picnic, according to Robert Hargreaves. She shouted that nobody liked me, not even my own mother, and that's why she left us – you and me . . .'

Her father shakes her head. 'Now, that part *is* nonsense, because both of us left you that afternoon, Ness.'

'You *both* left me? You both hated me?'

'No, no. Nothing like that. Look, Barbara Pritchard agreed to look after you, as both of us were . . . elsewhere.'

'But I remember – I remember it vividly! Mum coming up to me, telling me off about the state of my dress, dragging me home and washing my hands . . .'

Her father shakes his head. 'That didn't happen. It was Barbara Pritchard who brought you back here, and your mum – well, she got very angry with Barbara and shouted at her, and they've not spoken since.'

'What? Then why do I remember . . .'

He puts his arm around her. 'Love, you're a psychologist. You know as well as anyone that we misremember things, especially if those things are unhappy. The brain fills in the blanks. Your mum wasn't there, because she was . . .'

'I'd had a miscarriage,' her mother blurts. 'I needed hospital treatment, and was let out that afternoon. Barbara and her sister Lynette were hosting that bloody stupid awful picnic. Your dad told them my situation – in strictest confidence, of course – and they agreed to look after you, because that afternoon was when he was coming to pick me up. I'd been home less than an hour when the doorbell went, and Barbara handed you over, explaining what had happened – that you'd seen something unmentionable, had blurted out what you'd seen in front of the older children, and Blanche Wilkins had said something terrible to you, and you'd attacked her in response. I had a right go at Barbara, I'm afraid, and you were inconsolable. I suppose that's why Barbara took the blame for what you'd done. You were upset, I was upset, and I don't think Barbara anticipated the way the villagers would react to her admittance of guilt. I mean, the poor woman was ostracized for weeks . . .'

'The unmentionable thing I saw,' Vanessa whispers. 'I'm pretty certain I saw a couple having sex.'

Her mother nods. 'Everyone knew you were talking about Herbert Wilkins and Eleri Ellis, including Blanche – hence her excessive reaction.' She shakes her head. 'And then, just a few weeks later, Herbert and Eleri were killed in that terrible car accident. It was after that – when Barbara offered to pay for Eleri's funeral – that the villagers finally forgave her. I know I should have spoken out in Barbara's defence at the time, but I just couldn't face it – I had enough on my plate, what with losing the baby, and then being told I couldn't get pregnant again. I wasn't at all well, Ness. Wasn't myself for quite a while. I daresay Barbara has never forgiven me for the way I spoke to her. I wouldn't, if I was her. It's probably why she's selling the field behind this house for development. Getting her own back, even if it has taken twenty-odd years.'

'Mum, I'm so sorry.'

Vanessa's mother pats her hand. 'You've nothing to be sorry for. Except for using foul language.'

'I'm sorry you lost the baby. I'm sorry for what I said the other day, I'm sorry for what I did at the picnic, you must . . . you must both wonder what sort of person I am. I'm a rubbish psychologist and, it turns out, a rubbish person all round. No wonder you kept me apart from the other kids, you must have thought it was only a matter of time before I attacked one of them, too.'

'Don't be ridiculous!' Vanessa's mother hauls her into the mounds of her silk peignoir. 'You're not a rubbish person at all. You were a frightened little girl. I'd been away for three nights, nobody told you why, and then that horrible Blanche said that I'd abandoned you and your dad. But you see, people didn't talk about miscarriage back then. No wonder you lashed out.' She starts to cry. 'I lost all sense of proportion, for a while. Your dad and I – we got over-protective. We didn't stop you going into the village to play with the other children because we were snobs, or because we thought you'd attack them. We were frightened, that's all, after losing the baby and being told we could never have another. We – well, me mainly – I was terrified I might lose you, too.'

When Robert arrives an hour later, Vanessa is showered and dressed.

'There's a funny-looking car on the drive,' says her mother. 'Banana yellow. Ugly thing. Either of you expecting company?'

Her father looks up from his paper. 'It's that boy,' he says, 'from the Llanfair Arms. Nice chap. Looks a bit like Bob Geldof, on a good day. Used to work in insurance, been a bit aimless since his mum passed away. Rumour has it Blanche Marston's been having her wicked way with the poor sod. You seeing him, Ness?'

Vanessa's heart skips a beat as Robert Hargreaves emerges from his Ford estate, leathered of trouser and tousled of hair. She channels her inner Debbie-Marie Tunstall, rolling her eyes and muttering:

'No. Not really.'

52

Robert

10.15 a.m., inside his Ford estate

Robert is cruising in his car beside the woman of his dreams. He feels alive, giddy with life, the wind in his hair, a song in his heart – well, ear-worming its way into his head, as only 'I Just Called to Say I Love You' can. His gamble – turning up unannounced at Stockholm Villa – has paid off. Vanessa Bridges is in his passenger seat, laughing girlishly at his jokes, the outline of her Titian waves lit by the sun bouncing off the rear-view mirror. Robert makes a mental note to remove the furry dice.

It was that glorious, beautiful bird that did it. Speaking those thoroughly creepy words about Clive Marston, giving Robert an excuse to leap in his car and drive to Vanessa Bridges' house, because she seems to like sleuthing and clues, does Vanessa. As does Robert. He really likes them sleuthing together – likes them together, full stop.

Clive, Clive, let's be naughty, Clive . . . The moment he heard Llewelyn speak, Robert had the fleeting thought that the bird was mimicking his mother – that before her illness and death, Lynette Hargreaves and Clive Marston must have been having an affair. But Robert quickly dismissed that idea. His mother loathed Marston – the woman had some standards, after all – *and* there were at least thirty years between them. Besides (and this was the crucial part) Llewelyn didn't sound like Robert's mother at all. When he'd mimicked her voice in the past, the bird was uncannily accurate – not least because Lynette Hargreaves had a pronounced stammer and, when he copied her, so did Llewelyn.

This voice, on the other hand, was totally stammer-free. And sadly, unidentifiable. After twelve months of silence, Llewelyn was frustratingly rusty.

Robert winds down his window – it's humid this morning. After days of low, grey cloud, the Indian summer is back again – all cobalt skies and golden sunlight, a blindingly beautiful backdrop for the scarlet-berried rowan trees flanking the Llanfair pavements.

'I'd buy Barbara some grapes, but The Vicar, greedy bastard, will eat them all,' Robert laughs. 'You'd think someone from the village would bring him his own, especially as they nearly burnt the poor sod's house down.'

'*I'll* get The Vicar some grapes,' Vanessa says. 'I'll get some for him and for Barbara. Let's stop off at Sandy's – Lisa usually has some.'

'She won't have any Caramacs left, I can tell you that.'

They both laugh.

'Thank you,' he says.

'Thank you for what?'

'For agreeing to come out with me. It's a bit of a cheek, I know, turning up on your doorstep like that. But after what Llewelyn said this morning, I had to tell someone, and I couldn't think of anyone I'd rather share it with.' He looks sideways to check her reaction. She's smiling – thank God. 'Besides, I needed to visit Barbara, to take her some fresh clothes, and I know she'd love to see you, so I thought I'd kill two birds . . .'

'Not, I hope,' says Vanessa, 'the bird you want to talk to me about?'

Robert laughs. 'No, not that bird.'

He reverses into the lone space outside Sandy's, cricking his neck, wishing he had eyes in the back of his head. 'And you honestly didn't mind me calling for you this morning?' he says, wincing. *Calling for you.* He sounds ten years old! And what if she changes her mind and says, *Yes, Robert, I actually did. You've suddenly reminded me that I find you physically repulsive. Kindly stop the car, and let me out forthwith.*

But – 'I don't mind at all.' She smiles. 'Do you know, I actually feel quite happy this morning. I've made up with my mum after our big falling-out. And it turns out there was a lot more behind my dreadful behaviour at *that* picnic.'

'Sounds intriguing,' he says. 'You can tell me on the way to the hospital. Right, out you get. Grapes for Barbara and The Vicar.'

'What about the thing you wanted to tell me? About what Llewelyn said?'

'I can save it,' he says. 'For the journey. You tell me your news, then I'll tell you mine.'

She hops out of the car, leans in through the window. 'What'll you do when I'm buying the grapes?'

He nervously eyes the launderette. The door is ajar, the vibrating outline of an upright feline just about visible in the shadows. It'll be Mr Niblet, purring excitedly, anticipating his next assault. 'I've business to attend to,' Robert says. 'A pair of jeans to liberate.'

But the launderette is void of cats. Void of mess, too. For the first time in months, the floor is clear of mounds of unwashed clothes and bedding, swept of spilt washing powder, detergent balls and lint. The shelves are neatly stacked with magazines and healthy cactus plants; the feline shape revealed to be a rucksack propped against a tumble dryer going at full pelt. Robert opens the dryer door, and stares into the abyss.

'Mr Niblet?' he whispers. 'Nibsy?'

But the contents are a pair of jeans – his own – a mono-grammed handkerchief, three tangled pairs of ladies' tights and a mauve padded bra.

'Thought I'd get the place up and running again, now that Marston's finally out of the picture,' says a female voice from the doorway.

It's WPC Jane Gill, leaning against the architrave. 'What are you doing here, Robbie? Dropping off your dirty laundry? Washing away vital evidence?'

He glares at her. 'Evidence of what?'

She smirks. 'Let's just say that Blanche Marston gave me food for thought when I interviewed her in hospital after her "kidnap-ping". Mentioned one or two males that had an unhealthy interest in her. An obsession, you might say. Your name came up . . .'

He swallows hard. 'Blanche would have said no such thing. That's not what our relationship is like . . .'

'That's not what Blanchey says.'

'You're lying!'

She smiles and nods at the open drum. 'My tights and bra, nestling next to your jeans. Very cosy. That handkerchief's not yours though, is it? Not your initials, Robbie. Nicked it, did you? Oh, stop stressing, you clown. I'm just winding you up and having a laugh.'

'It's not funny though, is it, Jane?' Robert says.

Vanessa Bridges appears in the doorway, clutching two bunches of grapes. 'I got one of each, black and green,' she pants. 'Oh, hello, WPC Gill! Fabulous job you've done with the launderette. WPC Gill was here all yesterday evening, Robert, sprucing the place up with Twp Lisa and lots of other ladies from the village. Wasn't that lovely of them? Oh, and you've done Robert's laundry, WPC Gill! In fact, it looks like you've redone everyone's washing!'

'Had no choice,' Jane Gill says. 'Mr Niblet had a habit of crapping and peeing wherever he damn well pleased.'

'Good God,' says Vanessa, 'couldn't this Mr Niblet be made to clean up his own filth?'

'Yeah,' says Jane. 'That would've worked.'

'Oh, dear.' Robert pulls his shrunken jeans from the dryer. 'Well, I suppose I can stretch them into shape. And yes, this isn't my handkerchief – I didn't steal it though. Nurse Rose Pugh lent it to me when The Vicar took his overdose. But I do need to give it back.' He frowns, shaking his head. 'Not a clue how it got here, mind. Last time I remember seeing it was when I visited Blanche in hospital. You know, after she was found in that carpark in Barwood.' He shoves the hanky into his pocket and takes a deep breath, dreading the answer to the question he's about to ask. But ask it he must. 'What did you do with the cats, Jane? Tell me it was humane.'

'Of course it was! We called the RSPCA, who rehomed them at nearby farms. Feral buggers they were, but excellent mousers.' She smiles. 'We have our launderette back again, Robbie. No more talk of poncey wine bars. Your dad will be delighted.'

'He will at that,' Robert says. 'And the rats? What'll happen to them, now the cats have gone?'

'Local rat-catcher's dealt with them.' Jane nods knowingly. 'Got rid of quite a bit of vermin we have here in Llanfair of late, wouldn't you agree? Now, say hello to Debbie-Marie when you see her, and give her a flea in the ear from me. And tell her she's under house arrest until she apologizes to The Vicar.'

Robert is idling the car at the traffic lights, when Vanessa pipes up with – 'Oh! The bird. You were going to tell me about the bird!'

'And you were going to tell me about the picnic.'

'You go first.'

'Well, Llewelyn spoke. For the first time in over a year. He kept saying, "Clive, let's be naughty at your office on Monday". Over and over.'

'God!' Vanessa looks aghast. 'That's revolting, coming out of an animal's mouth!'

'If you'd known Clive Marston, you'd think it was revolting coming out of the mouth of any living thing. But think about it – all that "Clive, let's be naughty" stuff isn't coming from Llewelyn at all. He's mimicking someone – and I reckon he picked it up in the pub the Friday before Marston went missing. Four people were sitting around the table next to Llewelyn's cage. Marston himself, Blanche, Rose Pugh and Rachel Wilmslow.'

'A bit far-fetched, don't you think? He could have overheard it any time, from anyone. Who else could he have been listening into?'

'Well, me, of course. I was serving behind the bar and collecting glasses. And Dad. And Ingrid Tunstall, who cleans for us, though she wasn't there at the time – she'd been there earlier in the day, though, mucking out Llewelyn's cage. The pub was packed with all the usuals – Griffiths, Morris and Hoskins, propping up the bar as per, Gary and Julie from the hairdressers, Twp Lisa, Bug-eyed Thomas, WPC Jane Gill . . .'

'Was Clive there when Ingrid was cleaning?'

He shakes his head. 'Ingrid's hours are before opening time. Though I suppose their paths cross often enough in the pub.'

'Anyone else? Your aunt, perhaps?'

'Barbara rarely comes into the Llanfair Arms, because Utterson's banned from the public areas. Tried it on with one customer too many. Disturbing though, isn't it?'

'It's certainly that. But why do you think it's connected with Clive's murder?'

'Well, it sounds like someone was trying to coax Clive with a promise – a honeytrap! Imagine this: a woman lures Clive to his office on the Monday morning he vanishes, with the promise they'd be a bit "naughty". If Clive thought he'd be getting his end away, he'd have made some excuse to call his staff and tell them not to come in. Blanche told me that when she turned up to surprise him, the office was empty – no typists, no nothing. She reckoned he'd given them all the morning off.'

'Oh, I don't know . . . I just can't see it. The woman in question would be taking one hell of a risk . . .'

Vanessa's right, of course she's right. And now she'll realize that the whole Llewelyn stuff was a ruse – an excuse for Robert to pay her a visit, to persuade her to spend the day with him. Which means she'll hate him all over again.

But she's smiling down at Utterson, ruffling his ears. 'If only animals could speak,' she says. 'I mean, speak of their own accord. You're a wicked old soul,' she whispers in Utterson's ear. 'Good job you're not banned from the rest of the pub, or you'd have nowhere to stay while your mum's in hospital. Poor old Utterson.'

Robert shoots a look at the drooling dog nestled into Vanessa Bridges' bosom. He swears he's sniggering under his whiskers. Poor Utterson nothing.

'These bloody lights,' Robert mutters. 'Taking an age to change. I'd jump them, if I didn't already have three points on my licence.'

'Indicate right.' Vanessa speaks suddenly. 'Head for Aneurin Bevan Estate.'

'But the hospital . . .'

'Look, I've been thinking. Before I officially get the sack, I want to try and make things right between Debbie and your aunt. They need closure, both of them. Not forgiveness, not necessarily – that's asking a lot of Barbara . . .'

'And the impossible of Lewis Morgan, who'll more than likely be at Barbara's bedside in his striped pyjamas and wheelchair, guzzling her grapes.'

'But from Debbie's perspective, it would be good for her to meet and speak to the victims of her tale-telling. The Vicar being directly affected, but those indirectly affected, too – the Barbaras of this world, who try to do the right thing by people like Debbie, but get let down. It'll give Debbie a chance to face her mistakes and apologize. What do you think?'

'I think it's incredibly risky. Barbara has a weak heart, and The Vicar is a moody old bugger and unpredictable at the best of times. Given Debbie nearly got him killed by the village vigilantes, I think he's likely to swing for her. It's got disaster written all over it.'

'Not necessarily. I think it could be hugely beneficial. Look, all my professional life I've hidden behind academic papers because I'm scared of people and confrontation. With my previous patient – Miss X – I should have done right by her much, much sooner. She kept talking about a "monster" harassing her, and I thought she was speaking metaphorically, but what if she wasn't? What if it was a real person she had to face, and she ultimately ran away from that monster – literally throwing herself under a bus in the process? I don't want the same to happen to Debbie. She needs to confront Barbara and Lewis before it's too late, under my supervision, of course.'

Robert doesn't have the heart to say, I believe that what you're planning to do is potentially dangerous, and I think I really, really like you, and I don't want you to put yourself through this.

'I don't think you should do it,' he says. 'I think it could go badly wrong.'

'Well, you don't have to come with me, then.' She thrusts open the passenger door. 'You can drop me off here,' she says petulantly, 'and I'll get my own car . . .'

He places his hand over hers. 'Please don't. Let me come with you. I'll be there, I'll support you, if that's what you want.'

She leaves her hand where it is, under his. 'Thank you,' she says, turning to smile at him. 'Look, how about we keep Debbie outside the ward until we've spoken to Barbara and Lewis and prepared them for seeing her. What do you think?'

The lights change. The driver of the white Mini Metro behind them toots their horn.

'In or out?' Robert says. 'Better make your mind up, fast.'

She slams the door. 'In,' she says.

Robert holds his middle finger aloft through his open window, waggling it at the car behind. 'Dr Bridges,' he says. 'I believe we've reached a compromise.'

53

Debbie

11 a.m., inside Robert's car,
en route to the hospital

I was dead embarrassed when I answered the door just now, because I was plastered in conker pulp. I haven't washed since I smashed my new ones up. Dr Bridges and Rob just stood there and gawped, probably wondering what horrible disease I'd developed and whether they'd end up catching it, too.

'Bits of conker,' I said. 'I've been killing what's left of my conker collection.'

'And what,' Rob asked, 'has the innocent fruit of our nation's beloved horse-chestnut tree done to offend you, Deborah?'

'Nothing,' I said. 'I was bored, that's all.'

I was also very upset. I had completely destroyed them – every one of them – in a fit of anger and spite. My thumb hurt like buggery too, so I kept it hidden behind my back. It's felt even more painful since Rose Pugh pointed out just how bruised it is.

I didn't know what made me want to cry more – the pain

in my thumb, or the look on Dr Bridges' face, which was pity, I think.

'Hello, Debbie,' she said.

'I thought you were angry with me.'

'Well.' She shuffled from foot to foot. She was wearing brown leather clogs, which I personally wouldn't have put her in, because if I was her age and had legs like that, I'd wear high heels and mini-skirts all the time. 'I *was* angry, but not so much any more. I think you've suffered enough as it is, but you do owe Barbara and The Vicar an apology, and Robert and I would like to take you and your mum to the hospital to do so, if she thinks that's okay.'

'Mam's not here,' I said.

'Oh!' Dr Bridges looked disappointed. 'Well, I suppose we'll have to wait until she's back. How long will she be?'

I shrugged. 'Dunno. She didn't say. She's not talking to me. I don't know when I'll next see her.'

I wanted to add, 'Or if I'll ever see her again, because I reckon she'll do a runner one of these days, just like my dad.' But I knew if I said that, I'd cave in and blubber.

'Have you eaten today?' Rob asked.

I thought how to best answer this. I didn't want to say I'd not eaten in days, because that might get Mam into trouble. But I've been threatened with a thrashing if I lie again. I was what Barbara would describe as 'between a rock and a hard place'.

'Can't remember,' I said.

'I'll take that as a no,' Rob said. 'Can we come in?'

'I'm not sure. Mam doesn't like strangers coming and poking around and . . .'

'But we're not strangers,' Dr Bridges said. 'And I promise no poking. At worst, we'll poke around in your kitchen cupboards to see if we can rustle you up a sandwich or something. When did you last have a wash?'

'Dunno.' I bit my lip hard.

'Please,' Dr Bridges said gently, 'can we come inside, Debbie?'

I weighed up the pros and cons of this. And then I opened the door up properly, because I realized that by letting them in, I had nothing left to lose.

They said they'd make me a Dairylea sandwich, but only if I promised to have a wash and change my clothes before I ate. I must have looked and smelt bloody awful – sometimes I forget to wash and change unless Mam reminds me, which she hasn't for days, because she's not talking to me. So, I left them to it, and went into the bathroom and ran the tap for a bit, then tip-toed into the hall to listen to them talking in the kitchen.

I know that eavesdropping's naughty, and it's one of my nastier traits, but I needed to know what the pair of them were thinking and saying about me.

Dr Bridges was jabbering away – I couldn't make out exactly what she was saying, but I caught a few words – *neglect, abuse, we have to, we must do* . . .

Then Rob – *careful, accusations, Ingrid's had a hard time* . . .

Then Dr Bridges' voice, more clearly, 'Oh my word!'

'What?' said Rob.

I edged closer, so I was right outside the kitchen door and could hear them more clearly:

'This photo!' Dr Bridges exclaimed. 'Here, on the wall by

the cooker, next to the portrait of Debbie as a baby – at least, I think it's Debbie as a baby. It's all of us – look! As kids. I'm in it – standing at the front, holding hands with an older girl.'

She was talking about one of Mam's old photographs, taken when she was a teen. This particular one is in colour, but faded, with dozens of kids lined up in a field – Rob's in it and so is Blanche Marston, surrounded by girls of all ages and sizes: from primary-school kids to teenagers and everything in between.

'I swear it was taken at that bloody picnic!' Dr Bridges cried. 'Here's me at the front, the littlest one. God, the state of my dress – that puffed-up skirt and sash bow and my hair tied up in ringlets! I was plastered in blackberry juice by the end of the day . . .'

'That's Ingrid, holding your hand,' Rob said.

'What, that beautiful girl in the cropped jeans? Debbie-Marie's mother?! She looks like a young Audrey Hepburn!'

'Ingrid was stunning when she was younger, much to Blanche Marston's chagrin. And speaking of Blanche, there she is – in the row behind you, the young lady in the low-cut halter-neck dress. Thirteen going on thirty.'

'Christ! I see what you mean. The beehive, the heavy eye make-up . . . she looks so grown up, but she's only a child!'

'And there's me, standing next to her – the gap-toothed loon in short trousers and knee socks. I was eleven years old – just two years younger than Blanche, but there might just as well have been two decades between us.'

I heard Dr Bridges laugh. 'You poor little sod. And who's that girl standing on the other side of you – the one wearing glasses with the plaster over one lens?'

'My nemesis,' Rob said. 'Jane Gill, our friendly local PC. Class bully and teacher's pet. She hid her wickedness well, did Jane Gill – got away with murder, thanks to her pigtails, specs and demure gingham dresses. She's not mellowed with age, either.'

'Good God,' said Dr Bridges, 'I had no idea. I thought she must be an absolute angel, the way she's transformed the launderette – a pillar of the community. And she seemed so friendly just now! How old is she there?'

'Same age as me. Eleven.'

'And that little girl, just in front of Jane Gill? The one in the coat with her hood pulled up. What on earth was she wearing that for? The day was so hot!'

'Oh, that's Rose Pugh. Thirteen years old, looks about nine – the complete opposite of Blanche. She spent the whole summer wearing that coat, even when it was roasting. If anyone told her to take it off, she'd burst into tears. Claimed it protected her nurse's uniform; didn't want it to get dirty, she said, wanted to keep it nice and pure. Even then she was bloody obsessed with health and cleanliness.'

'Fascinating,' Dr Bridges said. 'Ingrid's changed beyond all recognition. Look at how happy she is – the way she's holding my hand, smiling down at me. She's a totally different person.'

I crept back to the bathroom after that, and washed my face and brushed my hair. It hurt my heart to hear how different Mam looked then. It's me who's made her sad and old; me, who's given her every single one of her wrinkles.

So, here I am, in the back of Rob's car with Utterson on my lap. We're going to the hospital, to visit Barbara, so that I can say sorry. And after that, we'll go to The Vicar's bedside, so

I can do the same with him. But Mam won't be with us. Dr Bridges left her a note to explain where I'd gone, and she asked me, as she was writing it – she said, 'Do you think your mum will mind us taking you out for a few hours, Debbie?'

'I daresay she won't give a toss,' I replied.

But there's a knot in my tummy and a lump in my throat, and sitting here on the back seat, even with Utterson to stroke, I'm scared of facing the people I could have killed with the stupid lies I told. I wish Mam was here after all. I need her, I really do, even though she's moody and downright nasty at times.

'Do you think,' I ask, 'that all girls turn out to be like their mothers?'

Dr Bridges doesn't reply. But Rob meets my eye in his rear-view mirror, and says:

'No. Some girls, I think, choose to be very different to their mothers. Just as I think some boys deliberately try to be the opposite of their fathers.'

'You're not at all like Dai,' I say.

Rob doesn't reply.

'I hope,' I say quietly, 'that I don't grow up to be like Mam. I think it must be very hard being her.'

54

Barbara

12 p.m., Ward H (Geriatrics),
Prince of Wales Hospital, Cardiff North

There are sixteen polystyrene tiles on the ceiling above Barbara's hospital bed. She knows this, because she's counted them, from one side of her bay to the other. She wishes Lewis would wake from his nap, but he's sparko in his wheelchair, snoring like a buffalo, leaving Barbara alone with her thoughts – thoughts that have been spiralling down shadowy staircases, sliding into a basement of doom. She's in danger of losing her mind – has been for several weeks now.

Although, when she really thinks about it, during these last few days in hospital, her memory has improved almost hour by hour – her head clearer than it has been in ages, which is quite remarkable, given how little sleep she's been getting. If she's not disturbed by the tea trolley, or someone wanting to give her a blanket bath, it's the ranting from the department store lift attendant diagnosed with kidney stones, drugged to the eyeballs on painkillers in the bay next door.

But gaps remain in Barbara's recall. There is something in particular she must remember, because it is important.

Something involving Lewis, an object of some sort she found on his person the day she found him lying on his front path, but the more she tries to trap the memory, the more it floats away from her grasp like a small red packet of . . . something.

It'll be visiting time soon enough. The last time he visited, Robert promised a change of clothing and a decent book. Barbara hopes it will be a very long book. The doctors won't discharge her until she eats a substantial meal, but her appetite is still off.

'I'm sick at heart, you see,' she tells the cheery young nurse who's arrived at her bedside to take her blood pressure.

'I know,' says the nurse – a young student type. Keen. Softly spoken. Angelic of face, wedged of fringe, crêped of sole and eager to please. 'You've had a nasty turn. But Doctor says you're doing ever so well.'

'I've had a heart attack,' Barbara replies. 'I don't call having a heart attack *doing ever so well.*'

'Heart attack?' the nurse laughs. 'Whatever gave you that idea?'

'The pains in my chest! The ambulance, I was blue-lighted, you know.'

The nurse shakes her head. 'I don't know, communication in this place. Has no one given you an actual diagnosis?'

Barbara thinks. 'Well, no one had to. I had a heart attack, everyone knows that!'

'Miss Pritchard, you had nothing of the sort. It says in your notes . . . that's it, rest your arm on the bed and think of something nice while I inflate this cuff . . . yes, it says in your notes that you had high levels of carbon monoxide in your blood. Not high enough to kill straight away, but enough to cause fatigue, chest pain, confusion and nausea. Does any of that sound familiar?'

'Good God,' says Barbara. 'That bloody boiler of mine! I thought I was dementing, or dying. Or both!'

'Well, isn't that smashing?' the nurse beams. 'Oh, look at this – fabulous blood pressure for a lady of your age. It's 125/82! Now, have you moved your bowels this morning?'

Thirty minutes later, and Robert's head pops around the curtain. 'Is it safe?' he asks.

Barbara reluctantly drags her attention away from the copy of *Lace* she's been reading, and glares at him. Not quite her usual choice of book – Lewis found it in the day-room – but she has to admit Shirley Conran has an extraordinary imagination, and she'll never look at a goldfish bowl in quite the same way ever again. 'Safe from what or from whom?' she enquires.

'Him.' Robert nods at The Vicar, snoring away in his wheelchair. 'I'd like a word with you before Rip Van Winkle rejoins the land of the living. And I have a surprise for you.'

'Have you finally thrown out those ghastly leather trousers?'

'Better than that.'

He pulls back the curtain. 'Ta da!'

And out steps the glorious Vanessa Bridges, dressed today in a green woollen pinafore, tatty brown jumper and tan leather clogs.

'You look like a fish wife,' Barbara says.

'You're feeling better, then,' Vanessa laughs.

'I am now. Do you know, I'm not dying? I've not got dementia, not had a heart attack. Turns out it was carbon monoxide poisoning. Isn't that bloody marvellous?'

Robert looks at her aghast. 'No!' he says. 'It is not! Carbon monoxide can kill! How on earth . . .'

'The boiler, I suspect. It's been on the blink for a while, as you know. Perhaps you should take a look at it, Robert.'

'Yep, no problem.'

'You'll do no such thing!' Vanessa cries.

'Keep your voice down,' Barbara hisses, gesturing at The Vicar. 'He can sleep through almost anything, including the raving from the unfortunate soul in the next bed, and I'd rather he remained in the land of nod while I catch up with the pair of you.'

'The boiler needs,' Vanessa hisses back, 'to be assessed by a professional. Do you have any idea what you're doing, Robert?'

Barbara gets in before Robert has a chance to open his mouth and ruin everything. 'Of course he does,' she says. 'He does odd jobs all the time, don't you, dear?'

Vanessa shakes her head. 'Robert's not going anywhere near that thing. No one's going anywhere near that thing until it's been assessed by someone who knows what they're doing.'

'Oh.' Barbara wafts her arm. 'Don't be such a fusspot. Robert is very handy, everyone in the village says so. Always fixing things at the pub or doing DIY jobs around the house for me. I've had a few requests, actually, from some of the ladies in the village, wanting to know when Robert can next give them a helping hand.'

'I bet you have,' Vanessa says. 'One of them being Blanche Marston, of course.'

Robert opens his mouth to protest, but Vanessa darts in front of him, side-stepping The Vicar's wheelchair, sitting on the bed, clasping Barbara's hand.

'For the first time in a very long time,' Barbara smiles, 'I don't feel the end of the world is nigh.'

'Don't speak too soon,' Robert grimaces. 'You've not seen surprise number two, lurking outside in the corridor. Now, I have to check whether you're up to this. I'm relieved to hear that you don't have a dodgy ticker after all, because the shock and horror might just . . .'

'Robert,' Vanessa says, 'before you unveil the surprise, I'd like a quick word with Barbara. It's about something that's been bothering me these last few days.' She leans forward, and Barbara thinks how glorious Vanessa Bridges always smells – of fresh air, violets and unspoiled youth, not of mildew, cabbage and old age, like her. 'I have concerns. About your over-investment in Debbie – that you consider her a genius. You've been very hurt by her once, as it is.'

'But Deborah *is* a genius!'

'Well, is she? Is she really? Robert showed me that piece of writing you wanted me to read . . .'

'The essay on *Lord of the Flies*?'

'But it's not, is it, Barbara? It's line after line of the fat cat sat on the mat . . . that's all it is.'

Barbara narrows her eyes. 'Where did Robert get the page of writing from?'

'I don't remember.' Vanessa turns to Robert. 'Do you?'

But Robert doesn't hear her. He's too busy checking behind the cubicle curtain.

'Well, I can guarantee,' Barbara sniffs, 'that it was on my coffee table, after falling out of my copy of *The Radio Times*, where it was placed by Twp Lisa before the delivery boy did his rounds. Twp Lisa who, incidentally, isn't *twp* at all, but is studying for a doctorate in Astrophysics, and works in Sandy's Newsagents to pay off her – ironically – astronomical debts to Clive Marston. We leave each other cryptic messages – she puts them inside my magazines; I send them back. The fat cat sat on the mat would, I believe, allude to Clive Marston, who is, or rather *was,* our local fat cat. The MAT refers to his company – Marston Accountancy and Tax Limited. The number of times the sentence was written, I suspect, refers to the number of occasions Marston visited Twp Lisa at her shop that particular week, threatening her if she didn't cough up the interest on the loan he "persuaded" her to take out to top up her scholarship fund. I could be wrong, of course. I haven't had a chance to check with Twp Lisa yet, for obvious reasons.'

'Could she not have just picked up the phone to tell you that?' Vanessa asks.

'And where on earth,' Barbara sniffs, 'would the fun be in *that*?'

Vanessa Bridges tries to say more, but Deborah Tunstall bursts through the cubicle curtain – a whirlwind of arms and legs, tangled hair and messy weeping. 'I'm so sorry,' she's saying. 'I couldn't wait in the corridor any longer. Please don't hate me, Barbara . . . you're my only friend . . . I didn't mean . . . I was scared but so stupid, so scared and so stupid . . .'

Barbara smiles, surprised at her capacity for forgiveness. She's going soft in her old age. 'It's all right, Deborah.' She opens her arms. 'Come and give me a hug, you mischief-making, tale-telling genius, you.'

A cough erupts from Barbara's bedside, followed by a growl. 'Mischief-making genius? I'll give her bloody mischief!'

'Ah, Lewis.' Barbara speaks through a knotted clump of Deborah's hair. 'You're back with us, I see.'

Deborah pulls away, wiping her nose with the back of her hand. She rises from Barbara's bed and stands, poker-straight, in front of The Vicar, tugging the fraying sleeves of her jumper over her hands, shuffling her feet and swallowing hard.

'Mr Vicar,' she says, 'I'm so very sorry. For everything I did to you. For taking that photograph of you and Rose Pugh, for blackmailing you, for breaking into the vicarage, for stealing your cigarettes and chocolates, for making you fall down the stairs, and for telling the terrible lie that got your house burnt down.'

'Jesus Christ.' Lewis shakes his head. 'When you put it like that, it really is quite a dossier of doom, isn't it, Deborah?'

'Yes, it is,' the child tearfully concedes. 'And I wouldn't blame you one bit if you hated my guts and told me to get out of your sight.'

'You know,' Lewis says with a heavy sigh, 'I've dealt with enough miscreants in my time to realize that very few people are born truly bad. Most are products of their environment. And you are one of those people, Deborah. Blackmailing me was bad, yes. But I understand that you believed I was doing a bad thing with Brown Owl, which is nobody else's business by the way, and does not excuse your behaviour. However, having been persecuted yourself, who could blame you for persecuting in return? As for breaking into my house . . . well, you had to find shelter, didn't you? And given how badly you were bullied, who can blame you for running away?'

'But the rest of the stuff I did! Making out that you kidnapped me. Not helping you when you were injured. Not telling anyone about Clive Marston.'

Lewis shakes his head. 'Not completely your fault. It was the fault of the adults who terrified you into using a lie to save yourself. They'd have done you serious harm that night outside the Llanfair Arms, from what Miss Pritchard's told me. As for my falling down the stairs . . . well. Did you push me? No. I tripped and fell, and may have done so, anyway, even if I'd not just discovered an eleven-year-old girl in my spare bed, up to her eyes and ears in Caramac wrappers.'

'All forgiven, then?' Robert asks, brightly.

'Apart from eating my packet of Smash, yes – Deborah is forgiven. Though I'd give my eye teeth to find the bastard who's been bumping off Llanfairians these last twenty-odd years. Whoever it is very nearly killed me, and tried to frame Deborah for that bloody morphine nonsense at the village fete. They started by killing Herbert Wilkins and Eleri Ellis, then that builder bloke who tried to do you over, Barb, and then he tried to get the Marston girls by poisoning their sandwiches. And Gwen Bridges! She was only spared a terrible death – death by green, it would have been, but she had the good grace to apologize. And now Clive Marston . . .'

Barbara shakes her head. 'Lewis, you're not making a word of sense. Are you developing a water infection?'

'No! I am not!'

'But The Vicar's right!' Deborah bounces excitedly on Barbara's bed. 'He's kept old newspaper cuttings and everything, and circled them in red marker pen!'

'Red marker pen?' Vanessa frowns. 'I know you were in hospital at the time, but my mother's car was vandalized with . . .'

'And it's all to do with the Seven Deadly Sins, isn't it, Vicar?'

Deborah interjects. 'You told me, didn't you, after you fell down the stairs.'

'Ah,' Robert says, knowingly.

'I wasn't concussed!' Lewis snaps. 'I've still got my marbles! I've been collecting a dossier on the murders for years.'

'You've never mentioned any murders to me,' Barbara says, offended. 'I thought we discussed everything to do with the village, Lewis. Though I suppose that explains why your sermons were so Deadly-Sin-centric. Trying to flush the perpetrator out, I presume?'

'I've been investigating in secret. Not a soul beyond suspicion, Barb. Not even you.'

'That's right!' Deborah exclaims. 'You said it yourself, Barbara. That I should never trust anyone, not even sweet little old ladies like you.'

'There's nothing sweet about *her*,' Robert mutters.

Barbara ignores him. 'What makes you think all these incidents are linked?' she barks at Lewis. 'They're just random deaths that happen in every community. One car accident, a choking tragedy several years later, I don't even know what happened to Gwendoline Bridges . . .'

'Her property was vandalized with green paint, after she complained about your Wales in Bloom win.'

'Well, that's hardly the work of a serial killer, is it?'

'It might be. Do you know how serial killers customarily behave? And what about my insulin overdose? I'm always incredibly careful. My medication system was tampered with. I'm sure of it!'

'If I may,' Barbara says, patting Lewis's hand to placate him, 'I'd like to return to the Marston girls and the morphine incident. Bear in mind, Lewis, they were the only girls poisoned at the fete. Why wasn't anyone else affected? It's taking a hell of a risk, is it not, using a buffet to target just two people? Their mother is a well-known attention-seeker, and their father – God rest his soul, assuming he has one – a known swindler with dubious connections. I wouldn't put anything past Blanche for attention, while any number of people would want to get back at Clive – and why not through his children?'

'Can we leave Blanche out of this?' Robert says hotly. 'She's not an attention-seeker. She's just a bit . . . dramatic, that's all.'

'Robert.' Barbara feels her shoulders sag. 'Now is not the time, but you and I need a serious talk regarding your relationship with Blanche Marston. It is, at best, inappropriate, and at worst downright grubby. She's a married woman, for heaven's sake. Albeit a widow now, but even so . . .'

'It's not grubby at all! You're making weird assumptions . . .'

'I think we understand the situation perfectly well,' Vanessa says crisply, rising from Barbara's bed. 'If you'll excuse me, I need to check on Utterson. We've left him tied to a post in the car park . . .'

'Oh, dear God,' Barbara mutters.

' . . . And the attendant promised to keep a close eye, but I don't think we can leave him for very much longer.'

Vanessa leaves in a clomping of clogs, Barbara shouting after her, 'Whatever's the matter? You don't seem your usual . . .' then Robert rises abruptly from the bed, stalking purposefully out of the ward, followed by Deborah Tunstall, yelling, 'What's up, Robbie? Can I come too?'

'They need time alone!' Barbara shouts. But Deborah's gone,

the splat-splat-splat of her sandals on lino gradually receding, followed by the distant ping of a lift.

Now it's just Barbara and Lewis again. Lewis, droning on about serial killers and working his way through what little is left of Barbara's grapes.

She snatches the bunch from his fingers. 'For God's sake,' she snaps. 'There is no evidence that one person and one person alone is bumping off the residents of Llanfair.'

'Yes, there is.' Lewis snatches the grapes back. 'The killer leaves a calling card, connected to the sin the victim has committed. That womanizer Herbert Wilkins – a wedding ring, lodged in his throat. Lust. That builder chappie who tried to swindle you. Choked, with a piece of sausage in his mouth. Greedy pig. Greed. Gwendoline Bridges – well, she was saved. But I can guarantee that had she not made a public admission of guilt, she'd have been found with something green and deeply unpleasant in her throat. Envy. And the Marston girls – poisoning. The brand of bread used in the sandwiches – and Deborah confirmed this – Mother's Pride. Carrie-Anne and Lucy Marston would have swallowed their mother's *pride*. The killer was out to punish Blanche Marston – and the other mothers too, quite possibly – through their children.' He folds his arms, smiling smugly. 'I rest my case.'

'Utter nonsense!'

But Barbara is struggling to keep her voice even. For the first time in their friendship, Lewis is unnerving her. 'Your own supposed targeting by the killer – did the ambulance drivers or doctors find anything stuck in your mouth or throat?' she says. 'No, they did not.'

But as she speaks, something pricks the recesses of Barbara's memory. There's an itch in her brain she just can't scratch. A spark of . . . something. In the bay next door, the lift attendant has woken from her afternoon nap. 'Ground floor,' she's shrieking, 'pet food, wallcoverings, Polaris missiles, going up!'

'As for Clive Marston.' Barbara has to raise her voice to be heard. 'He wasn't found with anything in his mouth or throat, either. The police would have said so.'

'I very much doubt it.'

'Well, Deborah, who found the body, would surely have seen something.'

'Not necessarily.'

'I'm reluctant to humour you, Lewis, but who do you suspect to be this *serial killer*? You must have theories.'

'Funny you should ask that, Barb. As I said before, no one is above suspicion. Not even you. So, there's you.'

'And you, Lewis. One could accuse you of bluffing us all – pretending to investigate a murderer while you are the murderer yourself.' She smiles. 'You know, this is actually fun! Oh, and then there's your unhealthy obsession with the Seven Deadly Sins – every single sermon, it seems, is based around one of them.'

'I am not obsessed,' he growls. 'It's just when I'm lacking inspiration, there's plenty of meat in the window behind me. A visual prompt card, if you like. Do you have any idea how hard it is coming up with moral instruction week after week?'

'Hmm.' Barbara eyes him suspiciously. 'Who else do you suspect?'

'WPC Jane Gill. A bad lot. Far too focused on law and order, and a bully.'

'I'll second that.'

'Dai Hargreaves.'

'Dai Hargreaves? The man can't keep his own teeth in, let

alone shove anything between those of his murder victims. And besides, he's not the type!'

'What is the type, Barbara?'

'Blanche Marston!'

'True. She's hard-nosed and nasty, when provoked.'

'Trust me, she doesn't need provocation.'

'Your nephew, Robert.'

'Too young at the time of Herbert and Eleri's deaths.'

'He'd have been the same age as Jane Gill. And no, not too young. A child could have caused that accident – running out in the road, perhaps. Causing a distraction.'

Barbara takes a deep breath. 'There's Ingrid, of course. She's been a troubled soul for years.'

'Rose Pugh?'

Barbara shakes her head. 'Why would she want to kill her mother? She was devastated by Eleri's death.'

'True.'

'And then, of course, there's Rachel.'

'You leave Rachel out of this! And she only moved to Uskshire five years ago.'

They sit in silence for a while. Barbara nibbles at the skin around her thumbnail, wondering how best to handle Lewis. Fun as it is to play detective, these revelations – well, ruminations – disturb her. She feels sick. And threatened. She feels afraid – of what? Of whom?

'Look,' she says finally. 'Perhaps you should talk to the police.'

He shrugs.

'Do I sense reluctance, Lewis. Because you know deep down that they'd discount your theory in a heartbeat?'

He shrugs again.

'Would they take you seriously? A handful of random deaths and incidents, spanning twenty years? Connected by one man with a ring in his mouth, another who choked on a chipolata, and a couple of girls eating sandwiches made from Mother's Pride and not Sunblest? And a selection of highly unlikely suspects – one of them your own good self?'

'I'm right. I know that I'm right.'

'Well, I think you're wrong. And *I* know that I'm right.'

He smiles. 'You usually are, Barb. You usually are.'

55

Vanessa

'I am not in love with Blanche Marston!'

Robert Hargreaves thumps his driving wheel in frustration. 'Never have been, never will be. For all sorts of reasons.'

Vanessa stares out of the passenger window, observing her own reflection chewing its lip in the wing mirror. If Robert Hargreaves prefers Blanche Marston, Vanessa wouldn't blame him. Every day is a bad-hair day for her, and not just regarding the hair on her head. She often forgets to shave under her arms and rarely tackles the hair on her legs. And if she's ever worn matching underwear, it's been by accident rather than design. Her bras are greying, her knickers sagging, and there's a dirty great hole in the seam of her tights. Her sensible 30-denier American Tan tights. Men like black stockings, don't they? She's never worn a pair of black stockings in her life.

'Please, Vanessa, can you say something? Something along the lines of, "Yes, I believe you, Rob"?'

She glances over her shoulder. Debbie-Marie and Utterson

are sprawled over the back seat, apparently asleep – a mass of entwined legs and paws, all black fur and tangled curls tumbling over a tartan blanket. To a casual observer, they'd look like a young family on the way home from an idyllic morning out.

'She's pretending to be asleep,' Vanessa hisses. 'I don't want her listening in. This is not a conversation for a child's ears. We'll discuss this later, Robert.'

'We're talking about Debbie-Marie Tunstall,' Robert hisses back. 'Her eyes and ears have seen and heard it all.'

Vanessa looks over her shoulder again. Utterson's ears are twitching. Debbie's, too – she'd bet her life on it.

'I just don't want to discuss the sordid details of your love-life in front of an eleven-year-old child,' Vanessa says. 'I'm annoyed with myself, actually, for allowing someone like you to take me out for the day.'

'Someone like me?!'

'Well, yes, given your reputation. Taking married women into the woods, and . . .'

'One married woman, actually. And . . . what? What do you think we do in there, Dr Bridges?'

'Well, you know. S-E-X.'

'I can spell, you know,' says a voice from the back.

'Christ's sake, she's awake!' Robert thumps the steering wheel again. 'Right. Well, I've nothing to lose from coming clean with the pair of you. I stand to lose a lot more by staying schtum.'

He swerves the car into the nearest layby, next to a field of cows. As he slams on the brakes and turns off the engine, a quizzical pair of yearlings saunter towards the fence, grinding the cud between their teeth like teenagers chewing bubblegum.

'Here's the deal,' Robert says, gruffly. 'Blanche and I meet in the woods every Monday. Not for S-E-X, no. It's so I can teach her karate – she's been scared stiff for the past few months, convinced someone's out to get her and the girls. Thought Clive was up to something murkier than usual, and it looks like she was right. In exchange, she teaches me ball-room dancing, so I can dance the waltz with my Auntie Barbara at the surprise eightieth birthday party my father and I will be throwing in six weeks' time, in her honour.'

'That's bizarre,' says the voice from the back.

'Bizarre it may be, but it's all true. In her youth, Auntie Barbara loved to dance, but hasn't danced in years – she says she's too old and has never found the right partner, but I know she still dreams of dancing with someone she loves. So, dancing with me at her birthday party will be my birthday gift to her. Blanche and I do what we do in the woods, because I want to keep the lessons a secret. If we did it in the pub, the Scout Hut – well, anywhere in Llanfair, some busybody would blab and ruin everything.'

'So,' Vanessa says incredulously, 'you meet in the woods because, you know, that won't set tongues wagging, will it?'

'Tongues didn't start wagging until Debbie started spying on us!'

'Morris the Butcher noticed, Robert. He practically said as much the night The Vicar's house burnt down. Do you honestly expect me to believe that you're not having S-E-X with Blanche Marston?'

'I can still spell,' says the voice from the back.

'I *do* expect you to believe that, yes, because it's the truth. Debbie?'

'What?'

'Utterson needs a poo.'

'No, he doesn't!'

'Yes, he does. You need to take him for a quick walk along the layby to let him do his business. Go on, out you get.'

'Whaaa?'

'I need to have a word with Dr Bridges. And I don't want you lugging in. Go on, out you get and don't come back until I tell you.'

With much huffing and puffing, Debbie-Marie hauls Utterson out of the car. 'This is cruelty to children and animals, it is,' she snarls.

'Further along the layby,' Robert shouts after her. 'Go on. Move.'

'How far along?'

'Until you're out of earshot.'

'Spoilsport!'

Robert winds up his window, turns to Vanessa, takes a deep breath. She tries to stay calm, but what a story this is – what an accomplished liar he must be! 'And you honestly expect me to believe all this?' she says.

'Yes, I do.'

'Because?'

'If I was having S-E-X with Blanche Marston, I'd be committing incest.'

Vanessa feels her jaw drop. 'God, I didn't see that one coming!'

Robert puts his head in his hands. 'My father is not Dai Hargreaves. My biological father is not alive any more. That is because he was Herbert Wilkins, Llanfair's resident tomcat. My mother told me, on her deathbed.' He raises his eyes heavenwards. 'Thanks, Mum, for dropping that particular bombshell just before you died.'

'Does Blanche know?'

'Only person I've told.' Robert smiles. 'My half-sister. It's taken a while for both of us to get our heads around it, but I think Blanche has finally accepted me. Which is why she's gone along with our mutual skill exchange. And that's why I'm so defensive when people say bad things about Blanche, however justified they may be.'

'Blimey.'

'Blimey indeed. Blanche has promised to keep our blood-tie secret, because if it got out, it would break Dai. He worshipped Mum, and this would destroy him. You know, I do love him, in spite of our differences. When all's said and done, Dai Hargreaves is my real father.'

He winds down his window and sticks out his head.

'You can get back in now,' he yells. 'And I thought I told you to move out of earshot.'

'I didn't hear nothing,' Debbie-Marie shouts back, popping up beside Vanessa's open window, pulling the back door open, shoving Utterson onto the seat. 'Can't see why you couldn't tell me, anyway, that Blanche Marston's your sister. No surprises there. You've got the same pudgy lips, mental hair and knock-kneed walk.'

'Oh, for Christ's sake!' Robert butts the steering wheel with his head. 'You keep all this to yourself, young lady. I only told Dr Bridges here because I didn't want her thinking I have designs on Blanche Marston.'

'Is that because you fancy Dr Bridges?' Debbie hauls Utterson onto her lap. 'Well, is it, Rob?'

Vanessa's heart somersaults. She stares down at her lap, holding her breath.

Robert restarts the engine. 'Mind your own bloody business,' he snaps.

Debbie pokes the back of Vanessa's seat. 'Do you fancy Rob back?' she enquires.

Vanessa says nothing, but looks sideways at Robert, steadily meeting his questioning eye.

They both smile.

56

Debbie

Just before midnight, Flat 4B,
Aneurin Bevan Estate, Llanfair

When Rob and Dr Bridges dropped me home, Mam was waiting on the front step – face like a smacked arse, not saying a word, which is never a good sign. She just held the door open, nudging her head for the three of us to get inside, thumbing at me to go straight to my room, which I did.

I crept out when Mam was mid-rant, and hid behind the kitchen bin. From there, I could watch the three of them having a right old ding-dong through the crack in the lounge door. Mam kept yelling she was going to call the police. Rob looked dead narked – jiggling his feet, pulling faces and fiddling with something in his jeans pocket. Dr Bridges looked a weird mix of glowy and bloody petrified, which makes sense, I suppose, because I think she's fallen in love.

'You took my kid without permission,' Mam said, glowering at glowy Dr Bridges, picking a spot on her chin with one hand, flicking ash from her fag with the other. 'You've crossed a line. I'm going to report you.'

'And I,' Dr Bridges replied, tossing her head, 'am going to

report *you*, for child neglect. Debbie was dirty and hungry when we found her. And there are bruises on her arm where you grabbed her . . .'

'She tried to run into the road,' Mam snapped. 'Outside the Dewi Sant Centre. She wanted to run after some girl she saw.'

It's strange. Even though Dr Bridges was defending me, I felt really cross with her for talking to Mam like that. Mam doesn't neglect me. She's tired and sad and she struggles, that's all. She needs help, not the police on her back.

Dr Bridges started to say, 'What sort of girl?' But Rob butted in.

'We took Debbie to see Barbara and The Vicar,' he said, touching Mam's arm with his hand, trying to calm her down. 'To apologize. All part of Debbie's therapy, isn't that right, Dr Bridges?'

'Therapy given,' Mam growled, staring at Rob's fingers like they were covered in crap, 'without my permission. And Debbie.' She raised her voice. 'I know you're out there, eaves-dropping. Go back to your room immediately, you nosy little sod.'

So here I am, alone in my room, minus my conkers, which are all smashed up. I'm without my people, without everything, really. I've never felt less loved than I do right now, and that's really saying something.

And Rob and Dr Bridges have gone. They left a good few hours ago. Left without saying goodbye to me. After everything that happened today, after all the three of us went through together. I thought they actually cared.

Because they made me a sandwich.

Because they made me wash and change my clothes.

Because they took me to see Barbara and Mr Vicar, to tell them both how sorry I was.

Because they really tried to make my brain feel better.

But, it turns out, they don't really care at all. They probably only spent time with me so they could spend time together. And now they know they're in love with each other, they won't need me any more. They used me, they did. That's all I am to anyone, a pawn in a game of chess. Worth very little, compared to all the other pieces on the board.

Although, when she was teaching me how to play, Barbara said that pawns are misunderstood – that people overlook them; that they think that they're 'expendable'. But, given the time and opportunity, she said, they can turn into *queens*.

After I heard Rob's car zoom off, I went into the lounge. It was a risky thing to do, I know, because Mam had told me to stay in my room. I could've made things much worse for myself by disobeying her.

She was sitting by the fireplace, looking even paler than usual. If she noticed me come in, she didn't let on. She was sitting up straight, her body stiff, hands gripping the arms of her chair, her knuckles white, her face like a mask – no expression there at all.

'They've gone, then,' I said.

No reply.

'Are you going to thrash me?' I asked. 'For going out without permission? For . . . I dunno. For the sake of it?'

No reply.

'Shall I go to bed, then?'

A shrug.

And it was that – the shrug – that finally finished me off.

I went back to my room to sit on the floor and wait until she'd gone to bed.

I left the house just before midnight. I've written my letters to Mam and Barbara. I've put Mam's in the kitchen, next to her bottle of Valium, and I'll hand-deliver Barbara's to Hollyhock Cottage on the way to the woods.

And when I get to the woods, I'll head for the quarry, where the moon will have cut a track through the lake – a rippling silver path that I'll swim through, until I'm completely out of my depth. And then I'll lie back and gaze up at the stars, pretending it's my bedroom ceiling at home; kidding myself that Dad put them there, that I'll always be his universe.

SUNDAY, 23 SEPTEMBER 1984

THE SOUTH WALES SUNDAY POST

Top Shrink Arrested in Connection with Marston Murder

By Margaret Lawrence,
Welsh Affairs Correspondent

In a dramatic turn of events yesterday evening, an arrest was made in Cardiff as a consequence of investigations into the murder of Llanfair businessman Clive Marston. WPC Jane Gill from Uskshire Police told *The South Wales Sunday Post*, 'A thorough search of Mr Marston's Cardiff offices uncovered evidence relating to black-market transactions involving prescription drugs, including amitriptyline, diazepam and morphine.'

The arrested man has been named as psychologist Professor Mark Murray, of Llandaff, Cardiff. *The South Wales Sunday Post* understands that another man, Peter Robinson, a haulier from Barwood, turned himself into police after discovering his haulage business was being used by Marston for drugs-trafficking purposes. Police are satisfied that Mr Robinson knew nothing of the illegal nature of Marston's activities, and he continues to assist officers with their inquiries.

57

Vanessa

9 a.m., a bench on Llanfair Common

She can't believe she's out and about this early on a Sunday morning, she says, but she simply couldn't sleep.

He kisses her again, for the umpteenth time, murmuring that he knows just how she feels – he couldn't sleep, either. He feels alive, he really does, for the first time in over a year. 'That's funny,' she says. 'I'm happier, too. For the first time in months, I wasn't afraid of the dark last night. And I'm not freaked out by the field behind my house any more. Not now I know what really happened the day of the picnic. And I've got you to thank for that.'

They smile down at the River Usk, cutting its glittering swathe through the golden valley beneath them. Rob says he was starting to think he'd never be happy again. He's been so down and dejected. Out of love with life.

'You lost your mum,' Vanessa replies. 'That would make anyone depressed. And you found out the man that you thought was your father actually wasn't.'

'And I lost my job.'

'Yep, and you lost your job.' She rests her head on his

shoulder. 'You need a new direction,' she says. 'And motivation.'

He laughs. 'Motivation. Rose Pugh said something similar to me a few weeks ago. She took one look at me in my dressing-gown – I'd gone over to Barbara's to shower, because Dad was bathing Llewelyn (don't ask) – and said, "It's well past midday, you're an absolute slob, Robert Hargreaves!" Then she waggled her finger at Barbara, who was still wearing her dressing-gown, too, and said, "For the love of God, you're a pair of sloths. Pull yourselves together! The devil makes work for idle hands."'

'Charming!'

'She's got a point, though.'

'What was Rose Pugh doing at your aunt's house?'

'Making tea. She's been popping in a lot these last few months, offering to make Barbara a cuppa. She must have sensed Barbara was out of sorts, and now we know the reason why – that bloody boiler!' He brushes a strand of hair from Vanessa's forehead. 'Now, where were we?'

'Motivation,' she says.

'Ah, yes. I've found mine, now, haven't I?'

She jumps up quickly, brushing him off.

'Something I said?' he asks, startled.

'No, no. Just a feeling I had . . .'

'Aw, that's natural, Ness, just go with it.'

'No, no. Not *that* kind of feeling. A feeling we were being watched.'

They look over at the kiddies' playground, and the rest of the common and road beyond, but there's not a soul to be seen.

'Look, do you think we can go?' Vanessa shivers. 'Besides,

you still haven't checked Barbara's boiler. Not that you should be meddling with it at all, but perhaps you should just make sure it's turned off.'

They drive around the village – deserted this morning. No church-goers, or early-morning walkers. Wilmslow's Pharmacy is all shut up, the launderette locked, the butcher shop window empty of meat – just plastic-grass fields littered with a few dead wasps.

Only Sandy's Newsagents is open.

'Can you stop the car, Rob?'

'Well, I was going to park outside Barbara's . . .'

'No, please. Stop the car now.'

He screeches to a halt, and Vanessa leaps out, heart in mouth, unable to believe her eyes. She plucks a copy of *The South Wales Sunday Post* from the newsstand, twirls to face Rob, pointing triumphantly at its headline –

'See this?' she shouts. 'Best bloody thing I've seen in months! Listen . . .' And she reads, out loud, '*Top Shrink Arrested in Connection with Marston Murder . . .*'

'Can you believe it?' she cackles, eventually putting the newspaper back on the newsstand, skittering back towards Robert's car, flashing him with a Cheshire-Cat grin. 'Mark Murray can't sack me now!'

'Are you sure?'

She clambers into the passenger seat, slamming the door. He restarts the engine. 'The whole thing stinks to high heaven,' she says. 'If Murray's not struck off for this, I'll eat my hat. And can you believe that the bloke "assisting the police with inquiries" is my ex-patient's dad? I knew all along they had a connection – something had to explain Miss X's off-the-record psychology sessions. And I wouldn't put Mark Murray past murdering Marston, either. He looks the type. Linen suit, sleeves rolled up. Floppy hair. Eyes too close together.'

'That's your considered professional opinion, is it?'

They both laugh.

'And then there's Murray's dodgy relationship with Blanche,' Robert says. 'Funny, isn't it, how Llanfair and Barwood are so inextricably linked?'

58

Debbie

I'm such a bloody muppet.

Fell asleep, I did, last night, on Barbara Pritchard's settee. I was tired and upset, and I said to myself, well, just a quick nap before you walk to the woods and vanish, Debbie-Marie. So, I took the spare key that Barbara always leaves under the flowerpot next to her porch, and let myself in.

It felt like I was coming home. As though Barbara might bustle out of her kitchen any moment with a plate of bourbon creams and Utterson nipping away at her ankles, and for the first time in days I felt bloody starving, and ended up emptying Barbara's cupboards. There was a packet of party rings I completely demolished, then I made myself a Spam and cheese sandwich, followed by a bowl of Smash. After that, I felt dead sleepy, so I curled up on Barbara's settee, draping Utterson's blanket over my shoulders because it was so chilly.

And now here I am, in broad bloody daylight, waking up covered in biscuit crumbs, with bits of Spam stuck to the roof of my mouth – and I've got a *shocking* headache. I also feel sick to my stomach, like I've eaten something really bad.

I can hear someone moving about in the kitchen – shuffling feet, the scraping of chairs. Bloody hell, is Barbara back already? She shouldn't be out of hospital yet, 'cos she's been so ill since her heart attack – the heart attack *I* gave her. That's what Mam's been saying these past few days, when she can be bothered to talk to me. *You broke poor Barbara's heart, and bit by bit, you're breaking mine . . .*

I sit up, letting Utterson's blanket slip to the floor. What if it's a burglar? A burglar on a Sunday morning, with the church just round the corner, and all the people going to Morning Worship?

But The Vicar's still in hospital. The church hasn't had a service in ages; the bells have been silent for weeks. Llanfair's as godless as hell just now, so someone burgling on a Sunday morning would fit right in, it really would.

The lounge door creaks open. A familiar figure stands in the hallway. Small, pudgy with blonde helmet hair, wearing a nurse's uniform. And on a Sunday morning, too! Does Rose Pugh never take a day off?

'Hello, Debbie,' she says with a smile.

I stand up too quickly, losing my footing. I'm feeling giddy – ever so whirly. 'I'm sorry,' I hear myself saying. 'Please don't tell . . .'

Nurse Pugh gives me a little smile. 'Your mummy's been on the phone to the world and its wife since the early hours of this morning, because you've gone missing again. But I won't tell her you've been here all night.' She helps me back onto Barbara's settee. 'This can be our little secret.'

'Our little secret,' I repeat, slumping back.

She plumps a cushion under my head, picks Utterson's

blanket off the floor, and tucks it around and under me. 'Gosh, whatever will Barbara say?' she's chuckling. 'You've left this place an absolute tip! We want it all nice and tidy, don't we? For when Barbara gets home. Now, go back to sleep, there's a good girl, while I do what needs to be done.'

I start to say that I honestly think Barbara wouldn't notice or care, but I clamp my mouth shut, because Rose Pugh suddenly looks ever so cross – there's an expression I've not seen on her face before. She's sticking her chin out, eyes bulging and glazed, glaring at the empty packets, the crumbs on the cushions, the bowl with crusted Smash stuck to its rim.

'Oh, Debbie-Marie.' She shakes her head. 'We were quite the glutton last night, weren't we?'

'You were, too?' I say. 'Well, I don't know about you, but I was starving.' My voice sounds like it's coming from far away, not from me at all. I feel . . . not myself. Not part of myself. And I'm so, so tired . . .

'I hadn't eaten properly in days,' I can hear myself saying. 'And now I feel sick and my head really hurts.'

Nurse Pugh nods, her lips tightening into a line. 'I see,' she says. 'That sounds about right. Let me have a look in my first aid kit. There'll be some medication for that.'

She sits down next to me, rootling around in the bottom of her nurse's bag.

'What sort of medicine?' I slur. 'I don't like taking tablets.'

'You'll take what's good for you,' she says firmly, pulling out a great big pill, shaped like a ball – the biggest pill I've ever seen in my life, impossible to swallow whole. 'Here,' she says. 'Your medication. Open wide!'

As her hand looms in front of my face, I can see it's not a

pill at all that she's holding, but a gobstopper, like the ones in Sandy's store – green, lime and peppermint flavour. Not my favourite, I won't lie. I try to stand up, but my legs won't work.

'No, I won't,' I say. 'I'm not taking no medicine. Not without Mam's say-so. I've only got a headache – just because you're a nurse doesn't give you the right . . .'

'I have every right,' she breathes into my ear, pressing her hand down onto my chest. And I can smell her perfume – strong and sickly, like it's covering up the stink of something rotten. 'You will take your medicine, Debbie-Marie Tunstall, if it's the last thing I do!'

I hear a car pull up outside, radio blaring *The Archers'* tune. The Sunday morning edition. When Mam's in one of her better moods, we'll listen to it together at breakfast. I thrash my head from side to side, trying to dodge the gobstopper. *Lalalalalalala* the music plays. *La-la-la-la-la-la-la* . . .

Nurse Pugh rolls the gobstopper over my lips, trying to prise them open, muttering quietly all the while, something that sounds like a prayer. Something I recognize from some time before, about a tongue and a tree of life . . .

'What, in the name of arse, is going on?'
Mam!
Standing in the doorway – strong and mighty – my outraged mam. Bloody *tamping*, she is. She swats Pugh to one side, hauls me into her arms, and I can feel it, can actually feel her heart leaping around like a frog in her chest, not weak and broken, the way it's been these last few years.

'I've been looking for you everywhere, Debbie-Marie!' she cries. 'I couldn't let you leave me again!'

She pulls away. Stares, first at me, then at Pugh. 'What the hell,' she growls, 'have you done to my daughter, you crazy bitch?'

'I haven't done anything!' Nurse Pugh cries. 'The child is ill! She has all the signs, actually, of very low blood sugar. I was encouraging her to take one of Susan's sweeties to give her a quick sugar boost, before I called for an ambulance. You're neglectful, Ingrid Tunstall! Debbie-Marie clearly hasn't eaten in days, and you've done nothing – absolutely nothing to help her . . .'

From the kitchen, I hear Dr Bridges shout, 'The outside flue's blocked with leaves – the bloody boiler's a death trap!'

I slump against Mam. All the shouting seems so very far away.

Then Rob – 'How the hell is it still turned on? I swear I switched it off when Barbara went into hospital. This place is full of carbon monoxide!'

I open my mouth to say, 'What's a flue?' just as Mam hauls me up by my arms, dragging me through to the kitchen, towards the back door.

Then everything goes fuzzy and static – my eyes can't see, my ears can't hear, like I'm slipping into the quarry lake. And I slide down into its velvety darkness, letting the water close over my face, everything around me all muffled and stifled, not important any more.

I hear Dad's voice. 'You ready now, Debs? You sure this is what you really want?'

I feel myself nod.

And we sink to the bottom, hand in hand, while the world above us drifts away. The way the world drifts into darkness, just before sleep.

Six Weeks Later

SATURDAY, 3 NOVEMBER 1984

59

Debbie

9.45 p.m., outside the Llanfair Arms

It's a clear, starry sky tonight. There'll be a heavy frost in the morning, making Llanfair look like a Christmas card, even though it's only November. The pavements will be too slippery for Barbara to take Utterson out for his walk, so Rob and Vanessa will do it instead. These days, those two do everything together. They'll stroll, hand-in-hand, towards Llanfair Woods, past the graveyard where jackdaws peck at the frozen mound covering Clive Marston's body, pausing for a moment when they reach the vicarage, to stare at the scaffolding holding it up. And then they'll follow the curve of the lane towards Stockholm Villa, admiring the line of birch trees glittering orange and pink as the sun starts to rise.

Just now, the pub windows are already misting up; from out here, in the car park, the people inside look jumbled up – a mass of heads and arms and colour, laughing and singing along to Rob's ghetto blaster. He's put on a cassette of Glenn Miller songs, because Barbara loves Glenn Miller. She once said his music takes her back to the war, when people lived on their wits, when there really was such a thing as society – everyone in the same boat, taking care of each other, rather than just themselves. I replied, *What – like now, with the Miners' Strike?* And Barbara said, no – not at all like now, because now we're all in different-sized boats. And some boats will get smaller as time goes by, while others get bigger. Just wait and see.

It's Barbara's eightieth birthday party, and it's been a lovely evening. We've had dancing, and speeches from Dai and Rob, and a few words from Mam that made me cry. She got up – wearing her poshest frock – to say Barbara always makes her feel equal. That in an unjust, unequal world, Barbara Pritchard always gives a helping hand to those who need it, and that makes her Barbara Lady Pritchard, with a capital 'L'. Then she read out a poem she'd written, and it really was very good indeed. I felt dead proud – I never knew Mam could write like that – and then I overheard her telling Barbara that she enters writing competitions on the sly. She even won two tickets, she said, to see Wrong Jones at the Llanfair Arms, and left a note in Barbara's diary as a jokey surprise. She was going to take Barbara with her, but then all the *Spotlight Cymru* stuff kicked off, and Mam couldn't be arsed with all that – her poem in *The South Wales Morning Post* had caused enough bad feeling as it was, she said, and she didn't want to risk being exposed. And Barbara said, Oh! So that's how Wrong Jones ended up in my diary – I honestly thought I was losing my mind! And they both had a good laugh about that.

Everyone loves a happy ending. Barbara reckons it's why grown-ups love fairy tales almost as much as kids do. 'It's because we all long for justice and order in an unjust and disordered universe,' she says.

And I think I know what she means by that. Because the world isn't always fair and ordered, and that makes us feel scared. Bad things happen to good people, and the other way around. Things don't always turn out the way that they should, though over the past few weeks, the universe seems to have been behaving itself for a change.

For a start, things have turned out fine for me. Better than fine, in fact.

I didn't die. I nearly did, because Barbara's boiler was blocked and churning out poison that I'd been breathing for hours, according to Mam. It was blocked by leaves jamming up its outside flue. I don't remember much about it at all – it's all a jumble of screaming and yelling and flashing blue lights in my head, but Mam's told me what happened, over and over, like a broken record, she is. I suppose she's still getting it out of her system, trying to make sense of it all. She keeps saying I'm lucky to be here. Even better, she says that *she's* lucky that I'm still alive.

Barbara's lucky to be alive, too. She thought she was dying or going doolally, and all because of a blocked bloody flue.

But a brush with death does have its upsides.

For a start, because I nearly died, almost everyone's been nicer to me, and when I went back to school, loads of kids came up to say hello. They said that they'd missed me, and for once in my life I kept my gob shut. If this whole sorry business has taught me anything at all, it's to not blurt out the very first thing that pops into my head. Especially if that thing is, 'Piss off, you've been shits to me for years and years, and I'm still the same person. Nothing's changed.' Which is the truth, God's honour, and it hurt not to say it, but I didn't say it, and I'm proud of myself for that.

Anyway, on my first day back at school, I went into class, and nearly cried. My desk was covered in conkers – the biggest, shiniest specimens you ever did see.

'A little bird told us your conker collection had met with a bit of an accident,' Bug-eyed Thomas said with a smile. 'So, we thought you might like a new one. A fresh start, if you like.' She hauled me against her ginormous boobs, and squeezed me tight. 'Welcome back, Debbie-Marie. Mr Griffiths has had a chat with us all, teachers included, and I think it's time that everyone turned over a new leaf.'

I smiled back, trying not to **gag**, because the smell of BO on her overalls was really rank. But I didn't say so. Six weeks ago, I'd have told her she stank, but not any more.

I'm a grown-up, now.

If you have very nearly died, everyone thinks you're the bee's knees. Maybe it's because you've almost met God, so that makes you practically God yourself. And it's weird, having people being nice to me. Nurse Pugh was always nice to me anyway, but she was particularly kind when she visited me in hospital. 'I feel terrible,' she kept saying, 'frightening you like that. But I only wanted to give you something sugary, because you looked so poorly and weak. I only wanted to help. I just can't help myself from helping people.'

Mam, who was there at the time, folded her arms and glared at Rose Pugh, and said: 'Helping people, my fanny. You're a busybody, Nurse Rose Pugh, and your busy-bodying nearly killed poor Debbie. Trying to shove a sweet into her mouth when you should have called an ambulance! And it shouldn't be allowed, professionals letting themselves into people's houses like that. Barbara needs to stop leaving her door key under her flowerpot.'

Pugh looked gutted, really she did. She twiddled a bit with her stethoscope, trying not to cry. She's only a nurse wanting to do good, even if she was scary at the time. So, I said it was fine, that I understood, and she patted my hand and said that I was a credit to my mother.

When she'd gone, Mam snorted and said, 'She's a one.'

'She's a what?'

'A piece of work. Always sticking her nose in where it doesn't belong. She and Susan have moved in with Blanche Marston, would you believe it? Says Blanche isn't coping at all since Clive's death, and Rose needs to look after her and the girls. Truth be told, Blanche does look awful – like she's aged at least twenty years – and she's completely away with the fairies most of the time. So maybe it's not such a terrible thing, having someone there, keeping an eye on things. But I don't know . . .'

'You don't know what?'

Mam shook her head. 'I never thought I'd hear myself say this, especially after the dreadful way she's treated us both, but I pity Blanche Marston, I really do. Losing her husband like that – even though there wasn't much love lost between them. Rumour has it she'll lose her house and all her money, too, because of Marston's misdealings and folk wanting to sue, and it turns out he had no life insurance, so Blanche has been left pretty much penniless. Which you might think serves her right, given how awful she is, but it's like she's being punished. A long, slow torture, if you like.'

I probably should feel sorry for Blanche, but I don't. And

I don't feel sorry for Carrie-Anne and Lucy, either. They've been dead sulky since I came back to school. Everyone reckons they're mourning their dad, but I dunno. The way that they glare at me – like I've stolen their thunder. And Carrie-Anne's face when Gary White asked me to partner him in country dancing (even though I told him to bog off, 'cos he was only asking me because I'm popular now). Well, she looked like she wanted to throttle me. It gave me the willies, it did. Still does.

Even so, I'd like to tell them that I'm sorry about their dad. That I know what it's like when you've got just a mam, and your mam's not really that well in the head. I want to tell them that I don't really like it – being really popular for a change. It's not as bad as being disliked, but it's knackering, it really is. Like tonight – everyone in the pub wanted to speak to me. Lots of ladies in sparkly dresses hugging me close and cooing, and sweaty, red-faced men in suits saying, 'Well, Deborah, here's to a fresh start.' And the smell of cigars and perfume made me feel like I wanted to puke.

Which is why I'm out here in the fresh air, having a bit of time by myself, sitting on the bonnet of Rob Hargreaves' car, freezing my arse off in a brand-new frock. Barbara bought it – dark blue denim, with a ra-ra skirt, but not too frilly, because that just isn't me.

When I first tried it on, Mam cried her eyes out. She said I looked utterly beautiful.

The door of the Llanfair Arms bursts open. I hear people laugh. I slip off the car bonnet and crouch by the bumper, just in time to see Rob and Dr Bridges lurching into the car park hand in hand, the pair of them drunk as lords. I crane my head around Rob's front wheel, to see them standing, heads pressed together, sharing one another's breath, swaying gently in the moonlight. They start to kiss. I look away. I don't want to spy. Not any more.

'Have I told you I love you?' I hear Rob say.

'At least a dozen times tonight,' Dr Bridges replies. 'Have I told you I love you, too?'

'Not yet.'

'Well, I do.'

There's silence for a minute or so, and I'm about to crawl out from my hiding place, because I'm feeling dead awkward about all of this, when I hear Rob say –

'It's rough about Blanche, though. She looks awful tonight. Fallen apart since Clive died. Given up on everything.' He strikes a match, and I hear it fizz. A tendril of cigarette smoke curls through the air towards my nostrils. 'Funny,' he says, breathing out heavily, 'because she was coping so well at first.'

'Delayed shock,' Dr Bridges says. 'And it can't be easy, now that Mark Murray's been charged with his murder. God knows what was going on there, but if your theory is correct . . .'

'That she and Mark Murray were having it away, and she's lost not just her husband, but her lover as well?'

'Exactly. And all the money and legal stuff that's come to light since Clive died – Blanche's life is ruined! She looks practically catatonic this evening. Whatever was Rose thinking of, bringing her to Barbara's party? It's humiliating for the poor woman. I never thought I'd feel sorry for Blanche, but I really do.'

'Thought it might do her some good, I suppose – trying to

snap her out of it.' I hear Rob exhale noisily. 'Rose is doing her best – thank God she's around to help take care of the girls. For now. Christ knows what Blanche will do when Rose flies out to Saudi. What do you make of that particular move?'

'I think Rose has made a sensible decision. She'll earn a small fortune out there – lots of British nurses do. And it'll be a nice change for her and Susan. I just hope Blanche is a bit more with-it before Rose leaves, for Carrie-Anne and Lucy's sake. What is it now – two weeks away? It's come around so quickly!'

'Just under. Rose reckons Blanche will be okay by then. "Never fear, Robert dear," she said, when I asked how she could be so sure. "The day that Susan and I touch down in Saudi, I can guarantee Blanche Marston will be in a much better place."'

'Well, if she can pull that one off, she's a better psychologist than I am!'

'No one's better than you.'

I hear slurping noises. They're probably kissing again. Bleugh! Then –

'Move in with me,' Rob says.

'Seriously?'

'Seriously.'

'Where? And when?'

'Rose's place. She's putting it up for rent when she moves to Saudi. Three-bed semi-detached, spacious garage – plenty of room for the banana-yellow estate. Enough room for a bloody bus, as it happens. In fact, I'm thinking about getting the band back together and using the garage as a rehearsal room.'

'You're not serious!'

Rob laughs. 'No, I'm not. I've made a decision, actually.

I'm going back to college. I've decided to follow in the footsteps of a certain Barbara Pritchard, and train to be a primary school teacher. To do what I can to help other young misfits. What do you think of that?'

'Oh, Rob!' Dr Bridges cries. 'You'd be perfect! I'm so proud of you!'

'Not as proud as I am of you. Taking on that permanent role at the Dewi Sant Centre . . .'

'Well, thanks to Debbie-Marie Tunstall, I've found my true calling in life. No more textbooks and case histories – it's grassroots psychology all the way!'

I pop my head over the bonnet to say, 'I'm proud of the pair of you, too!' But they've already headed back inside the pub, to the sound of Glenn Miller's 'In the Mood'.

Everyone's getting a happy ending. Apart from Blanche Marston, that is. And Mark Murray, who's since been charged with Clive Marston's murder, and I reckon he deserves everything he gets. Turns out that Clive was in some sort of drugs ring with Murray – a big-wig professor able to get his hands on all sorts of stuff. Then Clive double-crossed Murray, and Murray lost a six-figure sum. Murray was very cross about that, so he shot Clive Marston at point-blank range. I get all this from Rob, who hears it from Barry Parry, who hears it from his informers at Uskshire Constabulary. Llewelyn hears a lot of things, too – since he started talking again, he's been moved to Rob's bedroom, because every time Barry Parry walked into the pub, he'd shout out 'wanker'.

But Mam says Murray's arrest is 'too neat'.

I think it's too neat, too.

Because I keep thinking things. Remembering things that bother me. Things that I know are important enough to write in my Kajagoogoo notebook, even if Mam told me that if she ever caught me writing 'salacious musings' in my notebook again, she'd give me the thrashing of my life.

For a start, there's The Vicar, and that stuff he said about the Seven Deadly Sins and dead people having things pushed into their gobs, and Clive Marston having that fifty-pound note shoved inside his. I've not told a soul, and his fifty quid's still in my jewellery box, along with Clive's watch and Utterson's whisker and Mr Strong from Dad's keyring. I'll be in deep shit if I get found out, so I'll have to keep quiet for evermore. But it eats away at me, really it does, because I know that something's not right.

And it turns out the rug Clive's body was wrapped in came from the vicarage study, but Mark Murray is denying all knowledge of that. He's admitted the murder, but not the rug that Marston was dumped in, and Rob says rumour has it that Murray's protecting someone. I mean, what do you make of that? It's rattled The Vicar, and he tried to tell the police about his serial-killer theory, but the on-duty PC – the really young one with the bum-fluff face – looked at The Vicar like he was crackers, and said that this was Llanfair, not St Mary Mead, and if The Vicar wanted to go all Miss Marple and claim a serial killer was on the loose, he could conduct his own investigations in his own bloody time.

The Vicar reckons the serial killer is getting brazen – that he's having a laugh at us all, which means he'll eventually make a mistake. He's taking bizarre chances, like that stuff with The Vicar's rug; and being sloppy by leaving clues – like Clive

Marston's loafers turning up inside that van. And, even worse, he's being a lot less choosy about his victims. Targeting innocent children, The Vicar says, the way he did at the summer fete, really is plumbing new depths.

Which brings me to Barbara's boiler. Because what if the killer was targeting her? I mean seriously, how low could he go? Barbara's practically a saint! The carbon monoxide nearly killed me – it could have killed her, too – and all because of leaves in the outside flue? 'A not unheard-of problem', so Barbara tells me. But really? No one seems to want to think that a person might have stuffed the leaves in there on purpose. In fact, no one in Llanfair these days seems to want to *think* at all.

Because everyone who deserved to live lived, and the good people got their happy endings. So that's that, I suppose. Dr Bridges and Rob have fallen in love, and given up sleuthing in exchange for cosy nights together, watching TV. Barbara's back in her house with Utterson, Mam's getting help from social services *and* been given some counselling, and she's been a bit better these last few weeks. Even The Vicar's at it. Last month, he climbed into his pulpit – his first sermon since leaving hospital – and announced to everyone that Brown Owl's his daughter, the product of a short-lived affair. Then Brown Owl stood up, and said that The Vicar was moving into her flat while the vicarage was being rebuilt, and once that was done, she'd move in with him to make sure he didn't mess up his medication ever again. And at that, the whole congregation got to their feet and gave them a standing ovation.

I'm starting to like Brown Owl a bit more. She took over running Flicks N' Kicks, because Blanche is too out of it most of the time. I've been asked to audition for the chorus line, *and* invited to join the Girl Guides! Oh, and WPC Jane Gill – Rob's old bully – finally got her comeuppance. That chain-smoking Dr Jolly came forward to say he saw Gill shove a lit firework through The Vicar's letterbox the night the vicarage burst into flames. He saw her arrive before the rest of the mob while he was having a sneaky fag in The Vicar's side passage. It's his word against hers, it seems, with no actual evidence, but apparently Gill's locker was found to be crammed with confiscated goods – fireworks, cannabis, that sort of thing – and so she's been put on 'gardening leave' pending investigations. I think it's a bit crap, really, because she should be in prison or something like that after everything she's done, not planting bloody begonias.

Barbara's still planning on selling her field. Gwendoline Bridges must like it or lump it, she says, though Barbara is trying to ease the blow by choosing a 'socially conscious' developer, who's promised landscaped community gardens and an 'ecologically and aesthetically sympathetic design'.

The developer bloke is a millionaire, and when he's finally finished with us, he'll revamp the valleys, according to an article in *The South Wales Morning Post*. He says that when the coal mines close down, there'll be no unemployment at all, because he'll build 'boom towns' with factories making computers and stuff like that, and all the ex-miners will end up rich and live happily ever after.

Gwendoline Bridges was quoted as saying, 'What an absolutely smashing idea!' But when I asked Twp Lisa what she thought, she curled her lip and said, 'Yeah. Of course that'll happen.'

'What do you reckon, Debbie?' Twp Lisa said, handing me

an extra-large bag of flying saucers. I noticed she'd been doodling in bright red pen on a notebook by the till – 'kill the rich' and 'I hate Tories', that sort of thing. 'Do you think that the wanton destruction of the industrial heartlands of Wales will result in the creation of a technological "boom town" – a Silicon Valley of the South Wales Valleys, if you like – its prosperity shared by the common man and capitalists alike?'

I thought about this for a moment.

'No,' I said. 'Not really.'

Things between Barwood and Llanfair have improved. Mam says it's because we both share the shame of Clive Marston. Barwood bred him, Llanfair indulged him, so a truce of sorts has been called. Besides, the local journos have stopped stirring up shit between us – for now. Mam says it's because they've finally woken up to the fact that they've got more important stuff to worry about, like AIDS, the famine in Africa, and Indira Gandhi being shot. Mam says we're on a highway to hell, but at least she said it while she was making my tea – for the first time in months. Bangers and Smash and Angel Delight – my absolute favourites! She's still not how she was before Dad left, but she'll get there one day. I think.

But, I dunno. There's more stuff that bugs me.

Like the Flicks N' Kicks girls and the morphine poisoning. That one's never been solved. Everything weird that happened last summer's been pinned on Clive Marston; everything that's ever gone wrong in Llanfair, in fact, has been pinned on Clive Marston.

I said to Barbara when I went round for tea, I said – Barbara, it doesn't sit right with me. I think Mark Murray killed Clive of course, but there's more to all this than meets the eye. There's something rotten in Llanfair, like someone's playing a game of chess with us all, and no one – apart from The Vicar – has cottoned on to it yet.

Barbara looked puzzled, and then she said:

'Yes, Deborah. I think I know what you mean. I just wish my mind was sharper. There are things I can't quite grasp, you know. Memories I've lost, from when the boiler was leaking. There is something important I know that I saw, but I can't recall what it was. The more I try to grasp it, the slipperier the memory becomes. I daresay it'll come back to me by-and-by. Another custard cream, dear?'

She's not been the same, poor Barbara, since she got home from hospital. On the surface she's as sprightly as ever, but I know a light has gone out. She's not as sharp or as smart as she was. She seems a bit tired and frail. Sometimes, I worry that I was the one that took her light away.

But looking through the pub window just now, where someone's rubbed away the mist on the glass, I can see that tonight, Barbara's light is there for all to see. She's dancing in Rob's arms, rocking gently back and forth to Glenn Miller's 'Moonlight Serenade'. Even Dai Hargreaves has a grin on his face – *and* he's got his teeth in. He's agreed to let Utterson into the pub, as long as he behaves himself. Which Utterson has so far, thanks to Rob slipping him pork scratchings every so often.

The Vicar steps forward. 'A toast!' he shouts. 'I've a speech,' he laughs. 'I'll read it out. Hang on . . .'

He pulls loads of cards out of his pocket, all different colours. 'My prompt cards,' he booms. 'Red for the most important points, blue for jokes – which won't be blue, because I'm a man of the cloth – and green for tear-jerking moments. Now, let me just sort them into piles . . .'

I turn away, just as a girl steps out from the shrubbery behind Rob's car, into the shaft of light streaming through the pub window – a girl a little older than I am, with long dark hair, wearing a smocked dress and crocheted red cardigan. She moves quickly to stand in front of me, blocking my way.

'Hello,' I say. 'So, you've finally decided to talk to me. You've been following me these last few weeks. I keep seeing you. At school, in the lane outside my house . . .'

'I like playing conkers, too,' the girl says quietly.

'I thought that I was imagining things. That because I very nearly died, my brain had gone all funny and I was seeing ghosts. But I saw you once before, didn't I? Just for a second, in the Dewi Sant car park.' I reach out and touch her cardigan, just to make sure she's real.

'Please listen to me,' she says, grabbing my hand. And, with her other hand, she pulls a piece of paper out of her dress pocket, clears her throat, and starts to read:

'My name is Isobel Robinson. Peter and June Robinson's daughter; Dr Bridges' ex-patient. Once a promising swimmer, now a drifting nobody. I drift from Barwood to Llanfair and back again almost every day, my comings and goings barely noticed by my family, who stopped caring once it was clear I was never going to be an Olympic champion . . .'

She looks up. 'Your hand is shaking,' she says. 'I'm scaring you, aren't I?'

'Just a bit.'

'Please don't be scared. I'd never hurt you; I'm not the hurting kind. But a certain person *is*. Let me explain, and then you can tell Dr Bridges about it. Be my go-between. What do you think?'

'I think I want to go to the toilet.'

'Listen to me first. Please?'

And she tells me a story. That she was once a brilliant swimmer, but a woman in Barwood ruined all that. Put ideas into Isobel's head that she was proud and a sinner. And this woman was everywhere: in Isobel's school, at her swimming classes – watching from the side of the pool, waiting for her outside her home, in the park and the playground. And all the while, telling Isobel that she had to repent. But nobody noticed that someone was following Isobel, because of the woman's job. Because the woman was meant to be everywhere, because she was the district nurse.

'And she had a thing about mouths,' Isobel says. 'Sometimes, she'd quote from the Bible. Said it often enough that I can repeat it word for word – *a wholesome tongue is a tree of life, but perverseness in it . . .*'

'*. . . crushes the spirit.*'

She nods at me.

'Rose Pugh,' we say together.

The car park seems to give way. The girl starts talking terribly fast, barely catching her breath. 'On the day of my accident, I went shopping in Cardiff, just before my appointment with Dr Bridges. I was buying a record for my dad's birthday. His favourite song – "Red, Red Wine". And I saw Rose Pugh as I came out of Spillers – she'd followed me there, I'm sure of it, and was getting out of her red Mini, which she'd parked across the street. She was livid, because I'd won a major swimming gala the day before, and I was so excited to tell Dr Bridges. Anyway, as soon as I saw her, I panicked and started to run, didn't look where I was going and . . . oh!'

She hides her face in her hands. 'I've tried to tell Dr Bridges the truth – that she wasn't to blame. I found her number in the telephone book, and called her flat a few times, but lost my nerve at the last minute. I even waited outside her parents' house once, trying to pluck up the courage to talk to her. But I was so scared she wouldn't believe me, and would hate me for getting her into trouble. You see, things got much worse for poor Dr Bridges when a couple of witnesses gave their statements, and said a medical person drove right past the accident without offering help. Pugh always wears a stethoscope, and after she saw what she'd done, she drove away – I remember she was wearing a coat at the time, so no one would know whether she was a doctor or nurse; they'd just see the stethoscope and reach their conclusions. So, when the witnesses mentioned the "medical person", my dad thought they meant Dr Bridges, and I was too ill in hospital at the time to put him straight. But in fact, Dr Bridges called the ambulance, and stayed with me until it arrived.'

I lean against Rob's car, head spinning. I can't take this. Can't deal with this.

'Mark Murray, as you know, killed Clive Marston – not just because Marston double-crossed him and swindled him out of loads of money, but because Murray wanted to run off with Marston's wife. It's true – Murray's obsessed with Blanche Marston, to the point he'd take the full rap to save her from jail. I overheard my dad say so to my mum, and he should know because he's known Murray for years. And I was there in the woods the day you found the body, but I'm too scared to say what I heard and saw to anyone, in case Rose Pugh finds out and comes and gets me. So, you'll tell Dr Bridges what I'm about to tell you, and she can call the police for us, yes?'

'You were the thing in red! You scared the shit out of me!'

'I was spying on Dr Bridges' house,' Isobel says, 'when a white van pulled into the layby opposite the woods. Then a man in a yellow car turned up, and he went for a walk and when he was gone, two women in hats and masks got out of the van and dragged a rug from the back. I ran towards the quarry, and just before you get to where the woods dip down into a hollow, I slipped into my hiding place – a small gap between two rocks. Anyway, the two women carried the rug close to where I was hiding, and I clearly heard Rose Pugh's voice say, *You owe me, you do, Blanche Marston. Owe me big time for this, for your freedom with Mark bloody Murray.* The other woman – Blanche – was all out of breath and really struggling with the rug, and kept whining, *Why are we having to do this? Why can't Mark dump the body?* And Rose Pugh said, *Because he has to search Clive's offices for the missing cash and drugs before anyone realizes Clive's gone AWOL, stupid, and Mark knows what he's looking for. We don't.*

'Then Blanche told Rose to keep her effing voice down, because she didn't want Clown Face to hear them . . . who's Clown Face?'

'Rob,' I whisper.

Rob. The kindest man I've ever known. Who thinks his half-sister, Blanche, might actually give a stuff about him.

'Well, they were planning on framing this Rob man, I reckon, because Blanche started boasting that tongues were beginning to wag. Everyone thought that she and this Rob were having it away in the woods, and would think that he had murdered Clive and attacked her in a jealous rage. And if that didn't work, the plan with the van in the Texas Homecare car park would – that there were loads of people in Barwood who'd be glad to see Clive dead and his wife beaten up. And if Mark Murray was ever caught, he wouldn't grass Blanche up, because he was utterly smitten with her.'

I feel sick.

'After they dumped the rug,' Isobel's saying, 'Blanche Marston mentioned how scared she was about getting punched – that she knew she had to go through with it for appearances' sake, but was nervous as hell. She said, *Go gently on me, won't you, Rose?* And Pugh just laughed and said, *I'll try not to get carried away, Blanche my love, but you have such a slappable face.* They left after that, and I thought they'd gone and I nearly crawled out of my hiding place, but then Rose Pugh came back. I don't know what excuse she'd made to get away from Blanche, but she went to the rug, pulled it open, and did something to the body – something to its face – and I overheard her saying the weirdest thing. I remember it clearly: 'Well then, Mammy, that's another filthy sinner sent to keep you company. Bet you wish you'd kept your knickers on the day of the picnic, don't you?' Then she took the shoes off the body, and shoved them into her nurse's bag, before rolling the rug up again. Rose Pugh is small, but . . .'

'Strong as buggery,' I say, slowly. 'When she pulls my hair apart to look for nits, it bloody well hurts. It was Rose Pugh all along. Killing people. For years and years. Punishing them for their sins. Choking them with their sin as they died, or after they died. It doesn't matter when, because either way, she was shutting them down and shutting them up. For ever.'

I turn and peep through the pub window. I can see Nurse Pugh, chatting and laughing, sitting on the knee of Morris the Butcher, who's drunkenly singing and swaying away, not realizing he has the arms of a killer around him.

Always in bloody uniform, she is. Never takes a day off . . .

I turn back to say, 'Why don't we both talk to Dr Bridges and the police? We can back each other up!' But Isobel's gone.

The pub door opens.

Out trips Dr Bridges in her clogs, ruddy-faced and pissed as a fart. She smiles at me woozily. 'Out here all by yourself, Debbie-Marie? Come inside, into the warmth!'

And she takes my hand, and I walk beside her – robot-like – into the open arms of the party. The first person I see, sat in the corner, is Blanche, who's made my life hell these last few years. Blanche Marston, who's guilty of every sin going – pride, greed, envy, you name it. And murder. She helped get rid of her murdered husband's body, then tried to frame Rob and some innocent miners. It's only a matter of time before Rose murders her, too. Does Blanche have a clue what Rose has been up to with her Seven Deadly Sins stuff? I can't see how. If she did, she wouldn't let her near her, wouldn't let her anywhere near her precious girls.

'Debbie?' Dr Bridges frowns down at me. 'Whatever's the matter, my lovely?'

I could stay silent, I should say nothing, Isobel Robinson's crackers, that's all. None of this is true. And if it is, well – Blanche

Marston deserves all she gets, being 'looked after' by Nurse Rose Pugh. And those horrible daughters of hers. Girls who make other girls' lives miserable . . .

'Debbie?' Dr Bridges guides me to a seat. 'Do you need to sit down?'

But they're kids, the same as you, Debbie-Marie Tunstall. And whatever you do, they'll lose their mam. Either because Rose will kill her, or because the police will find out Blanche Marston helped do away with her own husband. And that means two kids left without a mam or a dad . . .

Whatever I do, I'm buggered.

Dr Bridges eases me down onto a stool, touches my cheek. 'Debbie? Are you okay?' she says. 'You're looking ever so pale!'

I brush off her hand to look over at Rob, who's just finished dancing with Barbara. The kindest man in the whole wide world is leading his aunt by the arm to a younger woman – Celia Owen from Barwood Library, according to Mam – sitting next to Blanche Marston on a red banquette. I watch him step back, as though he's handing Barbara over, and Barbara mouths *thank you*.

Dr Bridges is leaning over me, shouting into my ear: 'Debbie? Debbie-Marie? Do you need a glass of water?'

. . . then Celia Owen takes Barbara's hand. And Rob reaches into his trouser pocket, taking out a handkerchief, dabbing away his tears.

And at that moment, Blanche Marston, who's been dead-eyed all this time, bolts out of her seat, shrieking – 'Daddy's hanky! I bought it for him for his final birthday before he died! Embroidered, it is, with his initials – HW. Where did you get that, Robbie? Tell me, please!'

I feel dazed and dizzy, hot and cold. I turn from Rob, just

in time to see The Vicar, who's ready to make his speech, shuffling his cards into order, sticking a red one between his teeth.

And Barbara, who's holding Celia's hand, guiding her across the pub to introduce her to everyone, sees this and cries: 'Now I remember! Lewis – the prophylactic! Stuck between your teeth!'

And Celia Owen says with surprise, 'A *condom*, Barbara?'

And Barbara yells over the crowd, 'Lewis – you had a red Durex in your mouth!' But her words get lost, because everyone's singing 'The Green, Green Grass of Home'.

I should say something. I could say something. But who on earth would believe me? They'll say I'm a liar, Mam will thrash me, and I'll be back to square one, a right Nobby-no-mates. And I am beginning to enjoy having friends. I like to be liked.

Besides, Rose will be leaving in less than two weeks, and won't be a risk to Llanfair any more. She's a risk to Blanche Marston, that's all, and Blanche Marston deserves all she gets for betraying poor Rob, for being such a two-faced, bullying bitch . . .

But Lucy and Carrie-Anne – Blanche's kids. They'll suffer, whatever I do . . .

And life is good. *My* life is good. All this would cause a right rumpus, it would. And the village has been so happy of late.

'Debbie?' Dr Bridges crouches in front of me. 'Do you need to go home?'

I am a grown-up. I don't tell tales.

'Debbie? Are you all right?'

I am a grown-up, I don't tell tales.

I can hear Rose's cackling laugh, and Morris the Butcher singing away . . .

I don't tell tales!

Barbara pushes her way through the crowd, whispers in The

Vicar's ear, and he goes very pale indeed. Rob is shouting at Blanche Marston, waving his handkerchief in her face and pointing his finger at Rose, who's not noticed anything's up. She's too busy flirting with Morris the Butcher. Stroking his arm, nibbling his earlobe . . .

I WILL NOT tell tales.

Rose takes something out of her pocket, and dangles it in Blanche's direction, trying to catch her attention. It'll be her front door keys, I'll bet. She's trying to persuade Morris the Butcher to come back to hers for the night, I'm sure of it. I know I should tell him not to do it; that he'll be mincemeat if he does. He'll end up with mincemeat in his gob, for sure, for being a gluttonous alco.

'Blanche, my love,' Rose raises her voice, 'I'm taking Morris back to mine, to sober him up a little. Robert can see you home. I'll be back at yours in the morning.'

Blanche just stares at her, glassy-eyed, Rob whispering frantically in her ear.

'I said,' Rose repeats, lifting her keys in the air, jangling them for all to see, 'I'm taking Morris home.'

And that's when I see it. A leather fob holding three different-sized keys, and one Mr Happy. One yellow smiling face, with a scratch below its mouth. A scratched face I haven't seen in five long years.

Mam's Mr Happy. Trapped all this time, in Rose Pugh's nurse's bag. While my Mr Strong was locked away in my jewellery box at home, and Mr Lazy – what the hell happened to Dad's Mr Lazy?

Your father was a layabout, Debbie Marie . . . living off the public purse . . .

A sloth. He'd have been a sloth to her.

She'd have stopped Dad's mouth with his sin. Then taken what was left of his keyring. Keeping it as a souvenir.

'Debbie?' Dr Bridges' voice trails after me as I shove my way through the crowd.

She has no right, no right at all, to kill, to silence, to jam people's mouths shut, to choke them with their 'sin'. She has no right to play judge and jury, to decide who lives or dies. She took Dad's life, she took Mam's, too, and ruined everything for me . . . Got me blamed for stuff I never did. I bet it was her who gave the Marston girls morphine, and cut the brakes on Brown Owl's bike 'cos she thought she was having it off with The Vicar, the evil witch . . .

'I have something to say,' I shout, standing where Llewelyn's cage used to be. 'I have something important to tell you all. Something about all the things that have happened in Llanfair . . .'

Rob turns the music off. The pub goes quiet.

'Oh, Debbie-Marie!' Nurse Pugh jumps off Morris's lap with a little clap of her hands. 'You're giving a speech, after all!'

And I see it for the very first time, behind the pink-faced innocence, the nurse's outfit, the do-gooder smile. I see the flicker of a fork-tongued snake, a snake that's been hissing and laughing at us all this time.

'Got a tale to tell?' shouts Morris the Butcher. 'What lies you spewing now, Debbie-Marie?'

Everyone laughs.

Oh, what's the point?

'Shut it,' Dai Hargreaves growls. 'Let the child speak.'

I look around at all the faces, heart hammering in my chest.

Then Barbara comes and stands next to me. Then Rob.

Then Dr Bridges and The Vicar. Mam comes and joins them, taking my hand.

I'm surrounded by my beautiful people. My family and friends.

Barbara Pritchard nods at me. 'Will Nurse Rose Pugh like the tale you're about to tell us, Deborah?' she asks.

I open my mouth, take a deep breath.

'No,' I say. 'Not really.'

Acknowledgements

It's been a bumpy old ride, trying to write Book Number Two – in fact, there were many occasions when I wondered whether it would ever get written at all. This novel would not exist were it not for the following people. My agent, the wonderful Stephanie Thwaites at Curtis Brown – thank you for your faith in me, your wisdom, insight and for being such a joy to work with. To my publisher, Katie Loughnane at Pan Macmillan – thank you for your patience, professionalism and all-round loveliness. To my editor, Maddie Thornham – thank you for totally 'getting' Debbie-Marie, and for treating her story with so much love, care and compassion; and thank you, Daisy Dickeson, for managing the copy-editing stage with such proficiency, consideration and kindness. Thank you Susan Opie for your copy-editing expertise, and thank you, Pippa Wickenden, for your eagle-eyed proofreading. The inhabitants of Llanfair could not have been in more capable hands.

I am extremely grateful to the design team at Pan Macmillan for their hard work and creative wizardry, especially Kieryn

Tyler and Neil Lang; and to Zoe Coxon in marketing and Chloe Davies in publicity.

Heartfelt thanks to my first agent, Jo Unwin, and my first publisher, Wayne Brookes, for taking me on way back in 2022, and for helping me realize my childhood dream of becoming a published author. I am also deeply grateful to David Llewelyn of Triple L Consultancy for setting me on this path in the first place.

Special thanks to Steve Packenham and Drs Graham Taylor, Calum Macaulay and Tom Adler for their expert advice on the treatment of diabetes in the 1980s. Your input was invaluable.

Thank you to my family: Mark Williams, Rae Parkin, Elaine Mitchell, Ian Parkin, Sarah Parkin and Rich Parkin. Your interest in and support for my writing means so very much to me.

To the great loves of my life: H and E, you are magnificent young people, and I am so proud of everything the pair of you achieved while I was busy writing this book. And R: without your help, I honestly don't think I'd have found my way back to my desk, my keyboard and my writing mojo. Thank you so much for the – at times, quite literal – hand-holding. I love you more than words can say.

Lastly, this book is not just about serial murder and other nefarious goings-on. It is about the importance of friendship – however unlikely that friendship might be – and community. I am fortunate enough to count some truly amazing women among my friends, notably Jenny Smith, Jessica Ni Cheallaigh, Florence Barras, Caroline Hiscox, Cathy McDowell and Debbie Packenham, with a special shout-out to the lovely adult-ballet community at Firststeps School of Dance, and the magnificent Kit and Espe, who keep us all in line.

I am especially grateful to the girls I grew up with in Dinas Powys back in the 70s and 80s; girls who grew into women who have supported and cared about each other for over half a century – whether it be from the very next street, or from the other side of the world. So, here's to you, Isabel Sutherland, Helen Stoten, Michelle Baister, Diana Collins, Kate Leyburn and Helen Philip. Thank you for always being there, even when I was not.